Lafcadio Hearn's THE FACELESS GHOST AND OTHER MACABRE TALES FROM JAPAN

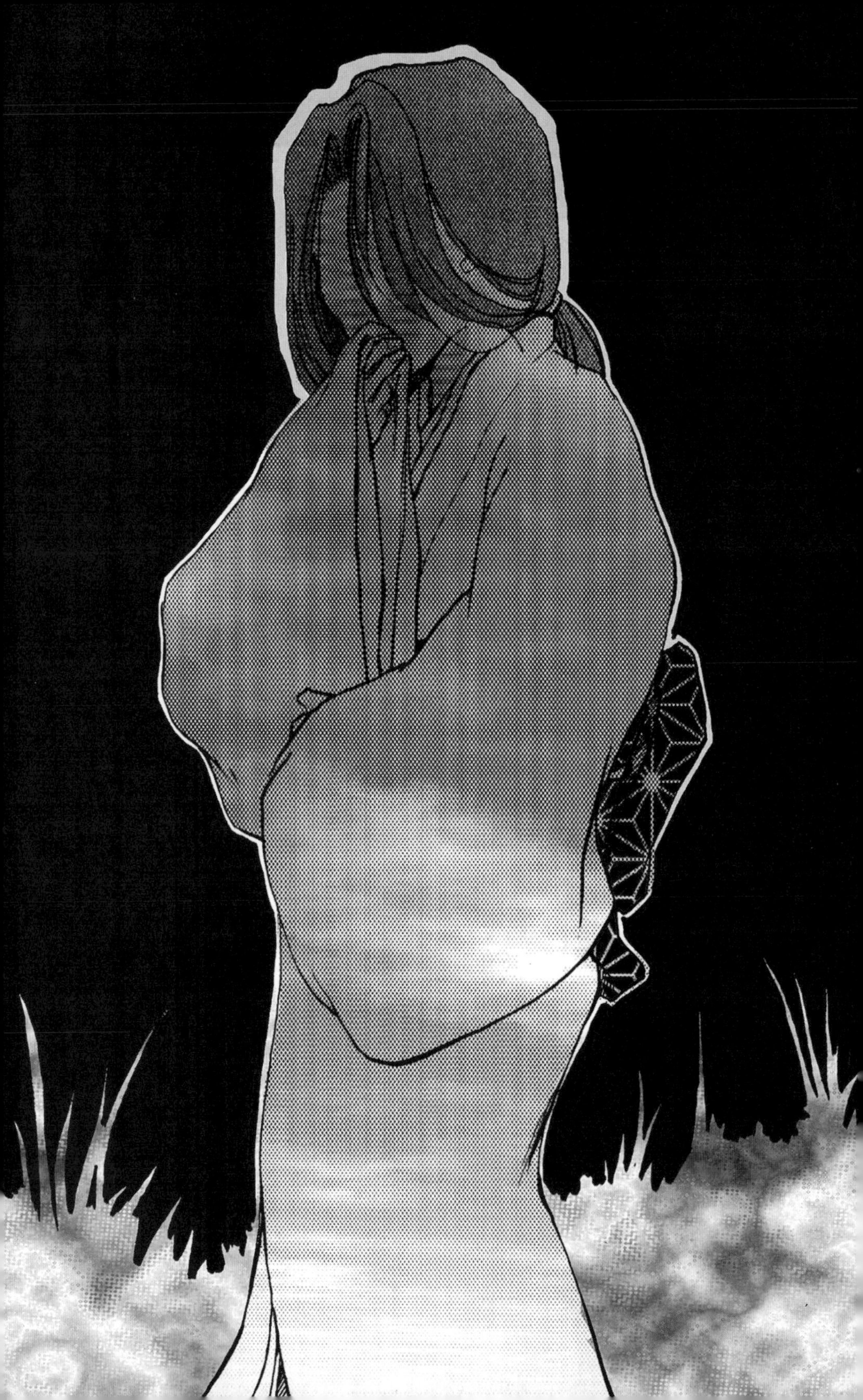

Lafcadio Hearn's THE
FACELESS GHOST
AND OTHER
MACABRE TALES FROM JAPAN

SEAN MICHAEL WILSON

ILLUSTRATED BY MICHIRU MORIKAWA

Shambhala · Boston & London · 2015

Shambhala Publications, Inc.
Horticultural Hall
300 Massachusetts Avenue
Boston, Massachusetts 02115
www.shambhala.com

9 8 7 6 5 4 3 2 1

First Edition
Printed in the United States of America

∞ This edition is printed on acid-free paper that meets the
American National Standards Institute Z39.48 Standard.
♻ Shambhala Publications makes every effort to print on recycled paper.
For more information please visit www.shambhala.com.

Distributed in the United States by Penguin Random House LLC
and in Canada by Random House of Canada Ltd

Library of Congress Cataloging-in-Publication Data

Wilson, Sean Michael, author.
Lafcadio Hearn's "the faceless ghost" and other macabre tales
from Japan: a graphic novel / Sean Michael Wilson;
illustrated by Michiru Morikawa.—First edition.
       pages   cm
ISBN 978-1-61180-197-2 (paperback: acid-free paper)
1. Horror comic books, strips, etc.—Japan. 2. Ghost stories, Japanese.
3. Horror tales, Japanese. 4. Graphic novels.
I. Morikawa, Michiru, 1973– illustrator. II. Title.
PN6737.W55F33 2015
741.5'9411—dc23
201500757

THE TALES

かけひき

DIPLOMACY

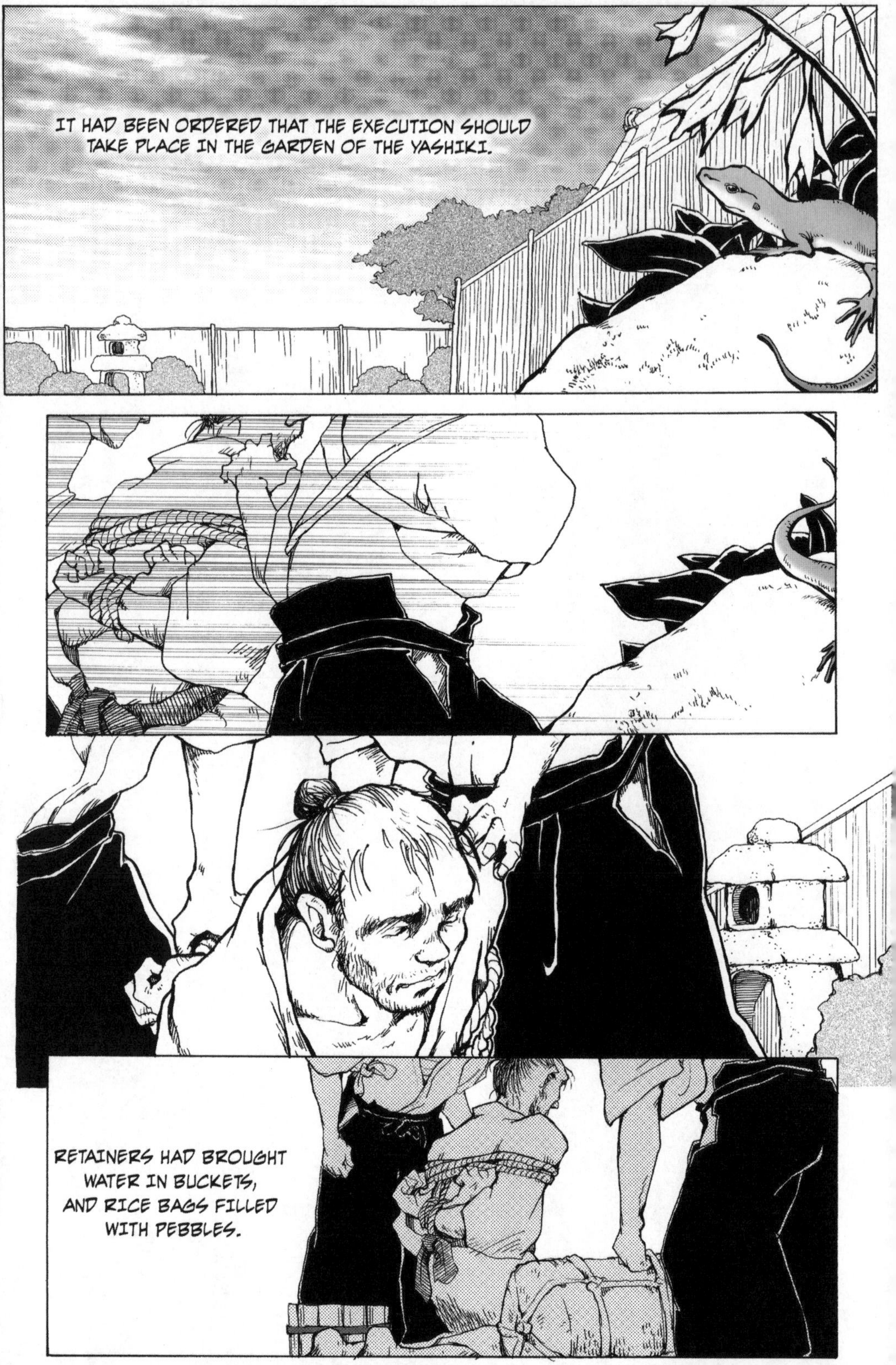
IT HAD BEEN ORDERED THAT THE EXECUTION SHOULD TAKE PLACE IN THE GARDEN OF THE YASHIKI.
RETAINERS HAD BROUGHT WATER IN BUCKETS, AND RICE BAGS FILLED WITH PEBBLES.

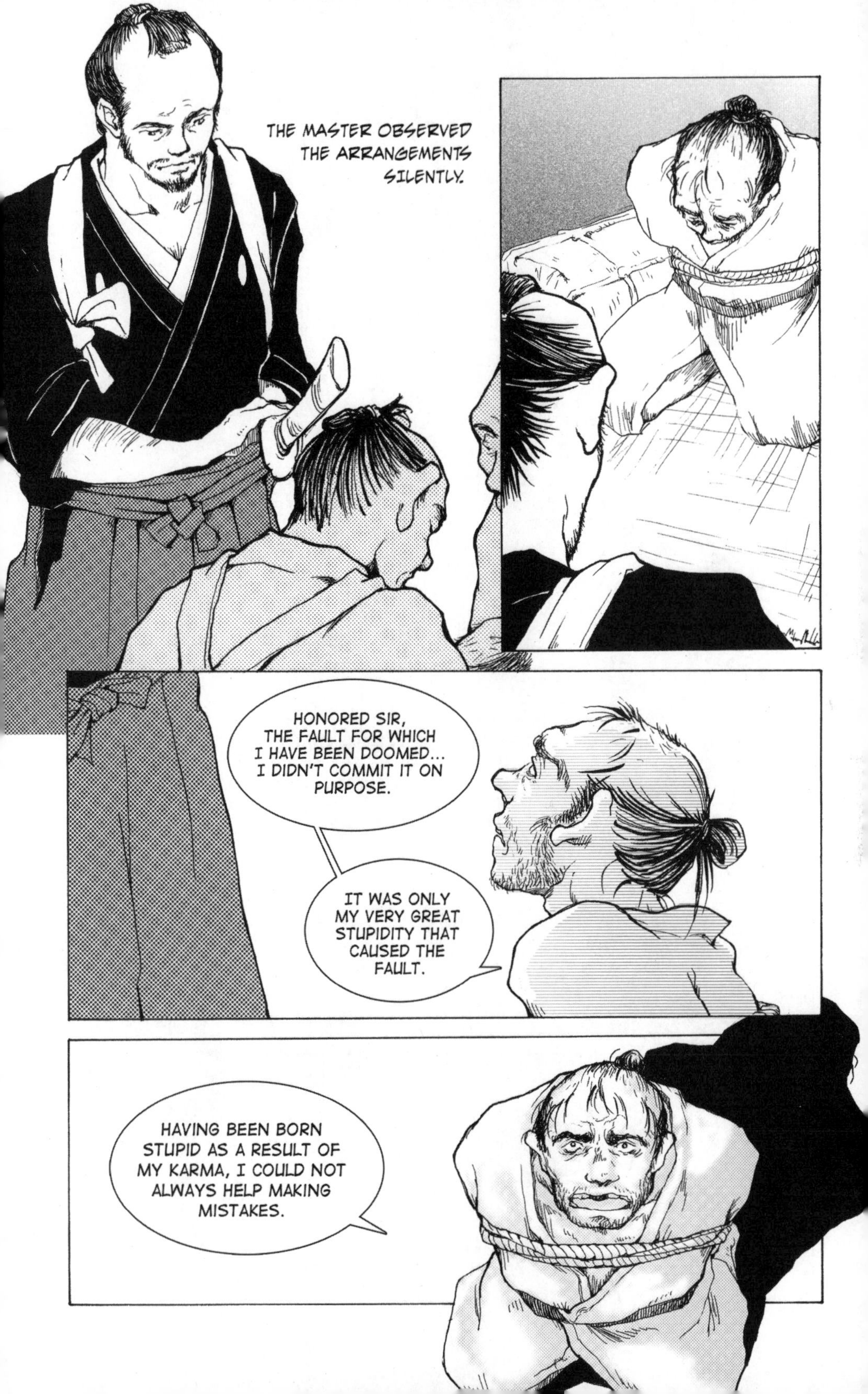
THE MASTER OBSERVED THE ARRANGEMENTS SILENTLY.
HONORED SIR, THE FAULT FOR WHICH I HAVE BEEN DOOMED... I DIDN'T COMMIT IT ON PURPOSE.
IT WAS ONLY MY VERY GREAT STUPIDITY THAT CAUSED THE FAULT.
HAVING BEEN BORN STUPID AS A RESULT OF MY KARMA, I COULD NOT ALWAYS HELP MAKING MISTAKES.

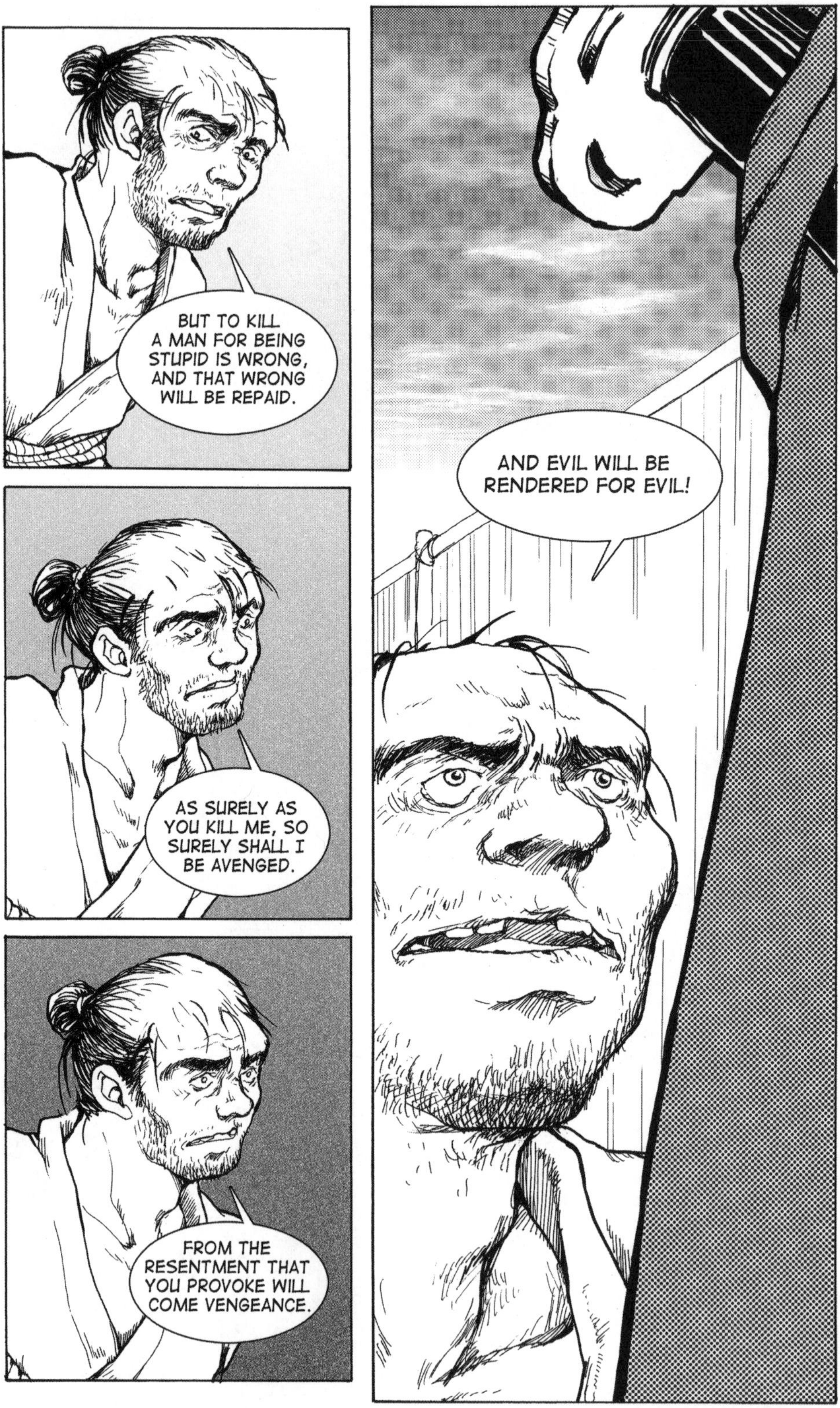
BUT TO KILL A MAN FOR BEING STUPID IS WRONG, AND THAT WRONG WILL BE REPAID.
AS SURELY AS YOU KILL ME, SO SURELY SHALL I BE AVENGED.
FROM THE RESENTMENT THAT YOU PROVOKE WILL COME VENGEANCE.
AND EVIL WILL BE RENDERED FOR EVIL!

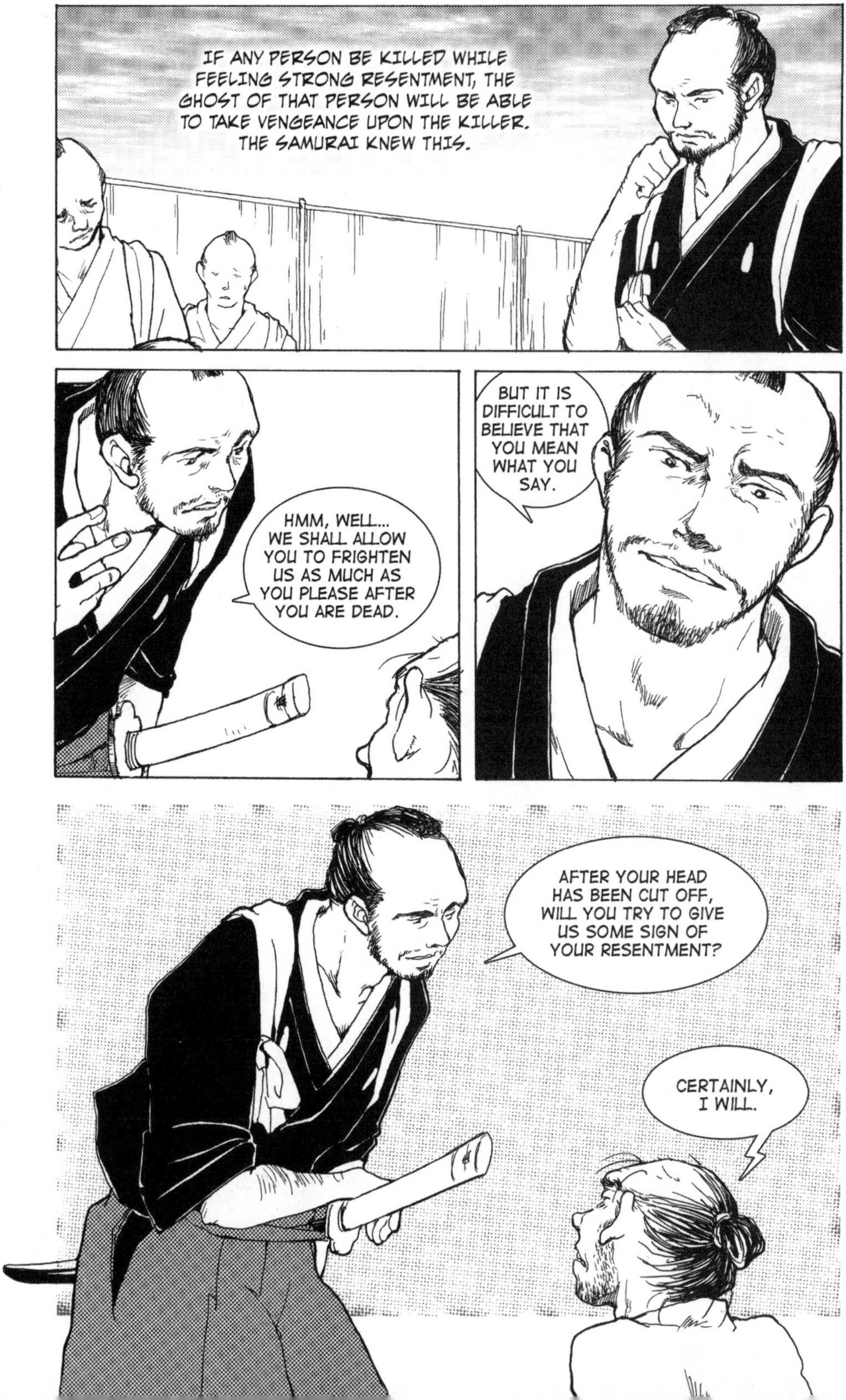
IF ANY PERSON BE KILLED WHILE FEELING STRONG RESENTMENT, THE GHOST OF THAT PERSON WILL BE ABLE TO TAKE VENGEANCE UPON THE KILLER. THE SAMURAI KNEW THIS.
HMM, WELL... WE SHALL ALLOW YOU TO FRIGHTEN US AS MUCH AS YOU PLEASE AFTER YOU ARE DEAD.
BUT IT IS DIFFICULT TO BELIEVE THAT YOU MEAN WHAT YOU SAY.
AFTER YOUR HEAD HAS BEEN CUT OFF, WILL YOU TRY TO GIVE US SOME SIGN OF YOUR RESENTMENT?
CERTAINLY, I WILL.

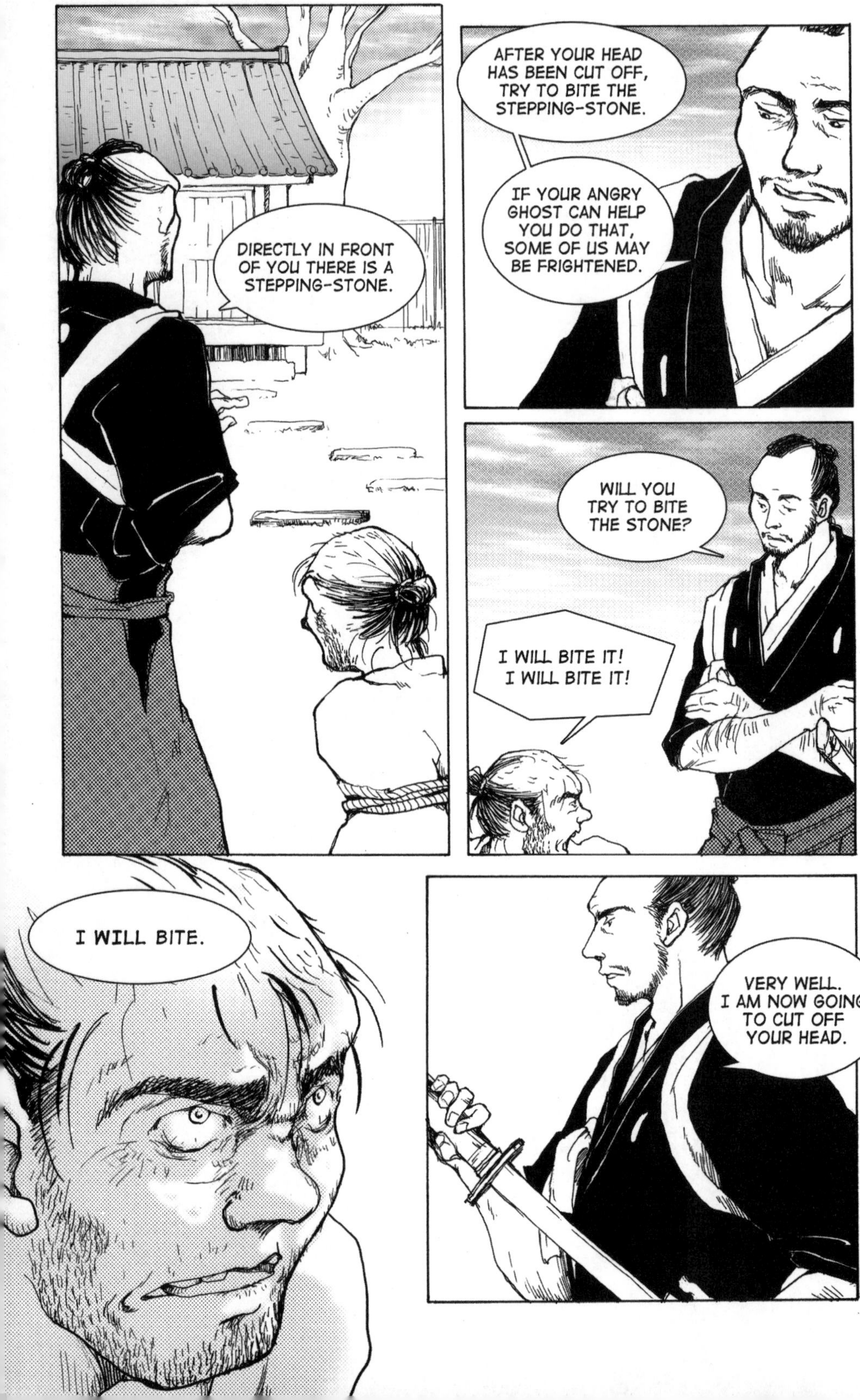

DIRECTLY IN FRONT OF YOU THERE IS A STEPPING-STONE.
AFTER YOUR HEAD HAS BEEN CUT OFF, TRY TO BITE THE STEPPING-STONE.
IF YOUR ANGRY GHOST CAN HELP YOU DO THAT, SOME OF US MAY BE FRIGHTENED.
WILL YOU TRY TO BITE THE STONE?
I WILL BITE IT! I WILL BITE IT!
I WILL BITE.
VERY WELL. I AM NOW GOING TO CUT OFF YOUR HEAD.

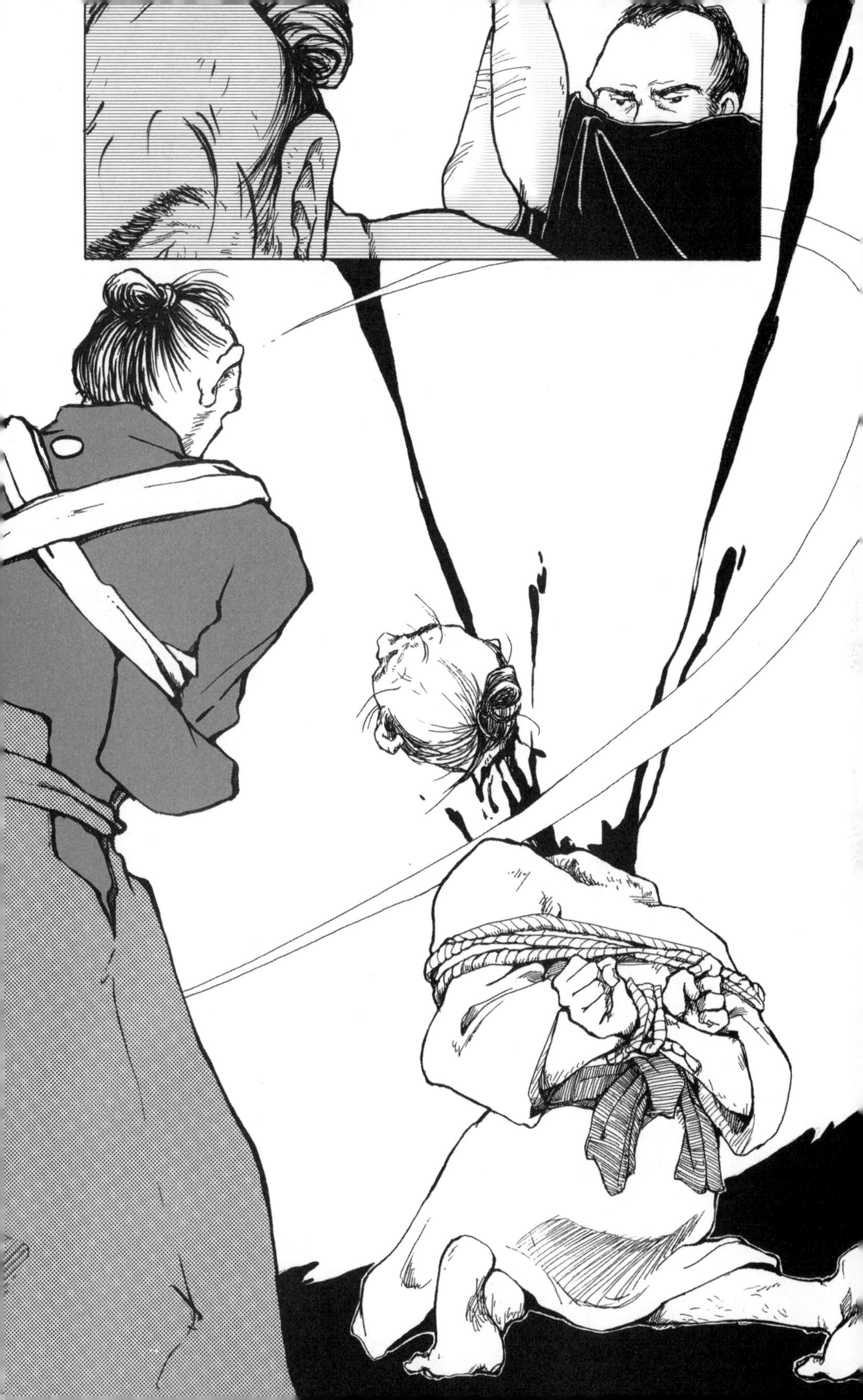

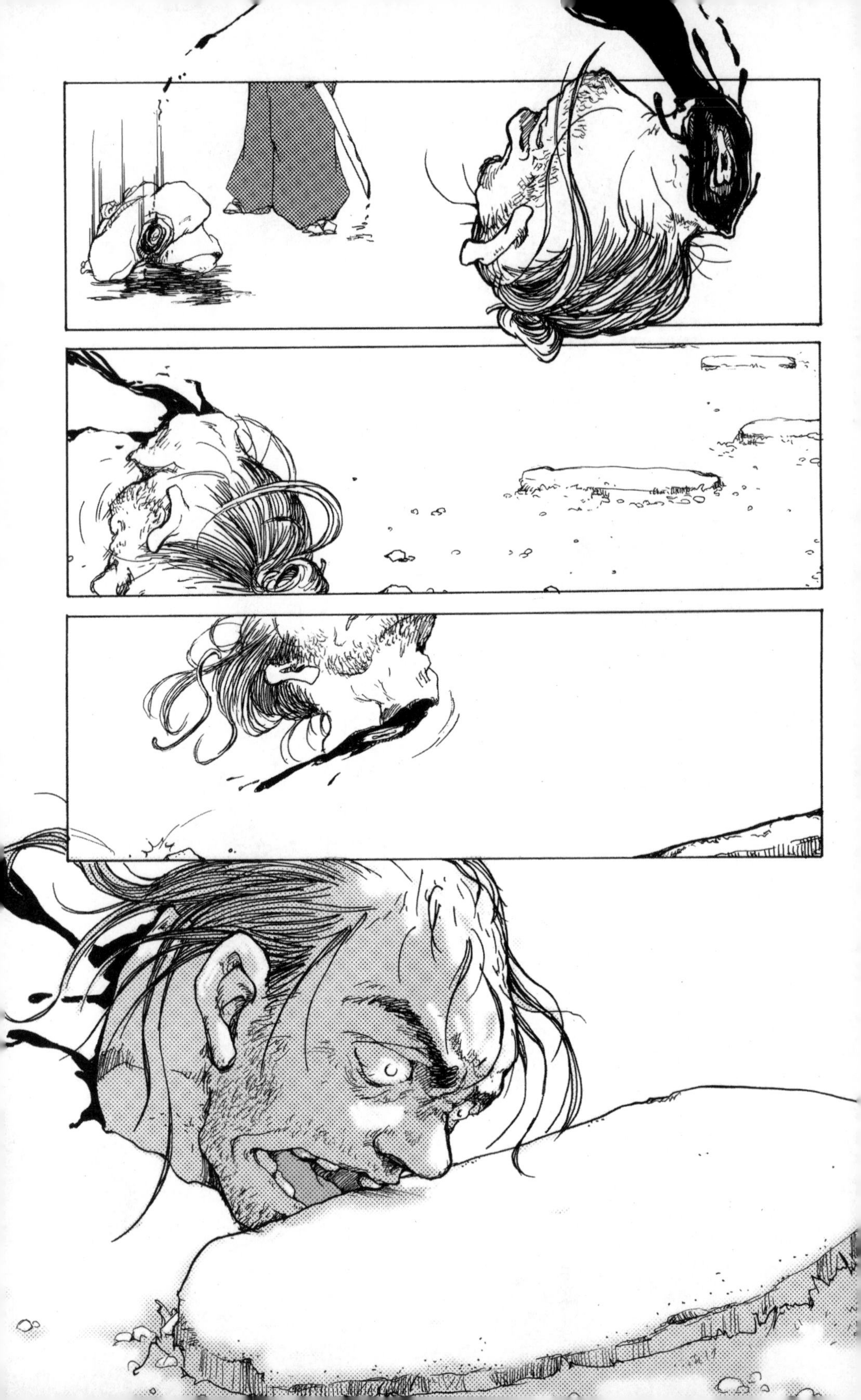

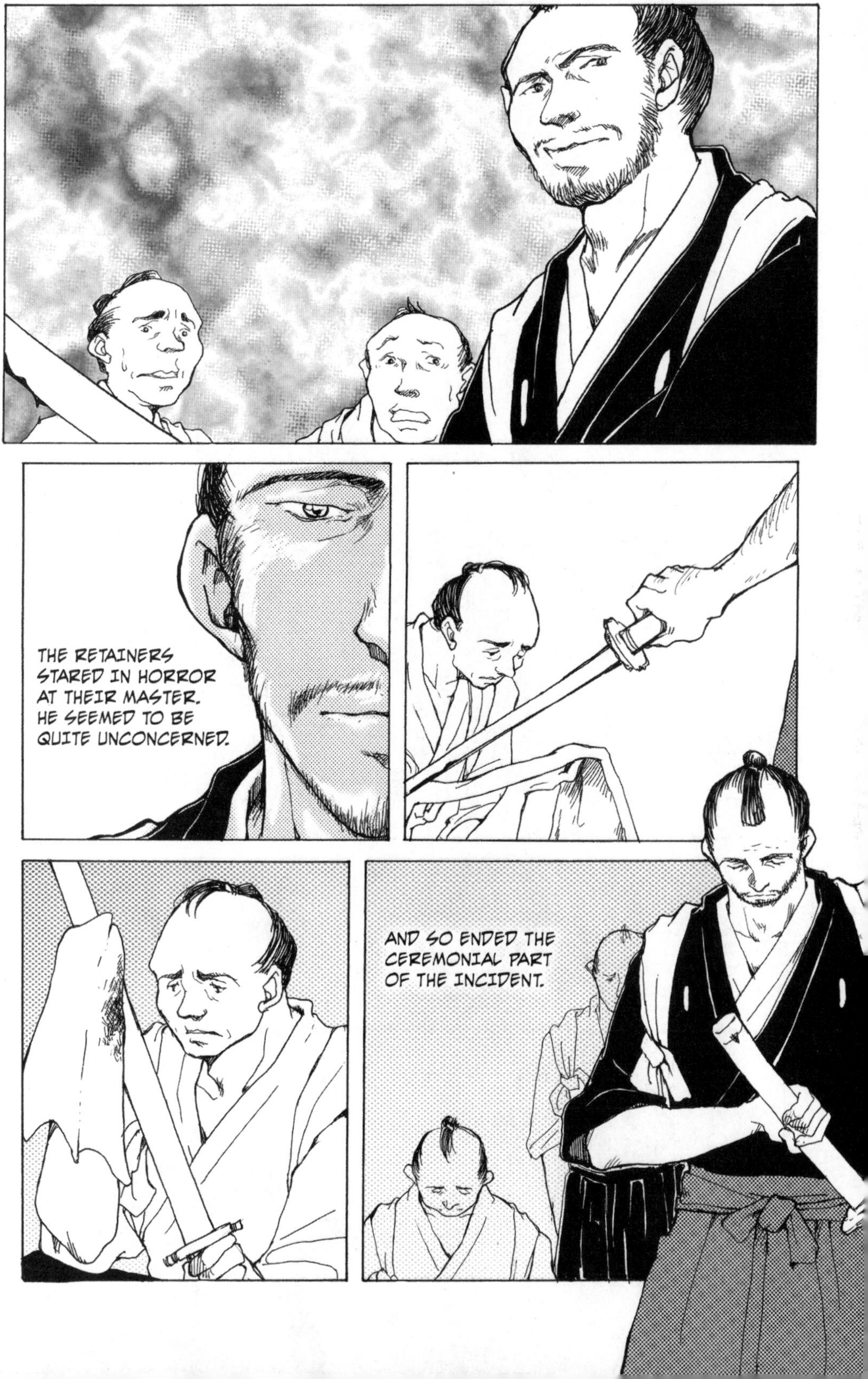
THE RETAINERS STARED IN HORROR AT THEIR MASTER. HE SEEMED TO BE QUITE UNCONCERNED.
AND SO ENDED THE CEREMONIAL PART OF THE INCIDENT.

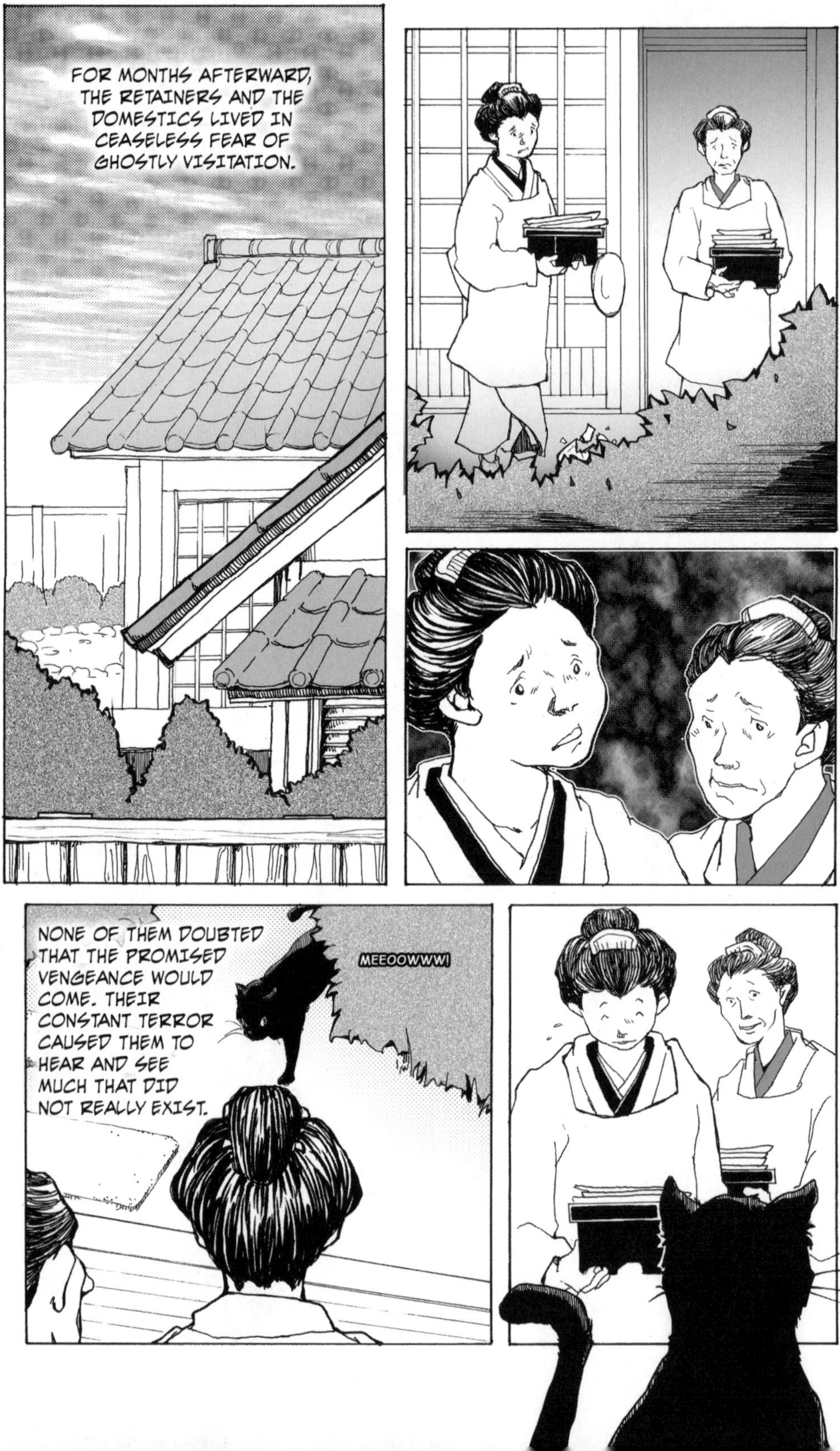
FOR MONTHS AFTERWARD, THE RETAINERS AND THE DOMESTICS LIVED IN CEASELESS FEAR OF GHOSTLY VISITATION.
NONE OF THEM DOUBTED THAT THE PROMISED VENGEANCE WOULD COME. THEIR CONSTANT TERROR CAUSED THEM TO HEAR AND SEE MUCH THAT DID NOT REALLY EXIST.
MEEOOWWW!

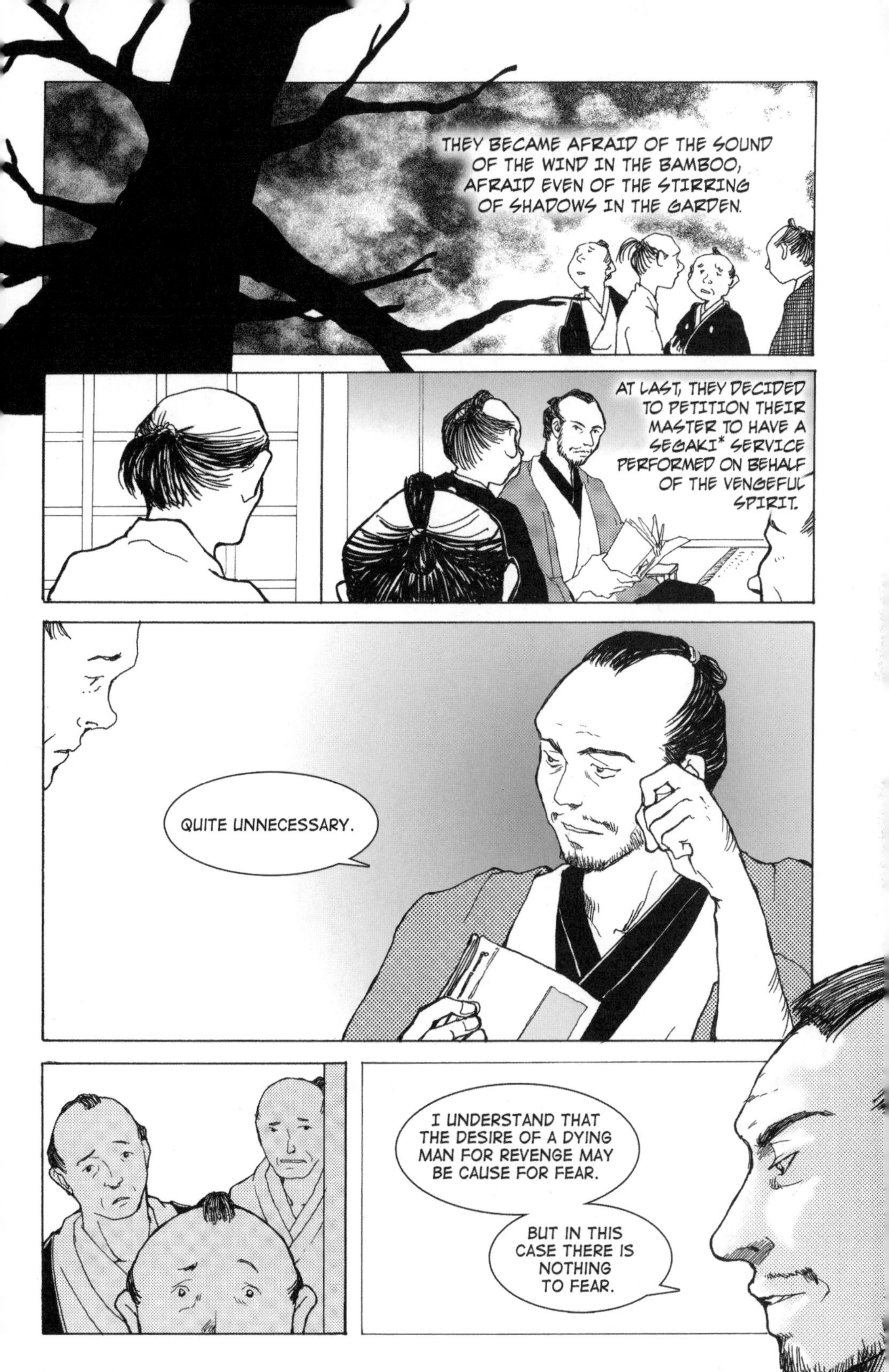
THEY BECAME AFRAID OF THE SOUND OF THE WIND IN THE BAMBOO, AFRAID EVEN OF THE STIRRING OF SHADOWS IN THE GARDEN.
AT LAST, THEY DECIDED TO PETITION THEIR MASTER TO HAVE A SEGAKI* SERVICE PERFORMED ON BEHALF OF THE VENGEFUL SPIRIT.
QUITE UNNECESSARY.
I UNDERSTAND THAT THE DESIRE OF A DYING MAN FOR REVENGE MAY BE CAUSE FOR FEAR.
BUT IN THIS CASE THERE IS NOTHING TO FEAR.

*SEGAKI: "FEEDING THE HUNGRY GHOSTS," A JAPANESE BUDDHIST RITUAL

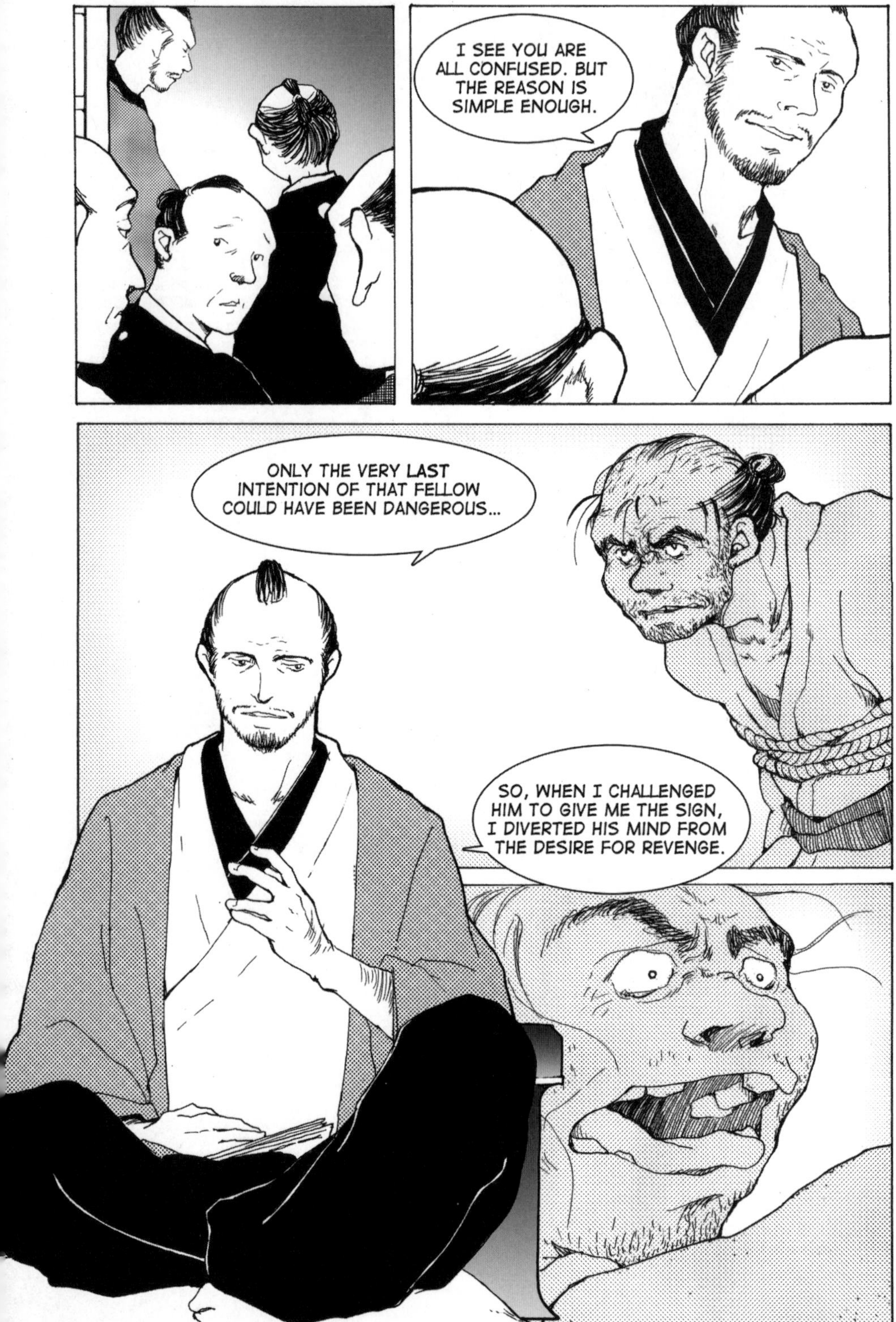
I SEE YOU ARE ALL CONFUSED. BUT THE REASON IS SIMPLE ENOUGH.
ONLY THE VERY LAST INTENTION OF THAT FELLOW COULD HAVE BEEN DANGEROUS...
SO, WHEN I CHALLENGED HIM TO GIVE ME THE SIGN, I DIVERTED HIS MIND FROM THE DESIRE FOR REVENGE.

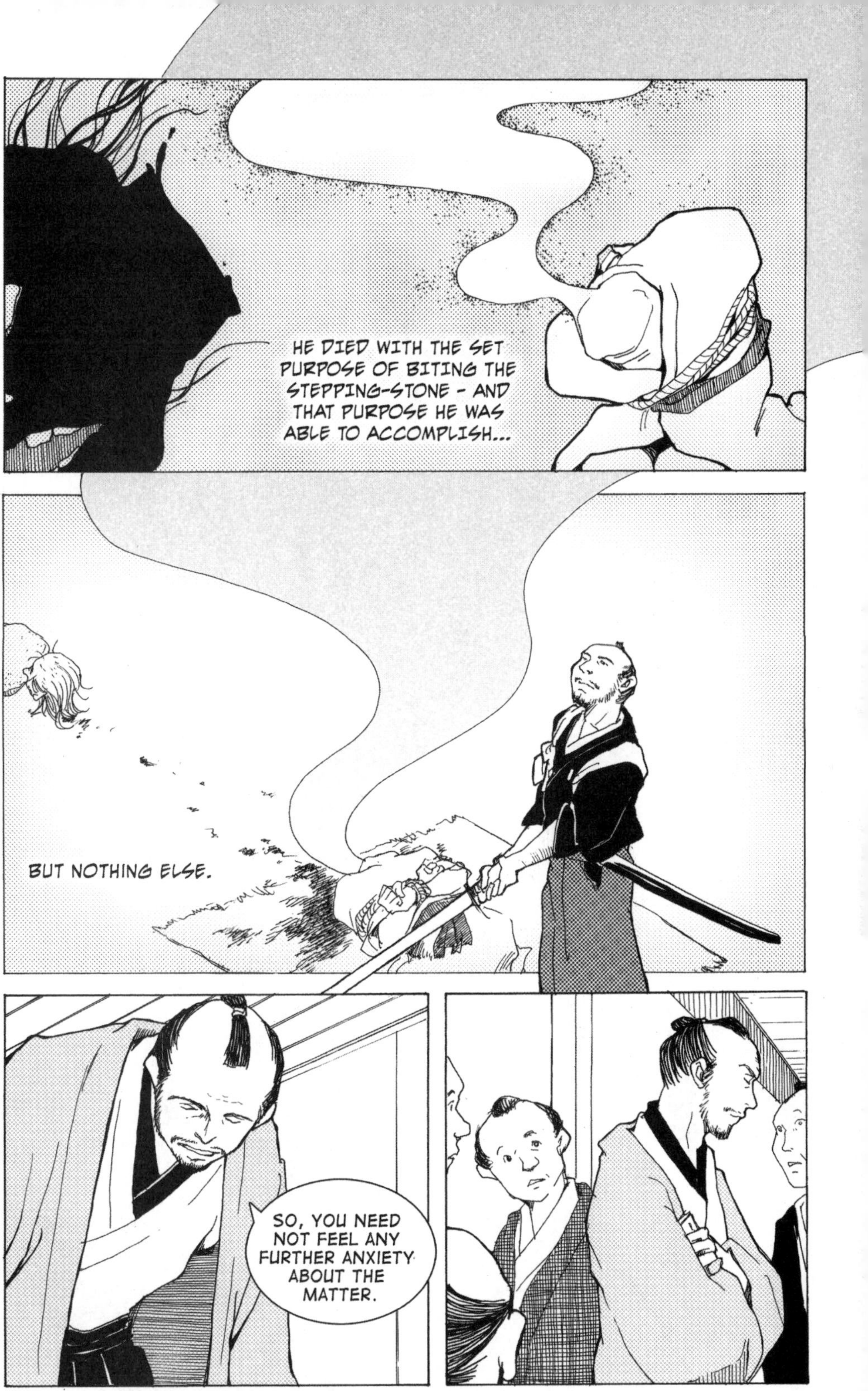
HE DIED WITH THE SET PURPOSE OF BITING THE STEPPING-STONE - AND THAT PURPOSE HE WAS ABLE TO ACCOMPLISH...
BUT NOTHING ELSE.
SO, YOU NEED NOT FEEL ANY FURTHER ANXIETY ABOUT THE MATTER.

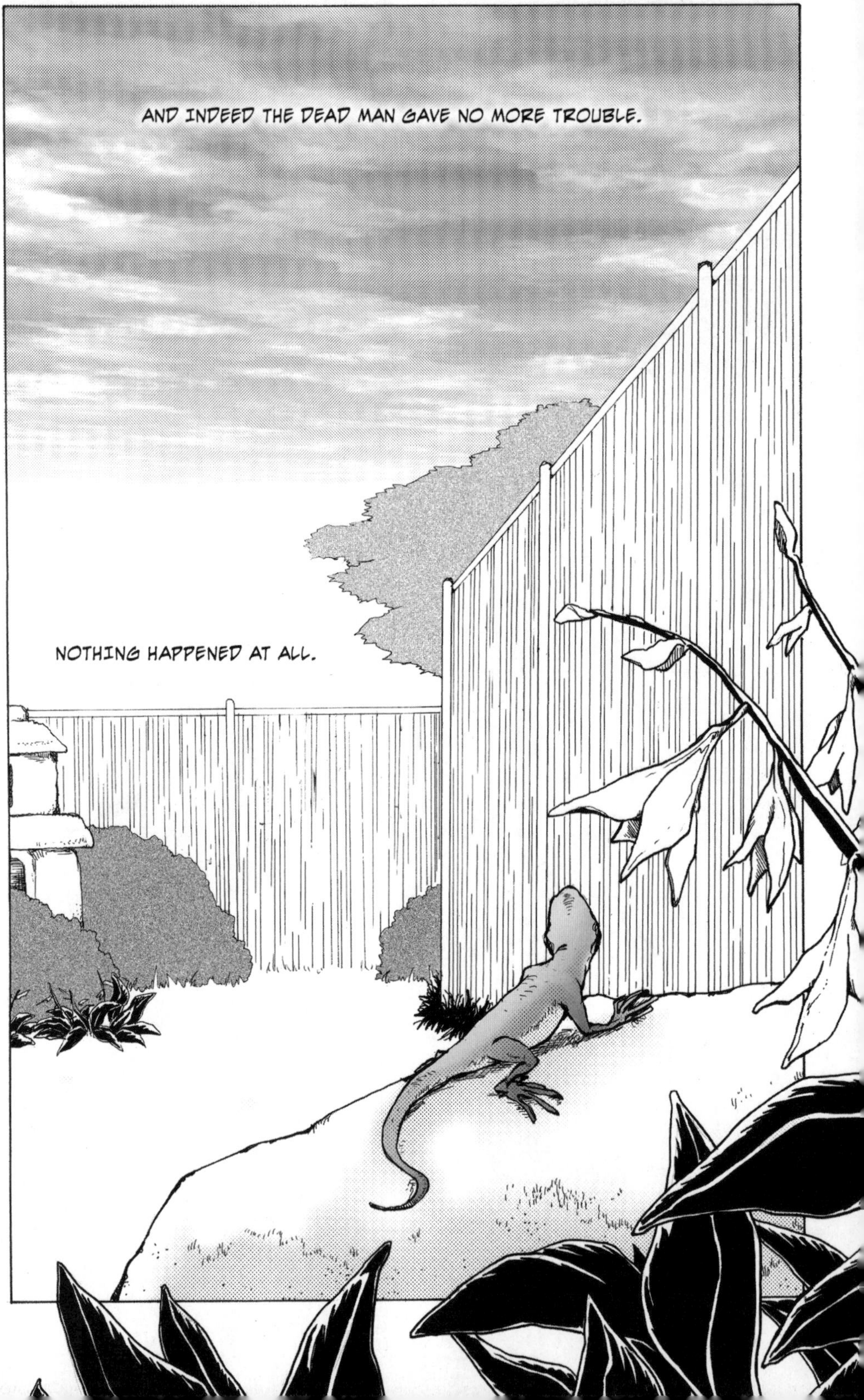
AND INDEED THE DEAD MAN GAVE NO MORE TROUBLE.
NOTHING HAPPENED AT ALL.

雪女

THE SNOW WOMAN

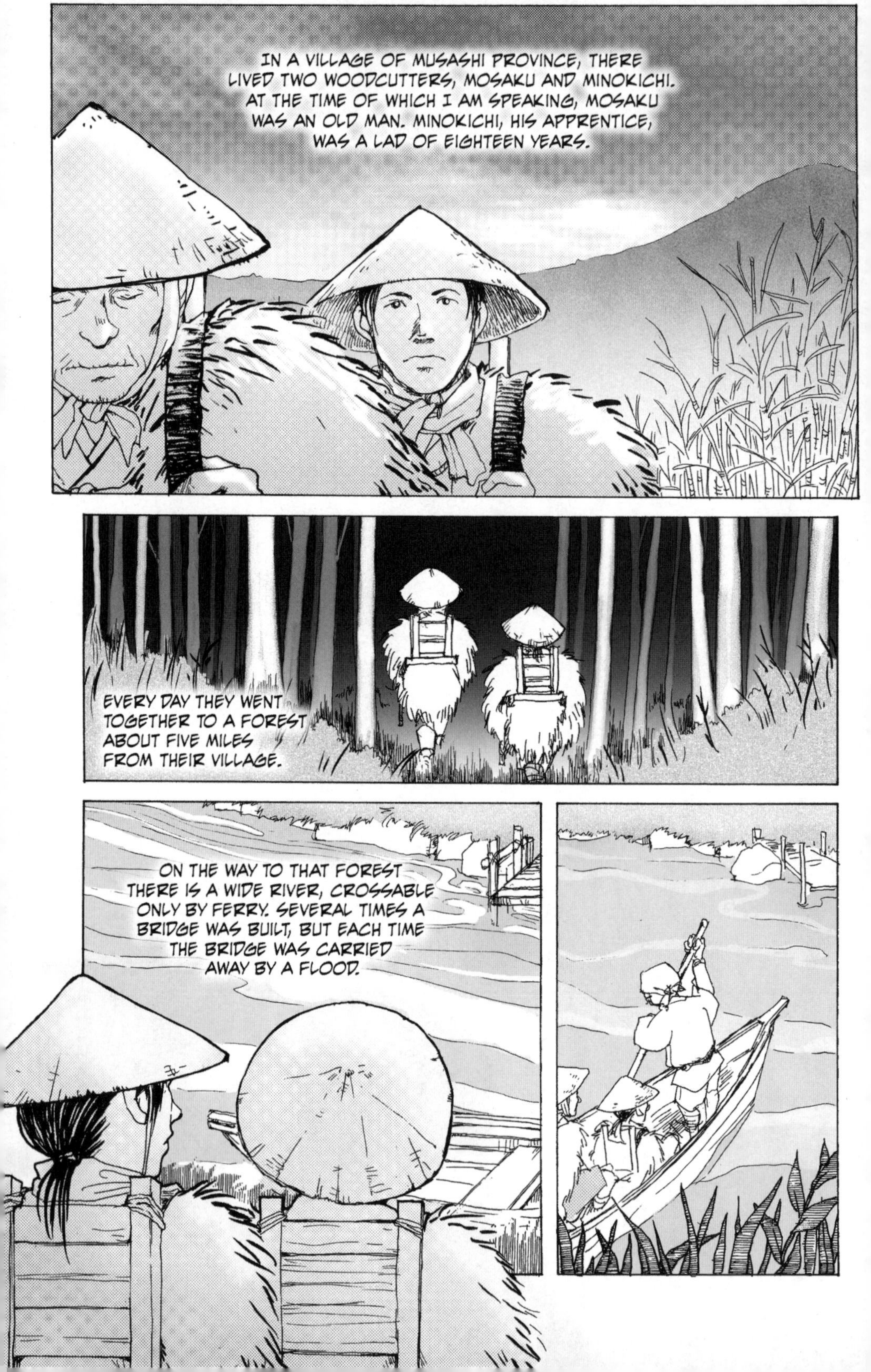
IN A VILLAGE OF MUSASHI PROVINCE, THERE LIVED TWO WOODCUTTERS, MOSAKU AND MINOKICHI. AT THE TIME OF WHICH I AM SPEAKING, MOSAKU WAS AN OLD MAN. MINOKICHI, HIS APPRENTICE, WAS A LAD OF EIGHTEEN YEARS.
EVERY DAY THEY WENT TOGETHER TO A FOREST ABOUT FIVE MILES FROM THEIR VILLAGE.
ON THE WAY TO THAT FOREST THERE IS A WIDE RIVER, CROSSABLE ONLY BY FERRY. SEVERAL TIMES A BRIDGE WAS BUILT, BUT EACH TIME THE BRIDGE WAS CARRIED AWAY BY A FLOOD.

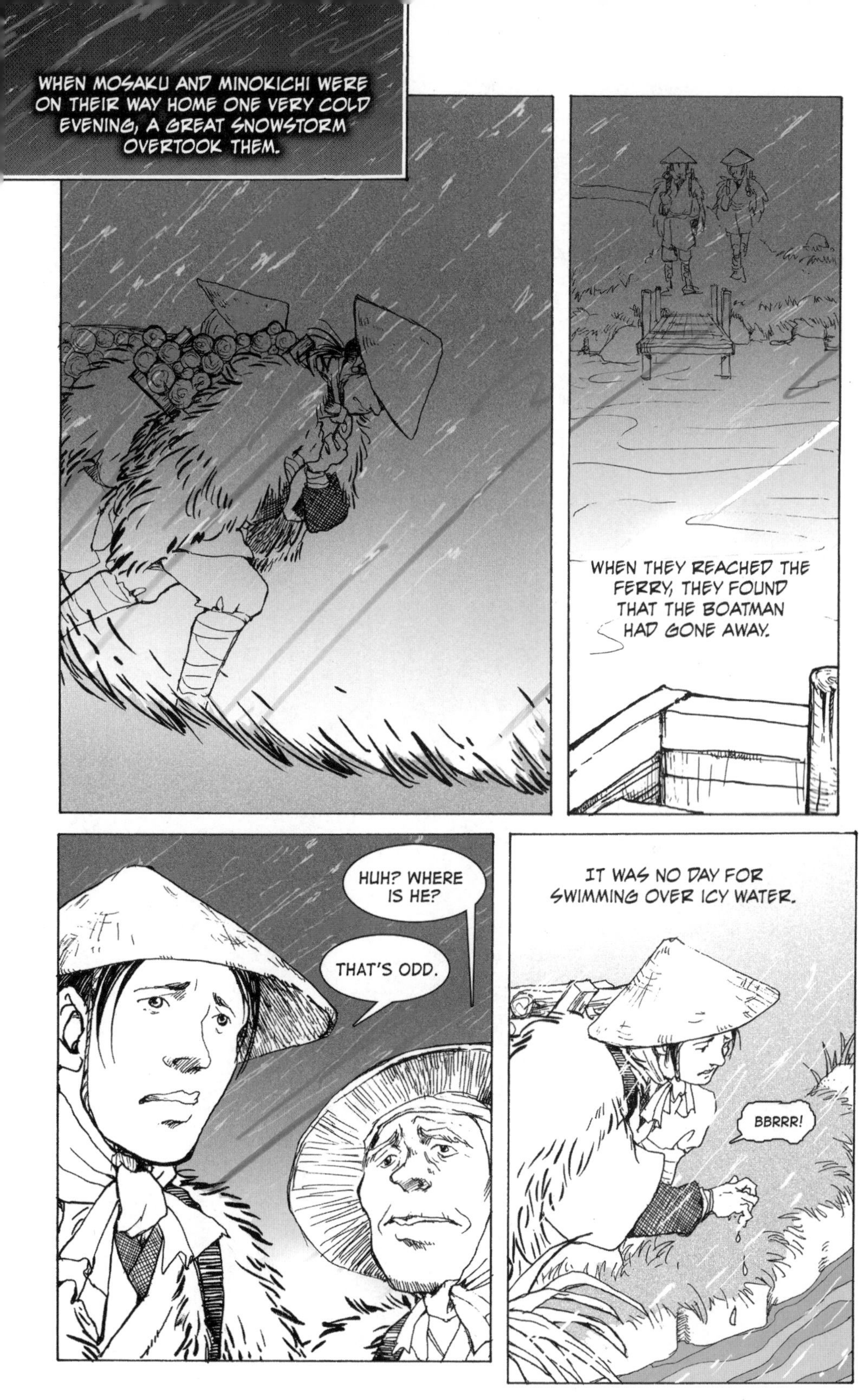
WHEN MOSAKU AND MINOKICHI WERE ON THEIR WAY HOME ONE VERY COLD EVENING, A GREAT SNOWSTORM OVERTOOK THEM.
WHEN THEY REACHED THE FERRY, THEY FOUND THAT THE BOATMAN HAD GONE AWAY.
HUH? WHERE IS HE?
THAT'S ODD.
IT WAS NO DAY FOR SWIMMING OVER ICY WATER.
BBRRR!

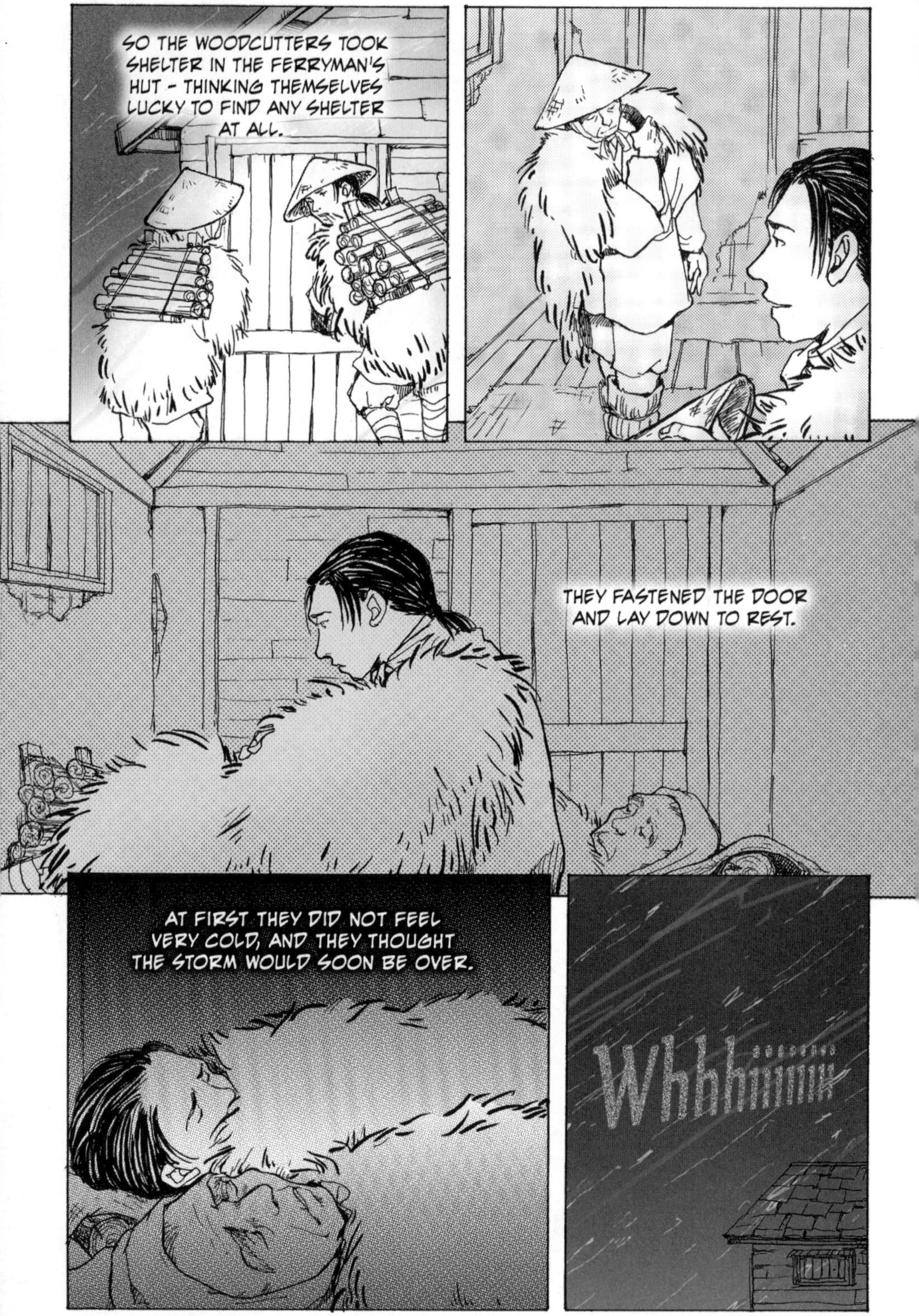
SO THE WOODCUTTERS TOOK SHELTER IN THE FERRYMAN'S HUT - THINKING THEMSELVES LUCKY TO FIND ANY SHELTER AT ALL.
THEY FASTENED THE DOOR AND LAY DOWN TO REST.
AT FIRST THEY DID NOT FEEL VERY COLD, AND THEY THOUGHT THE STORM WOULD SOON BE OVER.
Whhiiiiiiii

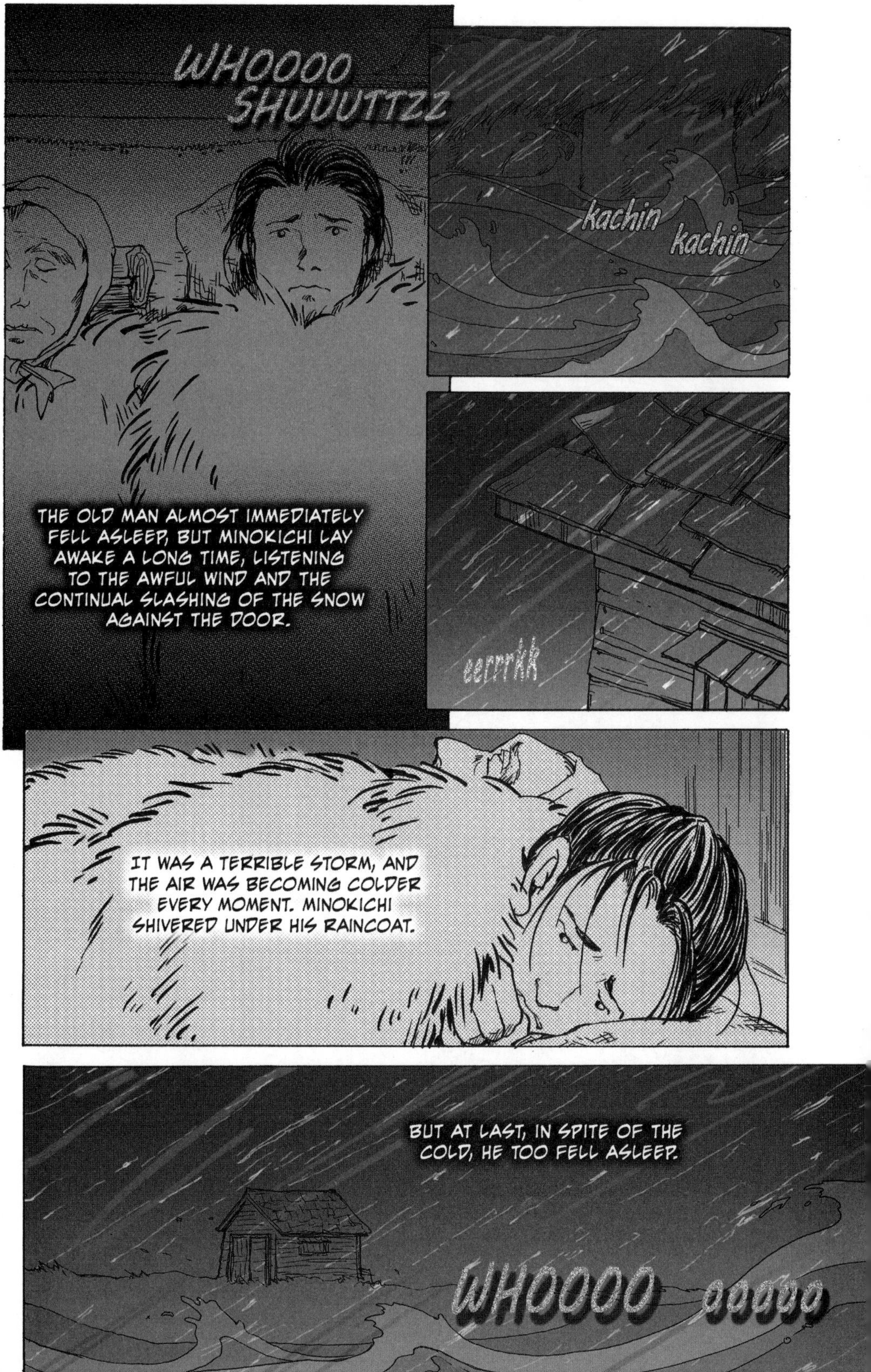
WHOOOO
SHUUUTTZZ
THE OLD MAN ALMOST IMMEDIATELY FELL ASLEEP, BUT MINOKICHI LAY AWAKE A LONG TIME, LISTENING TO THE AWFUL WIND AND THE CONTINUAL SLASHING OF THE SNOW AGAINST THE DOOR.
kachin
kachin
eerrrkk
IT WAS A TERRIBLE STORM, AND THE AIR WAS BECOMING COLDER EVERY MOMENT. MINOKICHI SHIVERED UNDER HIS RAINCOAT.
BUT AT LAST, IN SPITE OF THE COLD, HE TOO FELL ASLEEP.
WHOOOO
OOOOO

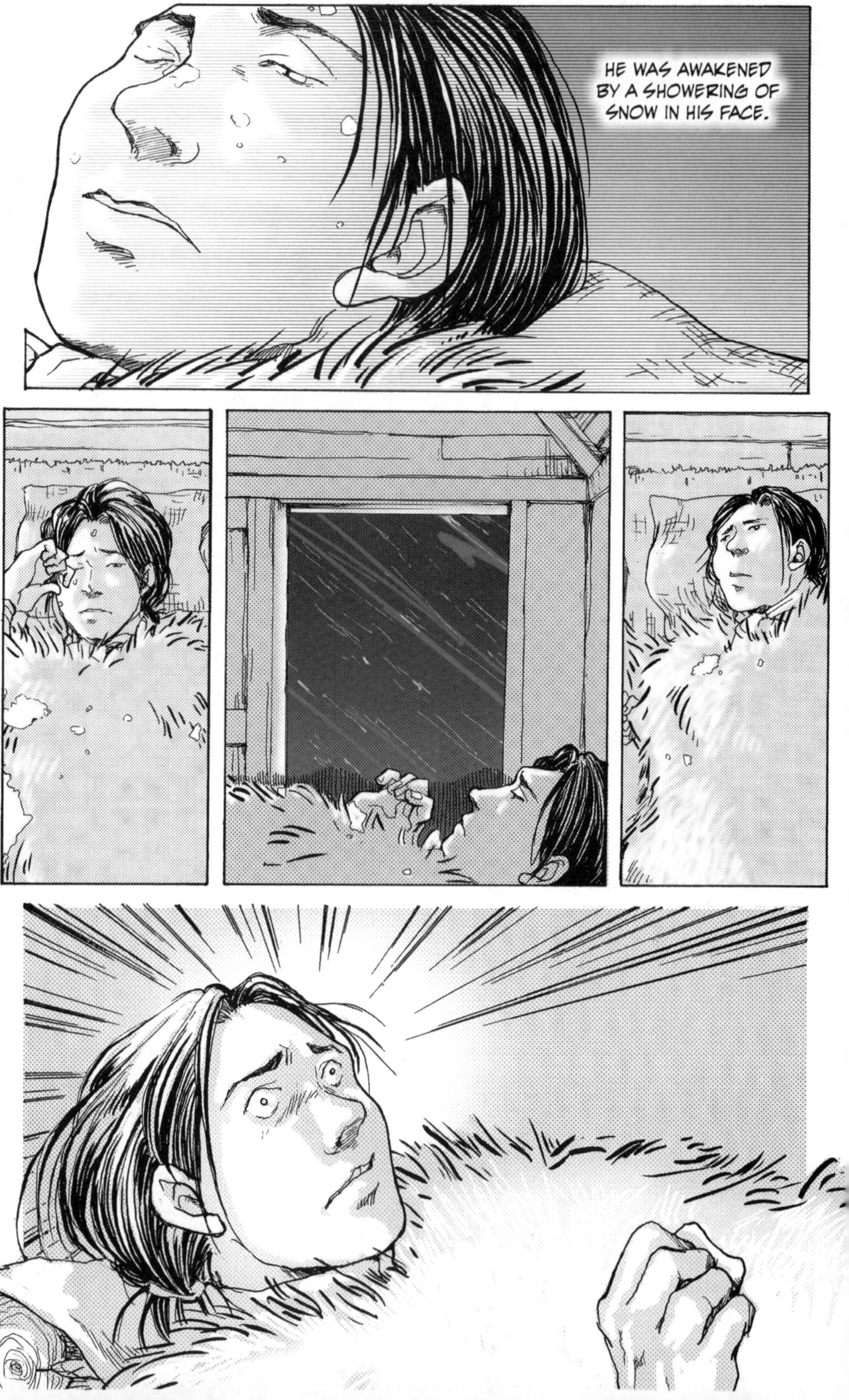
HE WAS AWAKENED BY A SHOWERING OF SNOW IN HIS FACE.

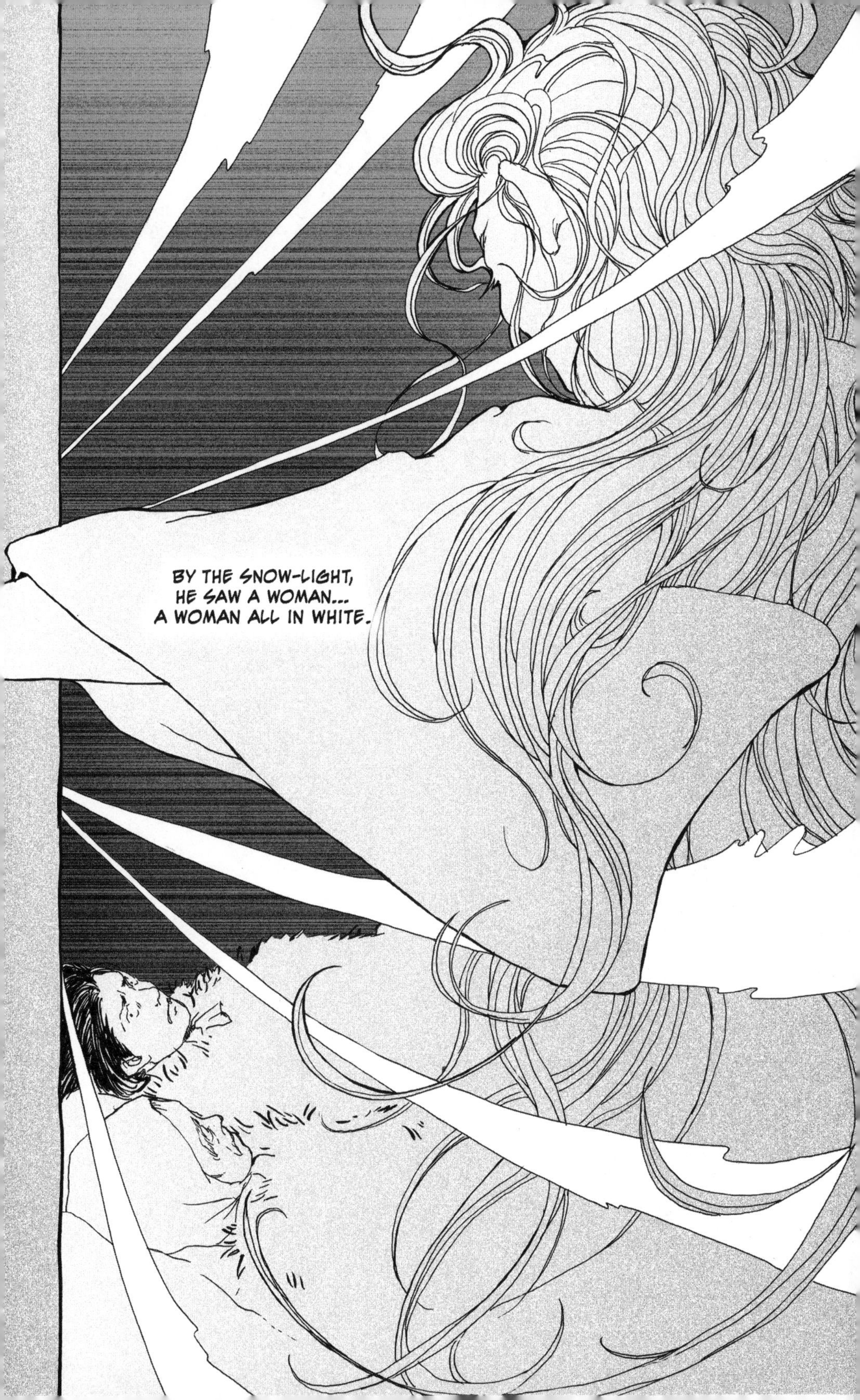
BY THE SNOW-LIGHT,
HE SAW A WOMAN...
A WOMAN ALL IN WHITE.

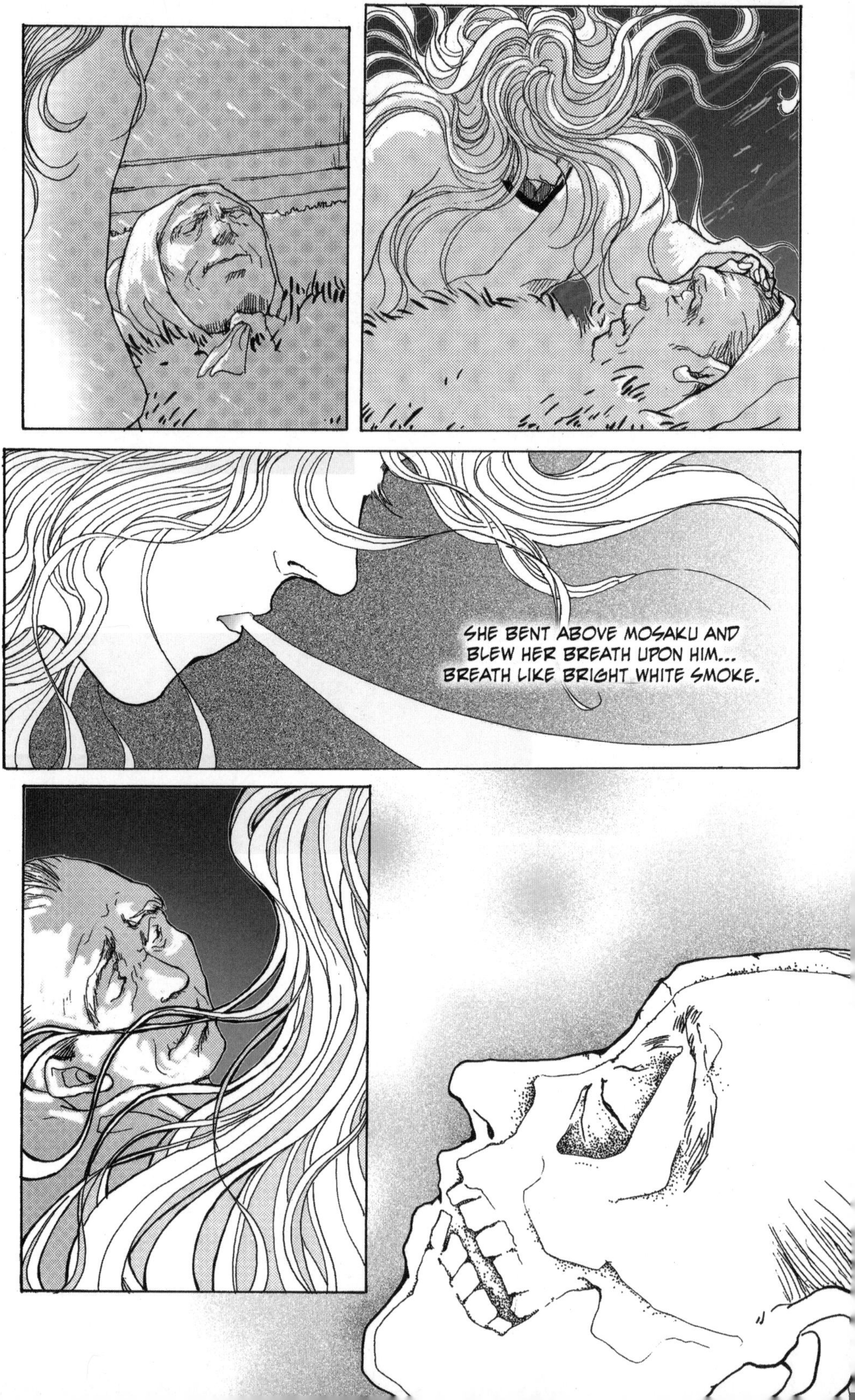
SHE BENT ABOVE MOSAKU AND BLEW HER BREATH UPON HIM... BREATH LIKE BRIGHT WHITE SMOKE.

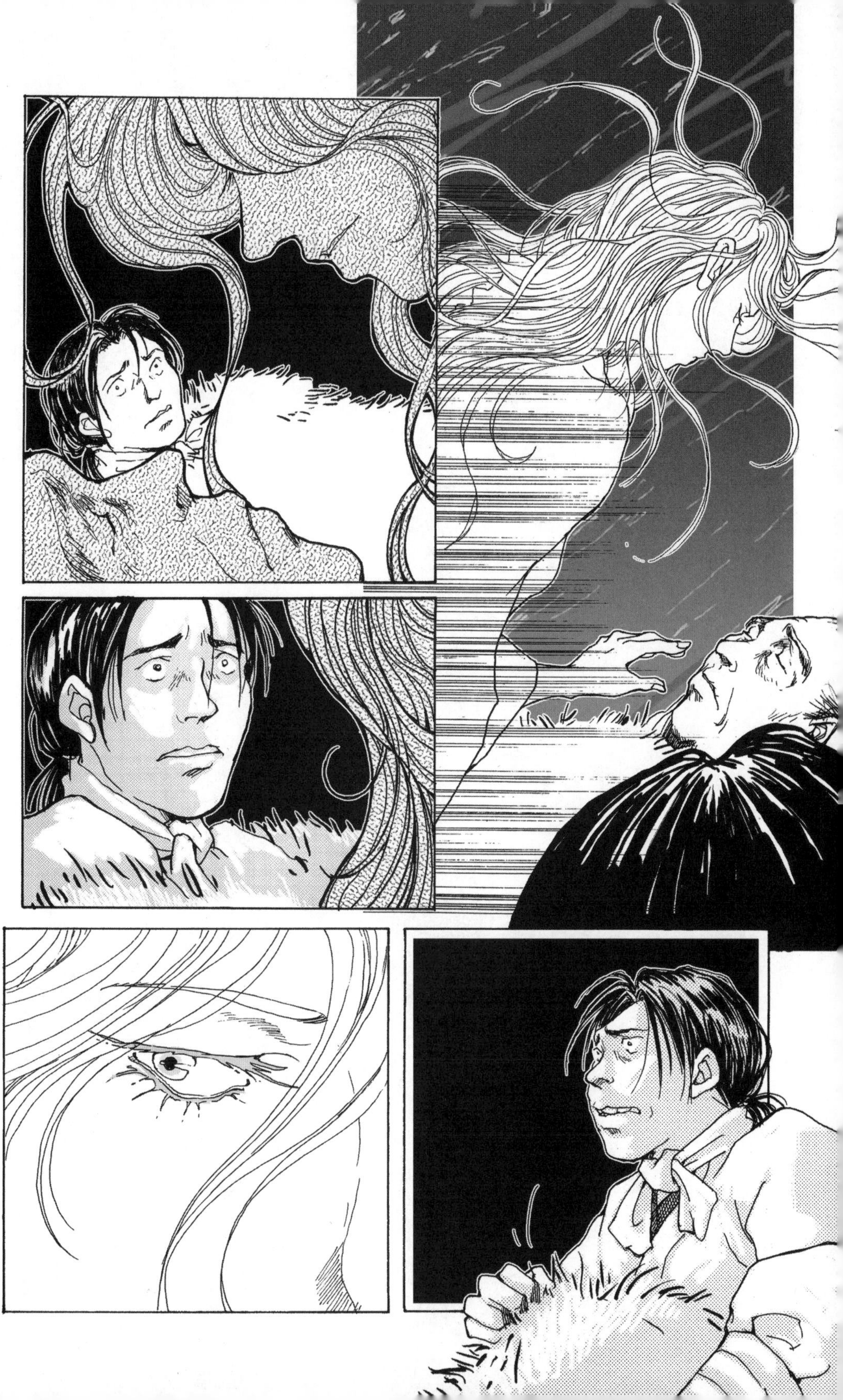

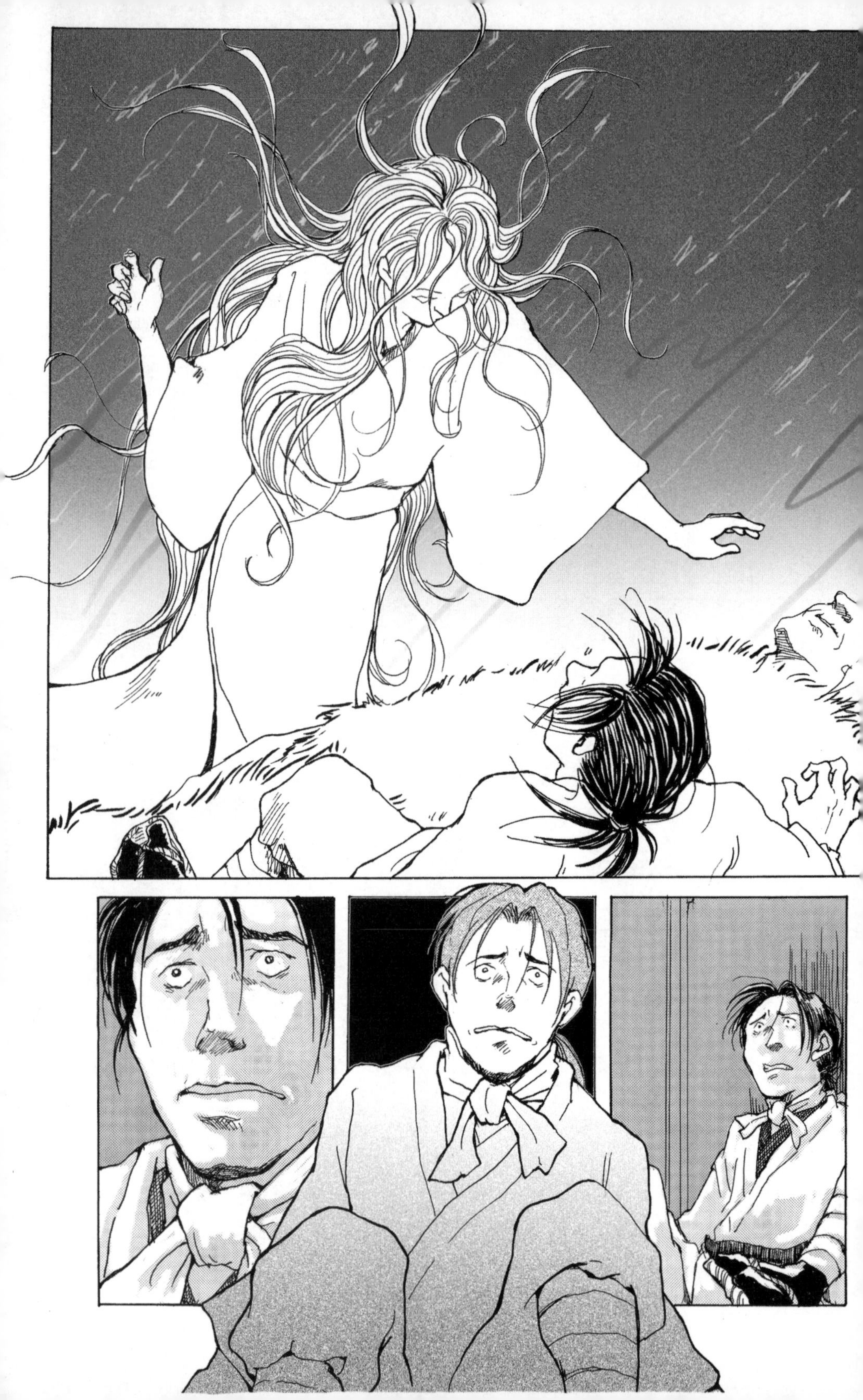

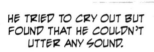
HE TRIED TO CRY OUT BUT FOUND THAT HE COULDN'T UTTER ANY SOUND.

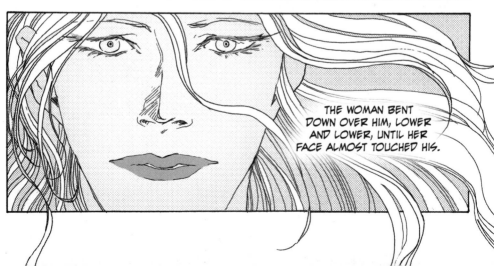
THE WOMAN BENT DOWN OVER HIM, LOWER AND LOWER, UNTIL HER FACE ALMOST TOUCHED HIS.

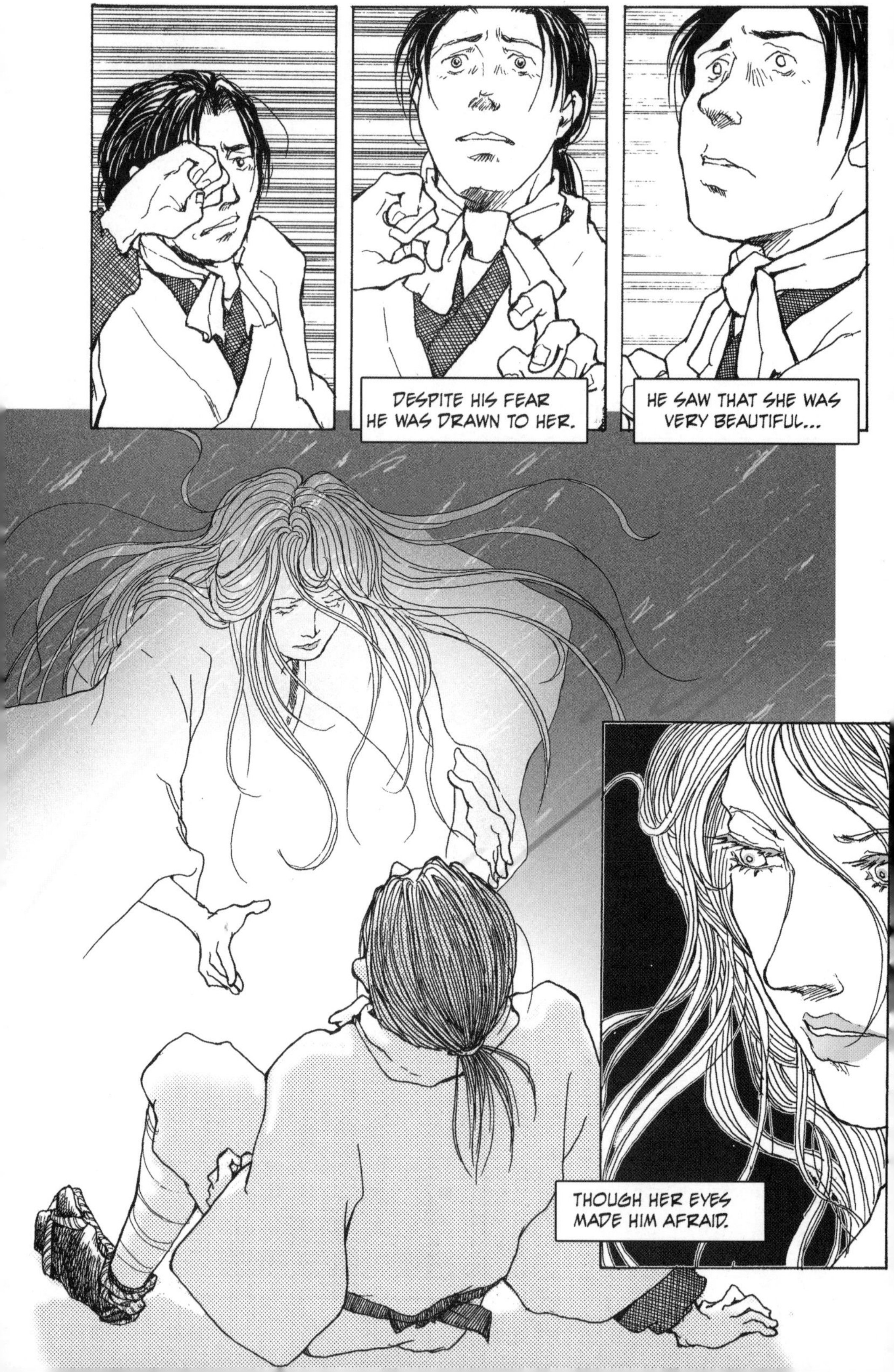
DESPITE HIS FEAR HE WAS DRAWN TO HER.
HE SAW THAT SHE WAS VERY BEAUTIFUL...
THOUGH HER EYES MADE HIM AFRAID.

SHE CONTINUED TO LOOK UPON HIM FOR A TIME, BUT THEN...

I INTENDED TO TREAT YOU LIKE THE OTHER MAN.

BUT I CANNOT HELP FEELING SOME PITY FOR YOU BECAUSE YOU ARE SO YOUNG AND HANDSOME.

YES, YOU ARE A PRETTY BOY, MINOKICHI. I WILL NOT HURT YOU NOW.

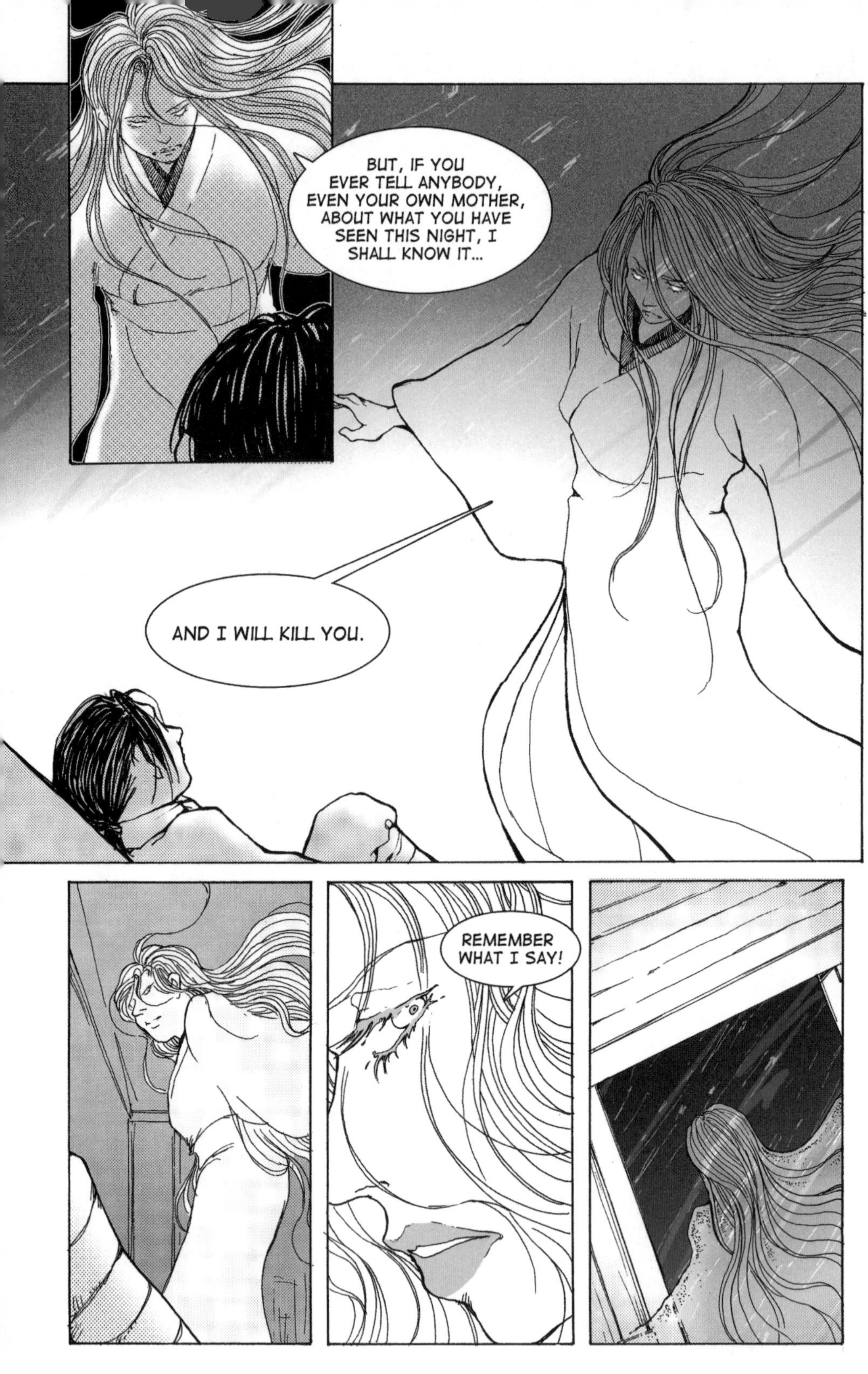
BUT, IF YOU EVER TELL ANYBODY, EVEN YOUR OWN MOTHER, ABOUT WHAT YOU HAVE SEEN THIS NIGHT, I SHALL KNOW IT...
AND I WILL KILL YOU.
REMEMBER WHAT I SAY!

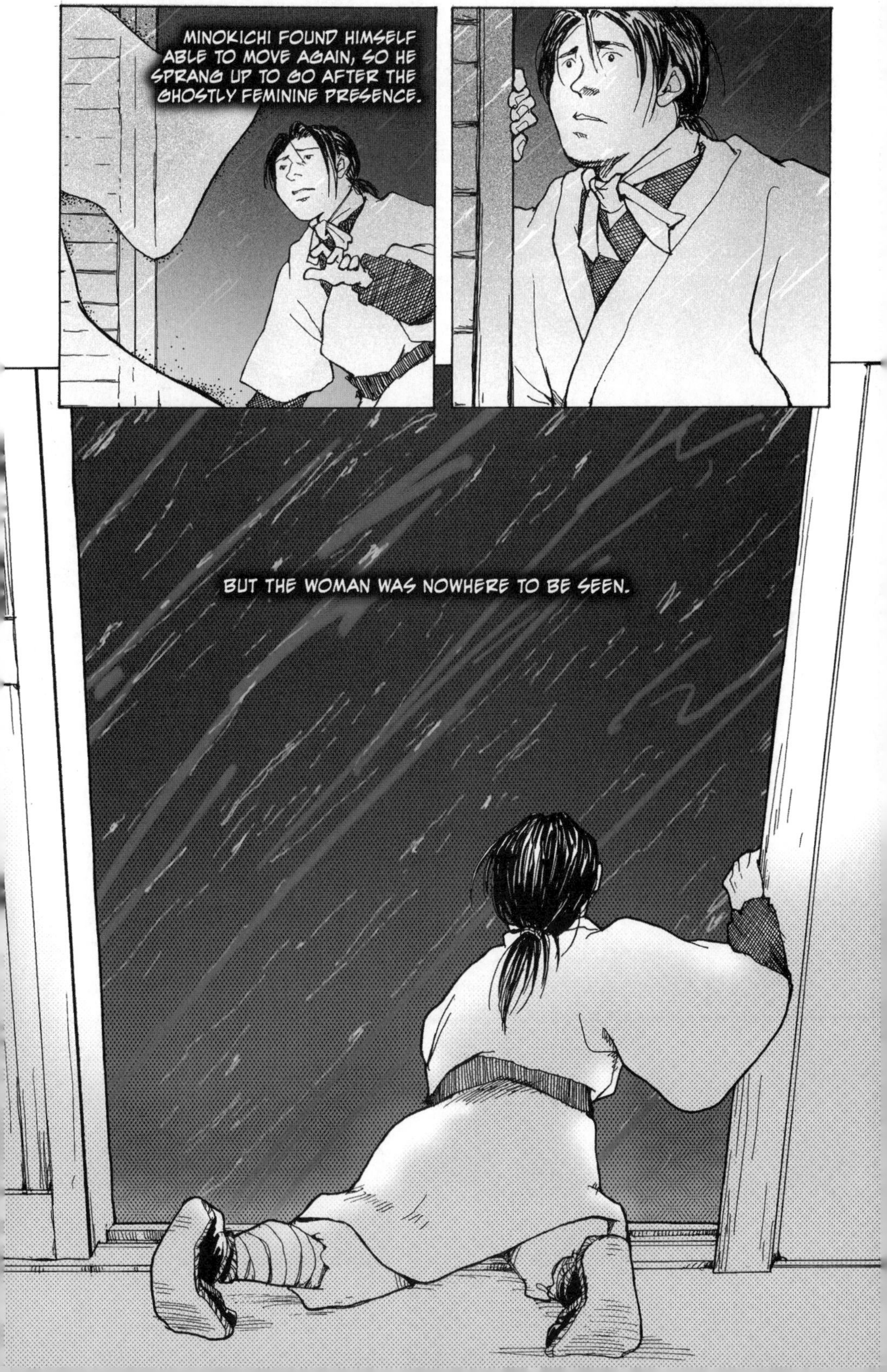
MINOKICHI FOUND HIMSELF ABLE TO MOVE AGAIN, SO HE SPRANG UP TO GO AFTER THE GHOSTLY FEMININE PRESENCE.
BUT THE WOMAN WAS NOWHERE TO BE SEEN.

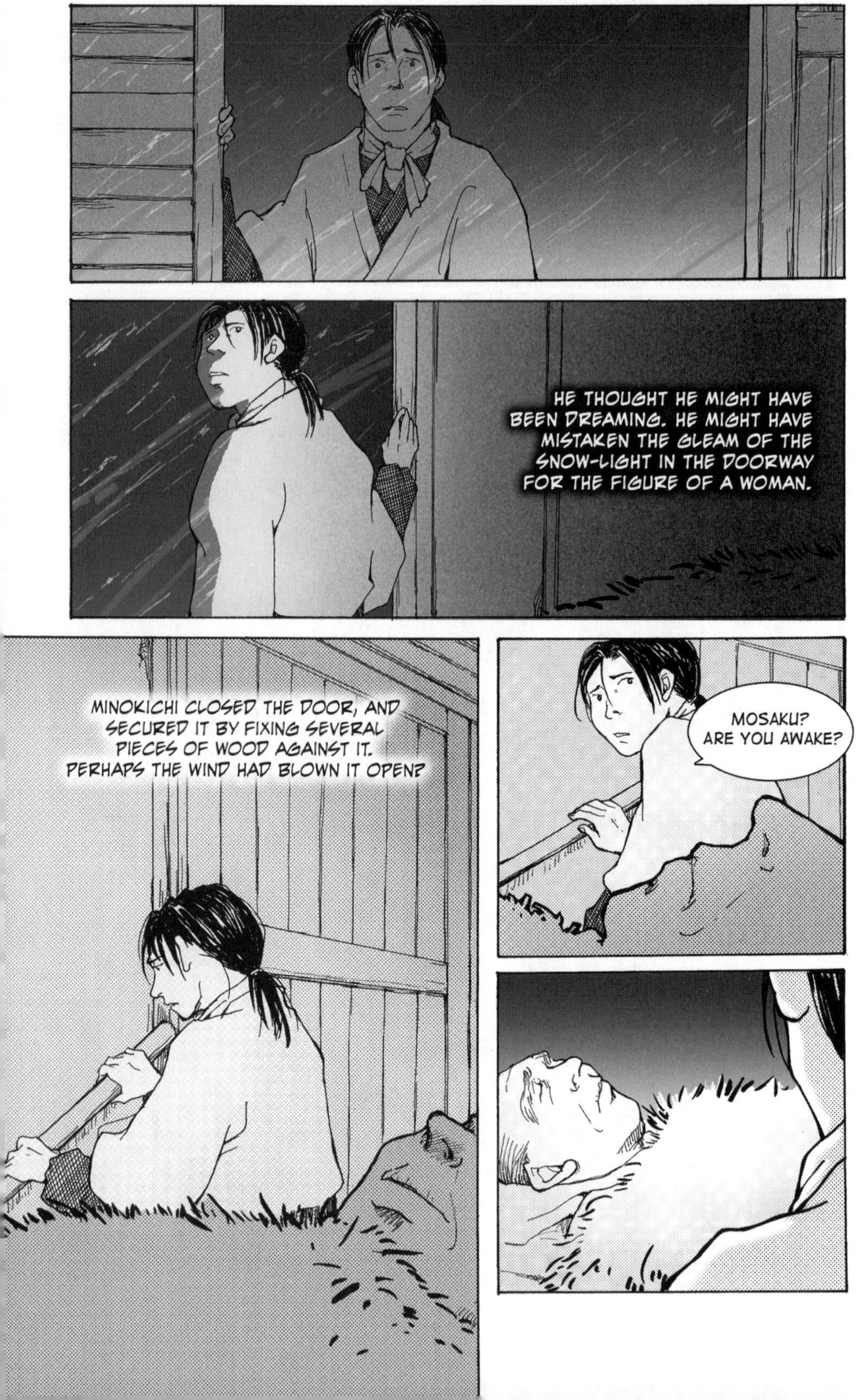
HE THOUGHT HE MIGHT HAVE BEEN DREAMING. HE MIGHT HAVE MISTAKEN THE GLEAM OF THE SNOW-LIGHT IN THE DOORWAY FOR THE FIGURE OF A WOMAN.
MINOKICHI CLOSED THE DOOR, AND SECURED IT BY FIXING SEVERAL PIECES OF WOOD AGAINST IT. PERHAPS THE WIND HAD BLOWN IT OPEN?
MOSAKU? ARE YOU AWAKE?

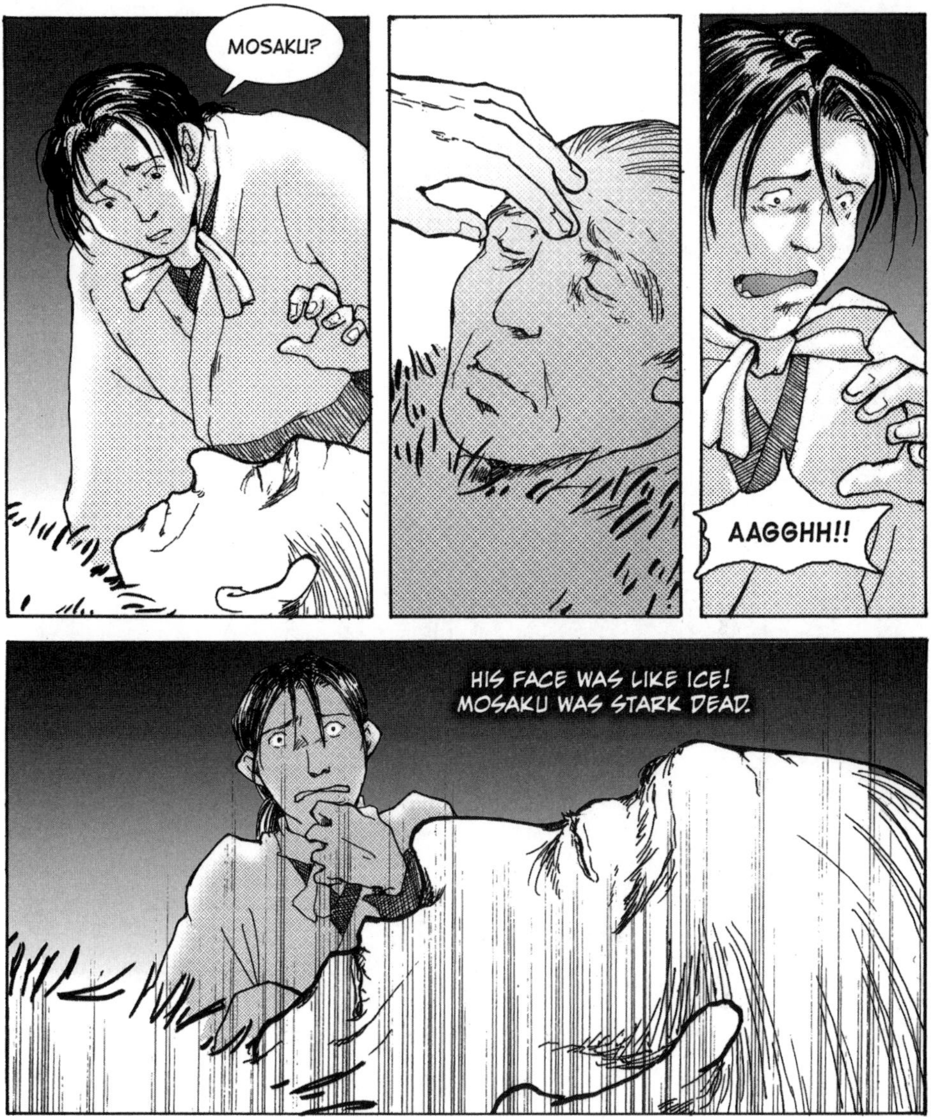
MOSAKU?
AAGGHH!!
HIS FACE WAS LIKE ICE!
MOSAKU WAS STARK DEAD.

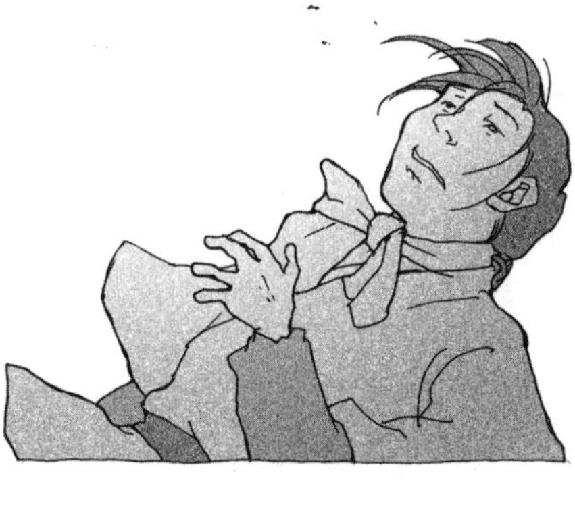

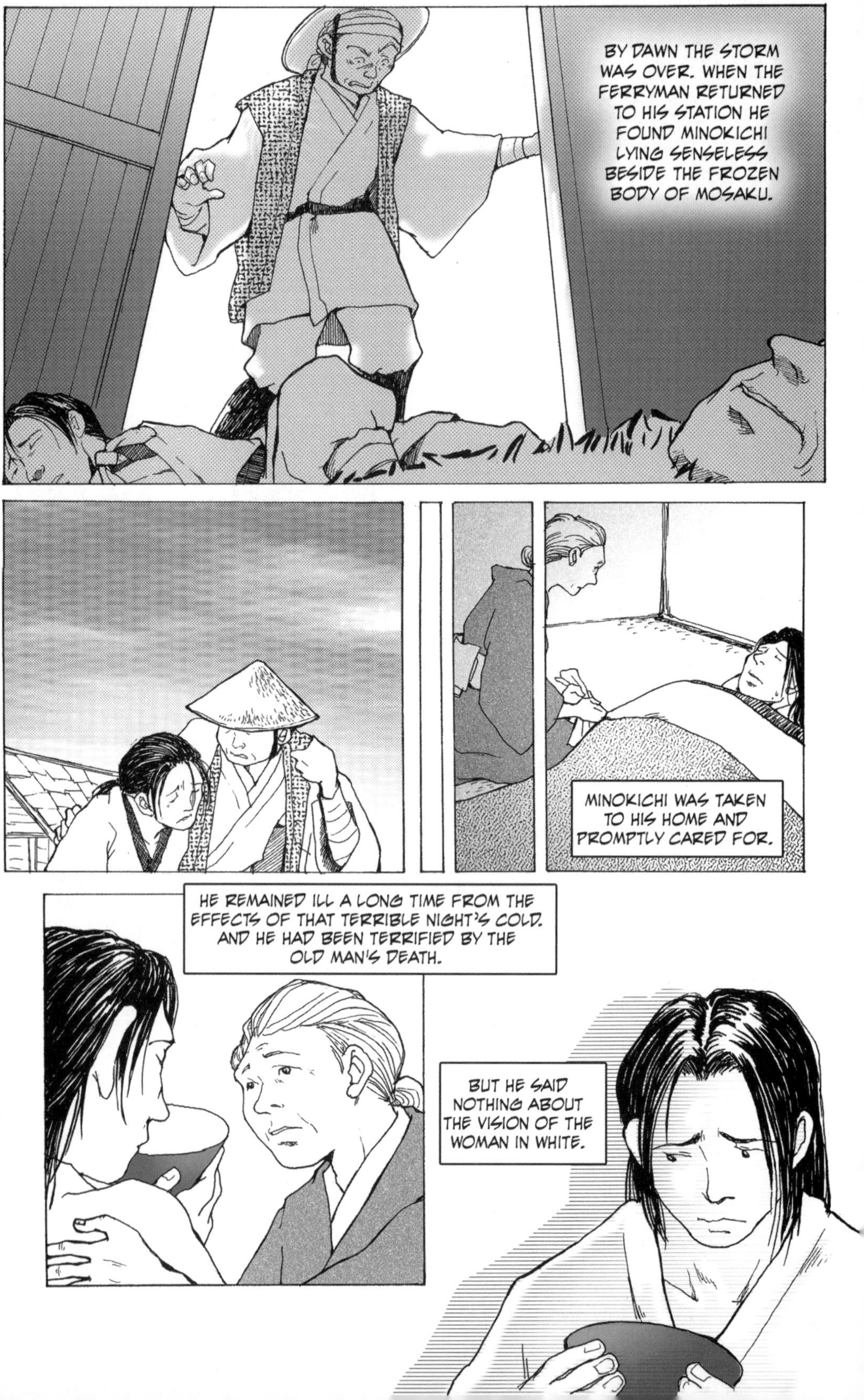
BY DAWN THE STORM WAS OVER. WHEN THE FERRYMAN RETURNED TO HIS STATION HE FOUND MINOKICHI LYING SENSELESS BESIDE THE FROZEN BODY OF MOSAKU.
MINOKICHI WAS TAKEN TO HIS HOME AND PROMPTLY CARED FOR.
HE REMAINED ILL A LONG TIME FROM THE EFFECTS OF THAT TERRIBLE NIGHT'S COLD. AND HE HAD BEEN TERRIFIED BY THE OLD MAN'S DEATH.
BUT HE SAID NOTHING ABOUT THE VISION OF THE WOMAN IN WHITE.

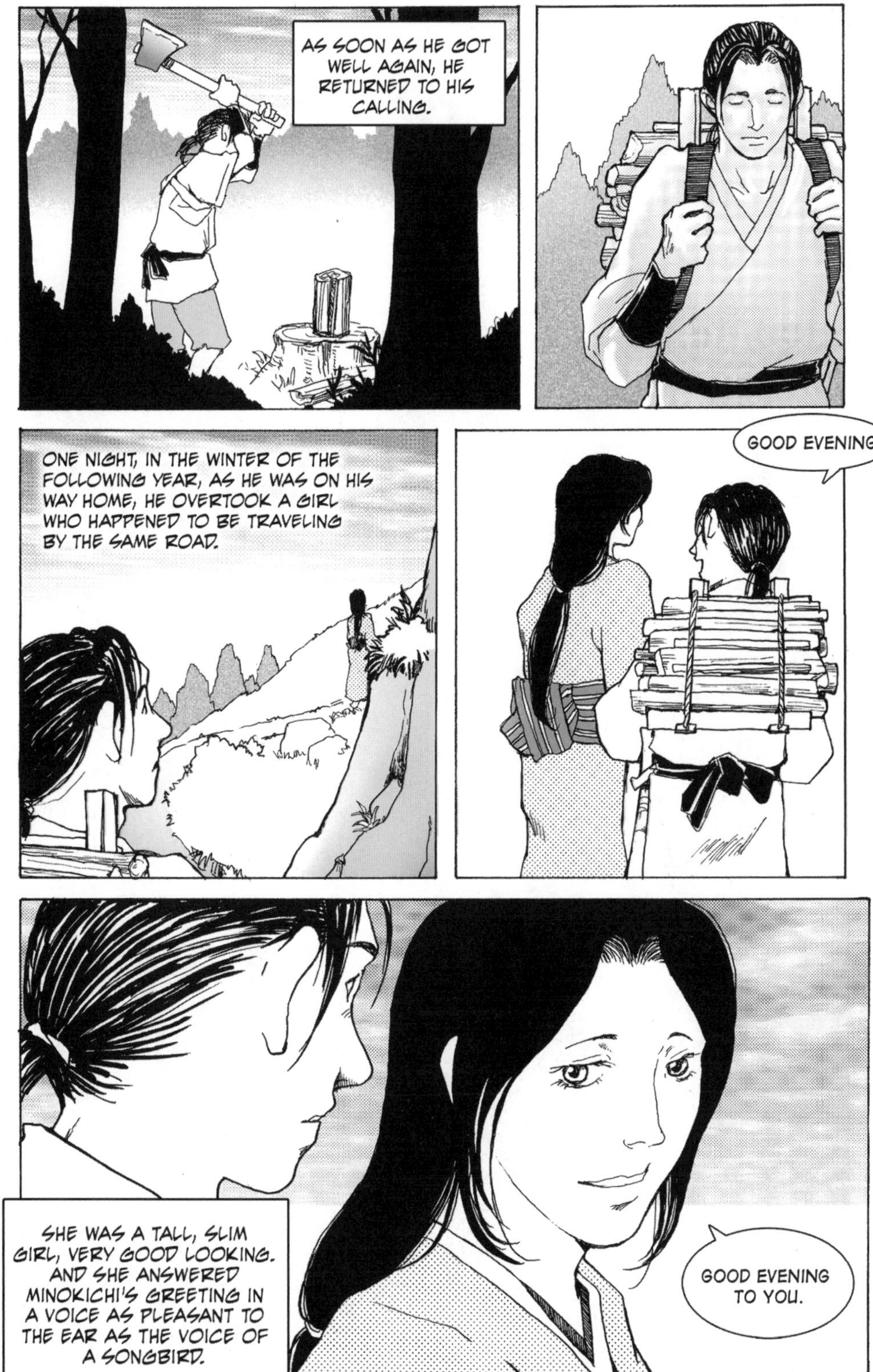
AS SOON AS HE GOT WELL AGAIN, HE RETURNED TO HIS CALLING.
ONE NIGHT, IN THE WINTER OF THE FOLLOWING YEAR, AS HE WAS ON HIS WAY HOME, HE OVERTOOK A GIRL WHO HAPPENED TO BE TRAVELING BY THE SAME ROAD.
GOOD EVENING.
SHE WAS A TALL, SLIM GIRL, VERY GOOD LOOKING. AND SHE ANSWERED MINOKICHI'S GREETING IN A VOICE AS PLEASANT TO THE EAR AS THE VOICE OF A SONGBIRD.
GOOD EVENING TO YOU.

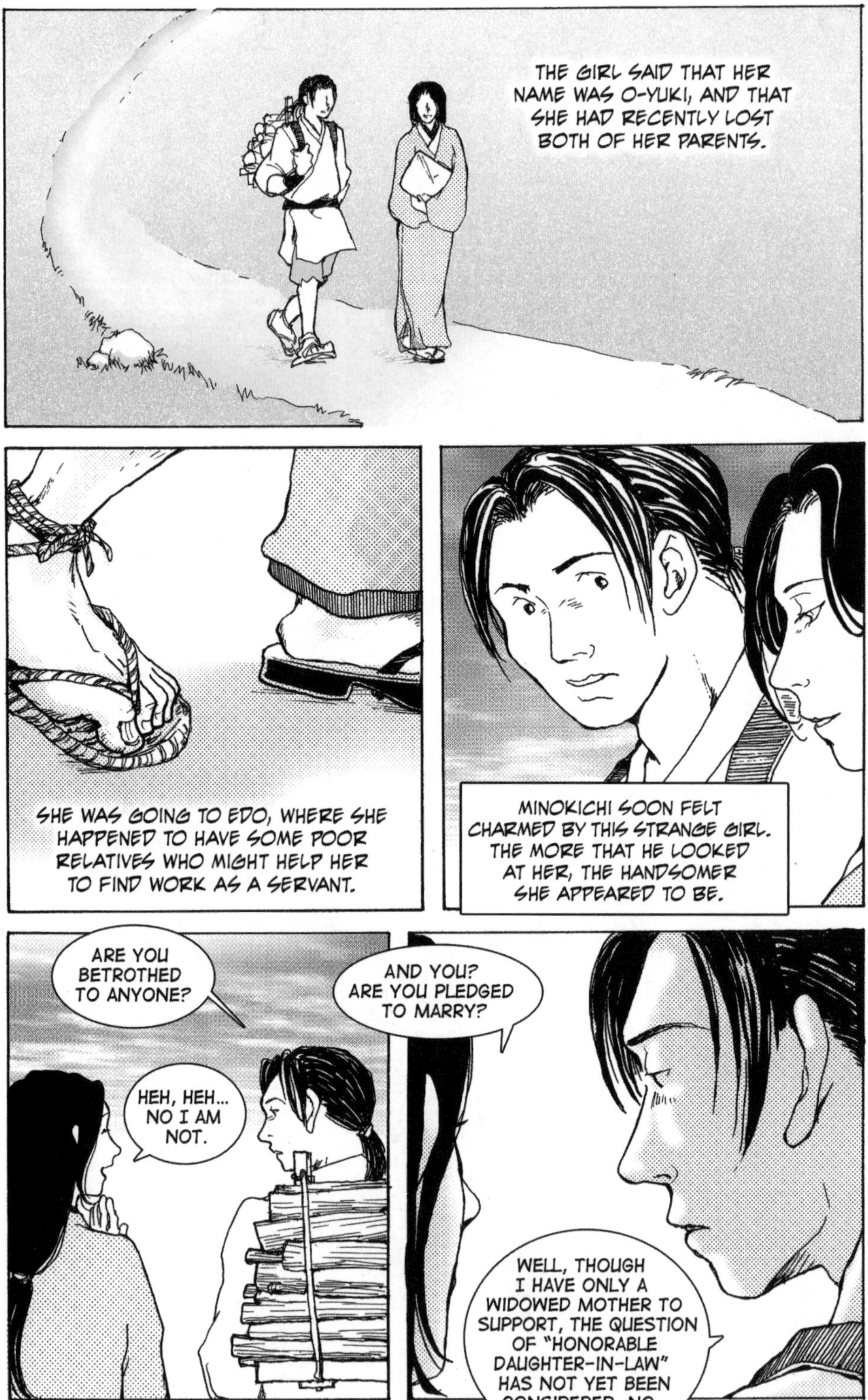
THE GIRL SAID THAT HER NAME WAS O-YUKI, AND THAT SHE HAD RECENTLY LOST BOTH OF HER PARENTS.
SHE WAS GOING TO EDO, WHERE SHE HAPPENED TO HAVE SOME POOR RELATIVES WHO MIGHT HELP HER TO FIND WORK AS A SERVANT.
MINOKICHI SOON FELT CHARMED BY THIS STRANGE GIRL. THE MORE THAT HE LOOKED AT HER, THE HANDSOMER SHE APPEARED TO BE.
ARE YOU BETROTHED TO ANYONE?
HEH, HEH... NO I AM NOT.
AND YOU? ARE YOU PLEDGED TO MARRY?
WELL, THOUGH I HAVE ONLY A WIDOWED MOTHER TO SUPPORT, THE QUESTION OF "HONORABLE DAUGHTER-IN-LAW" HAS NOT YET BEEN CONSIDERED, NO.

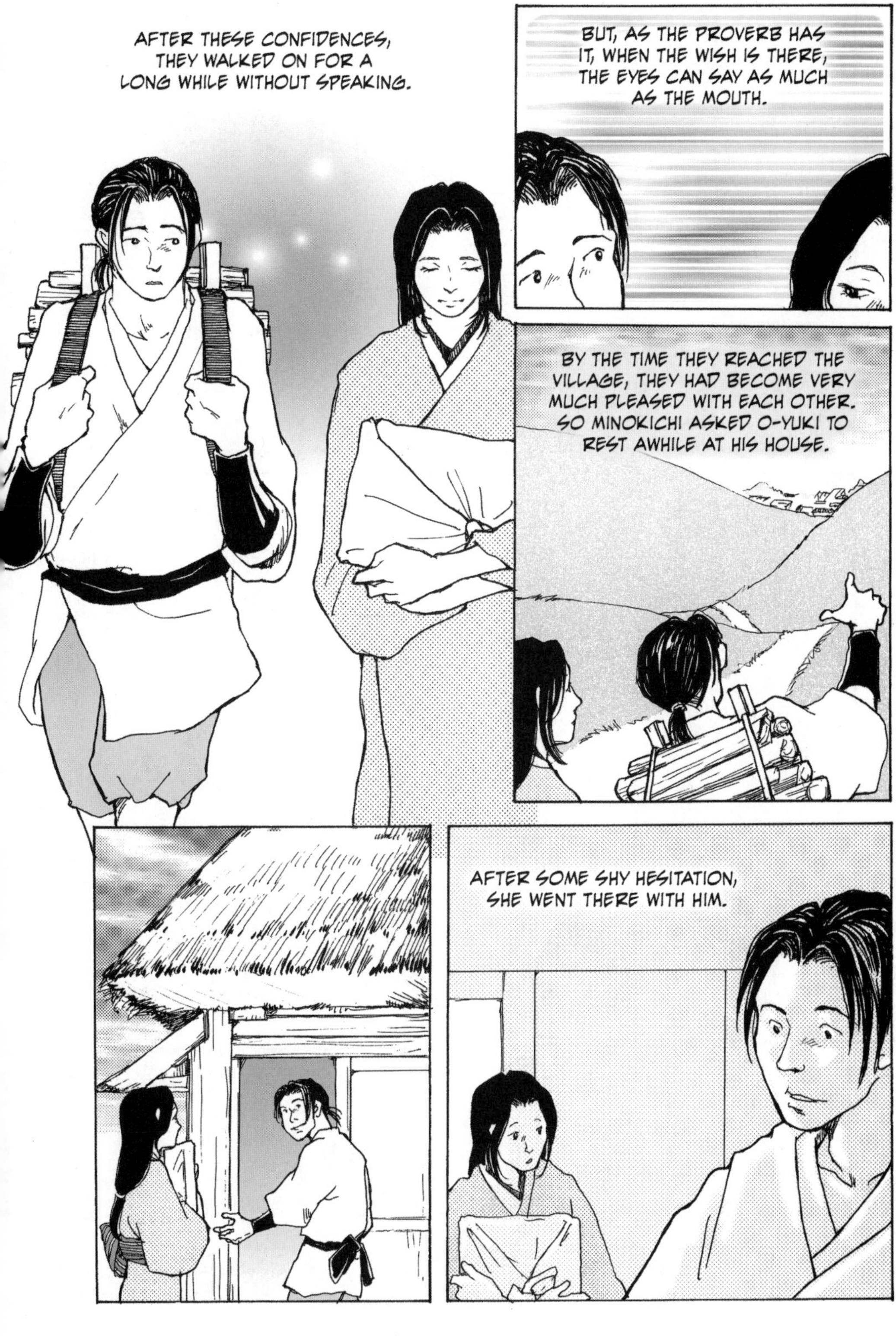
AFTER THESE CONFIDENCES, THEY WALKED ON FOR A LONG WHILE WITHOUT SPEAKING.
BUT, AS THE PROVERB HAS IT, WHEN THE WISH IS THERE, THE EYES CAN SAY AS MUCH AS THE MOUTH.
BY THE TIME THEY REACHED THE VILLAGE, THEY HAD BECOME VERY MUCH PLEASED WITH EACH OTHER. SO MINOKICHI ASKED O-YUKI TO REST AWHILE AT HIS HOUSE.
AFTER SOME SHY HESITATION, SHE WENT THERE WITH HIM.

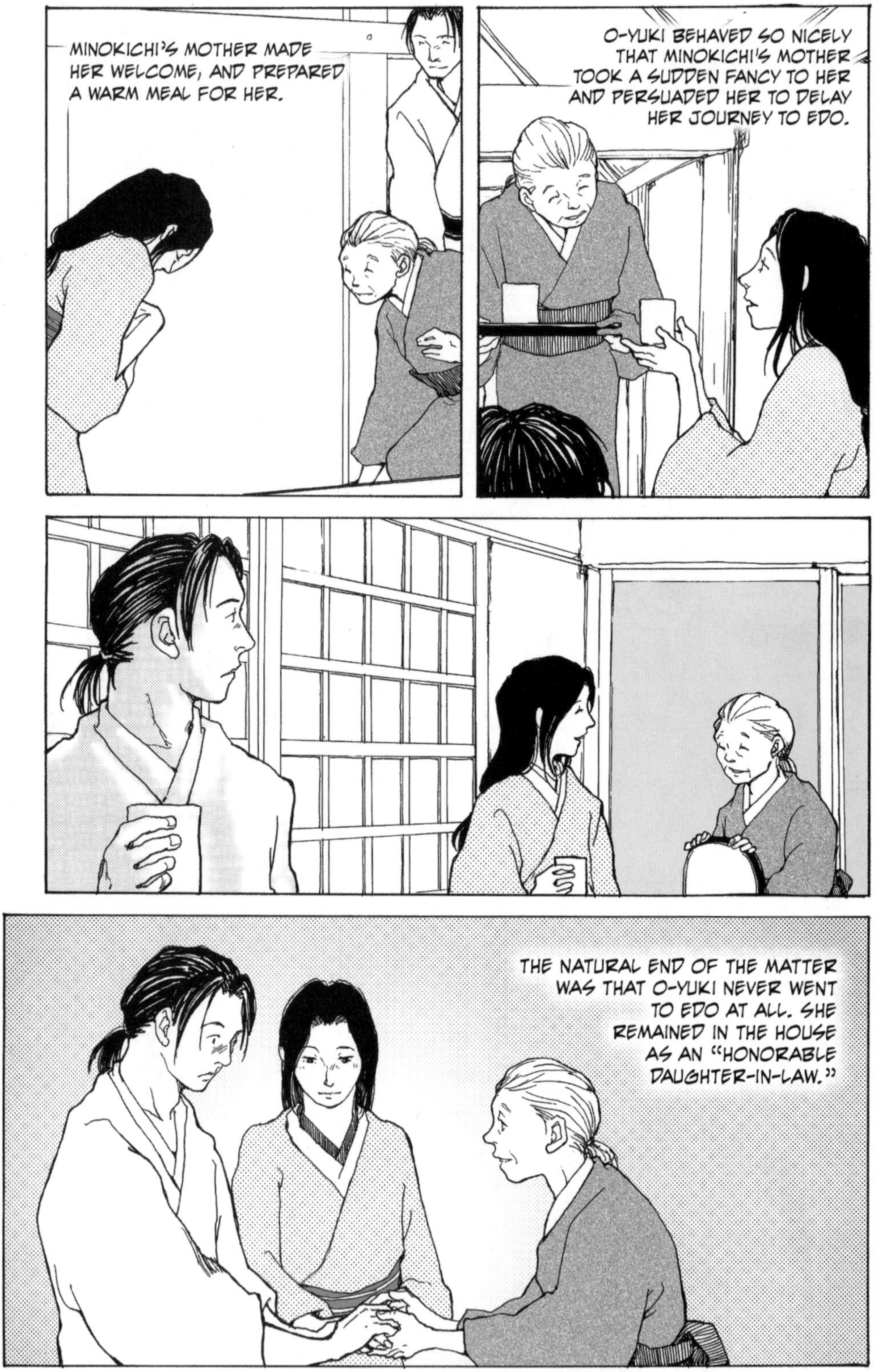
MINOKICHI'S MOTHER MADE HER WELCOME, AND PREPARED A WARM MEAL FOR HER.
O-YUKI BEHAVED SO NICELY THAT MINOKICHI'S MOTHER TOOK A SUDDEN FANCY TO HER AND PERSUADED HER TO DELAY HER JOURNEY TO EDO.
THE NATURAL END OF THE MATTER WAS THAT O-YUKI NEVER WENT TO EDO AT ALL. SHE REMAINED IN THE HOUSE AS AN "HONORABLE DAUGHTER-IN-LAW."

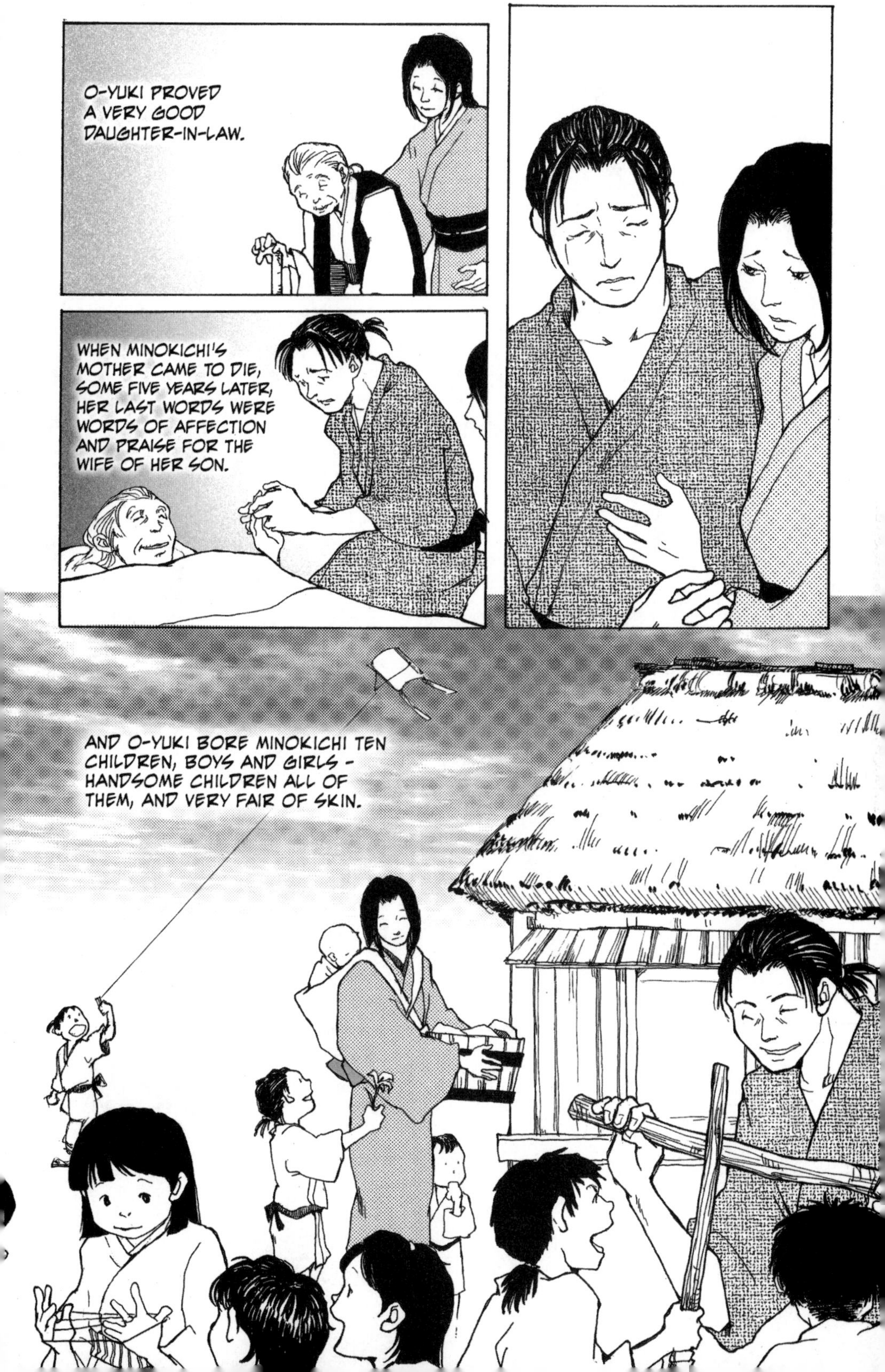
O-YUKI PROVED A VERY GOOD DAUGHTER-IN-LAW.
WHEN MINOKICHI'S MOTHER CAME TO DIE, SOME FIVE YEARS LATER, HER LAST WORDS WERE WORDS OF AFFECTION AND PRAISE FOR THE WIFE OF HER SON.
AND O-YUKI BORE MINOKICHI TEN CHILDREN, BOYS AND GIRLS - HANDSOME CHILDREN ALL OF THEM, AND VERY FAIR OF SKIN.

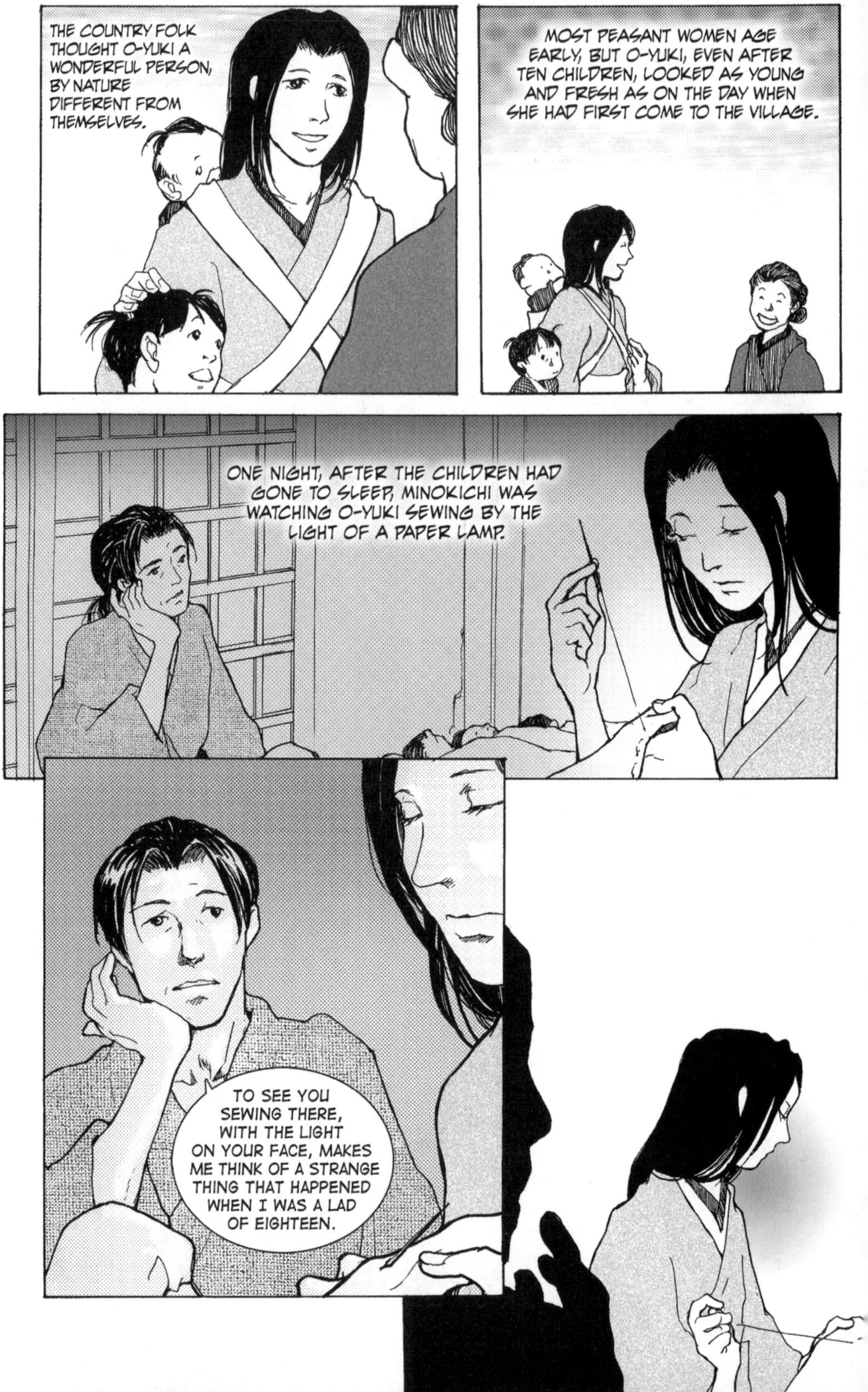
THE COUNTRY FOLK THOUGHT O-YUKI A WONDERFUL PERSON, BY NATURE DIFFERENT FROM THEMSELVES.
MOST PEASANT WOMEN AGE EARLY, BUT O-YUKI, EVEN AFTER TEN CHILDREN, LOOKED AS YOUNG AND FRESH AS ON THE DAY WHEN SHE HAD FIRST COME TO THE VILLAGE.
ONE NIGHT, AFTER THE CHILDREN HAD GONE TO SLEEP, MINOKICHI WAS WATCHING O-YUKI SEWING BY THE LIGHT OF A PAPER LAMP.
TO SEE YOU SEWING THERE, WITH THE LIGHT ON YOUR FACE, MAKES ME THINK OF A STRANGE THING THAT HAPPENED WHEN I WAS A LAD OF EIGHTEEN.

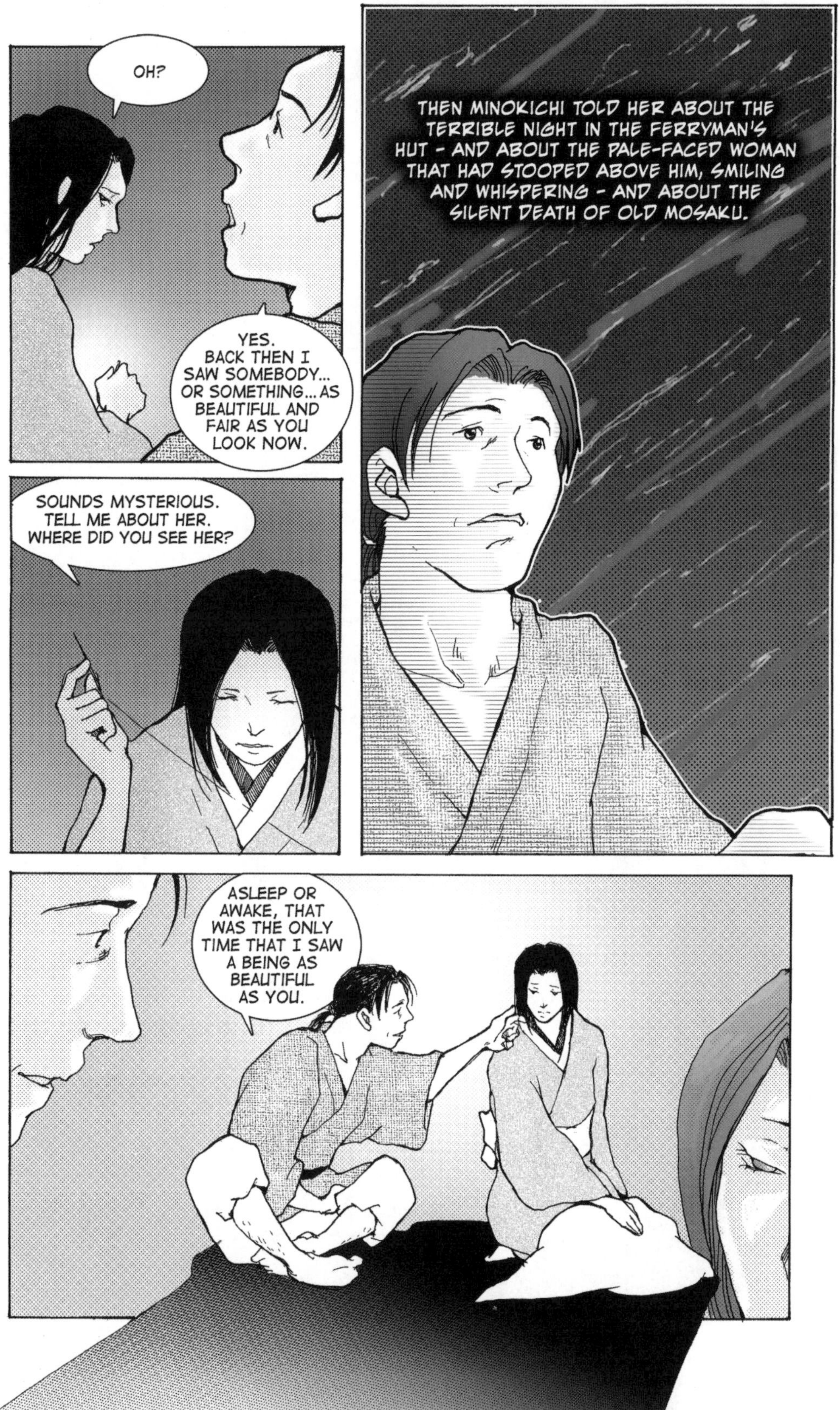
OH?
YES. BACK THEN I SAW SOMEBODY... OR SOMETHING... AS BEAUTIFUL AND FAIR AS YOU LOOK NOW.
SOUNDS MYSTERIOUS. TELL ME ABOUT HER. WHERE DID YOU SEE HER?
THEN MINOKICHI TOLD HER ABOUT THE TERRIBLE NIGHT IN THE FERRYMAN'S HUT - AND ABOUT THE PALE-FACED WOMAN THAT HAD STOOPED ABOVE HIM, SMILING AND WHISPERING - AND ABOUT THE SILENT DEATH OF OLD MOSAKU.
ASLEEP OR AWAKE, THAT WAS THE ONLY TIME THAT I SAW A BEING AS BEAUTIFUL AS YOU.

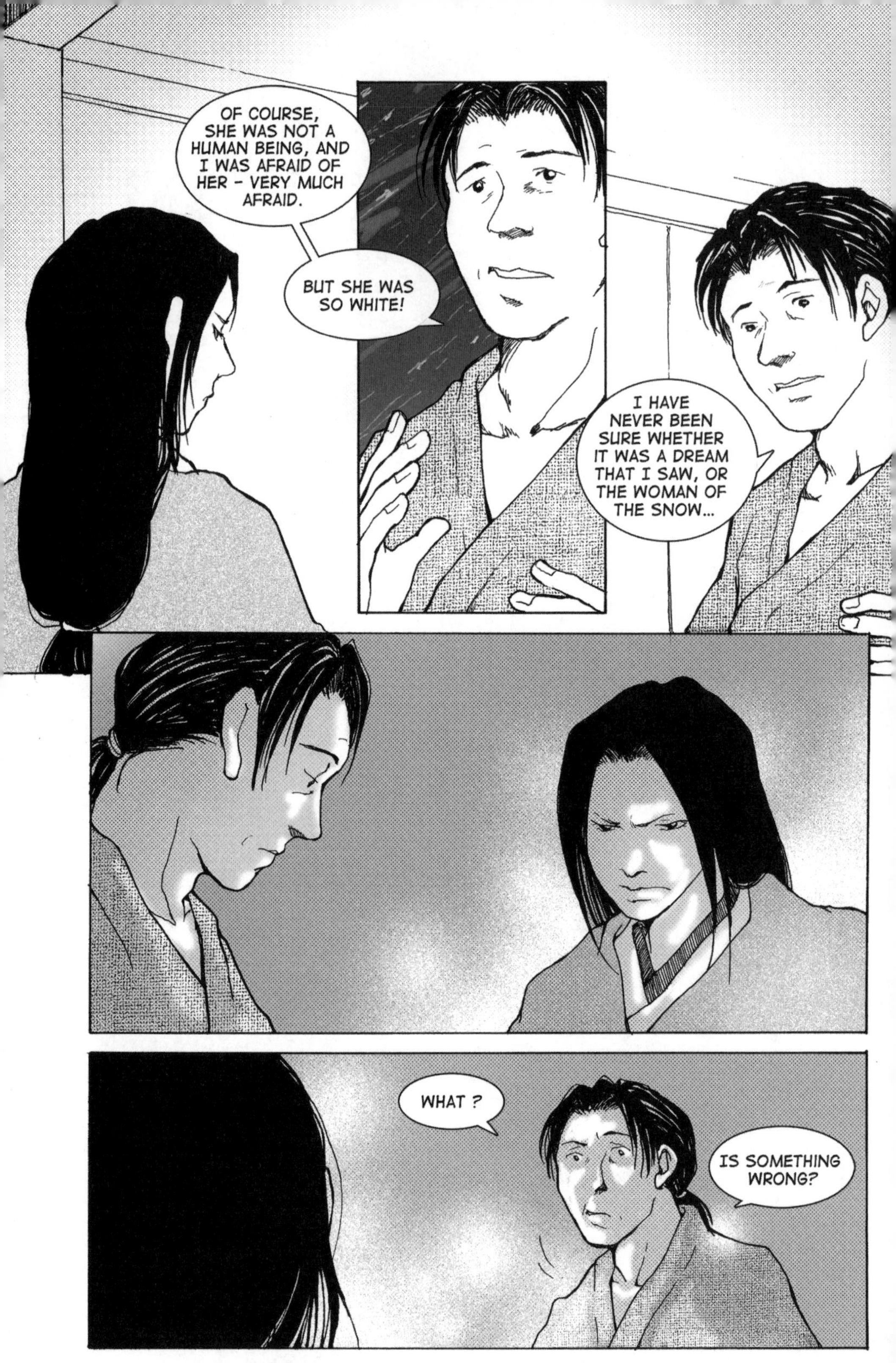
OF COURSE, SHE WAS NOT A HUMAN BEING, AND I WAS AFRAID OF HER - VERY MUCH AFRAID.
BUT SHE WAS SO WHITE!
I HAVE NEVER BEEN SURE WHETHER IT WAS A DREAM THAT I SAW, OR THE WOMAN OF THE SNOW...
WHAT ?
IS SOMETHING WRONG?

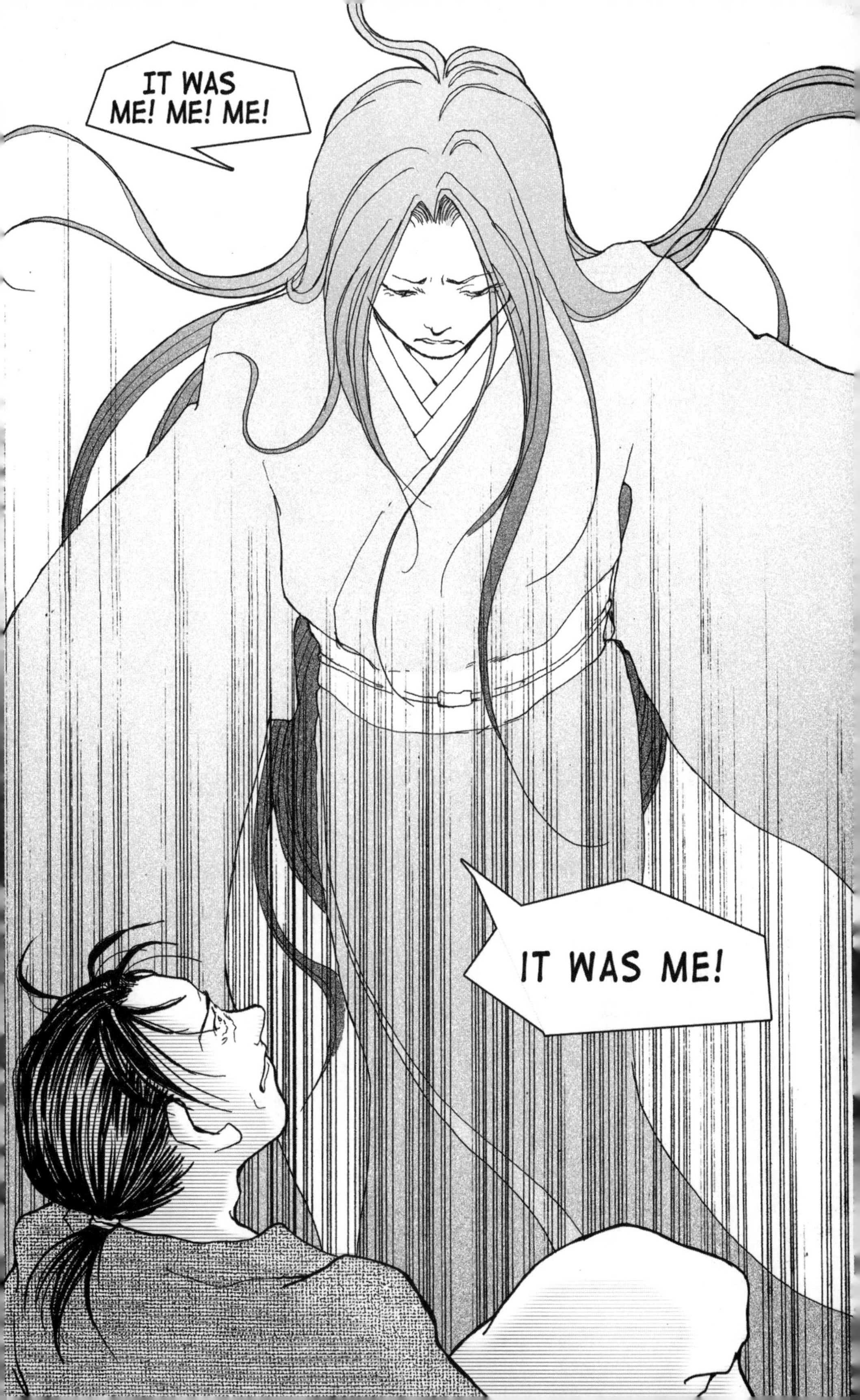
IT WAS ME! ME! ME!
IT WAS ME!

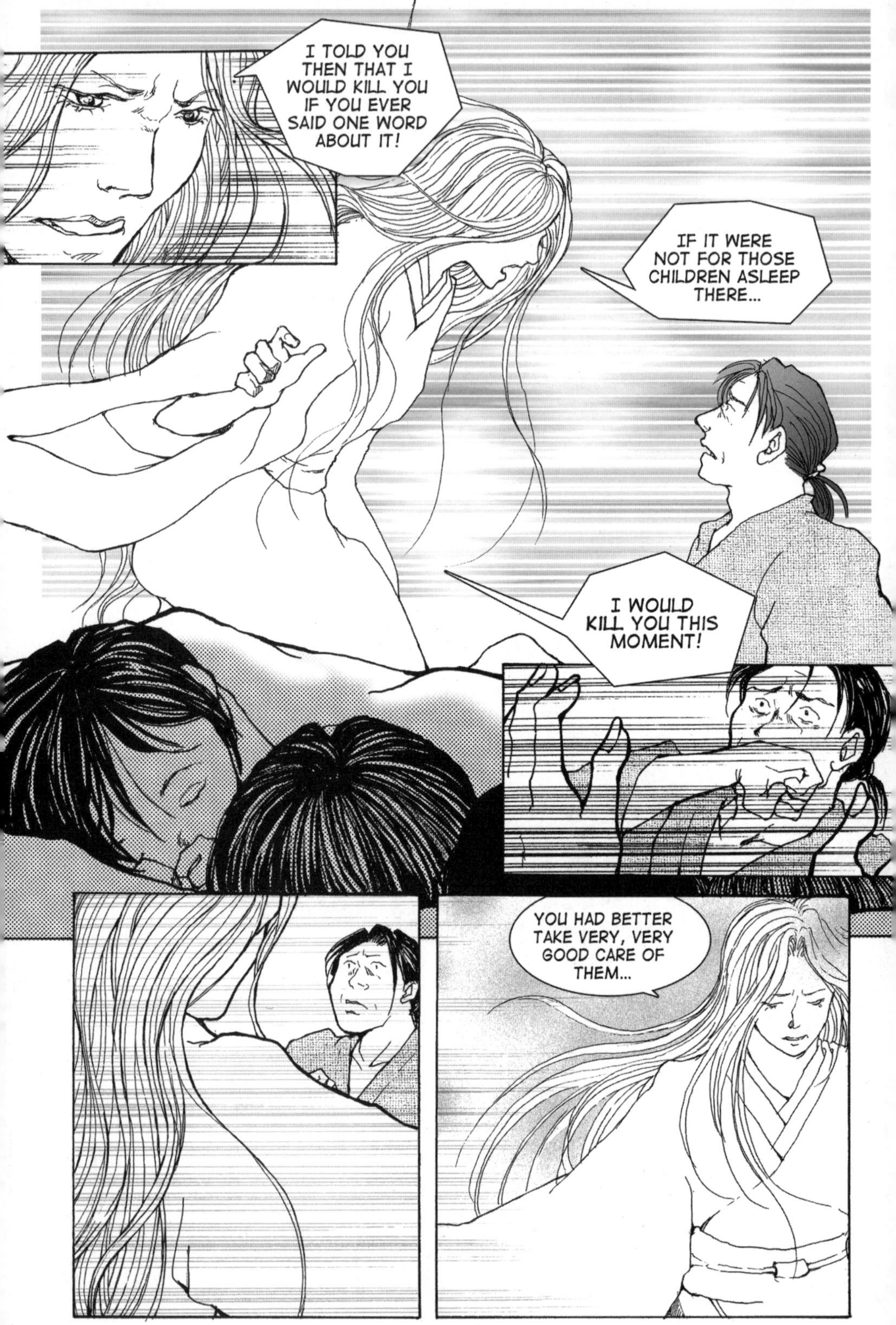

I TOLD YOU THEN THAT I WOULD KILL YOU IF YOU EVER SAID ONE WORD ABOUT IT!
IF IT WERE NOT FOR THOSE CHILDREN ASLEEP THERE...
I WOULD KILL YOU THIS MOMENT!
YOU HAD BETTER TAKE VERY, VERY GOOD CARE OF THEM...

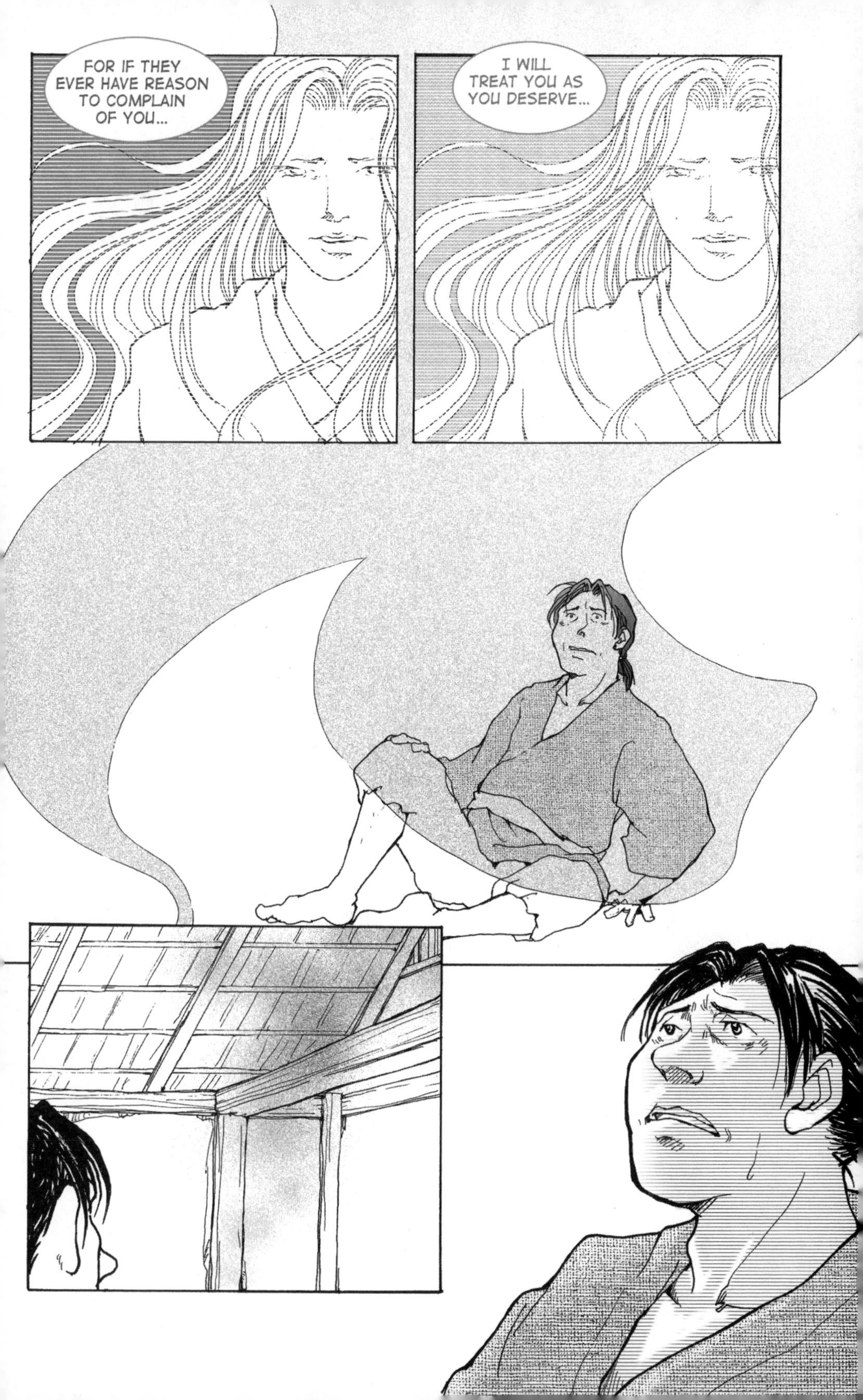
FOR IF THEY EVER HAVE REASON TO COMPLAIN OF YOU...
I WILL TREAT YOU AS YOU DESERVE...

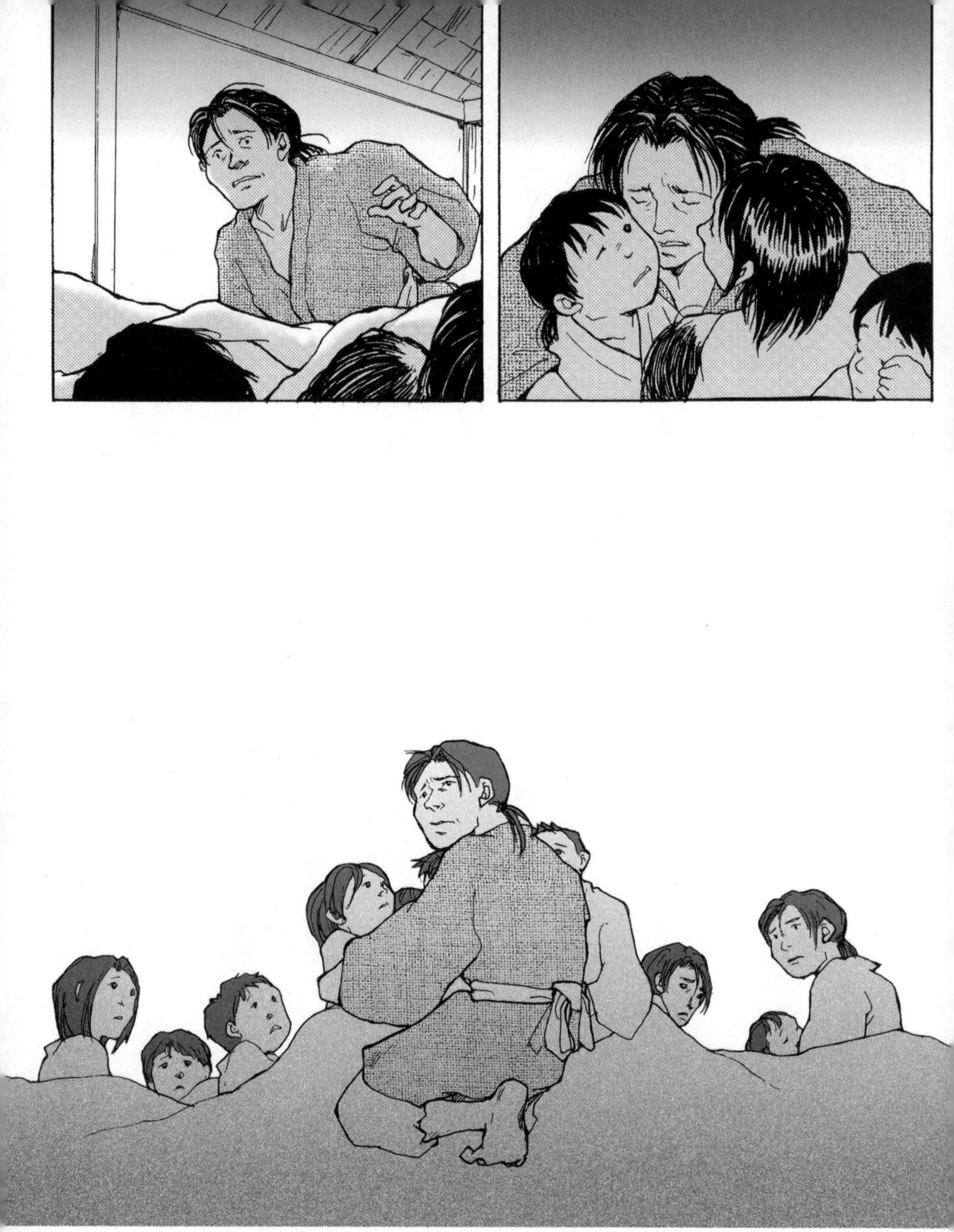

SHE WAS NEVER SEEN AGAIN.

鏡と鐘

OF A MIRROR AND A BELL

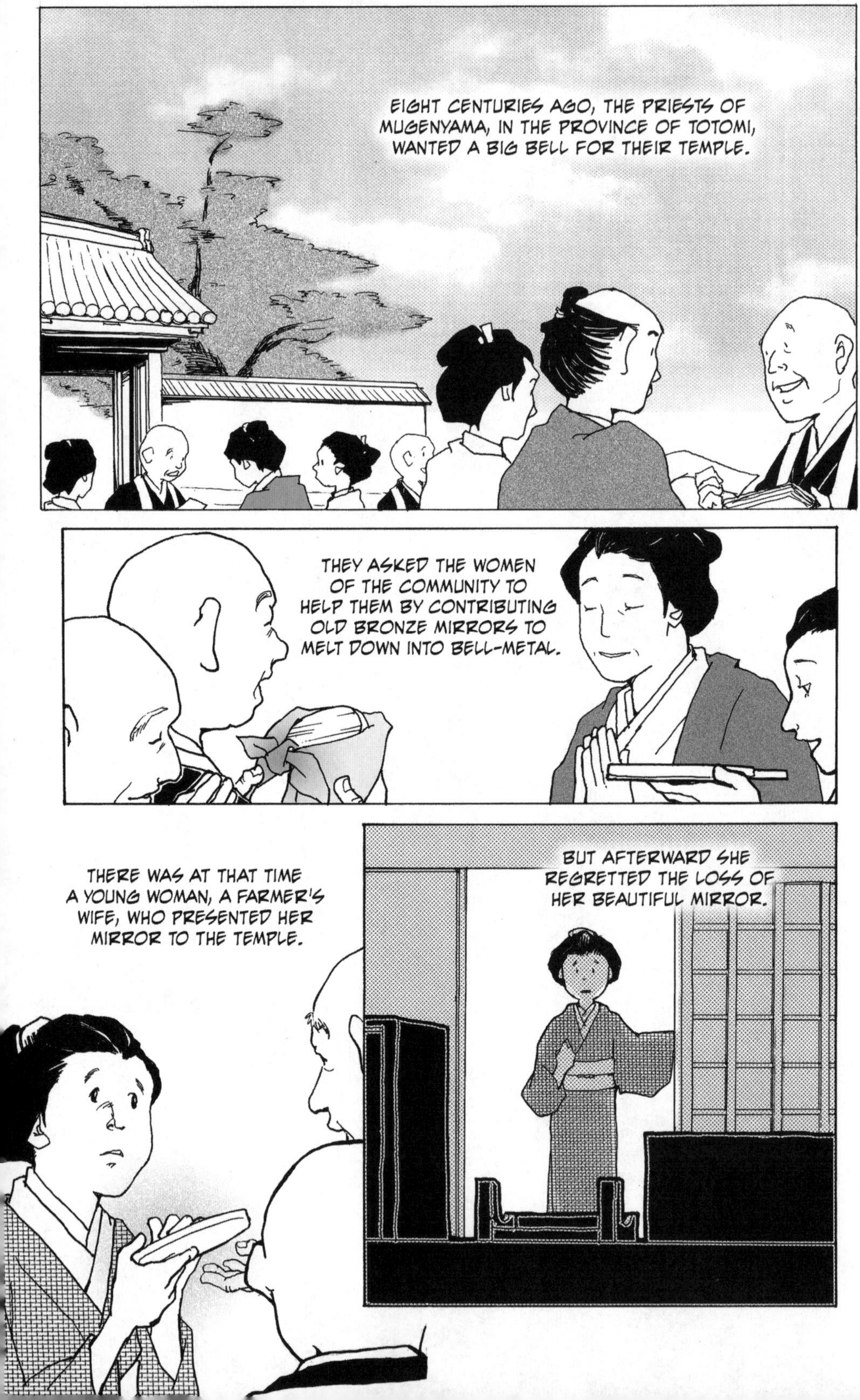
EIGHT CENTURIES AGO, THE PRIESTS OF MUGENYAMA, IN THE PROVINCE OF TOTOMI, WANTED A BIG BELL FOR THEIR TEMPLE.
THEY ASKED THE WOMEN OF THE COMMUNITY TO HELP THEM BY CONTRIBUTING OLD BRONZE MIRRORS TO MELT DOWN INTO BELL-METAL.
THERE WAS AT THAT TIME A YOUNG WOMAN, A FARMER'S WIFE, WHO PRESENTED HER MIRROR TO THE TEMPLE.
BUT AFTERWARD SHE REGRETTED THE LOSS OF HER BEAUTIFUL MIRROR.

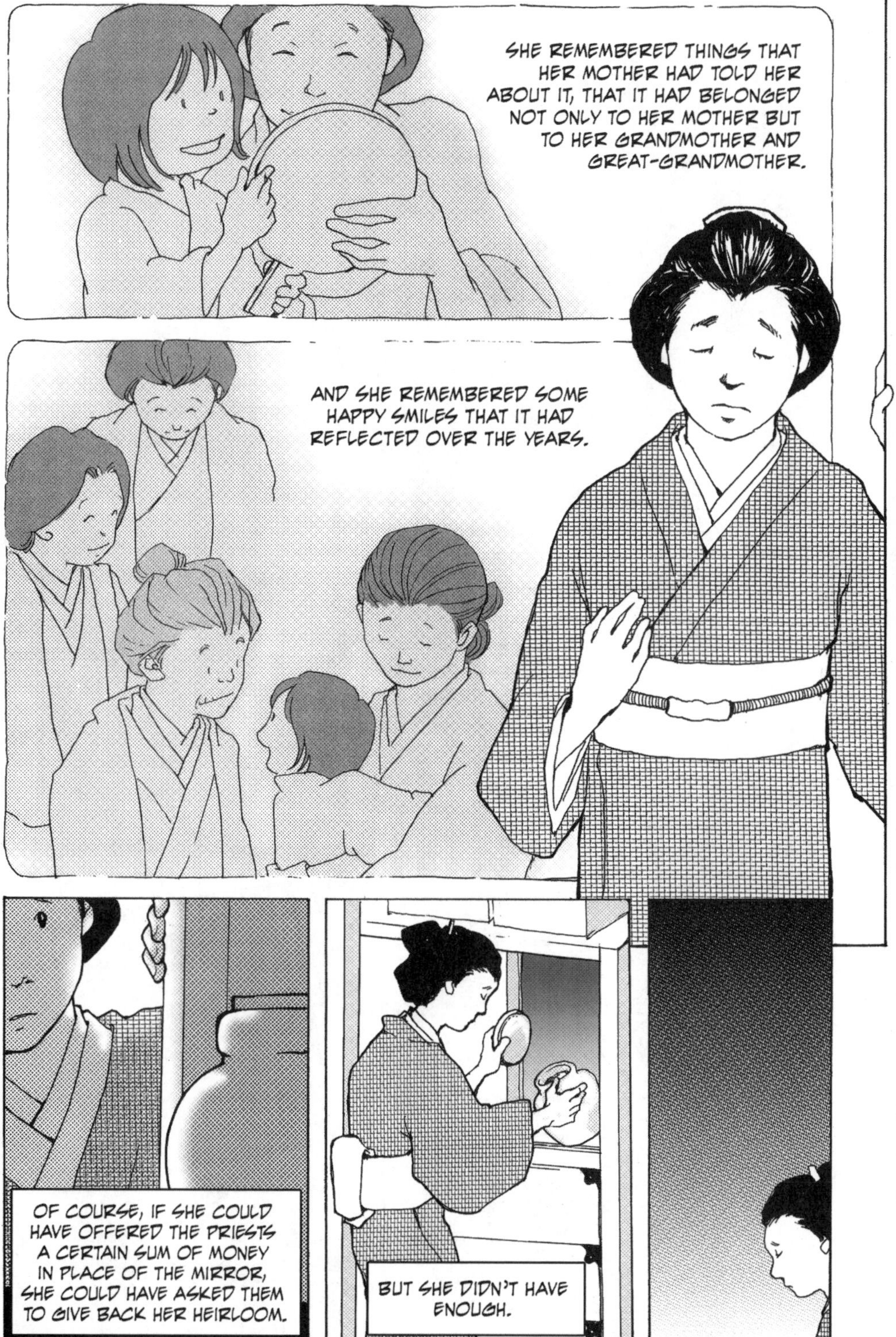
SHE REMEMBERED THINGS THAT HER MOTHER HAD TOLD HER ABOUT IT, THAT IT HAD BELONGED NOT ONLY TO HER MOTHER BUT TO HER GRANDMOTHER AND GREAT-GRANDMOTHER.
AND SHE REMEMBERED SOME HAPPY SMILES THAT IT HAD REFLECTED OVER THE YEARS.
OF COURSE, IF SHE COULD HAVE OFFERED THE PRIESTS A CERTAIN SUM OF MONEY IN PLACE OF THE MIRROR, SHE COULD HAVE ASKED THEM TO GIVE BACK HER HEIRLOOM.
BUT SHE DIDN'T HAVE ENOUGH.

WHENEVER SHE WENT TO THE TEMPLE, SHE SAW HER MIRROR LYING IN THE COURTYARD.

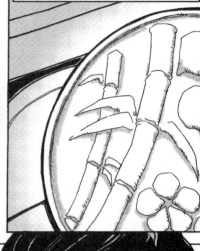

SHE KNEW IT BY THE IMAGE OF BAMBOO, PLUM, AND PINE ON THE BACK, WHICH DELIGHTED HER BABY EYES WHEN HER MOTHER FIRST SHOWED HER THE MIRROR.

SHE LONGED FOR SOME CHANCE TO STEAL THE MIRROR AND HIDE IT SO THAT SHE MIGHT TREASURE IT ALWAYS.

BUT THE CHANCE NEVER CAME, AND SHE BECAME VERY UNHAPPY.

IT FELT AS IF SHE HAD FOOLISHLY GIVEN AWAY A PART OF HER LIFE.

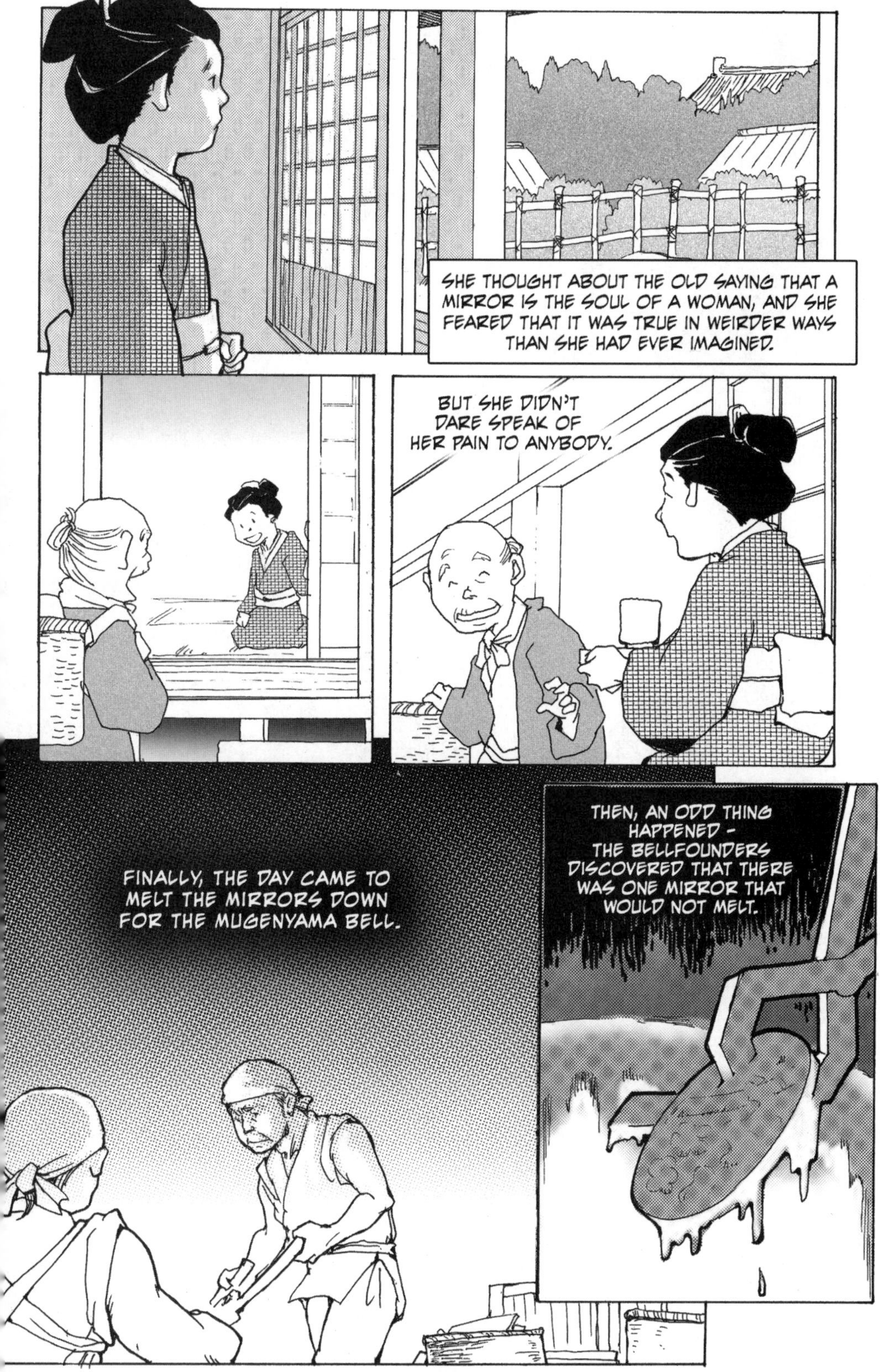
SHE THOUGHT ABOUT THE OLD SAYING THAT A MIRROR IS THE SOUL OF A WOMAN, AND SHE FEARED THAT IT WAS TRUE IN WEIRDER WAYS THAN SHE HAD EVER IMAGINED.
BUT SHE DIDN'T DARE SPEAK OF HER PAIN TO ANYBODY.
FINALLY, THE DAY CAME TO MELT THE MIRRORS DOWN FOR THE MUGENYAMA BELL.
THEN, AN ODD THING HAPPENED - THE BELLFOUNDERS DISCOVERED THAT THERE WAS ONE MIRROR THAT WOULD NOT MELT.

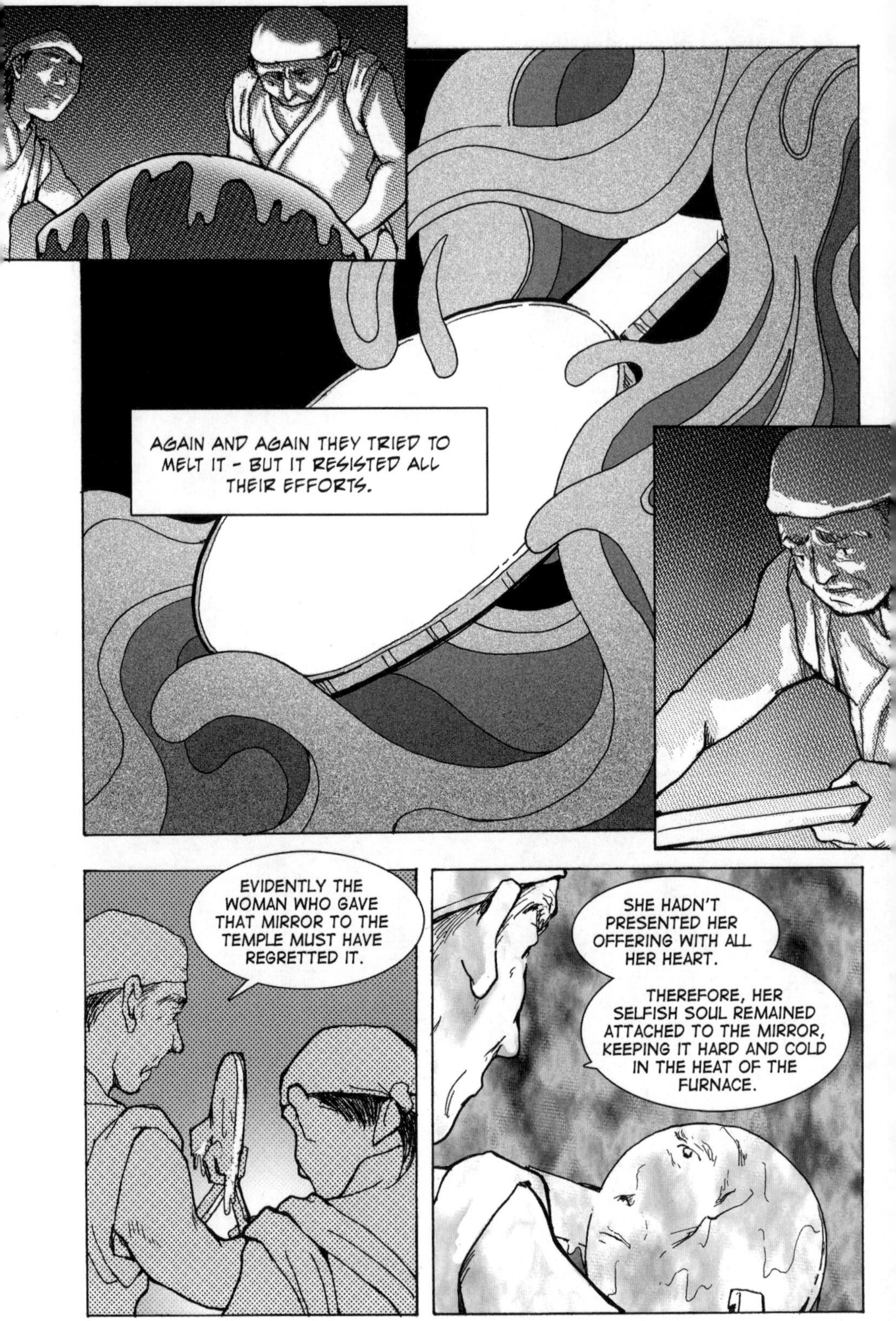
AGAIN AND AGAIN THEY TRIED TO MELT IT - BUT IT RESISTED ALL THEIR EFFORTS.
EVIDENTLY THE WOMAN WHO GAVE THAT MIRROR TO THE TEMPLE MUST HAVE REGRETTED IT.
SHE HADN'T PRESENTED HER OFFERING WITH ALL HER HEART.
THEREFORE, HER SELFISH SOUL REMAINED ATTACHED TO THE MIRROR, KEEPING IT HARD AND COLD IN THE HEAT OF THE FURNACE.

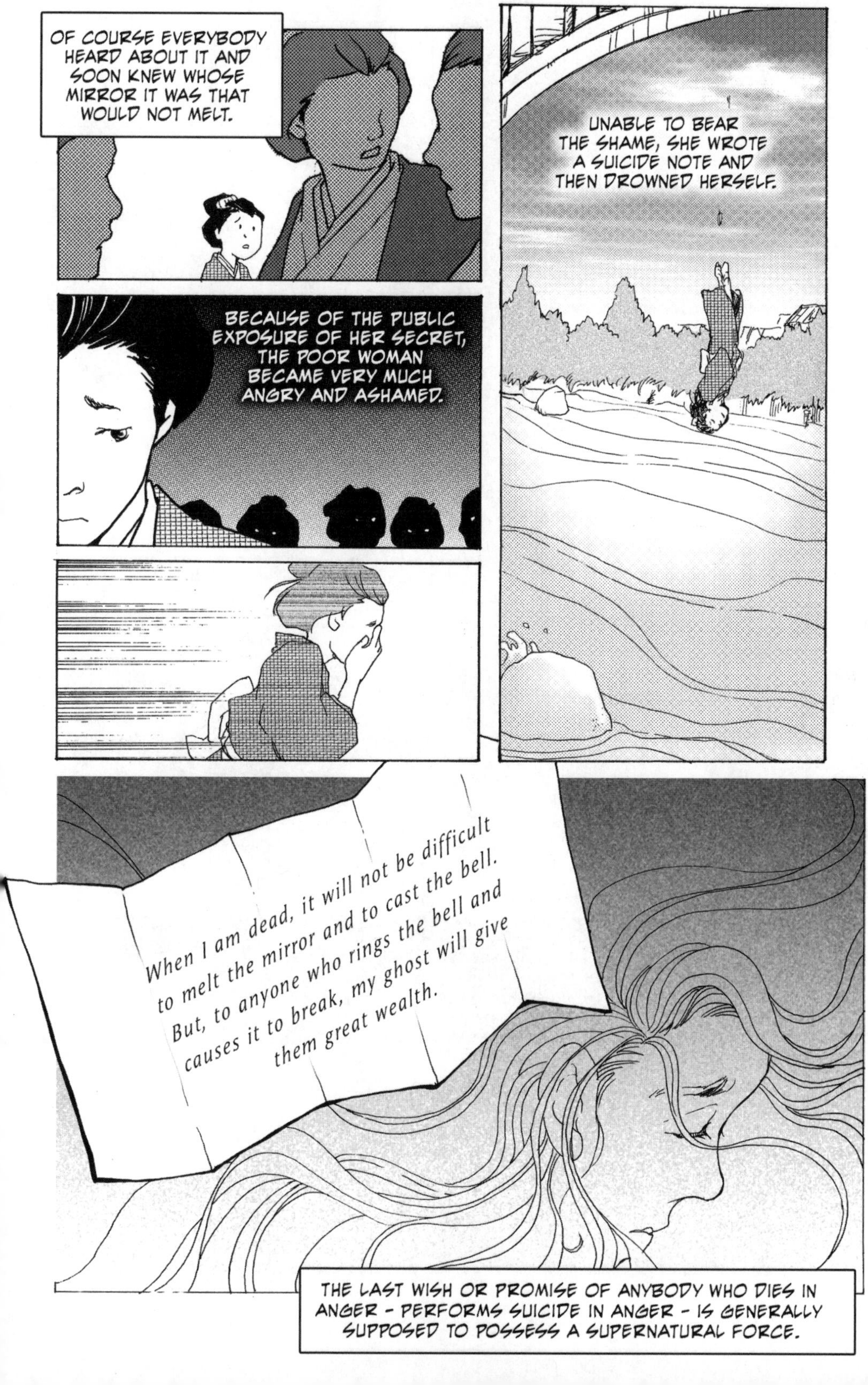
OF COURSE EVERYBODY HEARD ABOUT IT AND SOON KNEW WHOSE MIRROR IT WAS THAT WOULD NOT MELT.
BECAUSE OF THE PUBLIC EXPOSURE OF HER SECRET, THE POOR WOMAN BECAME VERY MUCH ANGRY AND ASHAMED.
UNABLE TO BEAR THE SHAME, SHE WROTE A SUICIDE NOTE AND THEN DROWNED HERSELF.
When I am dead, it will not be difficult to melt the mirror and to cast the bell. But, to anyone who rings the bell and causes it to break, my ghost will give them great wealth.
THE LAST WISH OR PROMISE OF ANYBODY WHO DIES IN ANGER - PERFORMS SUICIDE IN ANGER - IS GENERALLY SUPPOSED TO POSSESS A SUPERNATURAL FORCE.

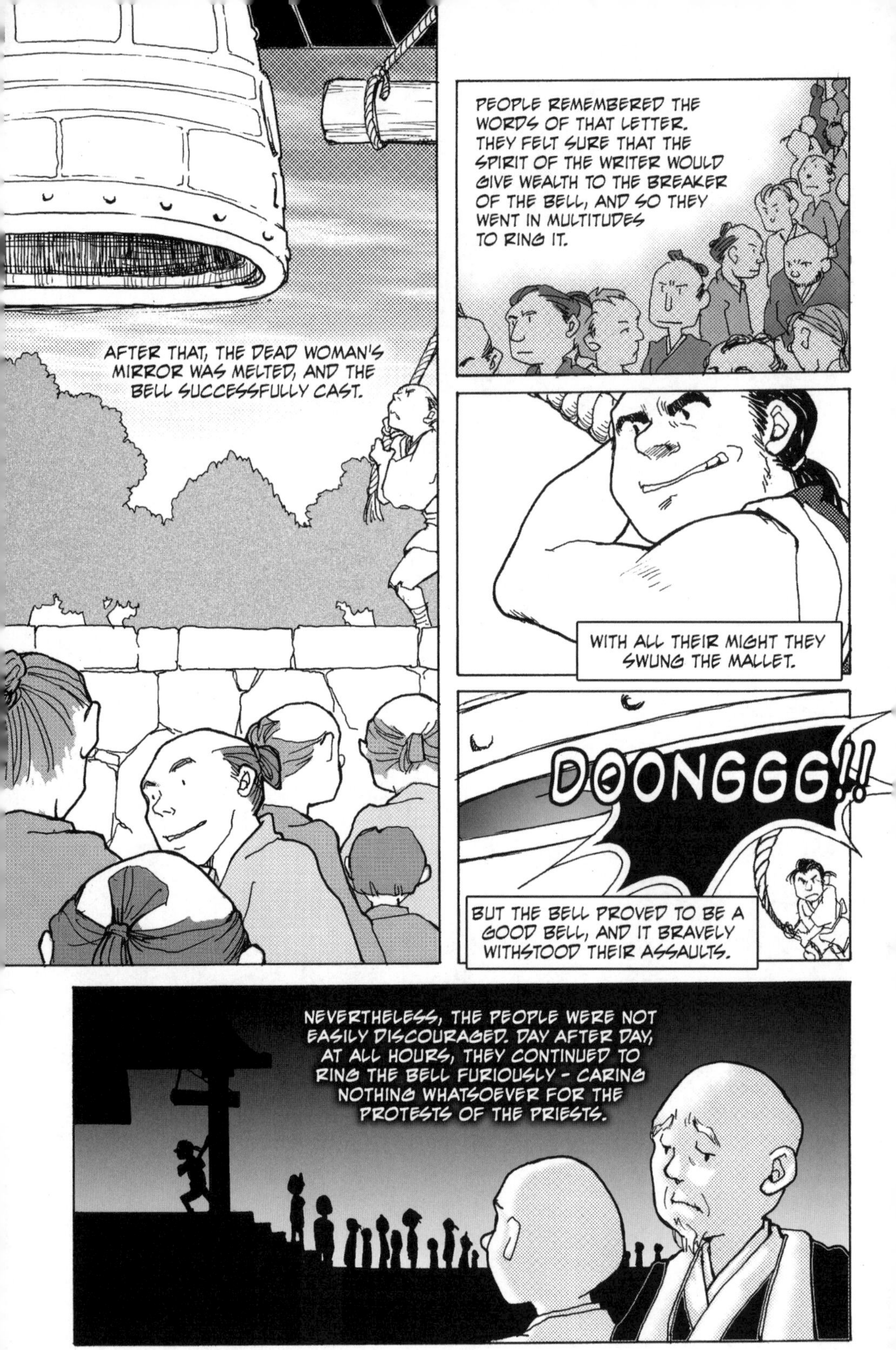

AFTER THAT, THE DEAD WOMAN'S MIRROR WAS MELTED, AND THE BELL SUCCESSFULLY CAST.
PEOPLE REMEMBERED THE WORDS OF THAT LETTER. THEY FELT SURE THAT THE SPIRIT OF THE WRITER WOULD GIVE WEALTH TO THE BREAKER OF THE BELL, AND SO THEY WENT IN MULTITUDES TO RING IT.
WITH ALL THEIR MIGHT THEY SWUNG THE MALLET.
DOONGGG!!
BUT THE BELL PROVED TO BE A GOOD BELL, AND IT BRAVELY WITHSTOOD THEIR ASSAULTS.
NEVERTHELESS, THE PEOPLE WERE NOT EASILY DISCOURAGED. DAY AFTER DAY, AT ALL HOURS, THEY CONTINUED TO RING THE BELL FURIOUSLY - CARING NOTHING WHATSOEVER FOR THE PROTESTS OF THE PRIESTS.

THE RINGING BECAME AN AFFLICTION AND THE PRIESTS COULD NOT ENDURE IT.

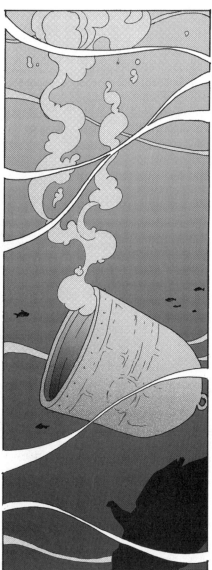

SO THEY GOT RID OF THE BELL BY ROLLING IT DOWN THE HILL INTO A SWAMP.

KASHIIING!

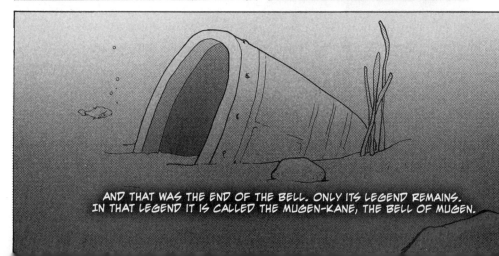
AND THAT WAS THE END OF THE BELL. ONLY ITS LEGEND REMAINS. IN THAT LEGEND IT IS CALLED THE MUGEN-KANE, THE BELL OF MUGEN.

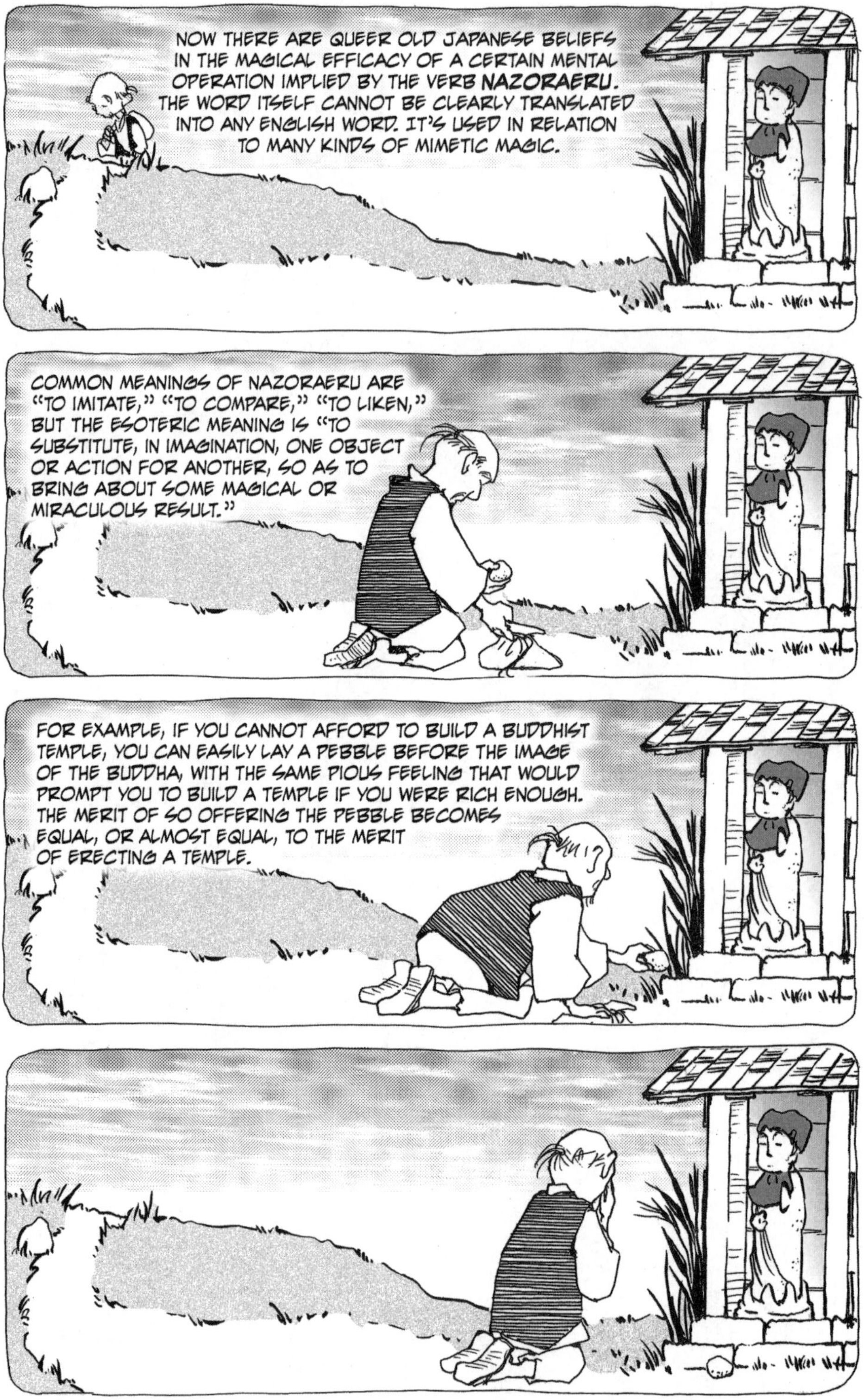
NOW THERE ARE QUEER OLD JAPANESE BELIEFS IN THE MAGICAL EFFICACY OF A CERTAIN MENTAL OPERATION IMPLIED BY THE VERB **NAZORAERU**. THE WORD ITSELF CANNOT BE CLEARLY TRANSLATED INTO ANY ENGLISH WORD. IT'S USED IN RELATION TO MANY KINDS OF MIMETIC MAGIC.
COMMON MEANINGS OF NAZORAERU ARE "TO IMITATE," "TO COMPARE," "TO LIKEN," BUT THE ESOTERIC MEANING IS "TO SUBSTITUTE, IN IMAGINATION, ONE OBJECT OR ACTION FOR ANOTHER, SO AS TO BRING ABOUT SOME MAGICAL OR MIRACULOUS RESULT."
FOR EXAMPLE, IF YOU CANNOT AFFORD TO BUILD A BUDDHIST TEMPLE, YOU CAN EASILY LAY A PEBBLE BEFORE THE IMAGE OF THE BUDDHA, WITH THE SAME PIOUS FEELING THAT WOULD PROMPT YOU TO BUILD A TEMPLE IF YOU WERE RICH ENOUGH. THE MERIT OF SO OFFERING THE PEBBLE BECOMES EQUAL, OR ALMOST EQUAL, TO THE MERIT OF ERECTING A TEMPLE.

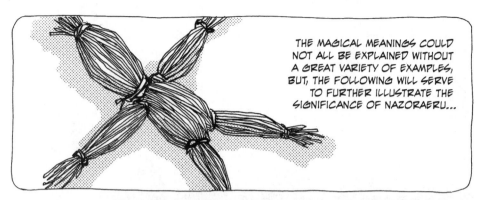

THE MAGICAL MEANINGS COULD NOT ALL BE EXPLAINED WITHOUT A GREAT VARIETY OF EXAMPLES, BUT, THE FOLLOWING WILL SERVE TO FURTHER ILLUSTRATE THE SIGNIFICANCE OF NAZORAERU...

IF YOU SHOULD MAKE A LITTLE MAN OF STRAW, AND NAIL IT, WITH NAILS NOT LESS THAN FIVE INCHES LONG, TO SOME TREE IN A TEMPLE GROVE AT THE HOUR OF THE OX, AND IF THE PERSON, IMAGINATIVELY REPRESENTED BY THAT LITTLE STRAW MAN, SHOULD DIE THEREAFTER IN ATROCIOUS AGONY...

OR, LET US SUPPOSE THAT A ROBBER HAS ENTERED YOUR HOUSE DURING THE NIGHT, AND CARRIED AWAY YOUR VALUABLES. IF YOU CAN DISCOVER THE FOOTPRINTS OF THAT ROBBER IN YOUR GARDEN, AND THEN PROMPTLY BURN A LARGE AMOUNT OF MOXA ON EACH OF THEM...

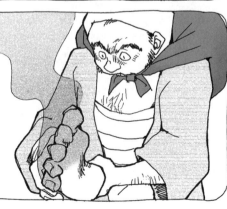

THE SOLES OF THE ROBBER'S FEET WILL BECOME INFLAMED AND WILL ALLOW HIM NO REST UNTIL HE RETURNS, OF HIS OWN ACCORD, TO PUT HIMSELF AT YOUR MERCY.

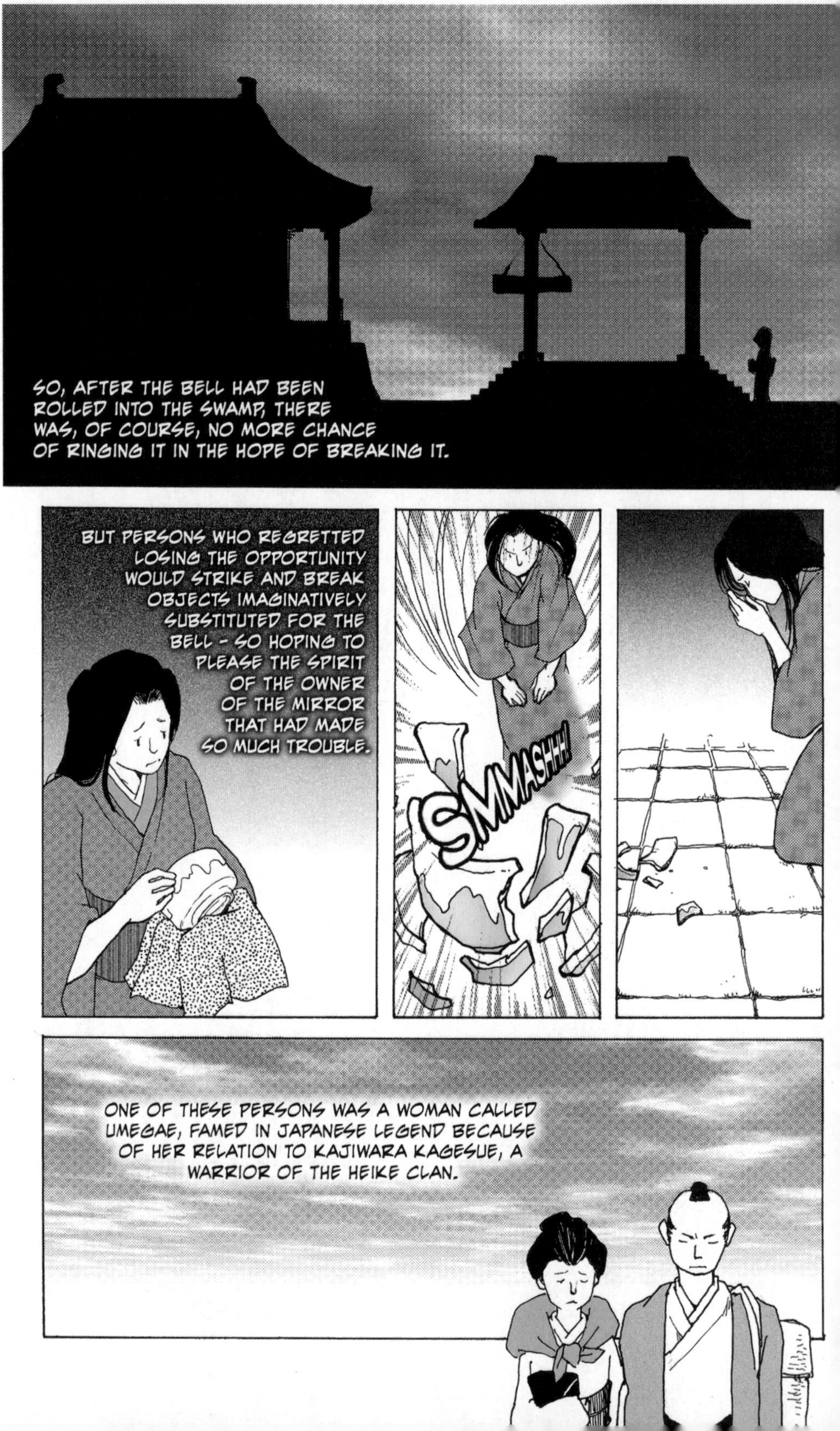
SO, AFTER THE BELL HAD BEEN ROLLED INTO THE SWAMP, THERE WAS, OF COURSE, NO MORE CHANCE OF RINGING IT IN THE HOPE OF BREAKING IT.
BUT PERSONS WHO REGRETTED LOSING THE OPPORTUNITY WOULD STRIKE AND BREAK OBJECTS IMAGINATIVELY SUBSTITUTED FOR THE BELL - SO HOPING TO PLEASE THE SPIRIT OF THE OWNER OF THE MIRROR THAT HAD MADE SO MUCH TROUBLE.
SMMASHH!
ONE OF THESE PERSONS WAS A WOMAN CALLED UMEGAE, FAMED IN JAPANESE LEGEND BECAUSE OF HER RELATION TO KAJIWARA KAGESUE, A WARRIOR OF THE HEIKE CLAN.

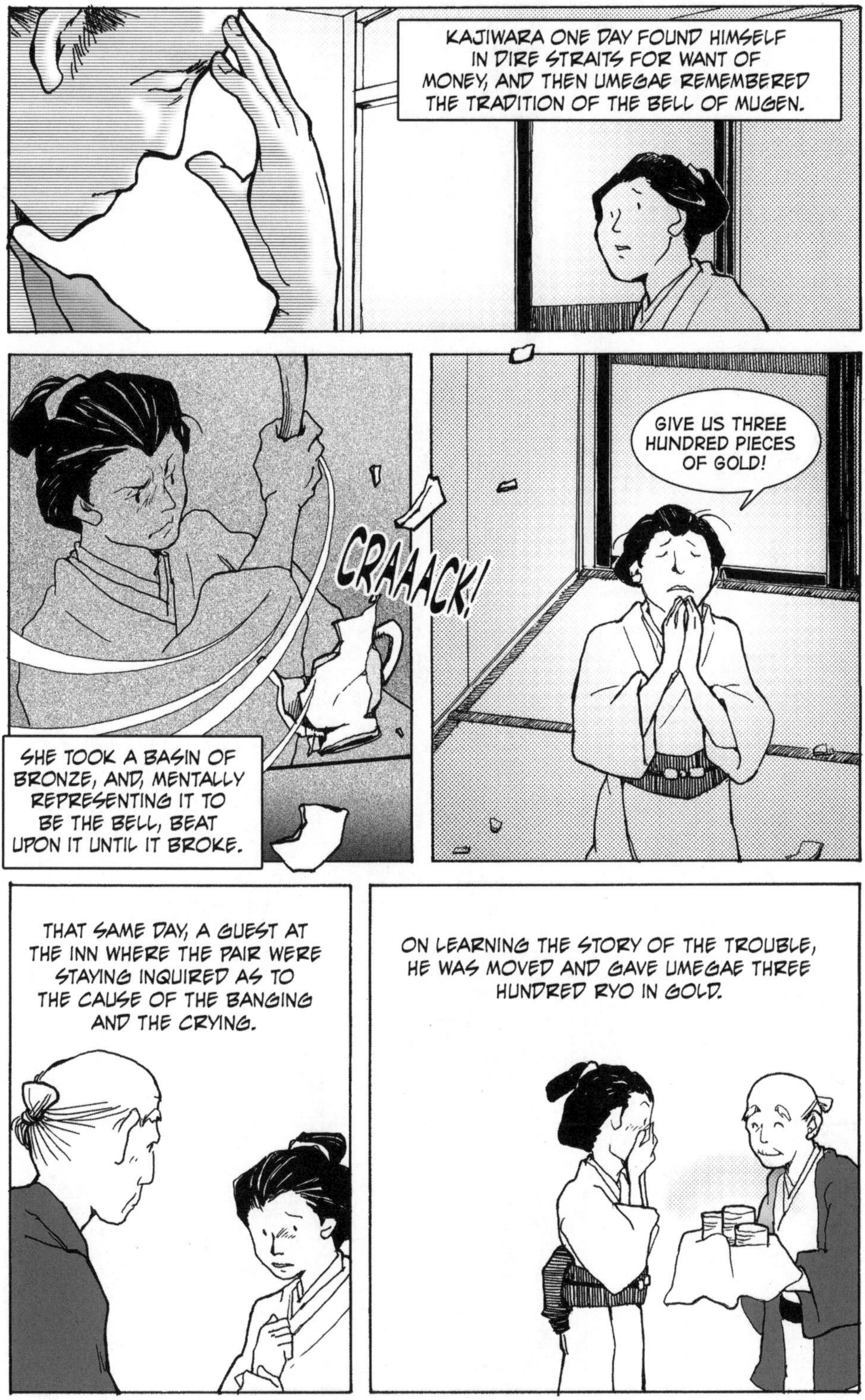

KAJIWARA ONE DAY FOUND HIMSELF IN DIRE STRAITS FOR WANT OF MONEY, AND THEN UMEGAE REMEMBERED THE TRADITION OF THE BELL OF MUGEN.
CRAAACK!
SHE TOOK A BASIN OF BRONZE, AND, MENTALLY REPRESENTING IT TO BE THE BELL, BEAT UPON IT UNTIL IT BROKE.
GIVE US THREE HUNDRED PIECES OF GOLD!
THAT SAME DAY, A GUEST AT THE INN WHERE THE PAIR WERE STAYING INQUIRED AS TO THE CAUSE OF THE BANGING AND THE CRYING.
ON LEARNING THE STORY OF THE TROUBLE, HE WAS MOVED AND GAVE UMEGAE THREE HUNDRED RYO IN GOLD.

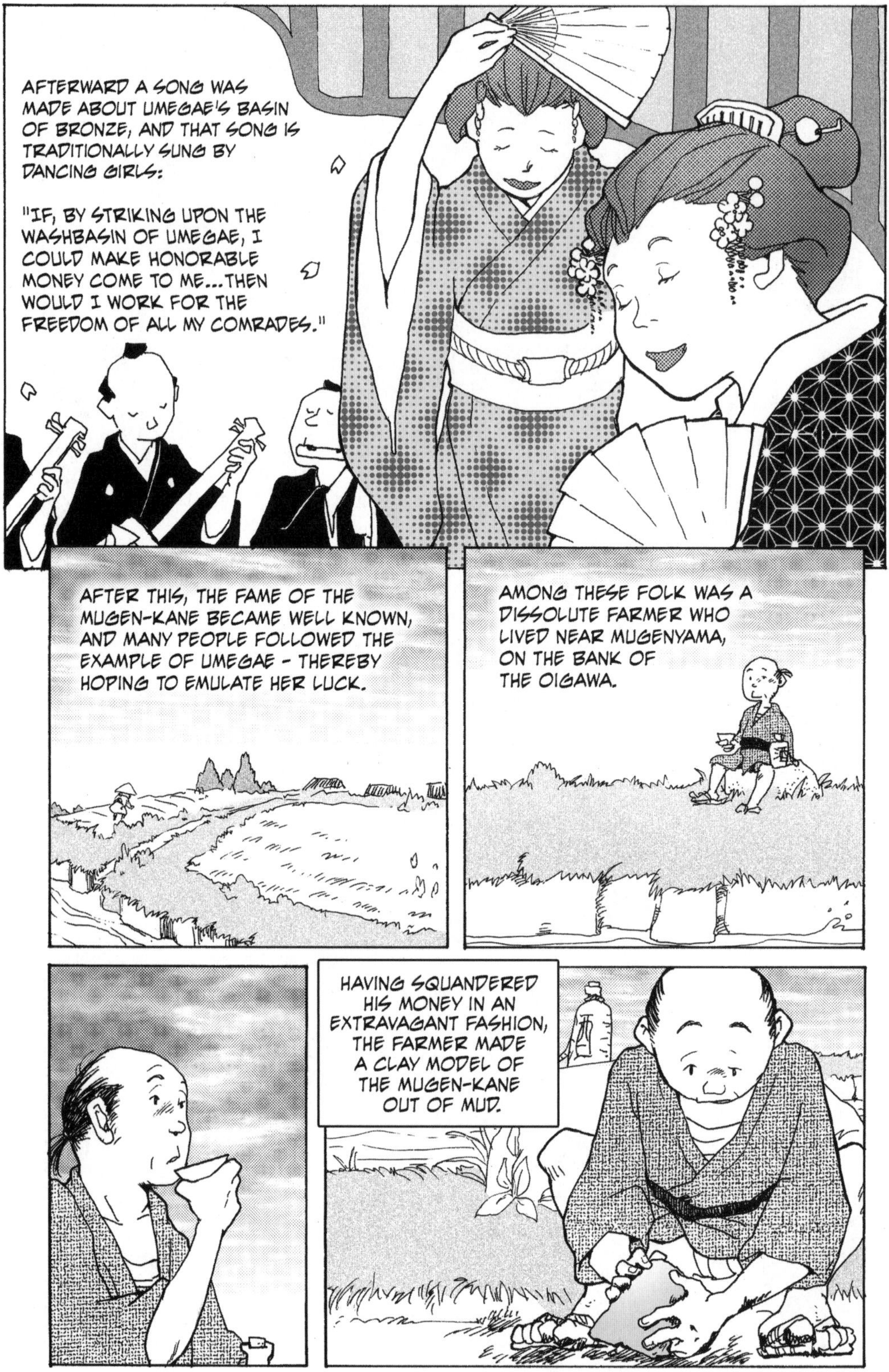
AFTERWARD A SONG WAS MADE ABOUT UMEGAE'S BASIN OF BRONZE; AND THAT SONG IS TRADITIONALLY SUNG BY DANCING GIRLS:
"IF, BY STRIKING UPON THE WASHBASIN OF UMEGAE, I COULD MAKE HONORABLE MONEY COME TO ME...THEN WOULD I WORK FOR THE FREEDOM OF ALL MY COMRADES."
AFTER THIS, THE FAME OF THE MUGEN-KANE BECAME WELL KNOWN, AND MANY PEOPLE FOLLOWED THE EXAMPLE OF UMEGAE - THEREBY HOPING TO EMULATE HER LUCK.
AMONG THESE FOLK WAS A DISSOLUTE FARMER WHO LIVED NEAR MUGENYAMA, ON THE BANK OF THE OIGAWA.
HAVING SQUANDERED HIS MONEY IN AN EXTRAVAGANT FASHION, THE FARMER MADE A CLAY MODEL OF THE MUGEN-KANE OUT OF MUD.

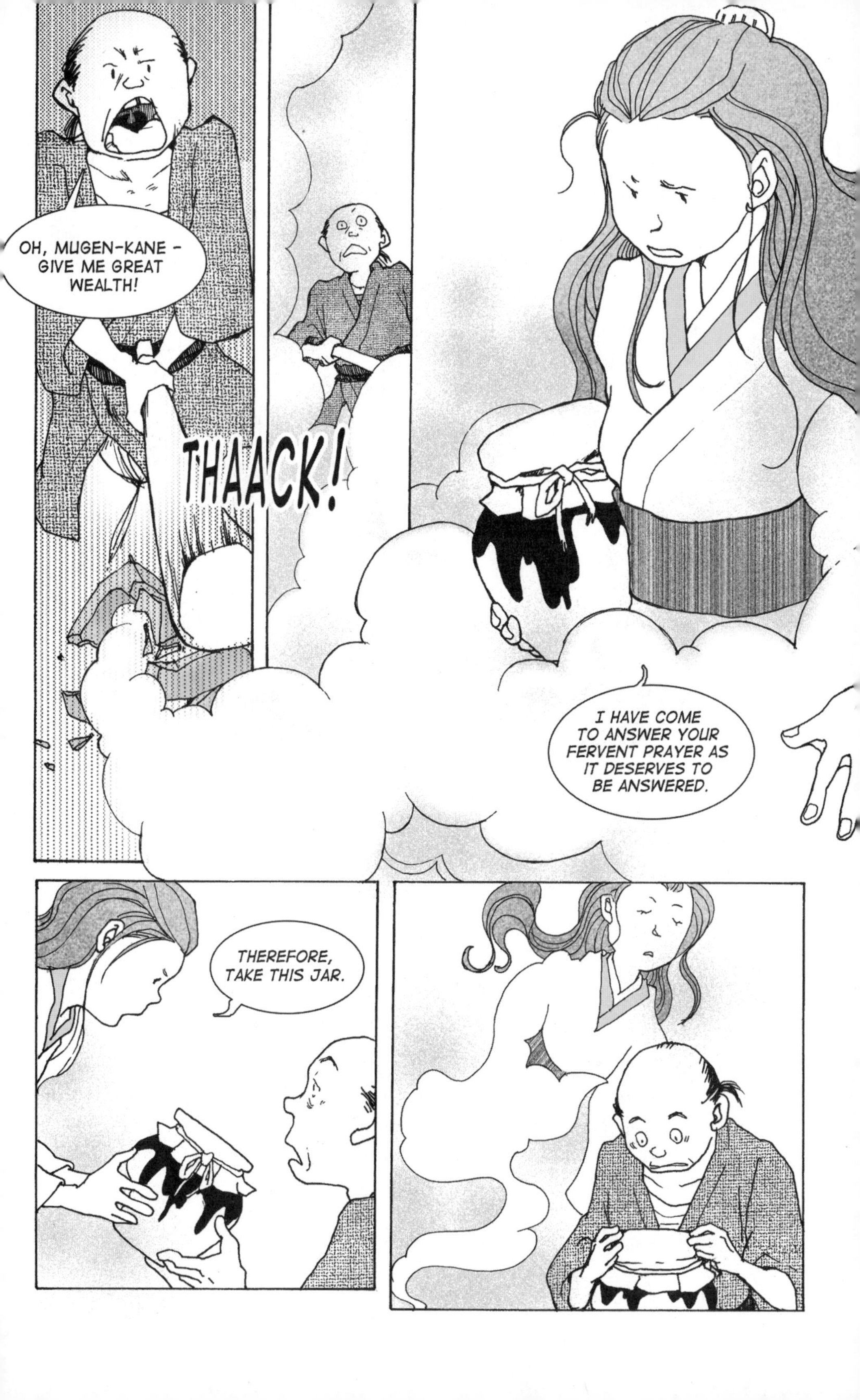
OH, MUGEN-KANE - GIVE ME GREAT WEALTH!
THAACK!
I HAVE COME TO ANSWER YOUR FERVENT PRAYER AS IT DESERVES TO BE ANSWERED.
THEREFORE, TAKE THIS JAR.

THE HAPPY MAN RUSHED INTO THE HOUSE TO TELL HIS WIFE THE GOOD NEWS.

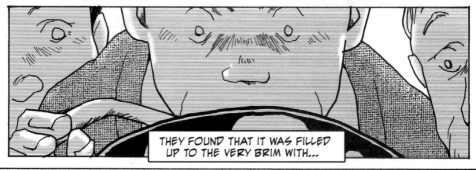

THEY FOUND THAT IT WAS FILLED UP TO THE VERY BRIM WITH...

BUT, NO... I REALLY CANNOT TELL YOU WITH WHAT IT WAS FILLED!

耳無し芳一

HOICHI
THE
EARLESS

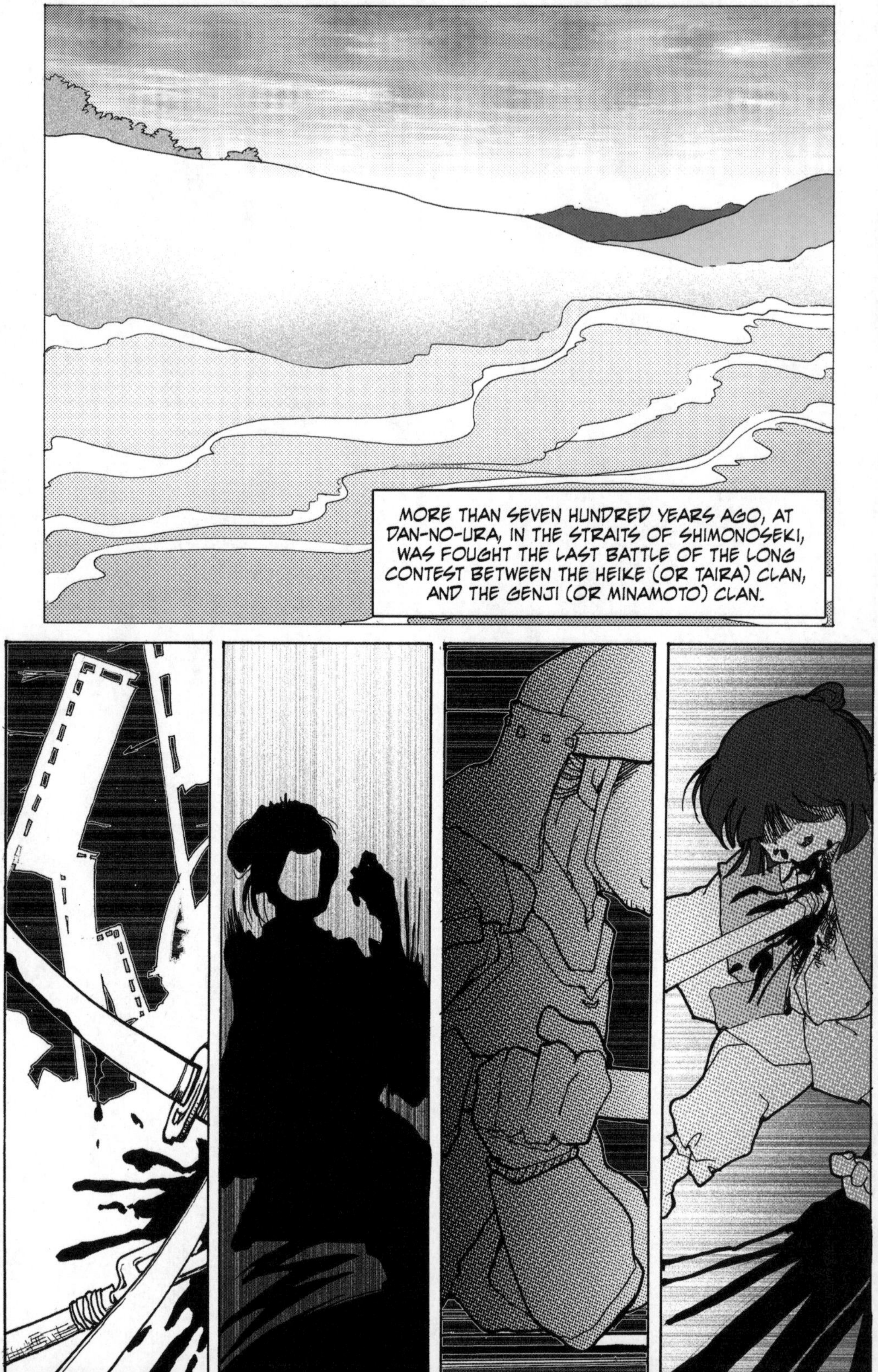
MORE THAN SEVEN HUNDRED YEARS AGO, AT DAN-NO-URA, IN THE STRAITS OF SHIMONOSEKI, WAS FOUGHT THE LAST BATTLE OF THE LONG CONTEST BETWEEN THE HEIKE (OR TAIRA) CLAN, AND THE GENJI (OR MINAMOTO) CLAN.

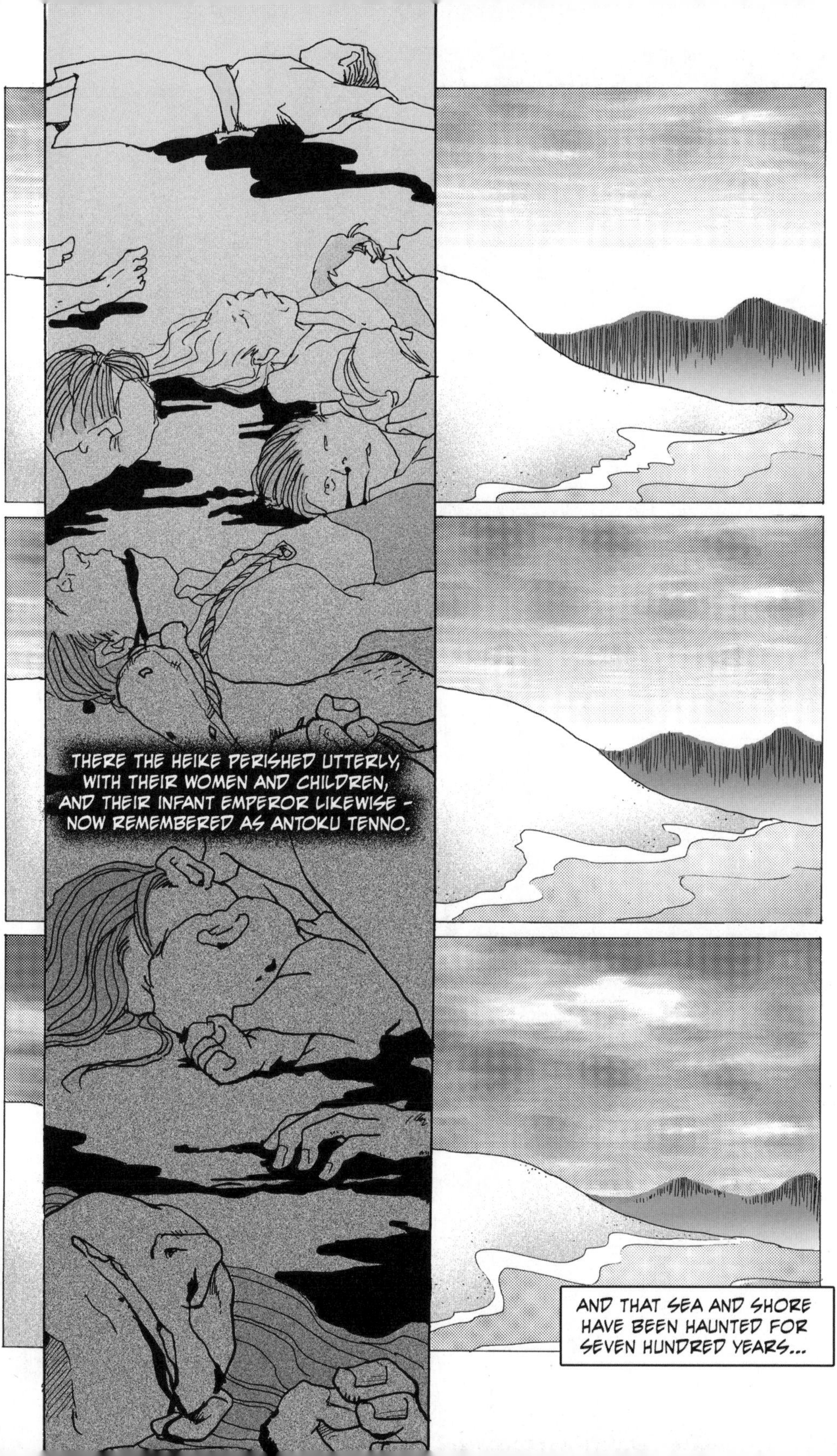

THERE THE HEIKE PERISHED UTTERLY, WITH THEIR WOMEN AND CHILDREN, AND THEIR INFANT EMPEROR LIKEWISE - NOW REMEMBERED AS ANTOKU TENNO.
AND THAT SEA AND SHORE HAVE BEEN HAUNTED FOR SEVEN HUNDRED YEARS...

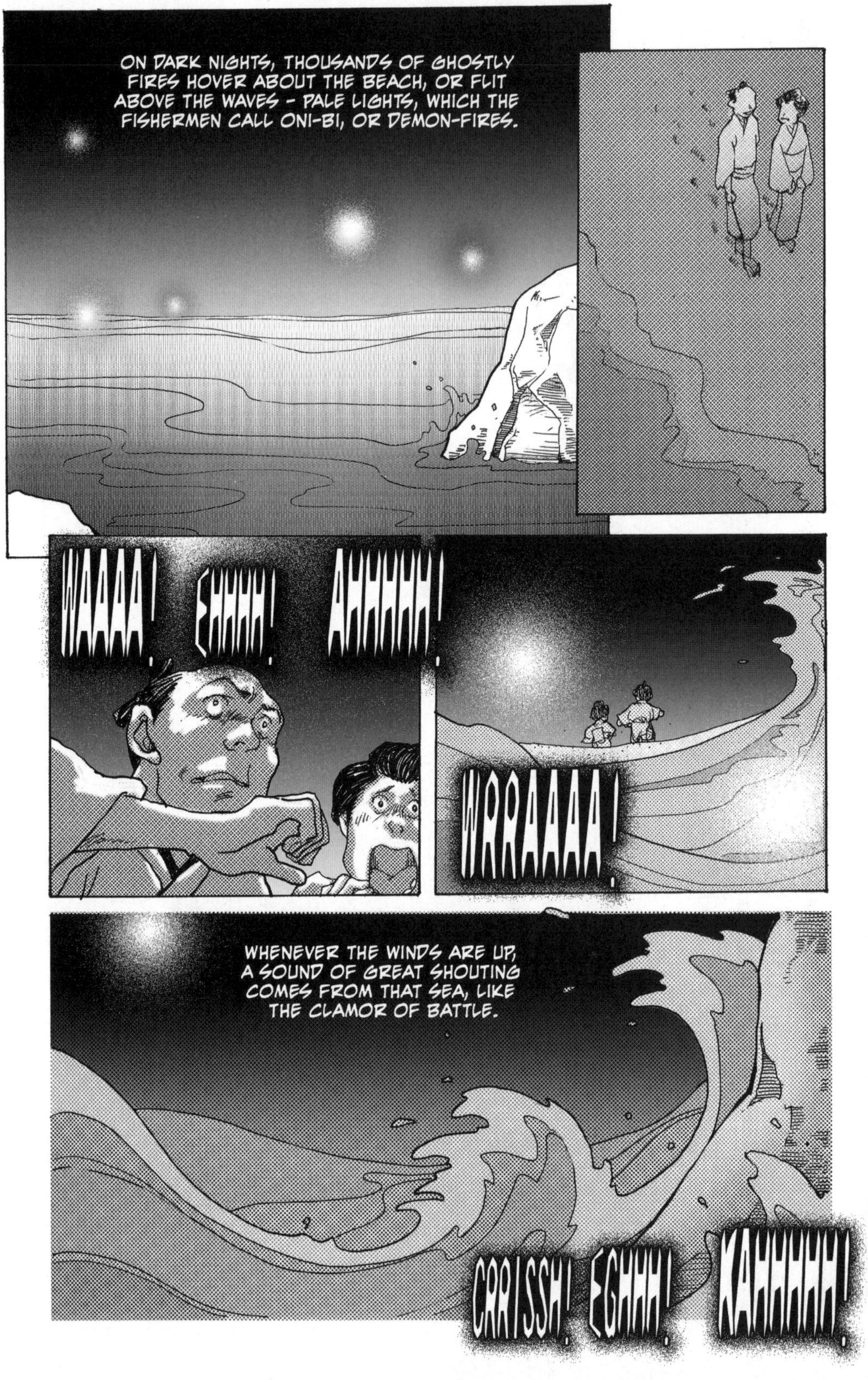
ON DARK NIGHTS, THOUSANDS OF GHOSTLY FIRES HOVER ABOUT THE BEACH, OR FLIT ABOVE THE WAVES - PALE LIGHTS, WHICH THE FISHERMEN CALL ONI-BI, OR DEMON-FIRES.
WAAAA!
EHHHH!
AHHHHH!
WRRAAAA!
WHENEVER THE WINDS ARE UP, A SOUND OF GREAT SHOUTING COMES FROM THAT SEA, LIKE THE CLAMOR OF BATTLE.
CRRISSH!
EGHHH!
KAHHHHH!

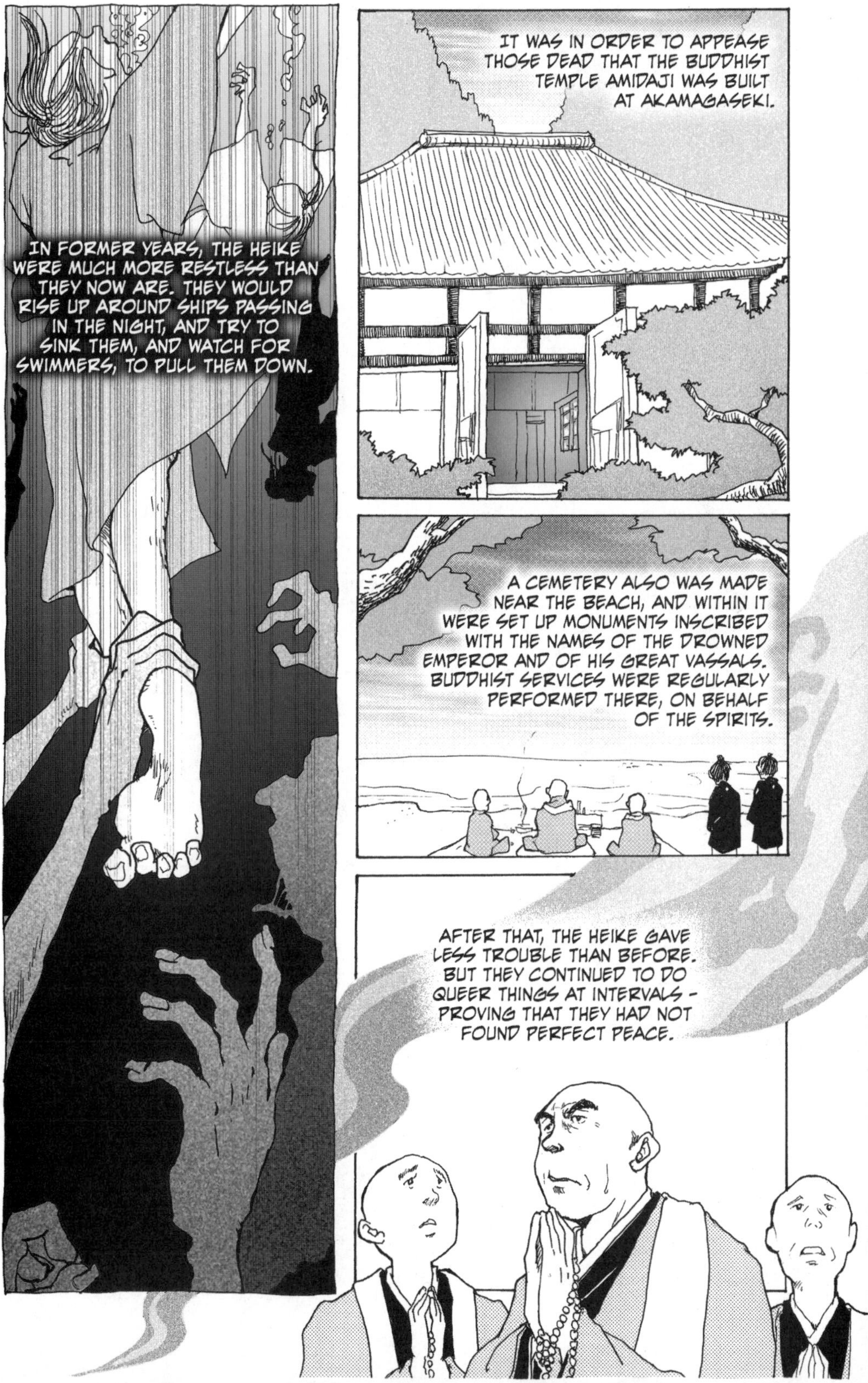
IN FORMER YEARS, THE HEIKE WERE MUCH MORE RESTLESS THAN THEY NOW ARE. THEY WOULD RISE UP AROUND SHIPS PASSING IN THE NIGHT, AND TRY TO SINK THEM, AND WATCH FOR SWIMMERS, TO PULL THEM DOWN.
IT WAS IN ORDER TO APPEASE THOSE DEAD THAT THE BUDDHIST TEMPLE AMIDAJI WAS BUILT AT AKAMAGASEKI.
A CEMETERY ALSO WAS MADE NEAR THE BEACH, AND WITHIN IT WERE SET UP MONUMENTS INSCRIBED WITH THE NAMES OF THE DROWNED EMPEROR AND OF HIS GREAT VASSALS. BUDDHIST SERVICES WERE REGULARLY PERFORMED THERE, ON BEHALF OF THE SPIRITS.
AFTER THAT, THE HEIKE GAVE LESS TROUBLE THAN BEFORE. BUT THEY CONTINUED TO DO QUEER THINGS AT INTERVALS - PROVING THAT THEY HAD NOT FOUND PERFECT PEACE.

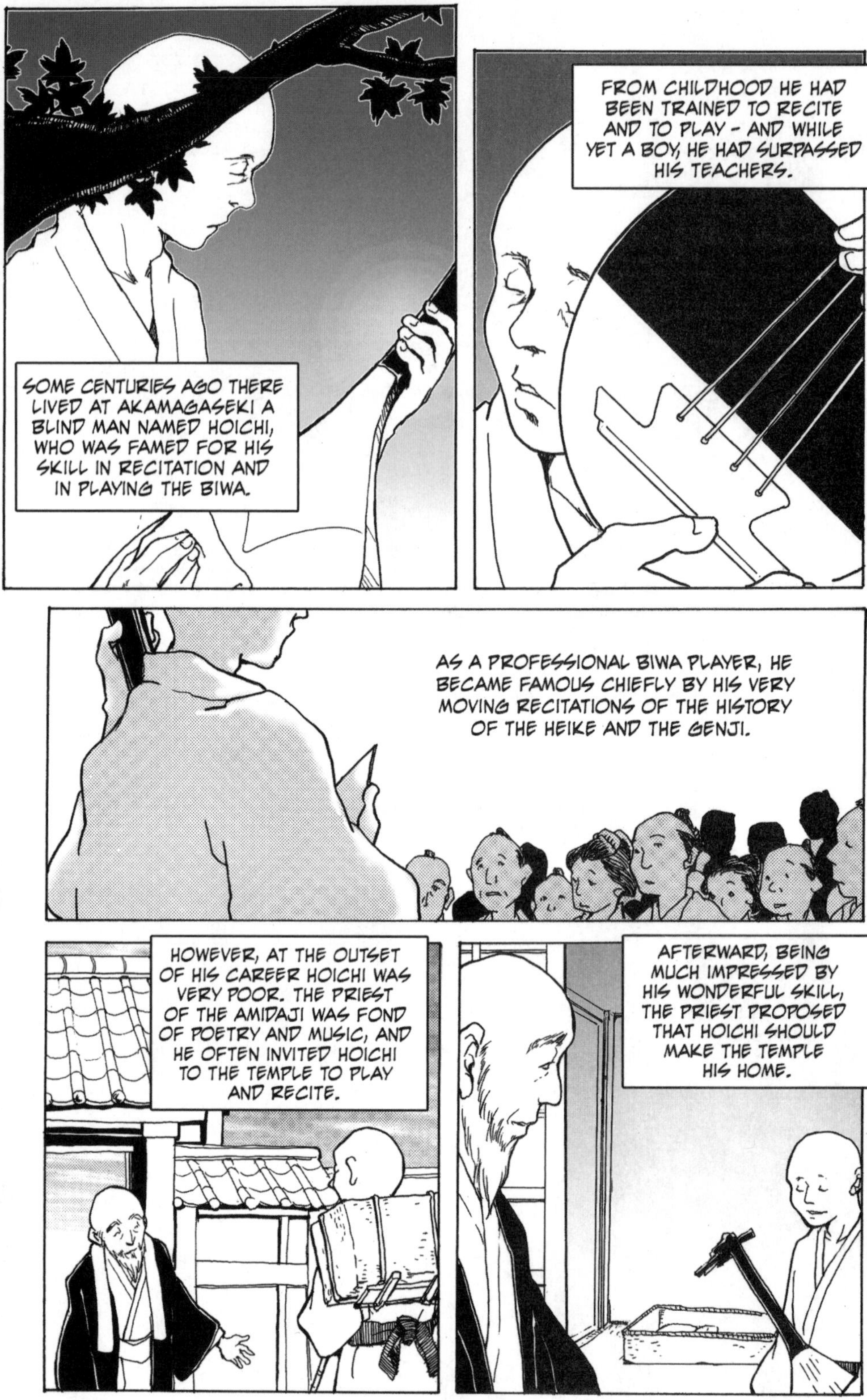
SOME CENTURIES AGO THERE LIVED AT AKAMAGASEKI A BLIND MAN NAMED HOICHI, WHO WAS FAMED FOR HIS SKILL IN RECITATION AND IN PLAYING THE BIWA.
FROM CHILDHOOD HE HAD BEEN TRAINED TO RECITE AND TO PLAY - AND WHILE YET A BOY, HE HAD SURPASSED HIS TEACHERS.
AS A PROFESSIONAL BIWA PLAYER, HE BECAME FAMOUS CHIEFLY BY HIS VERY MOVING RECITATIONS OF THE HISTORY OF THE HEIKE AND THE GENJI.
HOWEVER, AT THE OUTSET OF HIS CAREER HOICHI WAS VERY POOR. THE PRIEST OF THE AMIDAJI WAS FOND OF POETRY AND MUSIC, AND HE OFTEN INVITED HOICHI TO THE TEMPLE TO PLAY AND RECITE.
AFTERWARD, BEING MUCH IMPRESSED BY HIS WONDERFUL SKILL, THE PRIEST PROPOSED THAT HOICHI SHOULD MAKE THE TEMPLE HIS HOME.

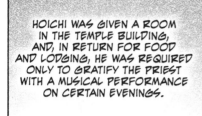

HOICHI WAS GIVEN A ROOM IN THE TEMPLE BUILDING, AND, IN RETURN FOR FOOD AND LODGING, HE WAS REQUIRED ONLY TO GRATIFY THE PRIEST WITH A MUSICAL PERFORMANCE ON CERTAIN EVENINGS.

ONE SUMMER NIGHT THE PRIEST WAS CALLED AWAY TO PERFORM A BUDDHIST SERVICE AT THE HOUSE OF A DEAD PARISHIONER, LEAVING HOICHI ALONE IN THE TEMPLE.

IT WAS A HOT NIGHT, AND HOICHI SOUGHT TO COOL HIMSELF ON THE VERANDAH BEFORE HIS BEDROOM.

THERE HE WAITED FOR THE PRIEST'S RETURN, AND TRIED TO RELIEVE HIS SOLITUDE BY PRACTICING HIS BIWA.

MIDNIGHT PASSED, AND THE PRIEST DID NOT APPEAR.

AT LAST HE HEARD STEPS APPROACHING FROM THE BACK GATE.

crunch crunch

SOMEBODY CROSSED THE GARDEN, ADVANCED TO THE VERANDAH, AND HALTED DIRECTLY IN FRONT OF HIM.

BUT IT WAS NOT THE PRIEST. A DEEP VOICE CALLED THE BLIND MAN'S NAME — ABRUPTLY AND UNCEREMONIOUSLY, IN THE MANNER OF A SAMURAI SUMMONING AN INFERIOR:

HOICHI!

HOICHI WAS TOO STARTLED, FOR THE MOMENT, TO RESPOND.

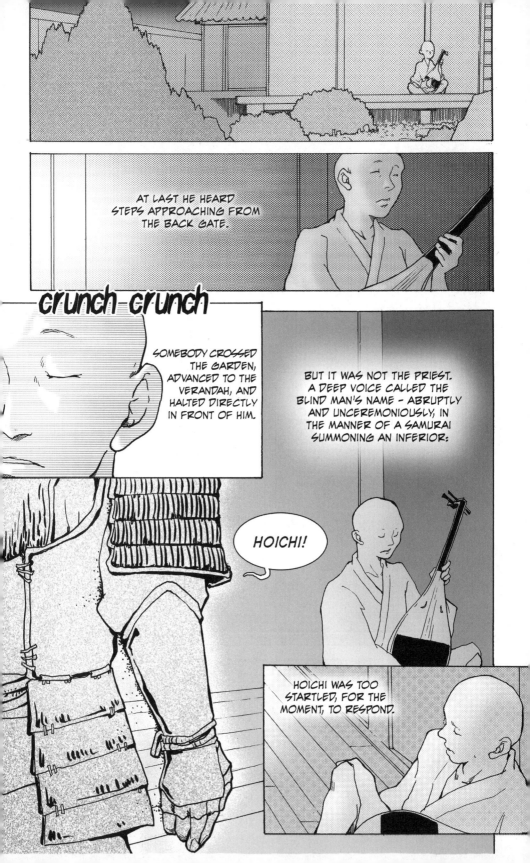

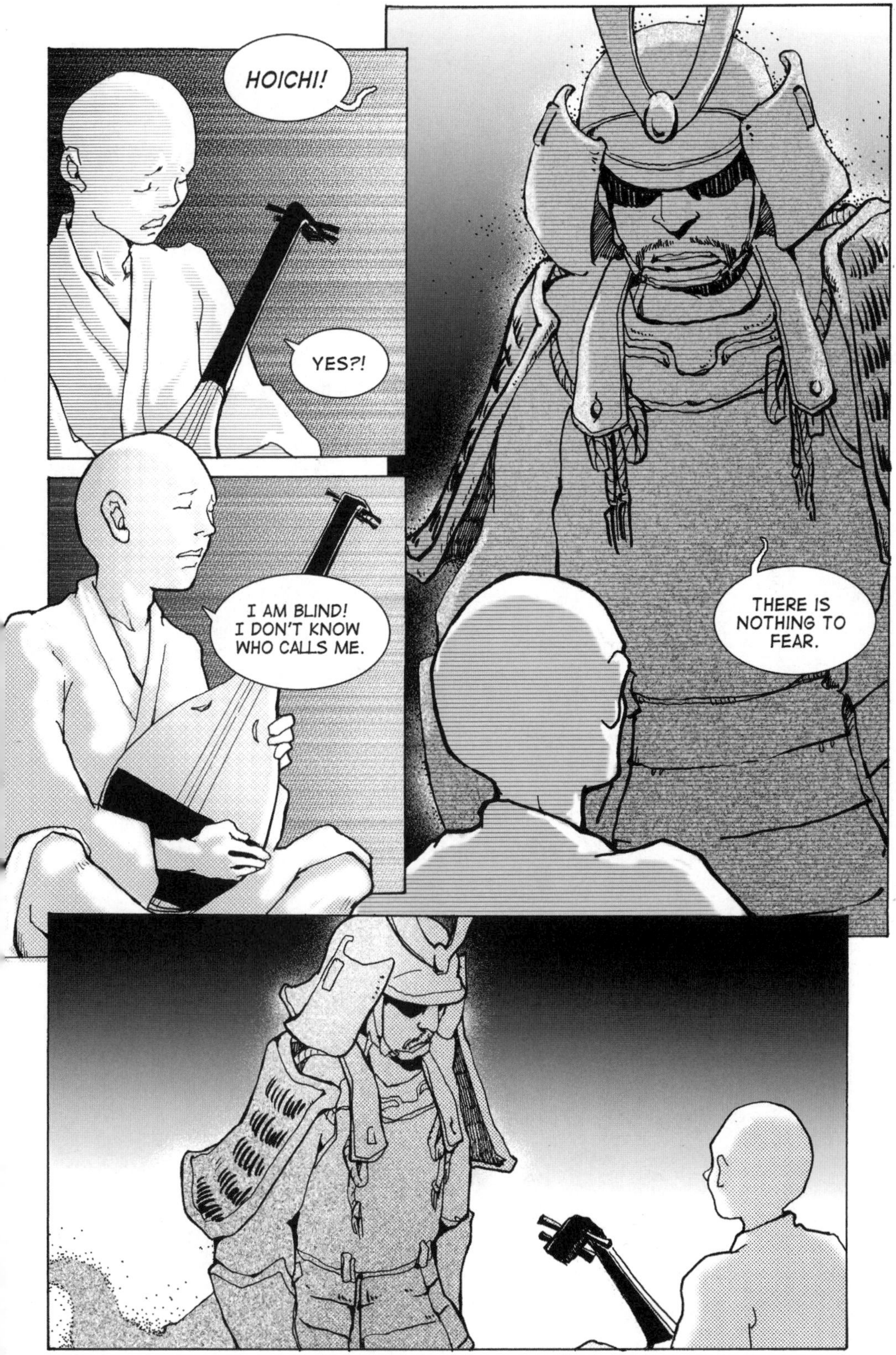
HOICHI!
YES?!
I AM BLIND! I DON'T KNOW WHO CALLS ME.
THERE IS NOTHING TO FEAR.

I HAVE BEEN SENT TO YOU WITH A MESSAGE.

MY LORD, A PERSON OF EXCEEDINGLY HIGH RANK, IS NOW STAYING IN AKAMAGASEKI, WITH MANY NOBLE ATTENDANTS.

HE WISHED TO VIEW THE SCENE OF THE BATTLE OF DAN-NO-URA, AND TODAY VISITED THAT PLACE.

HAVING HEARD OF YOUR SKILL IN RECITING THE STORY OF THE BATTLE, HE NOW DESIRES TO HEAR YOUR PERFORMANCE.

SO YOU WILL COME WITH ME AT ONCE TO THE HOUSE WHERE THE AUGUST ASSEMBLY IS WAITING.

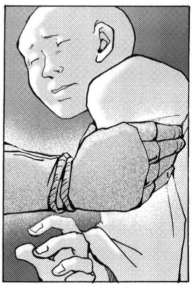

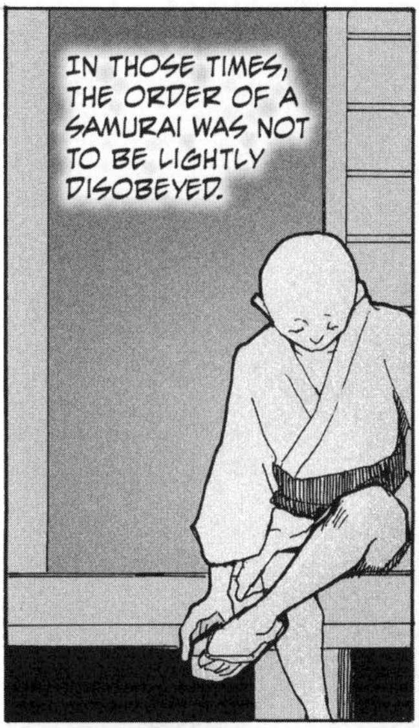
IN THOSE TIMES, THE ORDER OF A SAMURAI WAS NOT TO BE LIGHTLY DISOBEYED.

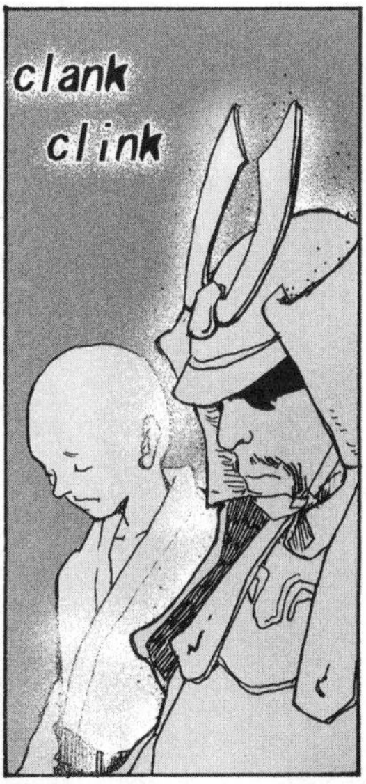
clank
clink

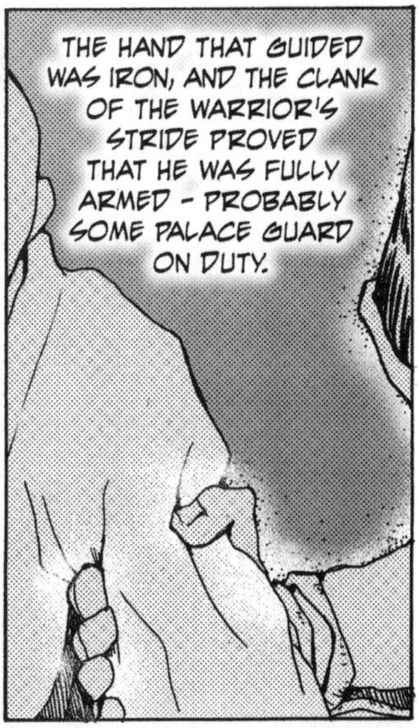
THE HAND THAT GUIDED WAS IRON, AND THE CLANK OF THE WARRIOR'S STRIDE PROVED THAT HE WAS FULLY ARMED - PROBABLY SOME PALACE GUARD ON DUTY.

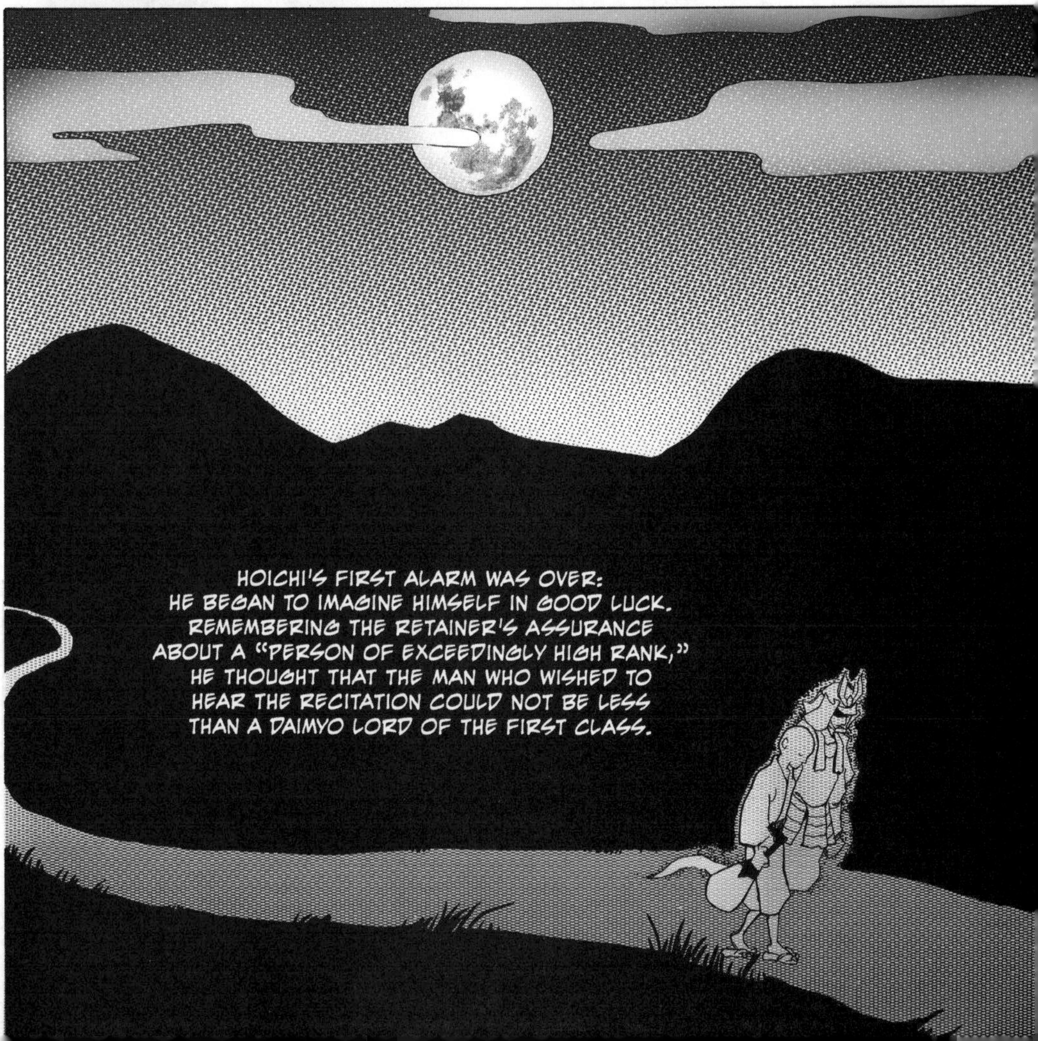
HOICHI'S FIRST ALARM WAS OVER: HE BEGAN TO IMAGINE HIMSELF IN GOOD LUCK. REMEMBERING THE RETAINER'S ASSURANCE ABOUT A "PERSON OF EXCEEDINGLY HIGH RANK," HE THOUGHT THAT THE MAN WHO WISHED TO HEAR THE RECITATION COULD NOT BE LESS THAN A DAIMYO LORD OF THE FIRST CLASS.

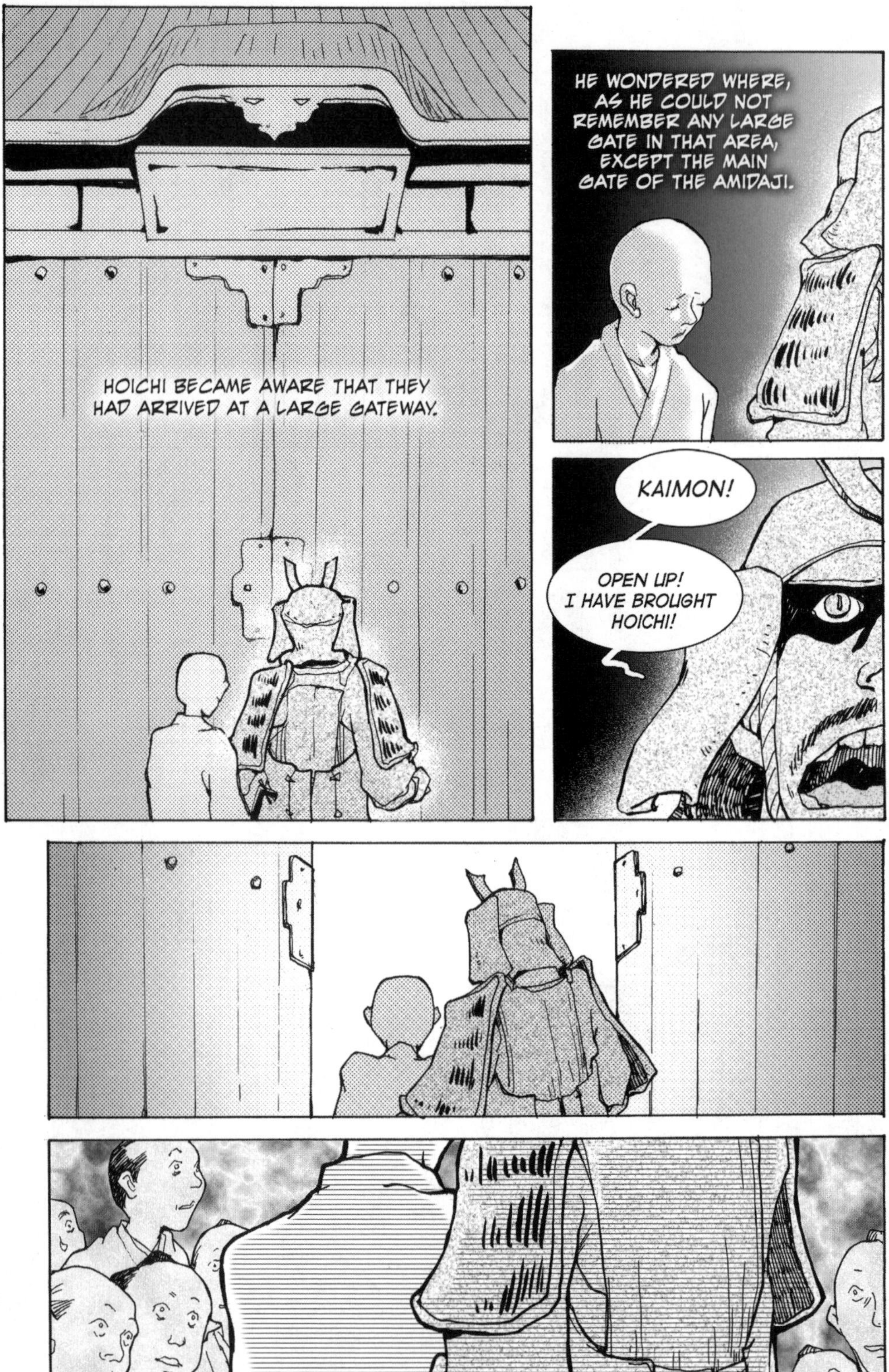
HOICHI BECAME AWARE THAT THEY HAD ARRIVED AT A LARGE GATEWAY.
HE WONDERED WHERE, AS HE COULD NOT REMEMBER ANY LARGE GATE IN THAT AREA, EXCEPT THE MAIN GATE OF THE AMIDAJI.
KAIMON!
OPEN UP! I HAVE BROUGHT HOICHI!

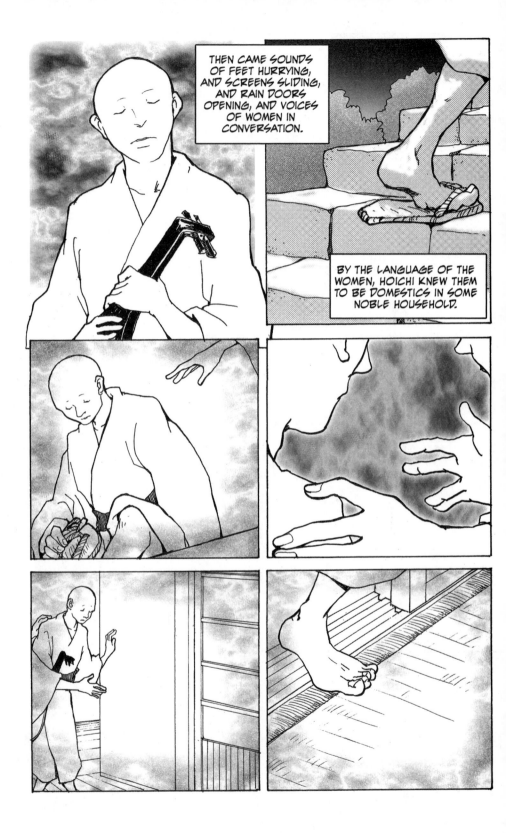

THEN CAME SOUNDS OF FEET HURRYING, AND SCREENS SLIDING, AND RAIN DOORS OPENING, AND VOICES OF WOMEN IN CONVERSATION.

BY THE LANGUAGE OF THE WOMEN, HOICHI KNEW THEM TO BE DOMESTICS IN SOME NOBLE HOUSEHOLD.

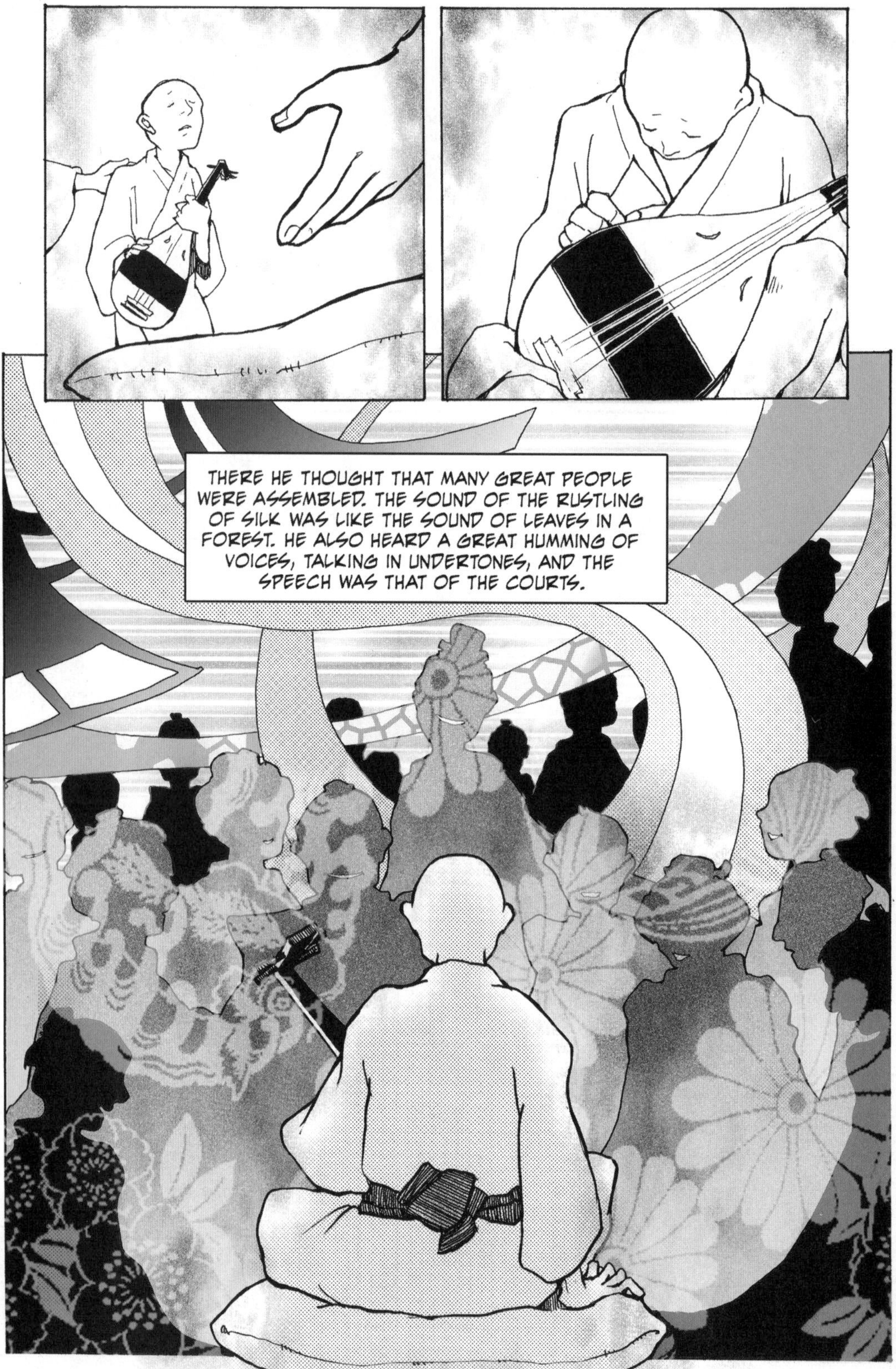
THERE HE THOUGHT THAT MANY GREAT PEOPLE WERE ASSEMBLED. THE SOUND OF THE RUSTLING OF SILK WAS LIKE THE SOUND OF LEAVES IN A FOREST. HE ALSO HEARD A GREAT HUMMING OF VOICES, TALKING IN UNDERTONES, AND THE SPEECH WAS THAT OF THE COURTS.

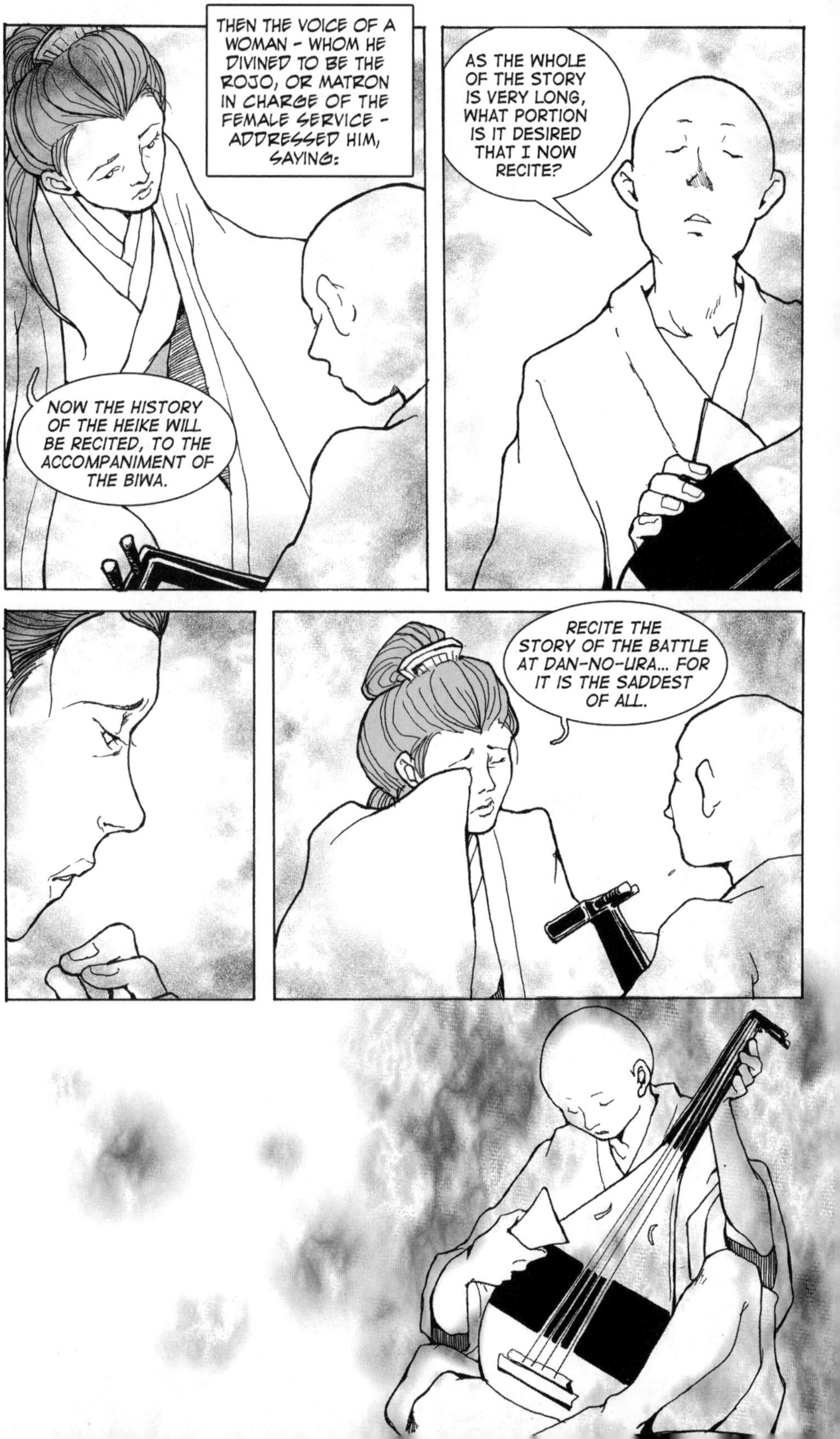
THEN THE VOICE OF A WOMAN - WHOM HE DIVINED TO BE THE ROJO, OR MATRON IN CHARGE OF THE FEMALE SERVICE - ADDRESSED HIM, SAYING:
NOW THE HISTORY OF THE HEIKE WILL BE RECITED, TO THE ACCOMPANIMENT OF THE BIWA.
AS THE WHOLE OF THE STORY IS VERY LONG, WHAT PORTION IS IT DESIRED THAT I NOW RECITE?
RECITE THE STORY OF THE BATTLE AT DAN-NO-URA... FOR IT IS THE SADDEST OF ALL.

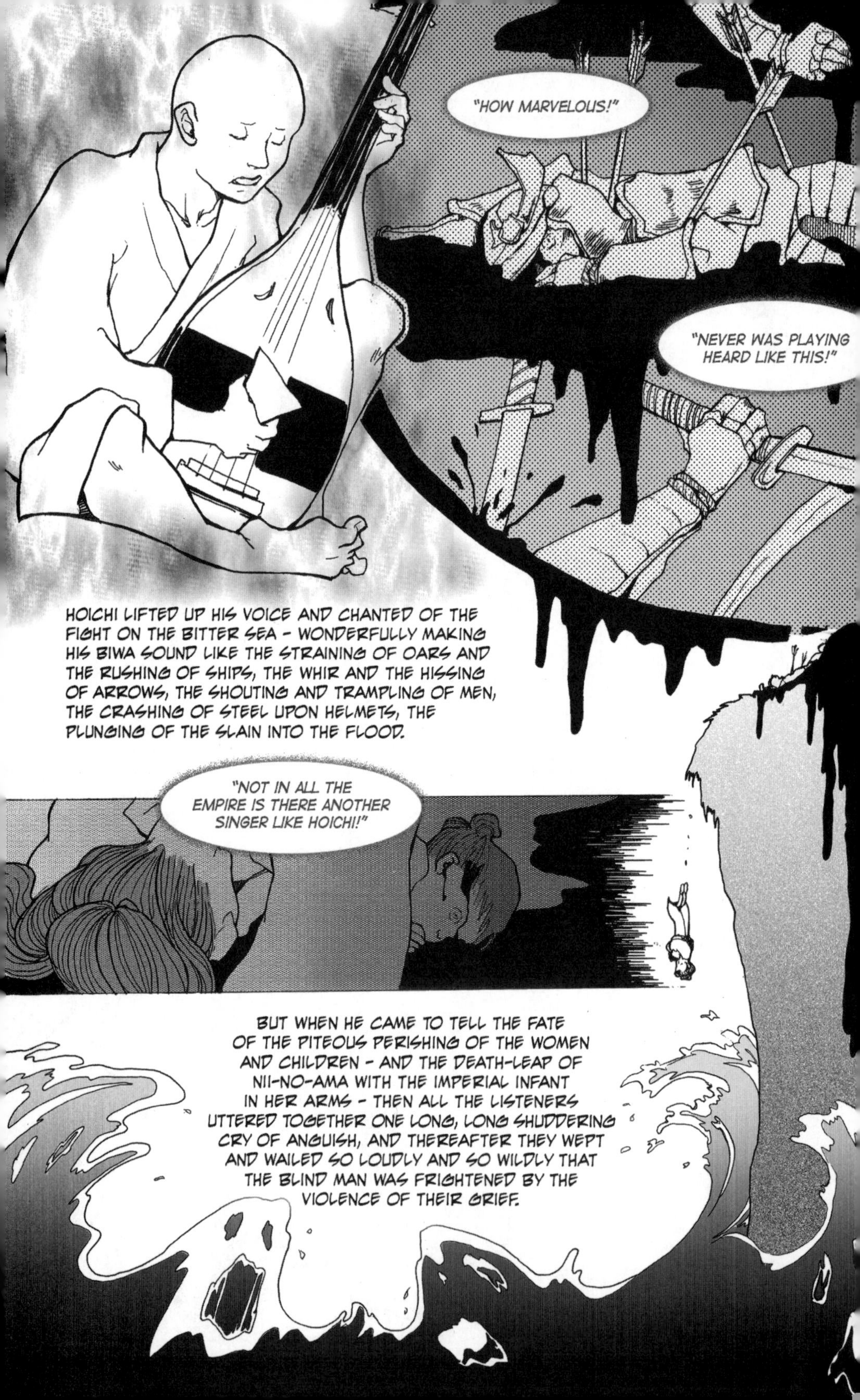
"HOW MARVELOUS!"
"NEVER WAS PLAYING HEARD LIKE THIS!"
HOICHI LIFTED UP HIS VOICE AND CHANTED OF THE FIGHT ON THE BITTER SEA - WONDERFULLY MAKING HIS BIWA SOUND LIKE THE STRAINING OF OARS AND THE RUSHING OF SHIPS, THE WHIR AND THE HISSING OF ARROWS, THE SHOUTING AND TRAMPLING OF MEN, THE CRASHING OF STEEL UPON HELMETS, THE PLUNGING OF THE SLAIN INTO THE FLOOD.
"NOT IN ALL THE EMPIRE IS THERE ANOTHER SINGER LIKE HOICHI!"
BUT WHEN HE CAME TO TELL THE FATE OF THE PITEOUS PERISHING OF THE WOMEN AND CHILDREN - AND THE DEATH-LEAP OF NII-NO-AMA WITH THE IMPERIAL INFANT IN HER ARMS - THEN ALL THE LISTENERS UTTERED TOGETHER ONE LONG, LONG SHUDDERING CRY OF ANGUISH, AND THEREAFTER THEY WEPT AND WAILED SO LOUDLY AND SO WILDLY THAT THE BLIND MAN WAS FRIGHTENED BY THE VIOLENCE OF THEIR GRIEF.

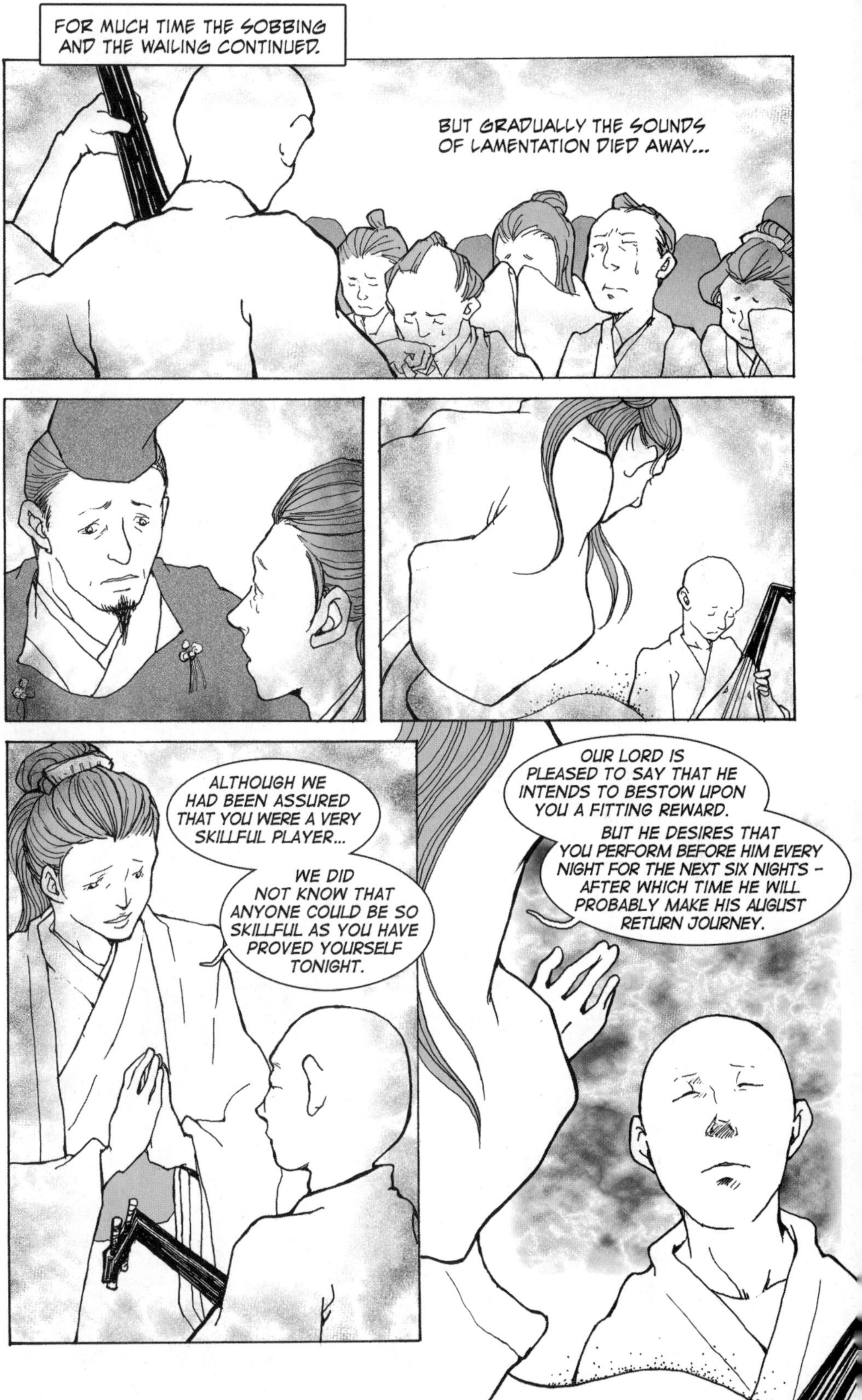
FOR MUCH TIME THE SOBBING AND THE WAILING CONTINUED.
BUT GRADUALLY THE SOUNDS OF LAMENTATION DIED AWAY...
ALTHOUGH WE HAD BEEN ASSURED THAT YOU WERE A VERY SKILLFUL PLAYER...
WE DID NOT KNOW THAT ANYONE COULD BE SO SKILLFUL AS YOU HAVE PROVED YOURSELF TONIGHT.
OUR LORD IS PLEASED TO SAY THAT HE INTENDS TO BESTOW UPON YOU A FITTING REWARD.
BUT HE DESIRES THAT YOU PERFORM BEFORE HIM EVERY NIGHT FOR THE NEXT SIX NIGHTS - AFTER WHICH TIME HE WILL PROBABLY MAKE HIS AUGUST RETURN JOURNEY.

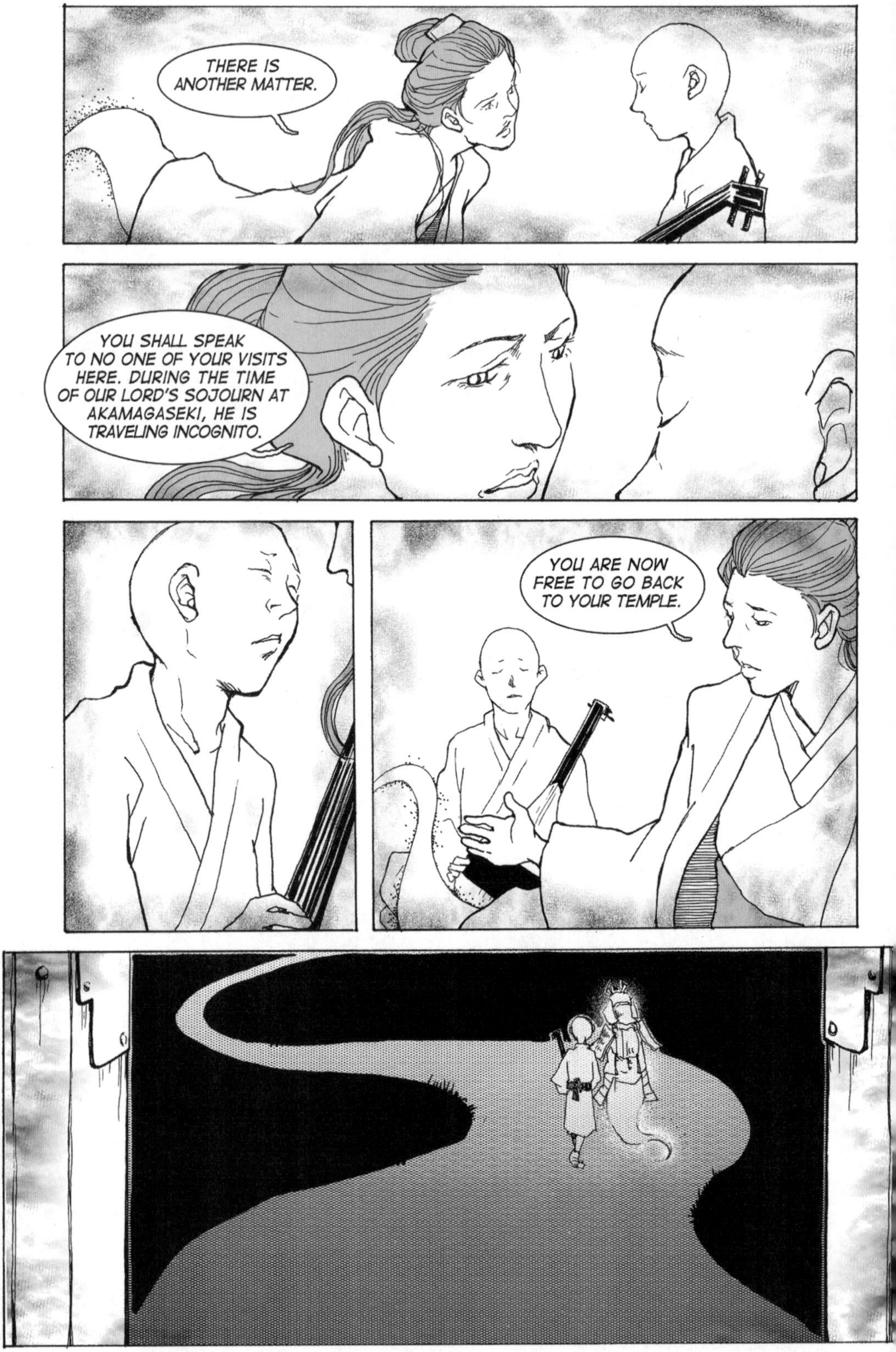
THERE IS ANOTHER MATTER.
YOU SHALL SPEAK TO NO ONE OF YOUR VISITS HERE. DURING THE TIME OF OUR LORD'S SOJOURN AT AKAMAGASEKI, HE IS TRAVELING INCOGNITO.
YOU ARE NOW FREE TO GO BACK TO YOUR TEMPLE.

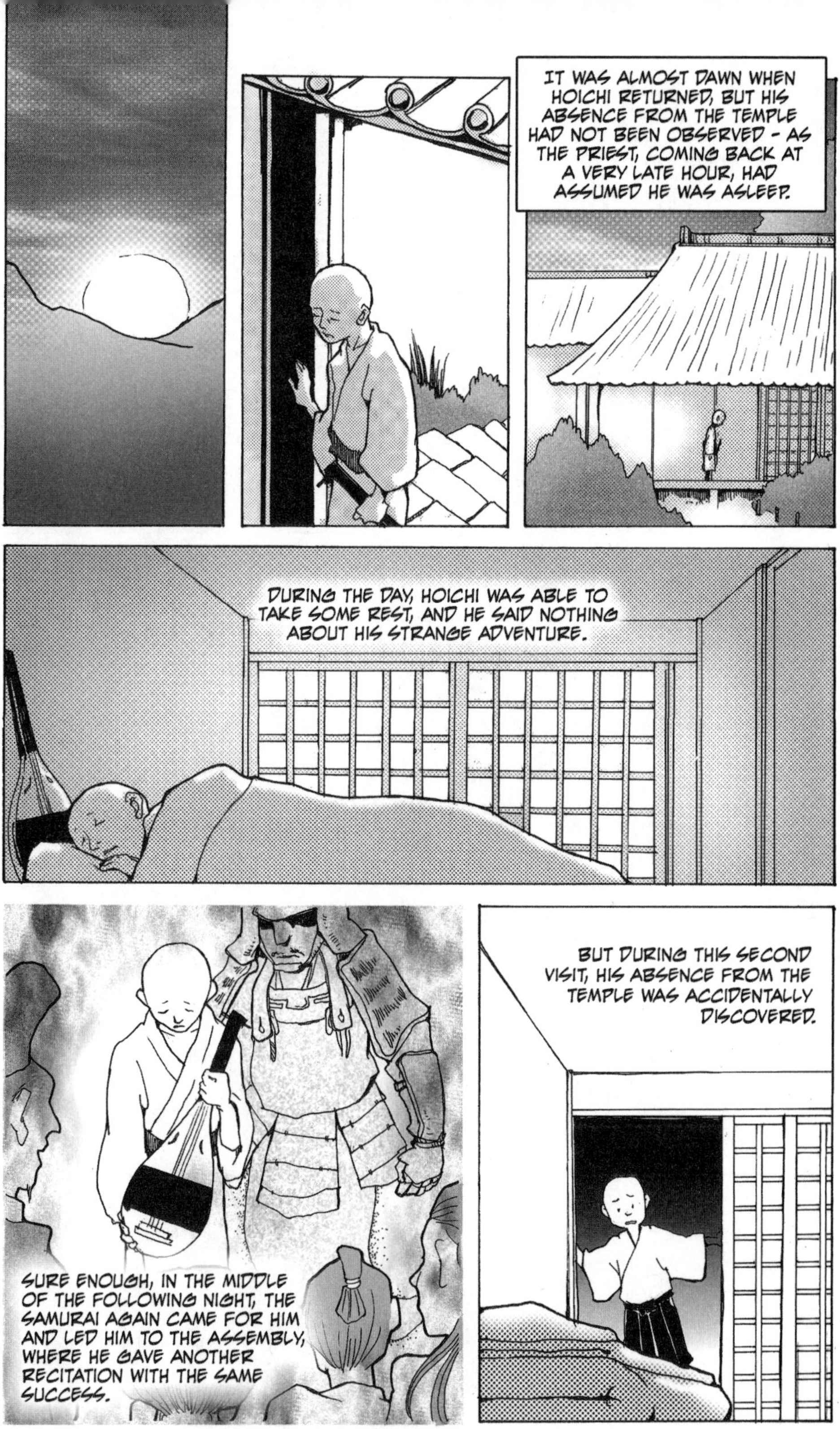
IT WAS ALMOST DAWN WHEN HOICHI RETURNED, BUT HIS ABSENCE FROM THE TEMPLE HAD NOT BEEN OBSERVED - AS THE PRIEST, COMING BACK AT A VERY LATE HOUR, HAD ASSUMED HE WAS ASLEEP.
DURING THE DAY, HOICHI WAS ABLE TO TAKE SOME REST, AND HE SAID NOTHING ABOUT HIS STRANGE ADVENTURE.
SURE ENOUGH, IN THE MIDDLE OF THE FOLLOWING NIGHT, THE SAMURAI AGAIN CAME FOR HIM AND LED HIM TO THE ASSEMBLY, WHERE HE GAVE ANOTHER RECITATION WITH THE SAME SUCCESS.
BUT DURING THIS SECOND VISIT, HIS ABSENCE FROM THE TEMPLE WAS ACCIDENTALLY DISCOVERED.

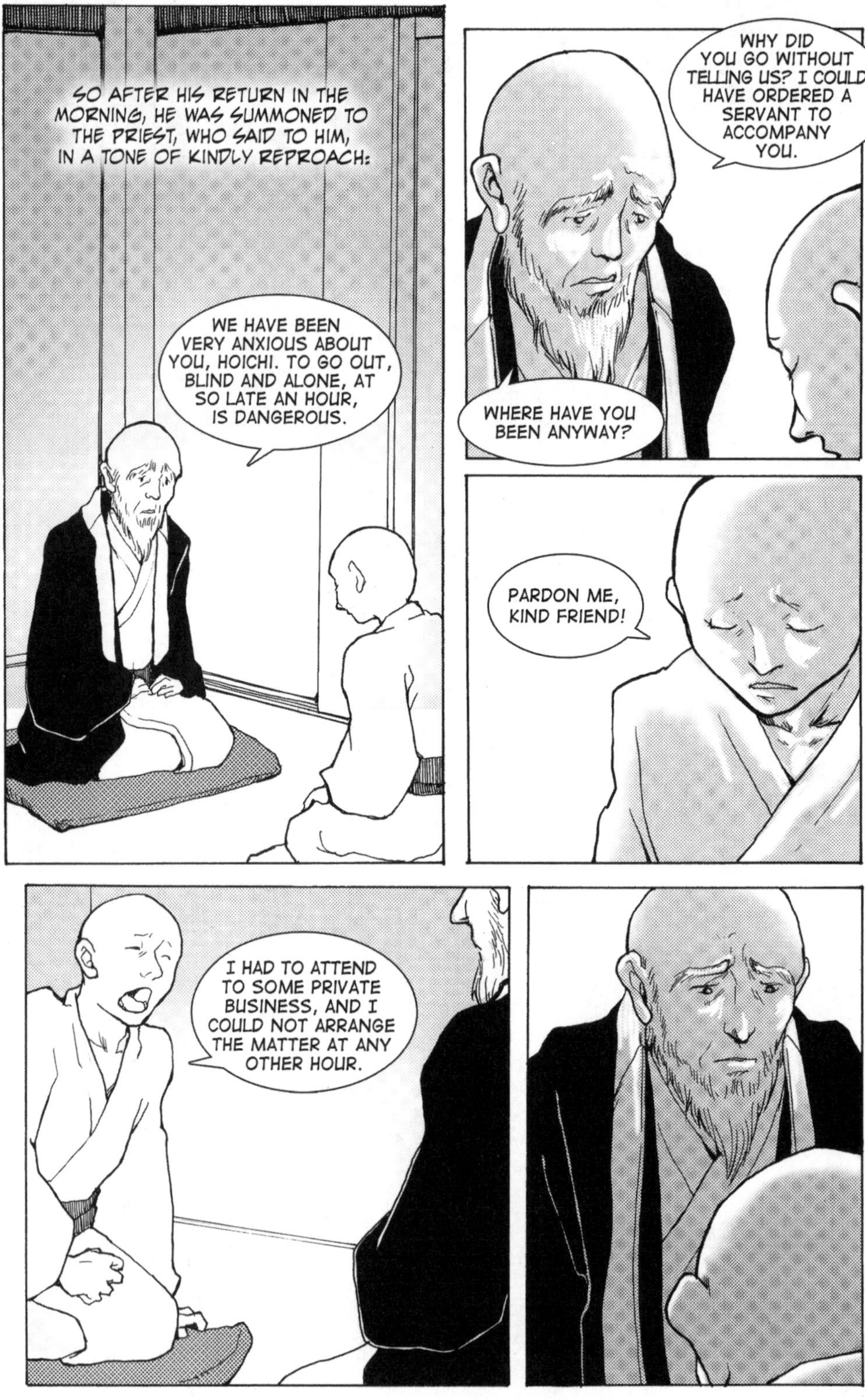
SO AFTER HIS RETURN IN THE MORNING, HE WAS SUMMONED TO THE PRIEST, WHO SAID TO HIM, IN A TONE OF KINDLY REPROACH:
WE HAVE BEEN VERY ANXIOUS ABOUT YOU, HOICHI. TO GO OUT, BLIND AND ALONE, AT SO LATE AN HOUR, IS DANGEROUS.
WHY DID YOU GO WITHOUT TELLING US? I COULD HAVE ORDERED A SERVANT TO ACCOMPANY YOU.
WHERE HAVE YOU BEEN ANYWAY?
PARDON ME, KIND FRIEND!
I HAD TO ATTEND TO SOME PRIVATE BUSINESS, AND I COULD NOT ARRANGE THE MATTER AT ANY OTHER HOUR.

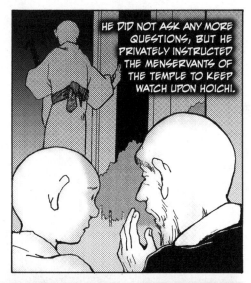

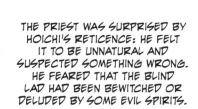

THE PRIEST WAS SURPRISED BY HOICHI'S RETICENCE: HE FELT IT TO BE UNNATURAL AND SUSPECTED SOMETHING WRONG. HE FEARED THAT THE BLIND LAD HAD BEEN BEWITCHED OR DELUDED BY SOME EVIL SPIRITS.
HE DID NOT ASK ANY MORE QUESTIONS, BUT HE PRIVATELY INSTRUCTED THE MENSERVANTS OF THE TEMPLE TO KEEP WATCH UPON HOICHI.
ON THE VERY NEXT NIGHT, HOICHI WAS SEEN TO LEAVE THE TEMPLE. THE SERVANTS IMMEDIATELY FOLLOWED AFTER HIM.
BUT IT WAS A DARK AND RAINY NIGHT, AND BEFORE THEY GOT FAR, HOICHI HAD DISAPPEARED.

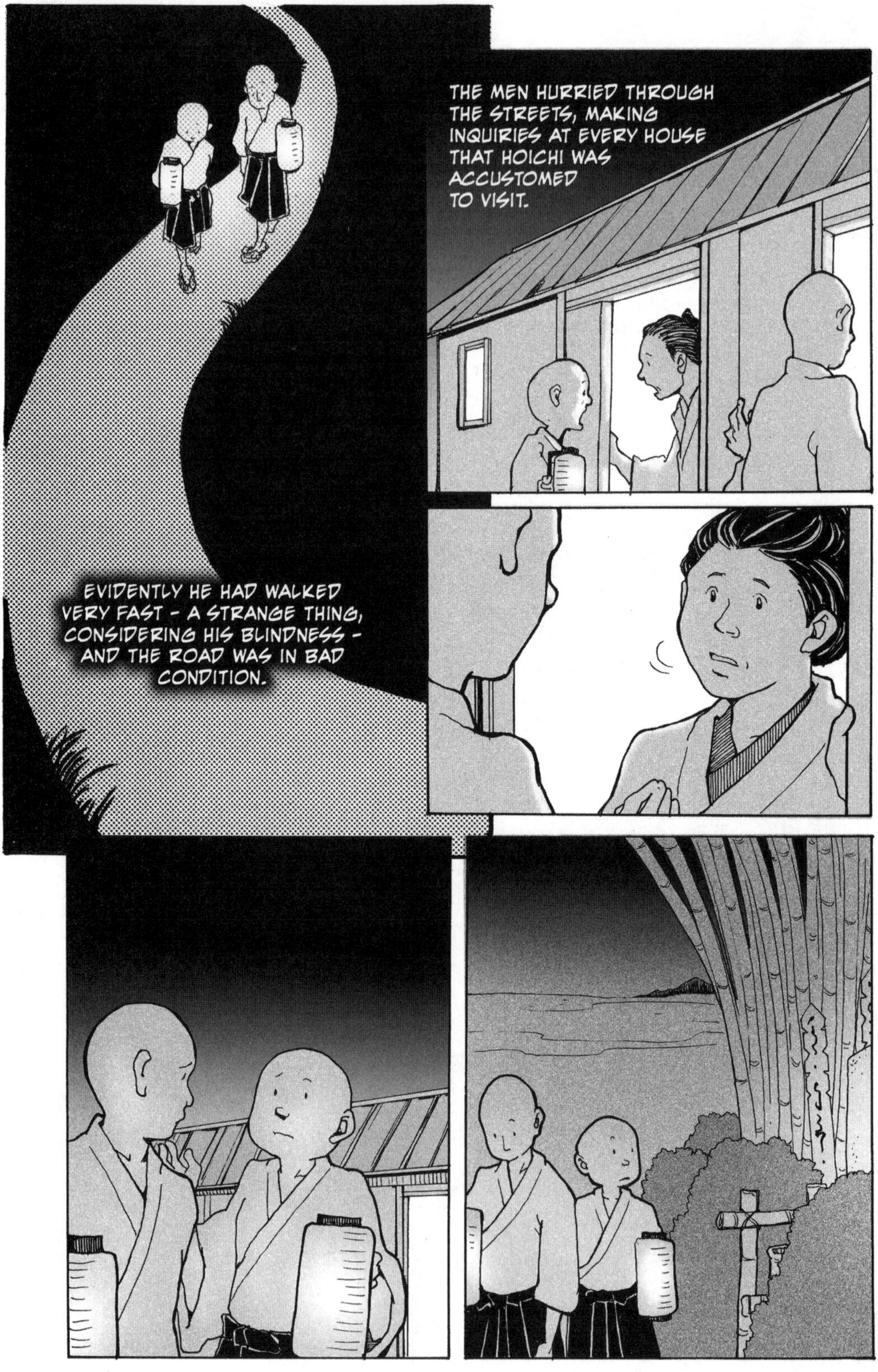
THE MEN HURRIED THROUGH THE STREETS, MAKING INQUIRIES AT EVERY HOUSE THAT HOICHI WAS ACCUSTOMED TO VISIT.
EVIDENTLY HE HAD WALKED VERY FAST - A STRANGE THING, CONSIDERING HIS BLINDNESS - AND THE ROAD WAS IN BAD CONDITION.

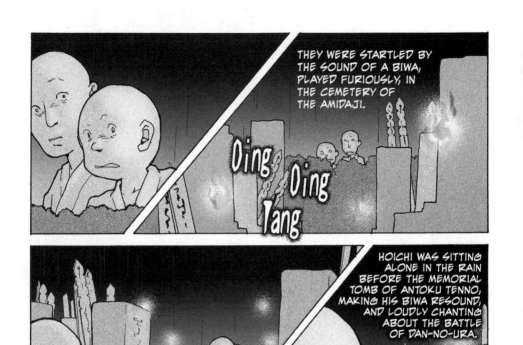

THEY WERE STARTLED BY THE SOUND OF A BIWA, PLAYED FURIOUSLY, IN THE CEMETERY OF THE AMIDAJI.

Oing Oing Tang

HOICHI WAS SITTING ALONE IN THE RAIN BEFORE THE MEMORIAL TOMB OF ANTOKU TENNO, MAKING HIS BIWA RESOUND, AND LOUDLY CHANTING ABOUT THE BATTLE OF DAN-NO-URA.

BEHIND HIM, ABOUT HIM, AND EVERYWHERE, THE FIRES OF THE DEAD WERE BURNING LIKE CANDLES. A GREAT HOST OF ONI-BI!

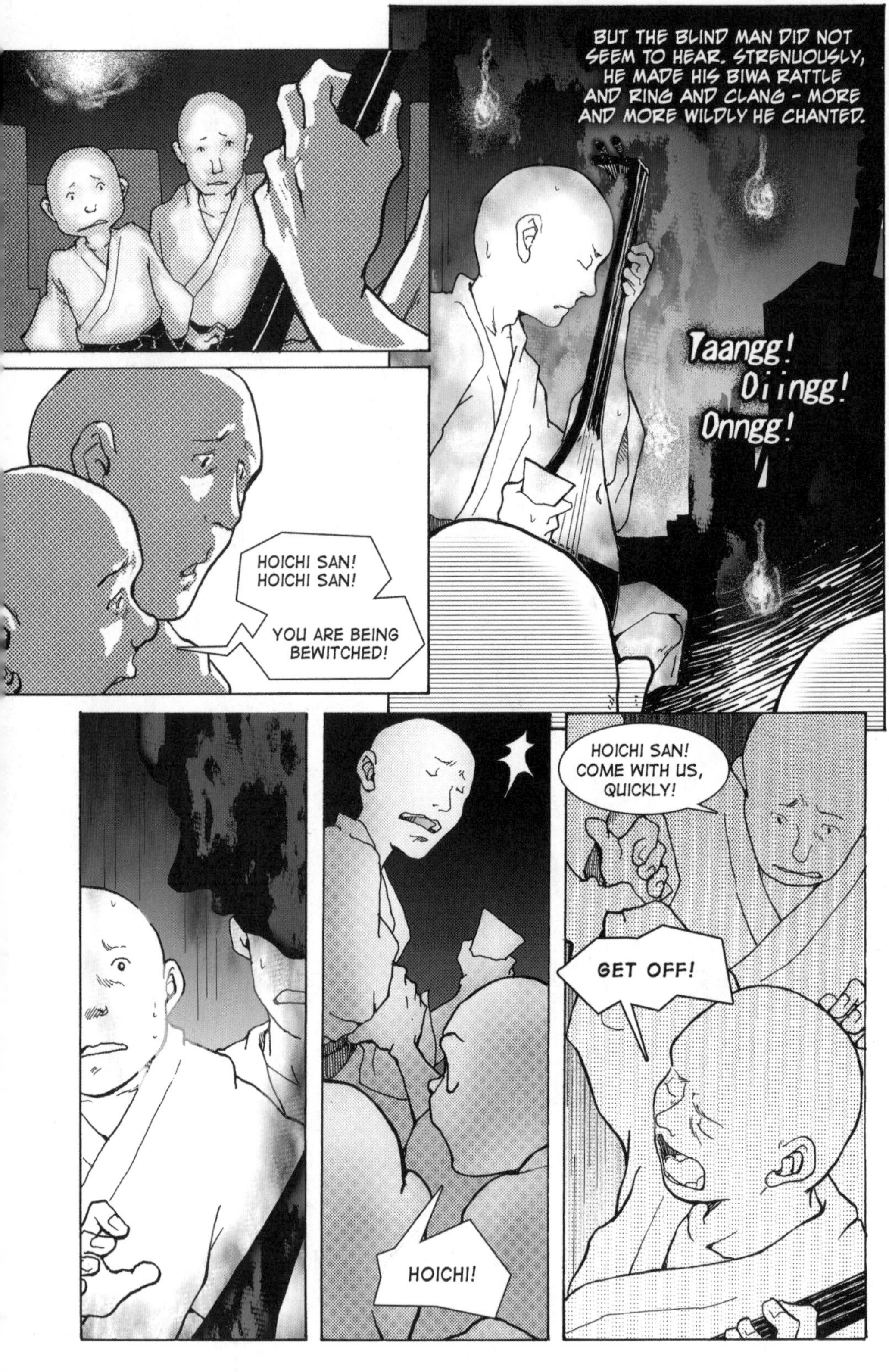

HOICHI SAN! HOICHI SAN!
YOU ARE BEING BEWITCHED!
BUT THE BLIND MAN DID NOT SEEM TO HEAR. STRENUOUSLY, HE MADE HIS BIWA RATTLE AND RING AND CLANG - MORE AND MORE WILDLY HE CHANTED.
Taangg!
Oiingg!
Onngg!
HOICHI!
HOICHI SAN! COME WITH US, QUICKLY!
GET OFF!

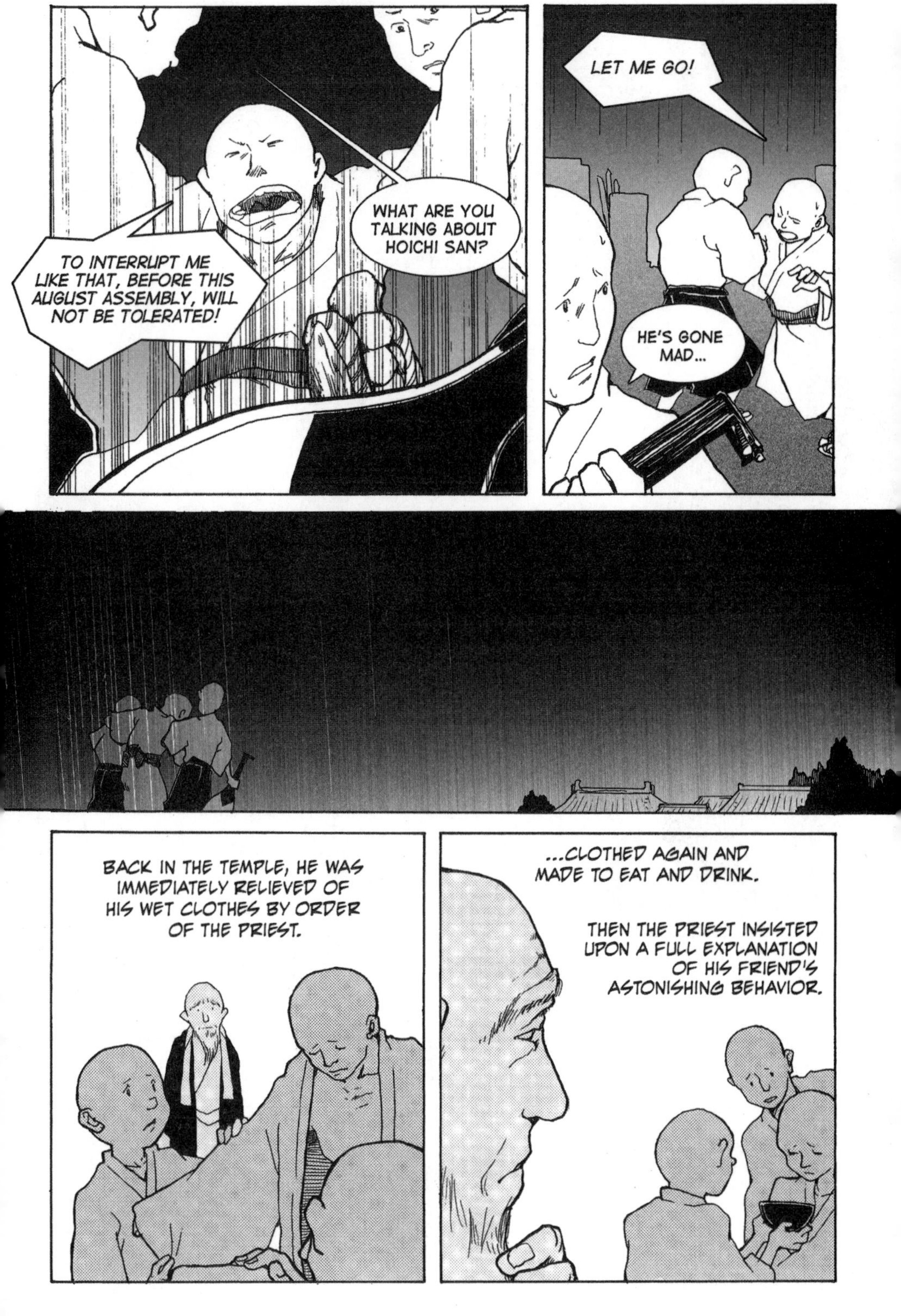
TO INTERRUPT ME LIKE THAT, BEFORE THIS AUGUST ASSEMBLY, WILL NOT BE TOLERATED!
WHAT ARE YOU TALKING ABOUT HOICHI SAN?
LET ME GO!
HE'S GONE MAD...
BACK IN THE TEMPLE, HE WAS IMMEDIATELY RELIEVED OF HIS WET CLOTHES BY ORDER OF THE PRIEST.
...CLOTHED AGAIN AND MADE TO EAT AND DRINK.
THEN THE PRIEST INSISTED UPON A FULL EXPLANATION OF HIS FRIEND'S ASTONISHING BEHAVIOR.

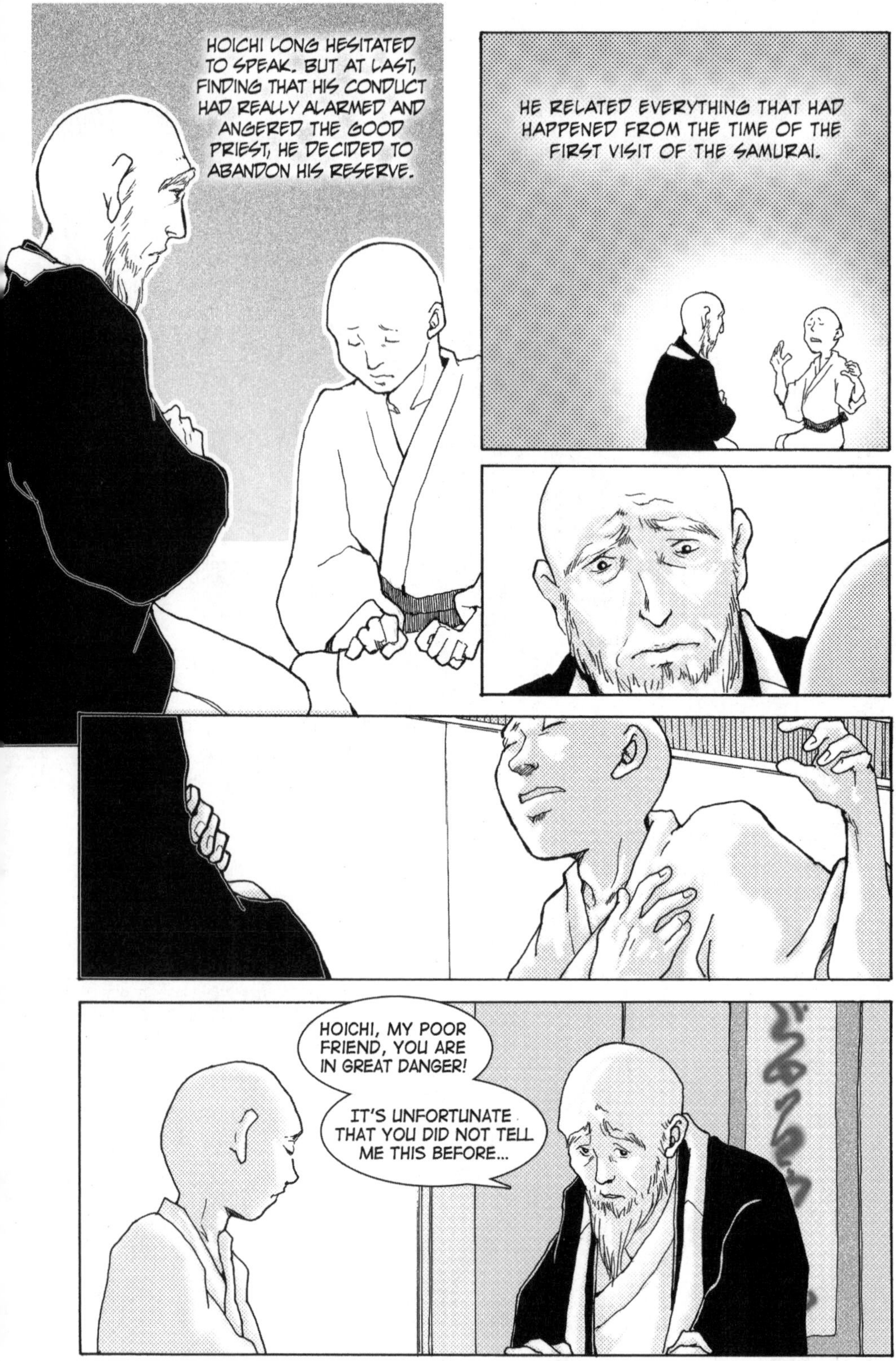
HOICHI LONG HESITATED TO SPEAK. BUT AT LAST, FINDING THAT HIS CONDUCT HAD REALLY ALARMED AND ANGERED THE GOOD PRIEST, HE DECIDED TO ABANDON HIS RESERVE.
HE RELATED EVERYTHING THAT HAD HAPPENED FROM THE TIME OF THE FIRST VISIT OF THE SAMURAI.
HOICHI, MY POOR FRIEND, YOU ARE IN GREAT DANGER!
IT'S UNFORTUNATE THAT YOU DID NOT TELL ME THIS BEFORE...

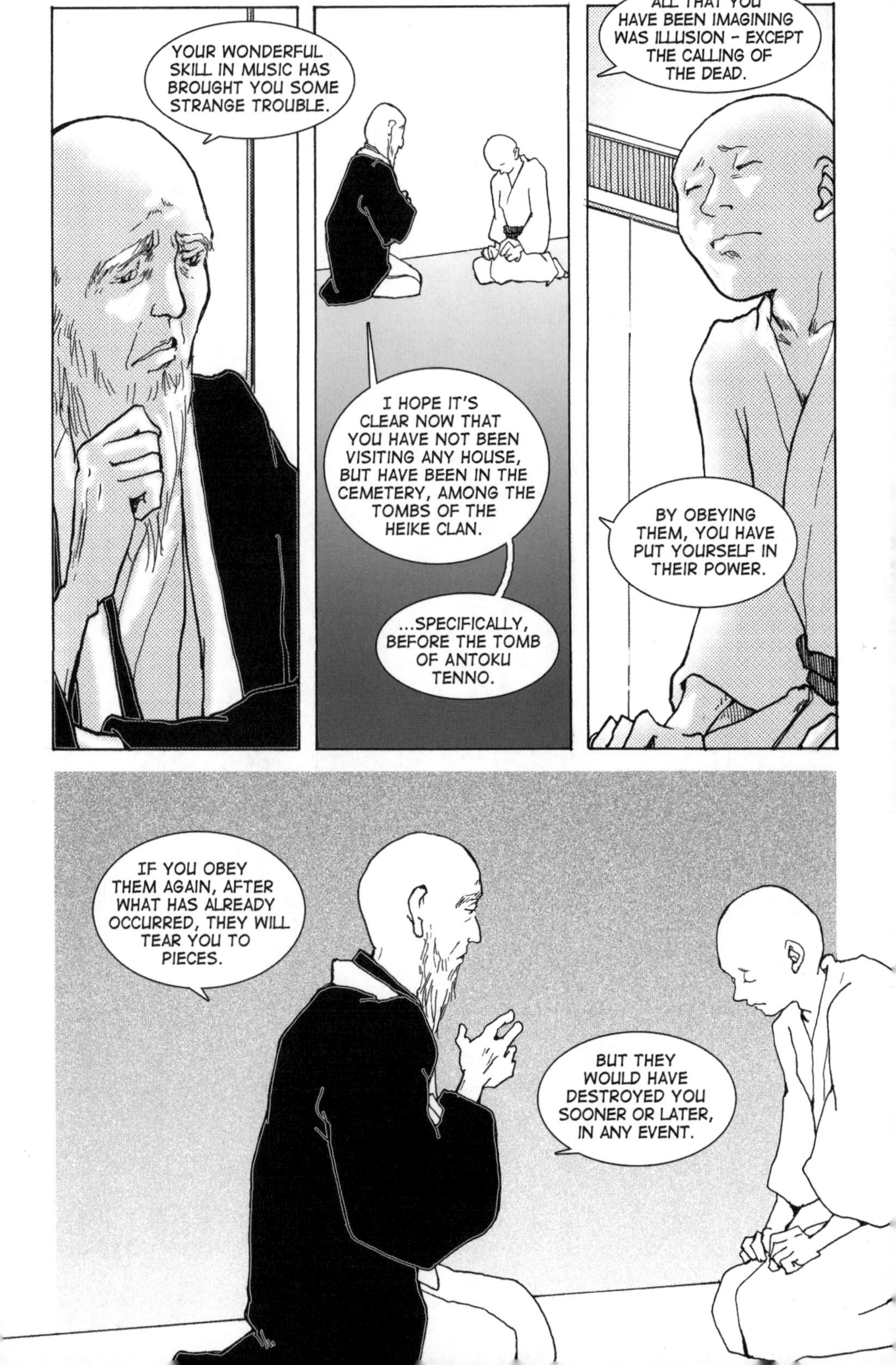
YOUR WONDERFUL SKILL IN MUSIC HAS BROUGHT YOU SOME STRANGE TROUBLE.
I HOPE IT'S CLEAR NOW THAT YOU HAVE NOT BEEN VISITING ANY HOUSE, BUT HAVE BEEN IN THE CEMETERY, AMONG THE TOMBS OF THE HEIKE CLAN.
...SPECIFICALLY, BEFORE THE TOMB OF ANTOKU TENNO.
ALL THAT YOU HAVE BEEN IMAGINING WAS ILLUSION - EXCEPT THE CALLING OF THE DEAD.
BY OBEYING THEM, YOU HAVE PUT YOURSELF IN THEIR POWER.
IF YOU OBEY THEM AGAIN, AFTER WHAT HAS ALREADY OCCURRED, THEY WILL TEAR YOU TO PIECES.
BUT THEY WOULD HAVE DESTROYED YOU SOONER OR LATER, IN ANY EVENT.

NOW I SHALL NOT BE ABLE TO REMAIN WITH YOU TONIGHT...

IT'S VERY UNFORTUNATE THAT I HAVE ALREADY BEEN CALLED AWAY TO PERFORM ANOTHER SERVICE.

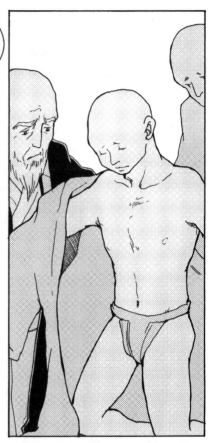

SO, BEFORE I GO, IT'S NECESSARY TO PROTECT YOUR BODY BY WRITING HOLY TEXTS UPON IT.

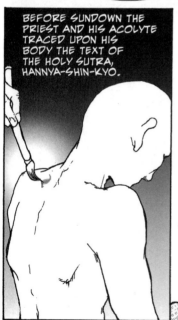

BEFORE SUNDOWN THE PRIEST AND HIS ACOLYTE TRACED UPON HIS BODY THE TEXT OF THE HOLY SUTRA, HANNYA-SHIN-KYO.

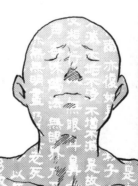

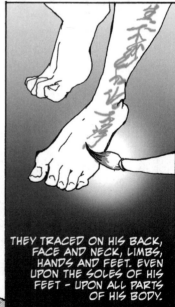

THEY TRACED ON HIS BACK, FACE AND NECK, LIMBS, HANDS AND FEET. EVEN UPON THE SOLES OF HIS FEET - UPON ALL PARTS OF HIS BODY.

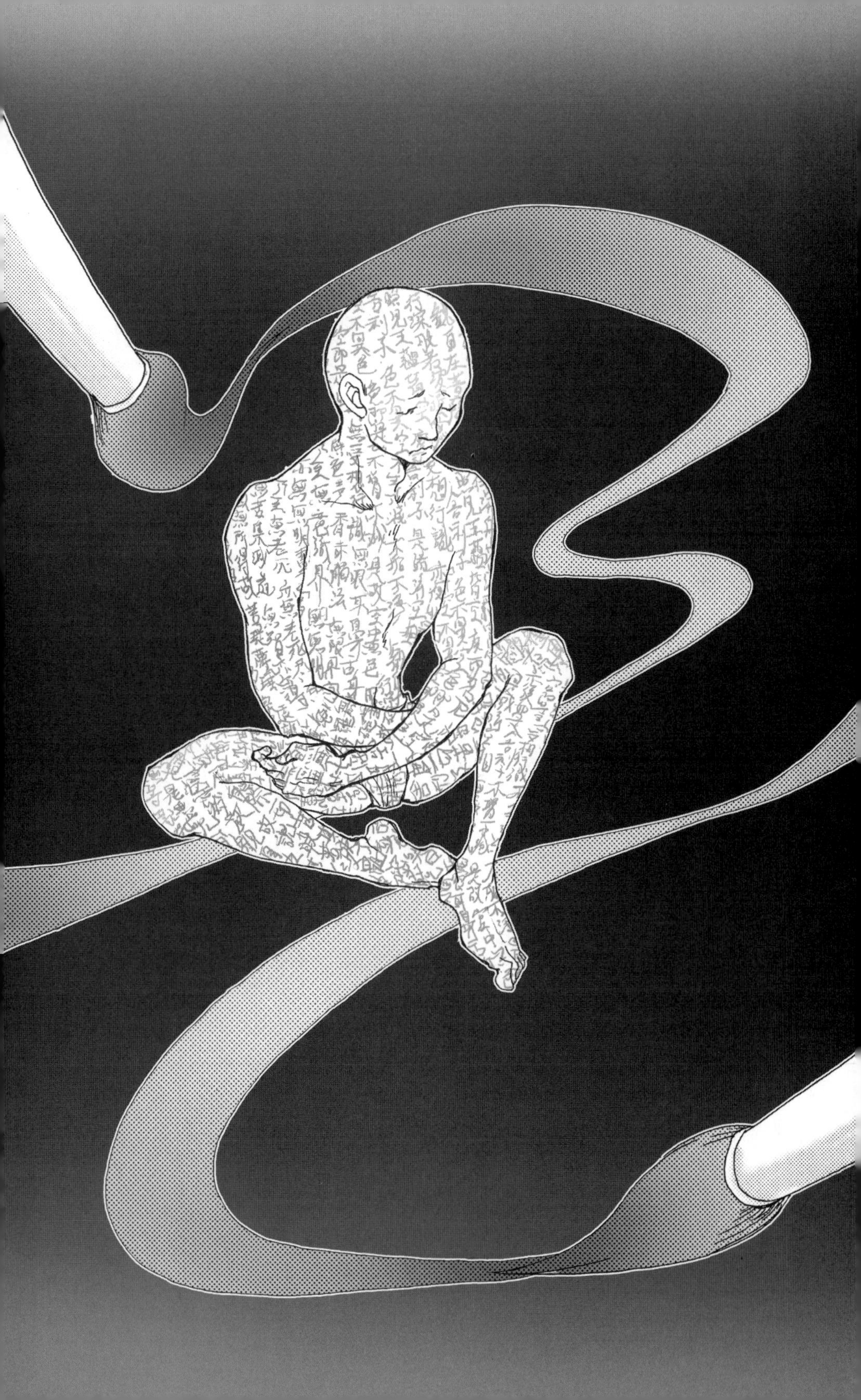

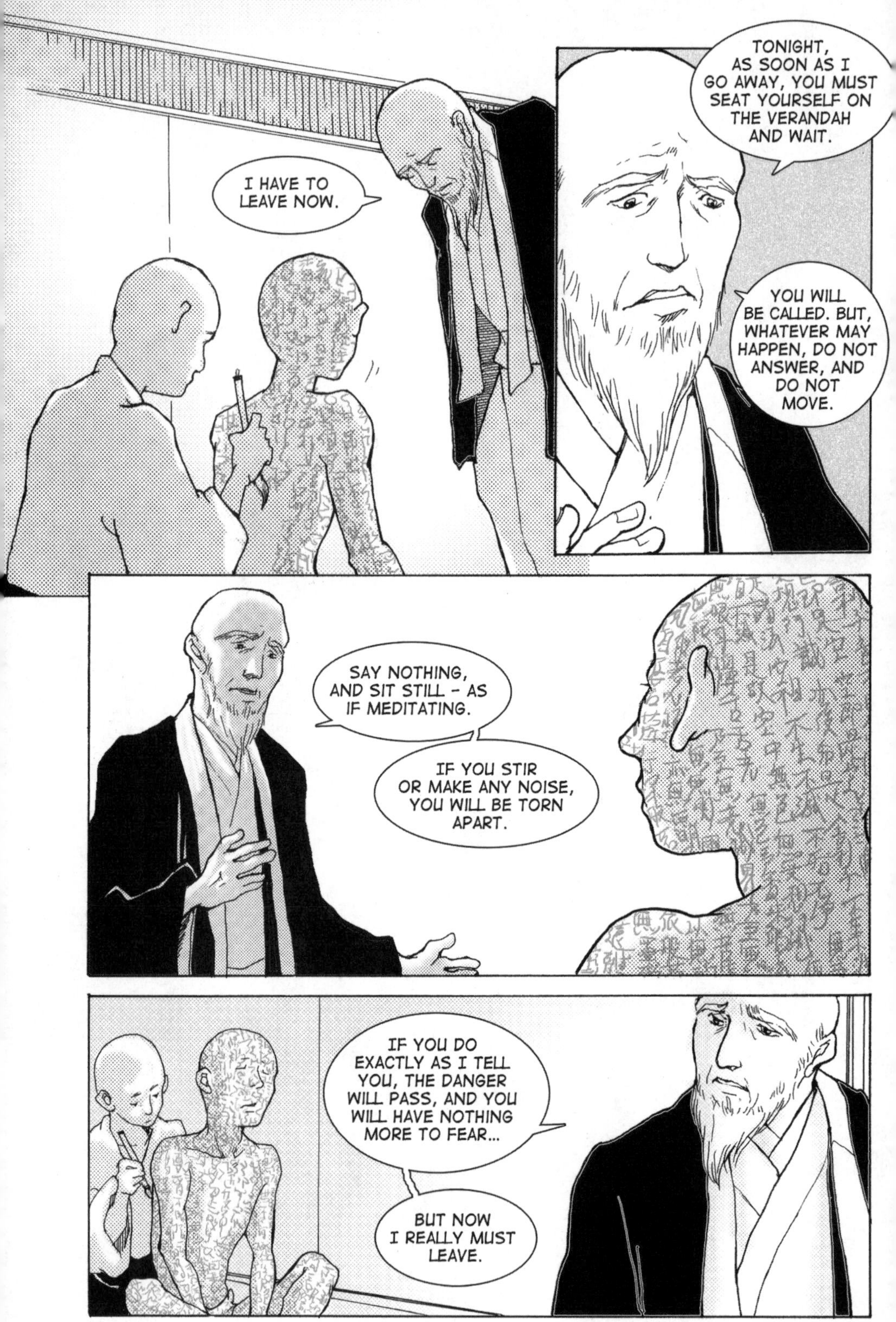
I HAVE TO LEAVE NOW.
TONIGHT, AS SOON AS I GO AWAY, YOU MUST SEAT YOURSELF ON THE VERANDAH AND WAIT.
YOU WILL BE CALLED. BUT, WHATEVER MAY HAPPEN, DO NOT ANSWER, AND DO NOT MOVE.
SAY NOTHING, AND SIT STILL - AS IF MEDITATING.
IF YOU STIR OR MAKE ANY NOISE, YOU WILL BE TORN APART.
IF YOU DO EXACTLY AS I TELL YOU, THE DANGER WILL PASS, AND YOU WILL HAVE NOTHING MORE TO FEAR...
BUT NOW I REALLY MUST LEAVE.

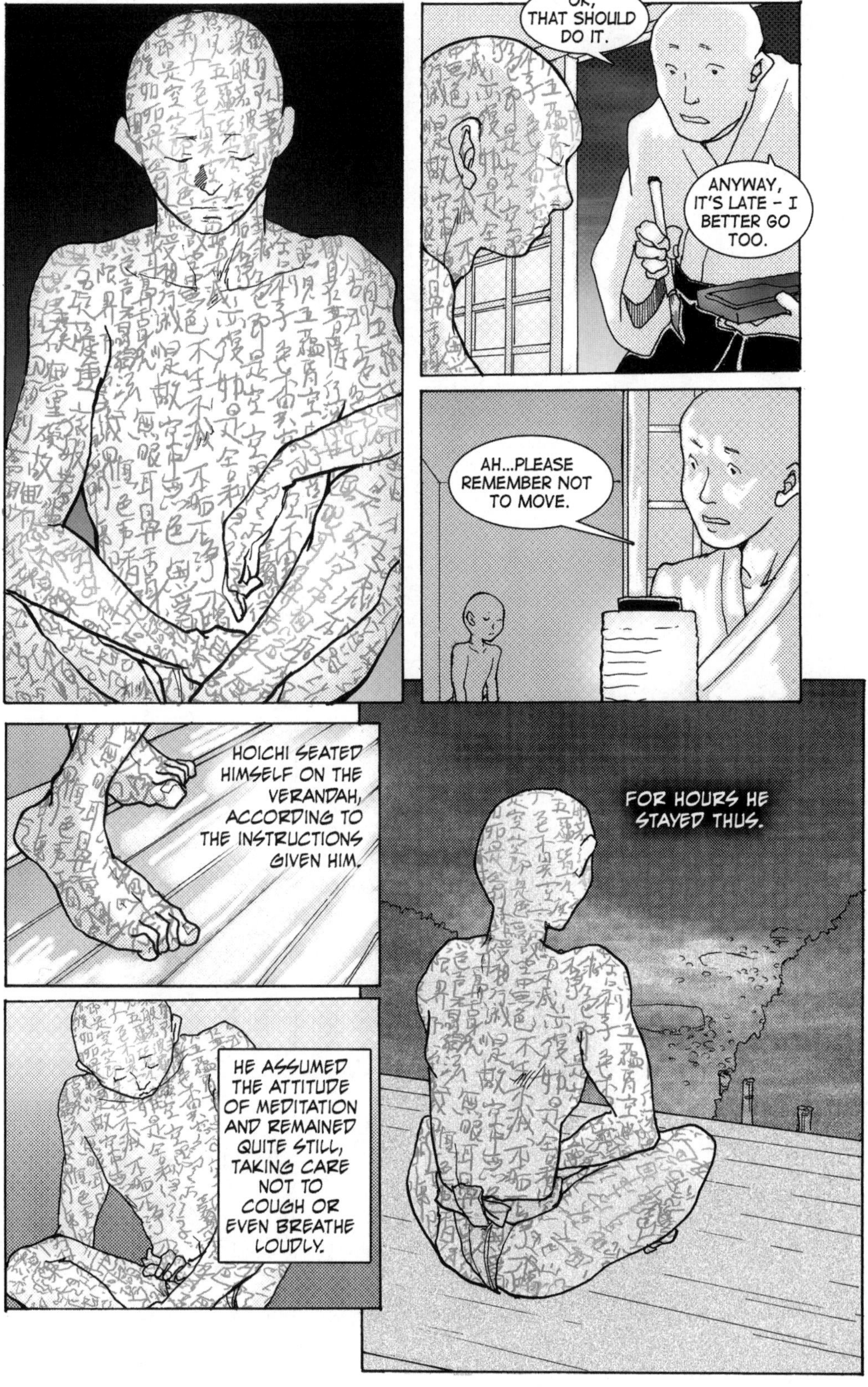
OK, THAT SHOULD DO IT.
ANYWAY, IT'S LATE – I BETTER GO TOO.
AH...PLEASE REMEMBER NOT TO MOVE.
HOICHI SEATED HIMSELF ON THE VERANDAH, ACCORDING TO THE INSTRUCTIONS GIVEN HIM.
HE ASSUMED THE ATTITUDE OF MEDITATION AND REMAINED QUITE STILL, TAKING CARE NOT TO COUGH OR EVEN BREATHE LOUDLY.
FOR HOURS HE STAYED THUS.

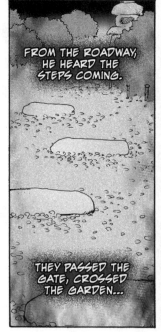

FROM THE ROADWAY, HE HEARD THE STEPS COMING.

THEY PASSED THE GATE, CROSSED THE GARDEN...

APPROACHED THE VERANDAH...

THEN STOPPED – DIRECTLY IN FRONT OF HIM.

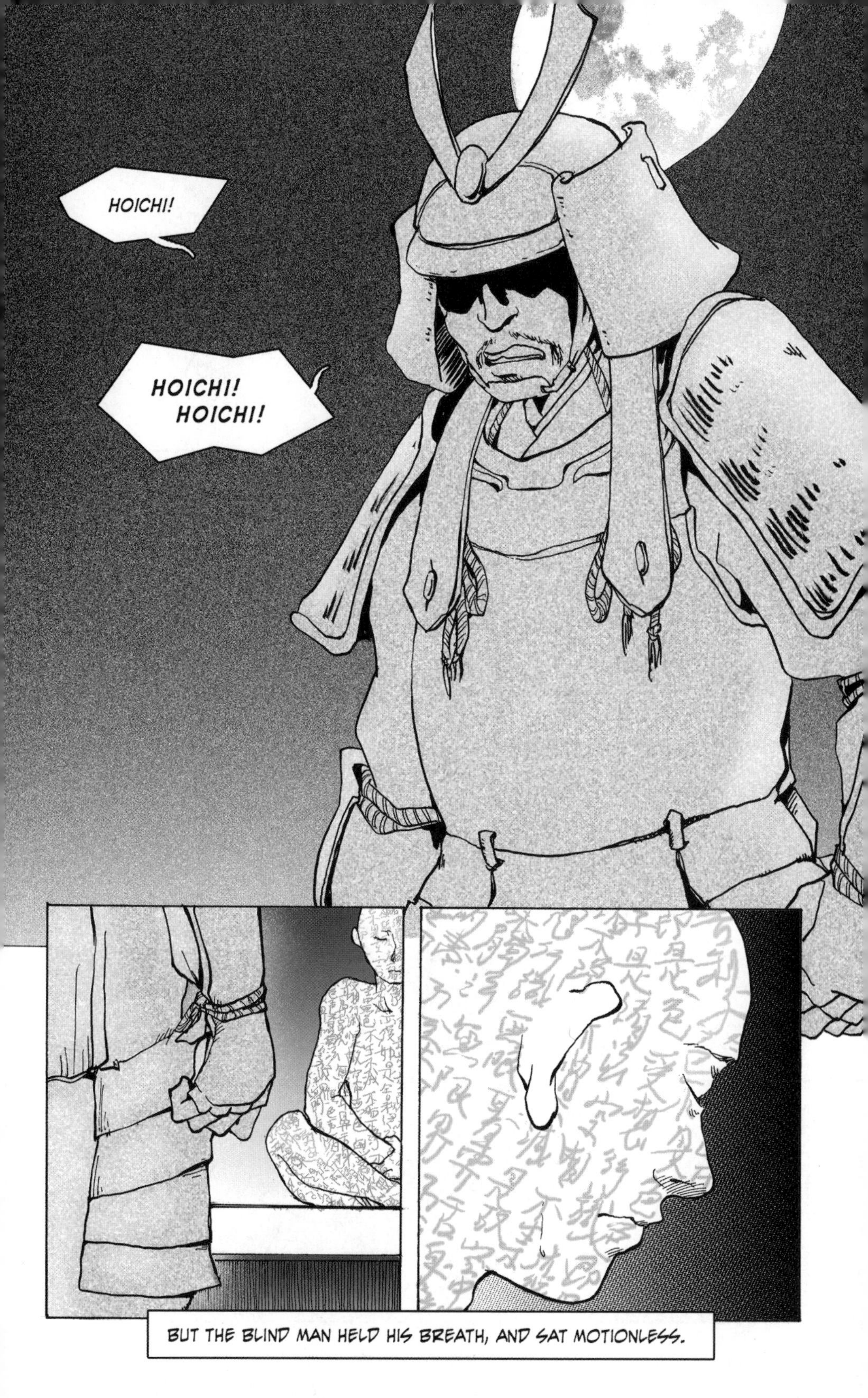
HOICHI!
HOICHI! HOICHI!
BUT THE BLIND MAN HELD HIS BREATH, AND SAT MOTIONLESS.

NO ANSWER!

THAT WON'T DO.

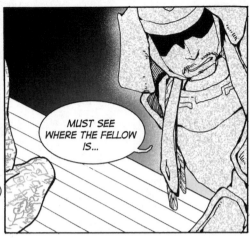

MUST SEE WHERE THE FELLOW IS...

THERE WAS A NOISE OF SOMETHING MOUNTING THE VERANDAH AND HALTING BESIDE HIM.

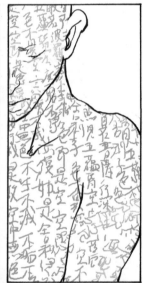

THEN, FOR LONG MINUTES — DURING WHICH HOICHI FELT HIS WHOLE BODY SHAKE TO THE BEATING OF HIS HEART — THERE WAS DEAD SILENCE.

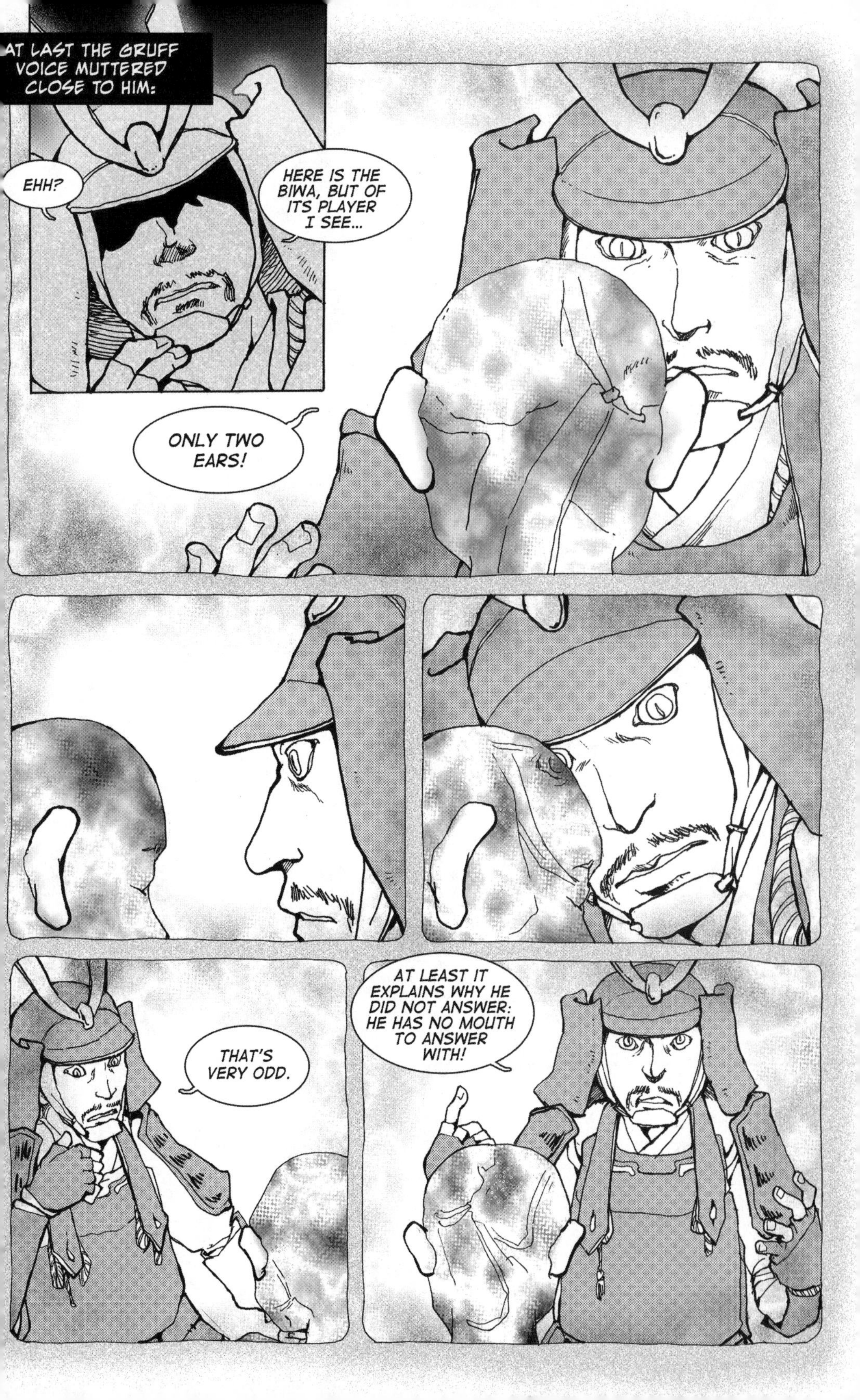
AT LAST THE GRUFF VOICE MUTTERED CLOSE TO HIM:
EHH?
HERE IS THE BIWA, BUT OF ITS PLAYER I SEE...
ONLY TWO EARS!
THAT'S VERY ODD.
AT LEAST IT EXPLAINS WHY HE DID NOT ANSWER: HE HAS NO MOUTH TO ANSWER WITH!

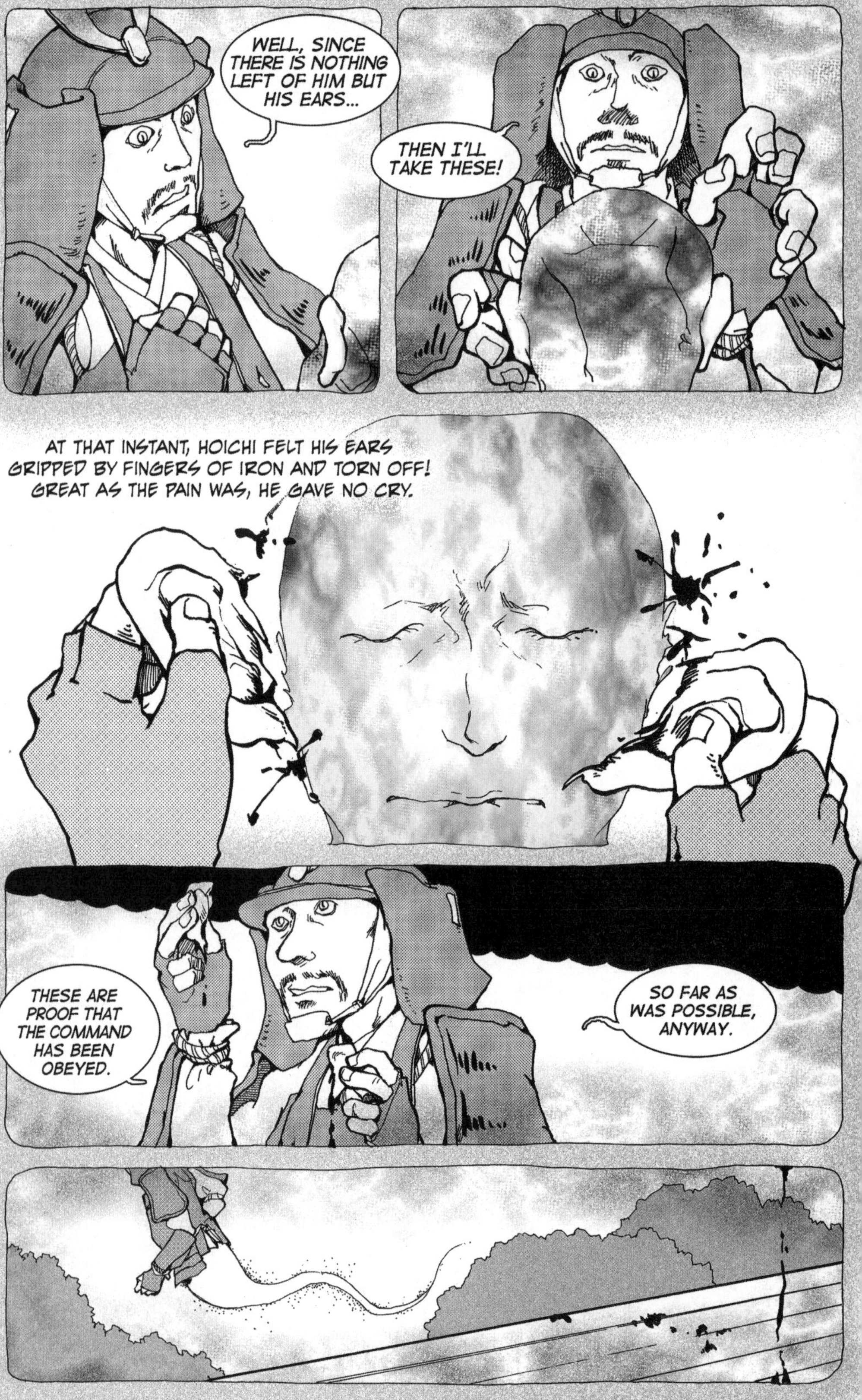
WELL, SINCE THERE IS NOTHING LEFT OF HIM BUT HIS EARS...
THEN I'LL TAKE THESE!
AT THAT INSTANT, HOICHI FELT HIS EARS GRIPPED BY FINGERS OF IRON AND TORN OFF! GREAT AS THE PAIN WAS, HE GAVE NO CRY.
THESE ARE PROOF THAT THE COMMAND HAS BEEN OBEYED.
SO FAR AS WAS POSSIBLE, ANYWAY.

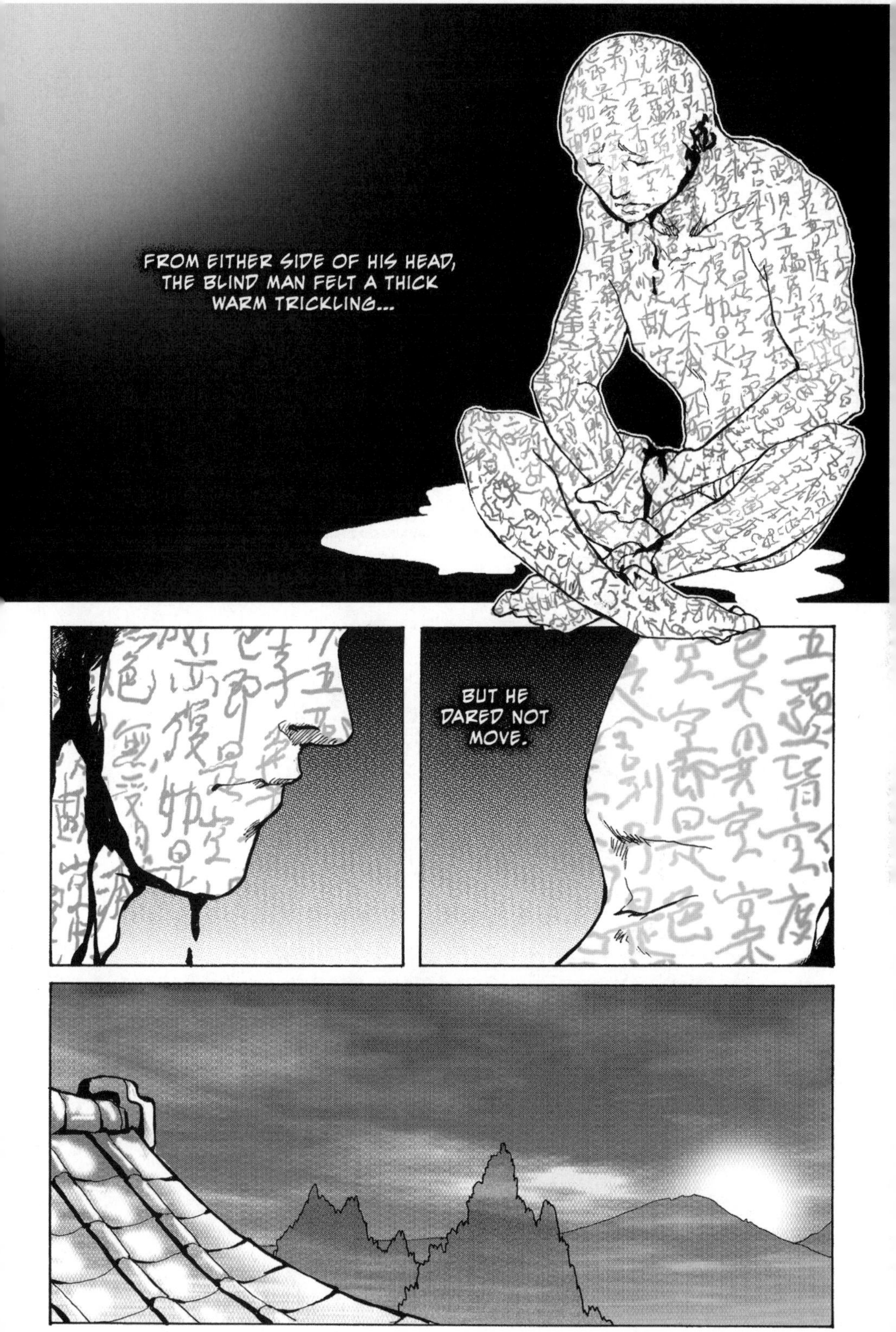
FROM EITHER SIDE OF HIS HEAD, THE BLIND MAN FELT A THICK WARM TRICKLING...
BUT HE DARED NOT MOVE.

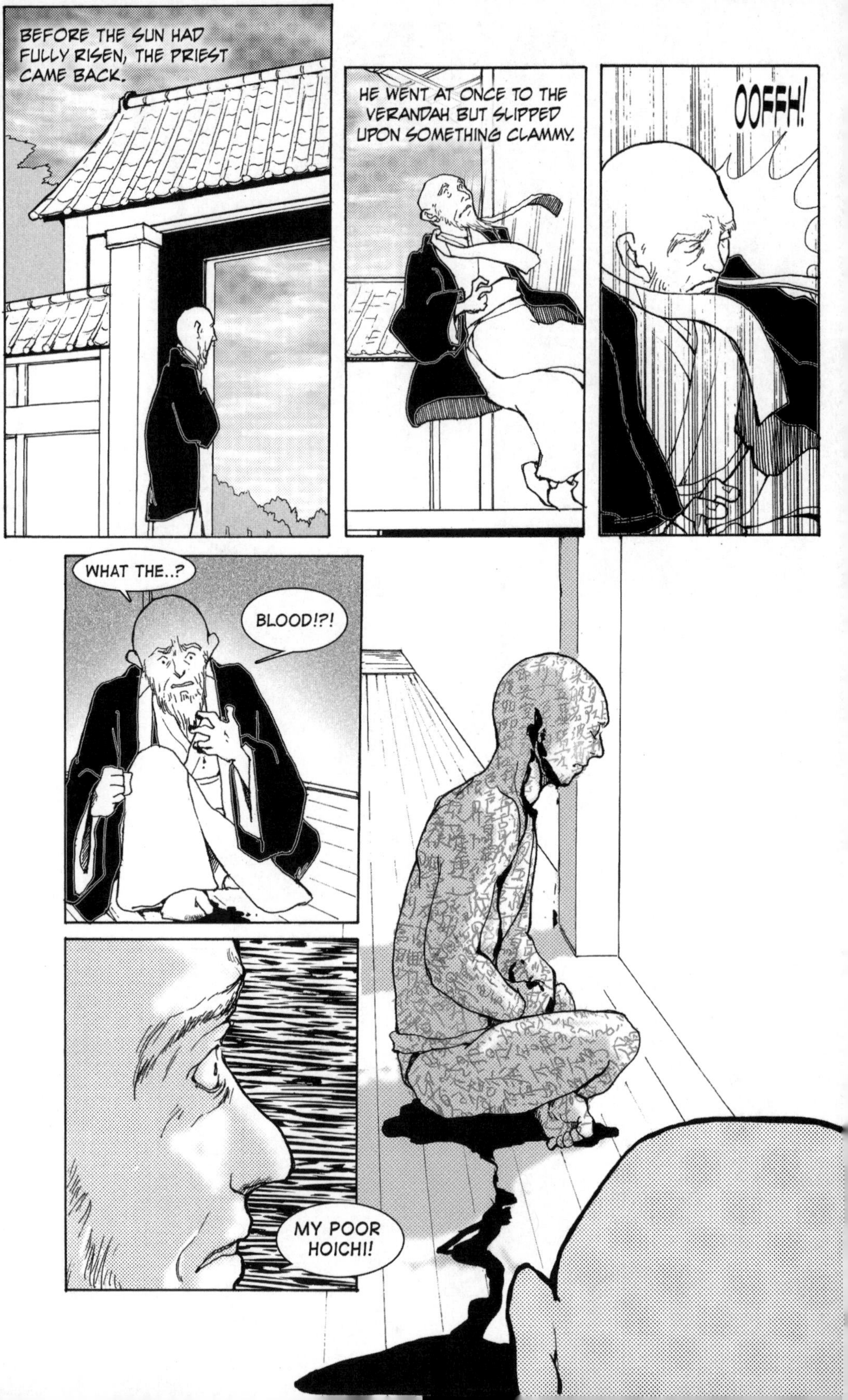
BEFORE THE SUN HAD FULLY RISEN, THE PRIEST CAME BACK.
HE WENT AT ONCE TO THE VERANDAH BUT SLIPPED UPON SOMETHING CLAMMY.
OOFFH!
WHAT THE..?
BLOOD!?!
MY POOR HOICHI!

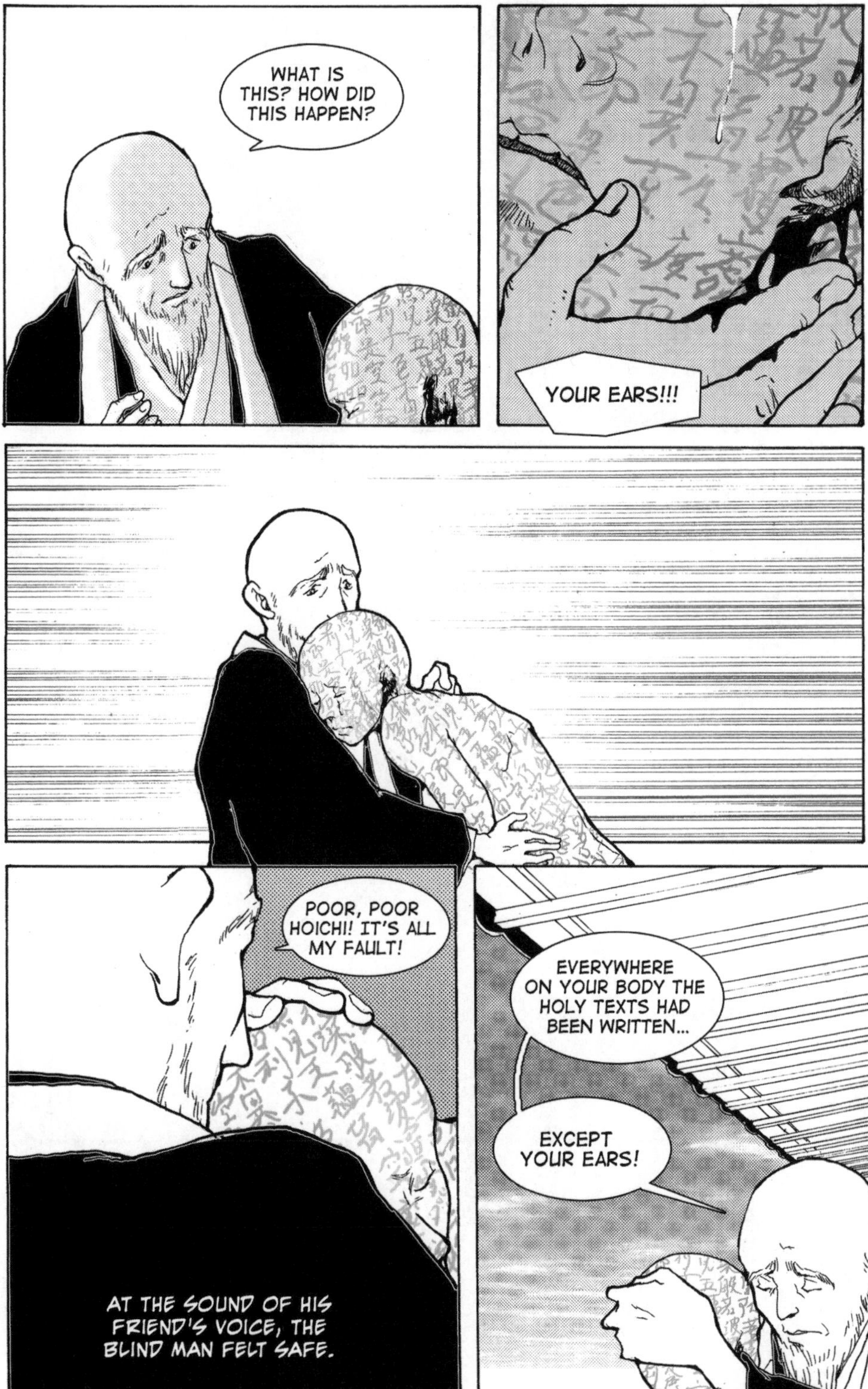
WHAT IS THIS? HOW DID THIS HAPPEN?
YOUR EARS!!!
POOR, POOR HOICHI! IT'S ALL MY FAULT!
AT THE SOUND OF HIS FRIEND'S VOICE, THE BLIND MAN FELT SAFE.
EVERYWHERE ON YOUR BODY THE HOLY TEXTS HAD BEEN WRITTEN...
EXCEPT YOUR EARS!

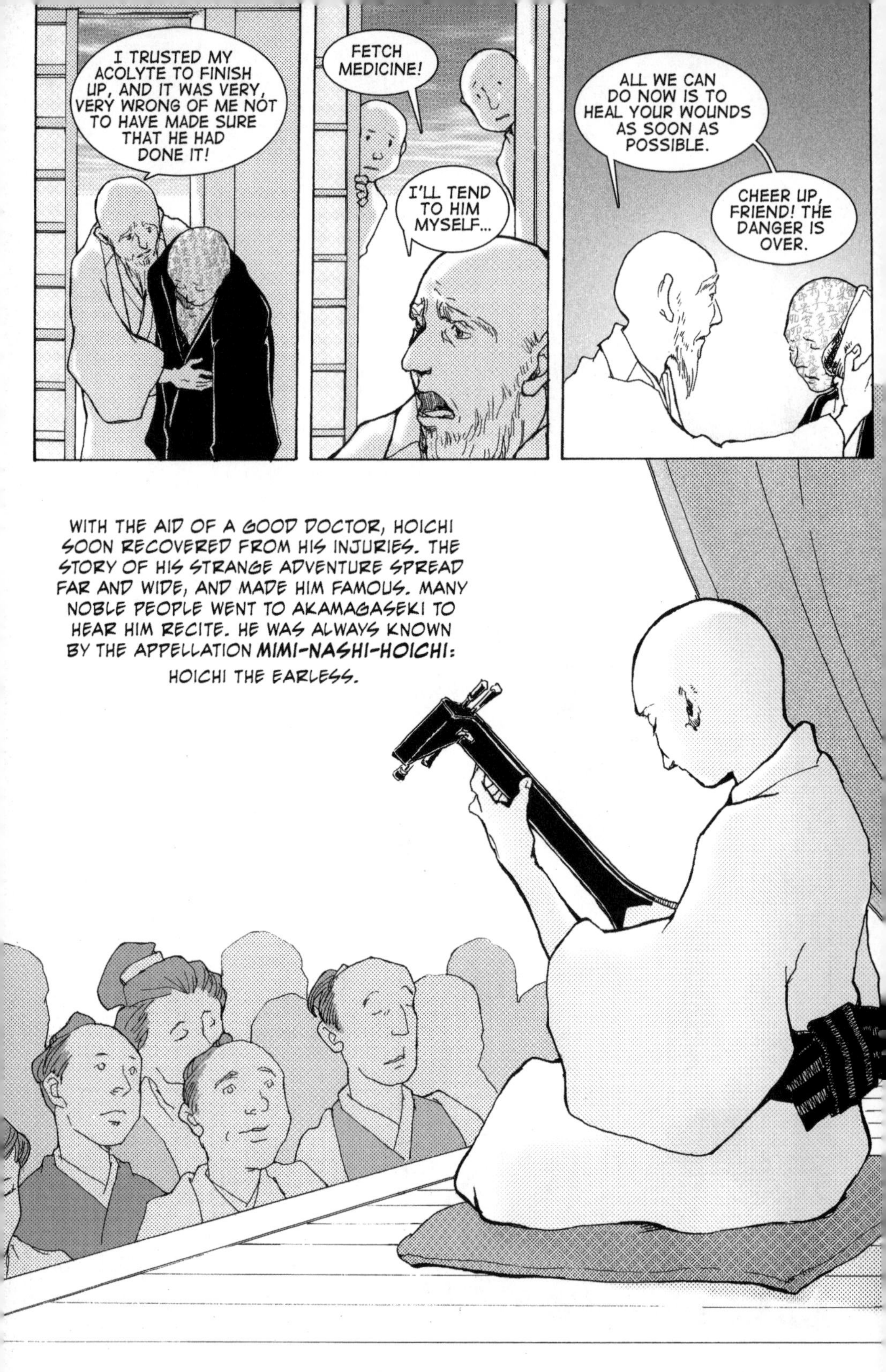
I TRUSTED MY ACOLYTE TO FINISH UP, AND IT WAS VERY, VERY WRONG OF ME NOT TO HAVE MADE SURE THAT HE HAD DONE IT!
FETCH MEDICINE!
I'LL TEND TO HIM MYSELF...
ALL WE CAN DO NOW IS TO HEAL YOUR WOUNDS AS SOON AS POSSIBLE.
CHEER UP, FRIEND! THE DANGER IS OVER.
WITH THE AID OF A GOOD DOCTOR, HOICHI SOON RECOVERED FROM HIS INJURIES. THE STORY OF HIS STRANGE ADVENTURE SPREAD FAR AND WIDE, AND MADE HIM FAMOUS. MANY NOBLE PEOPLE WENT TO AKAMAGASEKI TO HEAR HIM RECITE. HE WAS ALWAYS KNOWN BY THE APPELLATION **MIMI-NASHI-HOICHI**:
HOICHI THE EARLESS.

むじな

THE
FACELESS
GHOST

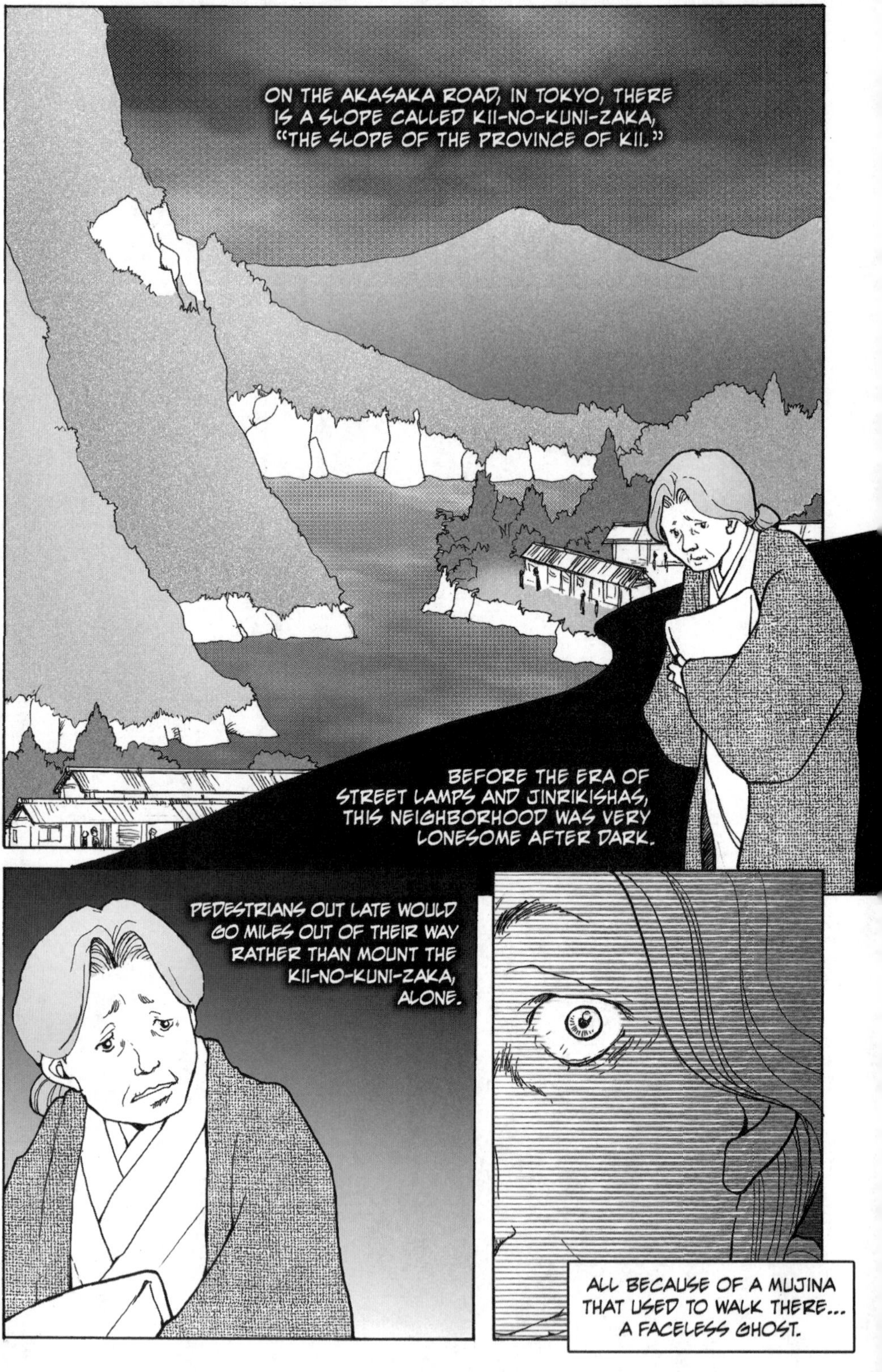
ON THE AKASAKA ROAD, IN TOKYO, THERE IS A SLOPE CALLED KII-NO-KUNI-ZAKA, "THE SLOPE OF THE PROVINCE OF KII."
BEFORE THE ERA OF STREET LAMPS AND JINRIKISHAS, THIS NEIGHBORHOOD WAS VERY LONESOME AFTER DARK.
PEDESTRIANS OUT LATE WOULD GO MILES OUT OF THEIR WAY RATHER THAN MOUNT THE KII-NO-KUNI-ZAKA, ALONE.
ALL BECAUSE OF A MUJINA THAT USED TO WALK THERE... A FACELESS GHOST.

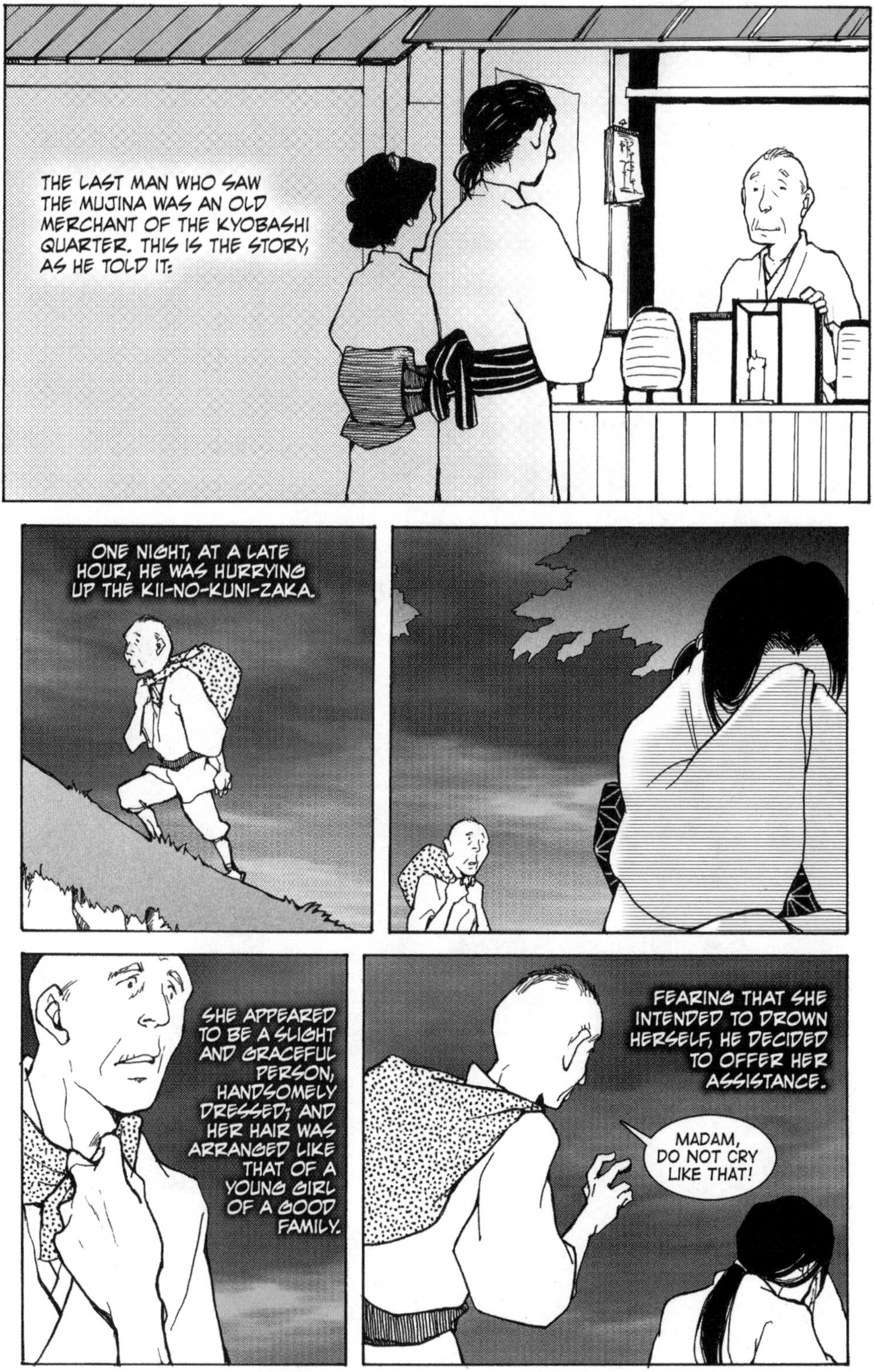
THE LAST MAN WHO SAW THE MUJINA WAS AN OLD MERCHANT OF THE KYOBASHI QUARTER. THIS IS THE STORY, AS HE TOLD IT:
ONE NIGHT, AT A LATE HOUR, HE WAS HURRYING UP THE KII-NO-KUNI-ZAKA.
SHE APPEARED TO BE A SLIGHT AND GRACEFUL PERSON, HANDSOMELY DRESSED; AND HER HAIR WAS ARRANGED LIKE THAT OF A YOUNG GIRL OF A GOOD FAMILY.
FEARING THAT SHE INTENDED TO DROWN HERSELF, HE DECIDED TO OFFER HER ASSISTANCE.
MADAM, DO NOT CRY LIKE THAT!

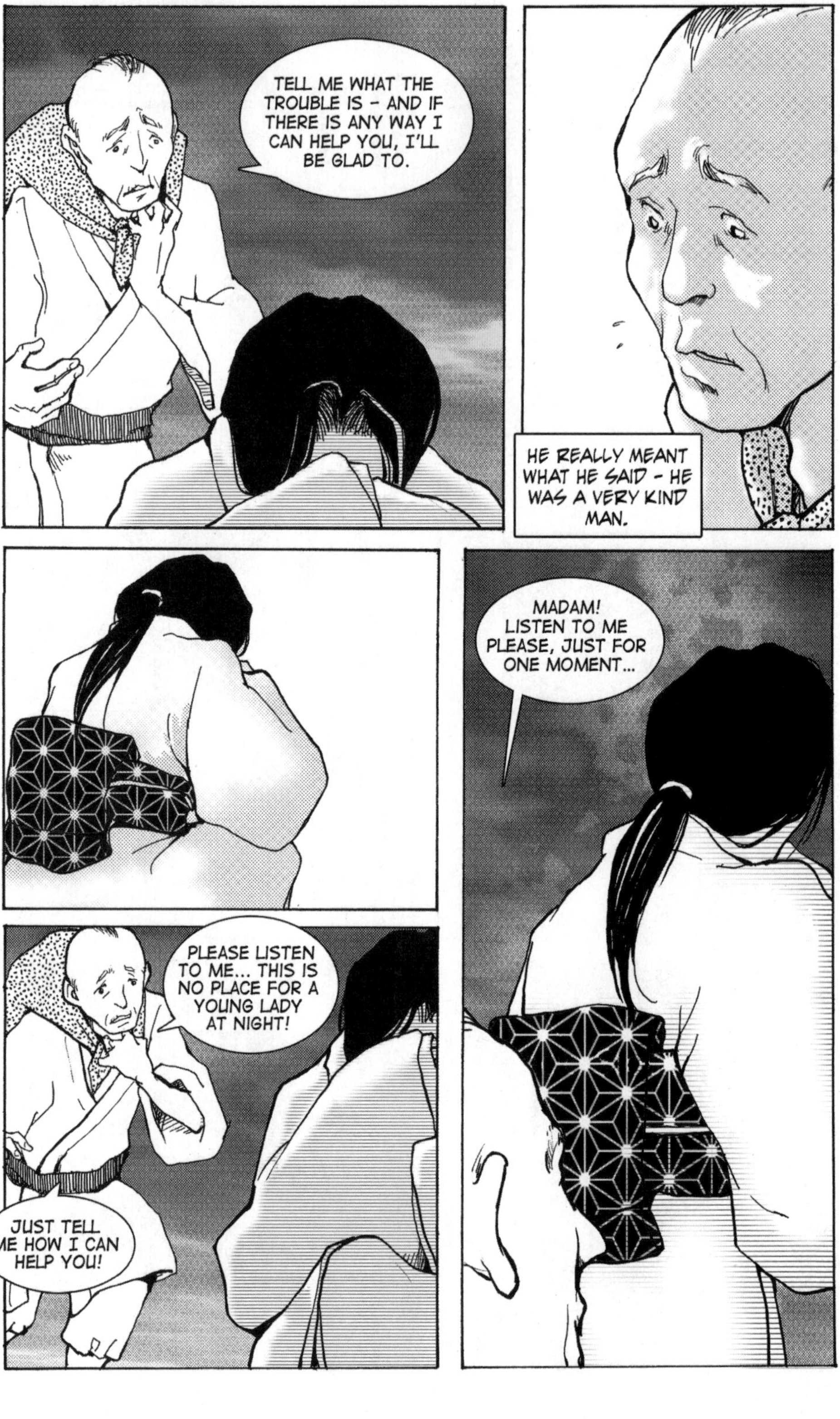
TELL ME WHAT THE TROUBLE IS - AND IF THERE IS ANY WAY I CAN HELP YOU, I'LL BE GLAD TO.
HE REALLY MEANT WHAT HE SAID - HE WAS A VERY KIND MAN.
PLEASE LISTEN TO ME... THIS IS NO PLACE FOR A YOUNG LADY AT NIGHT!
JUST TELL ME HOW I CAN HELP YOU!
MADAM! LISTEN TO ME PLEASE, JUST FOR ONE MOMENT...

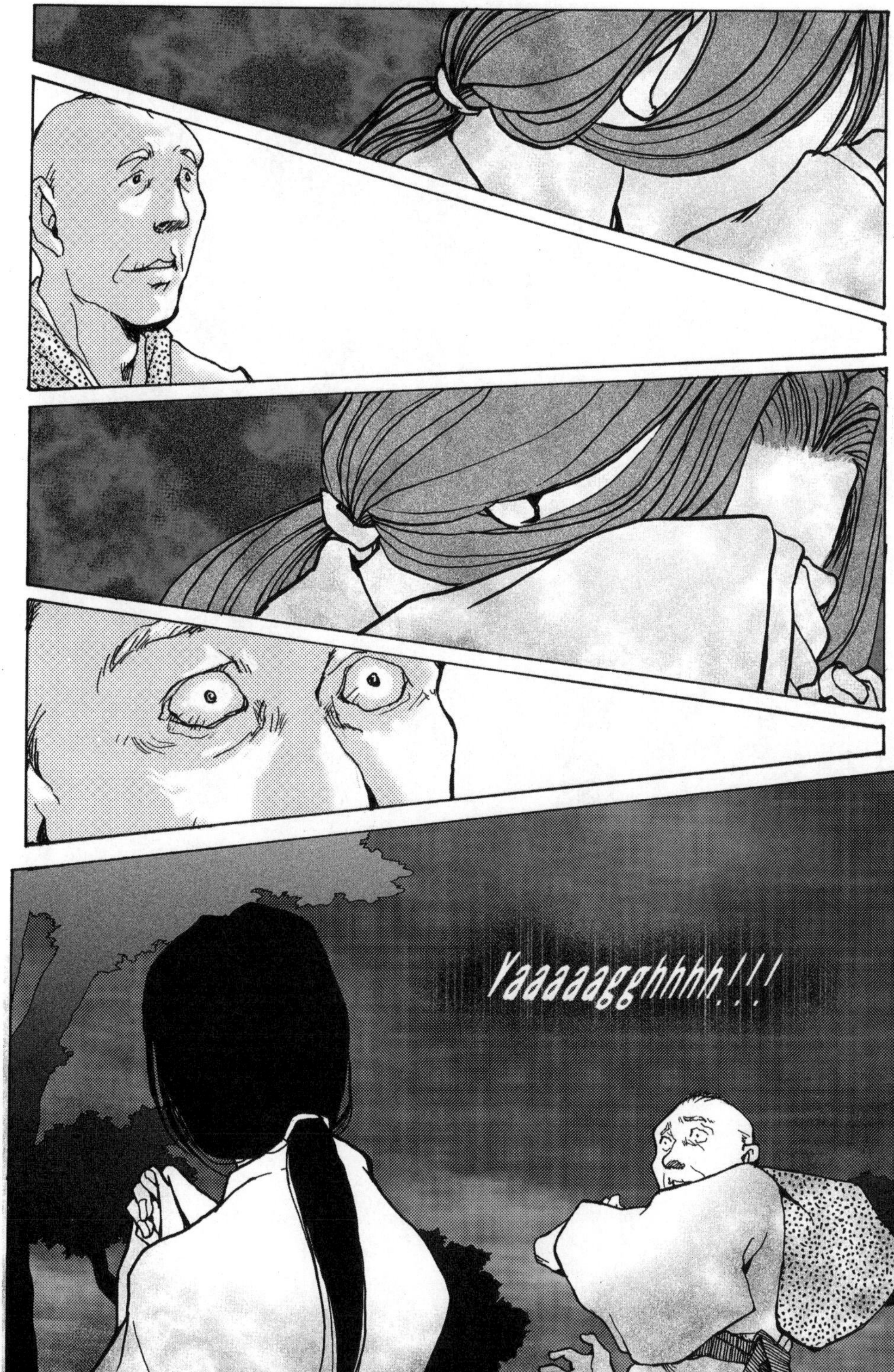
Yaaaaagghhhh!!!

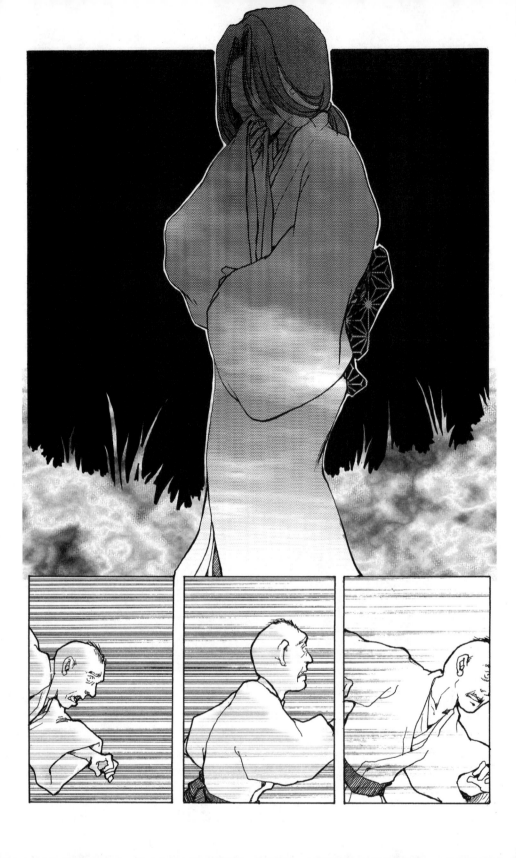

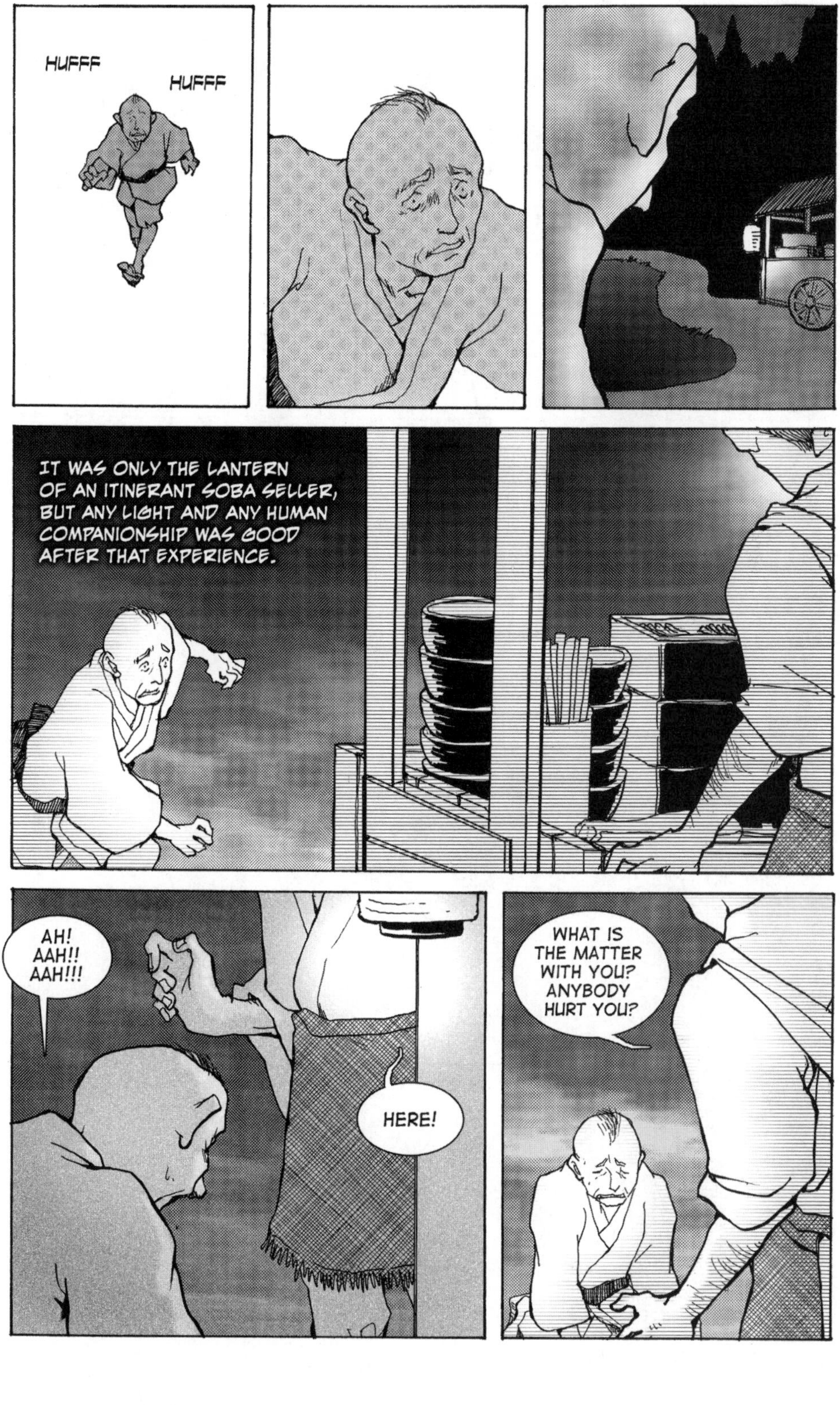
HUFFF
HUFFF
IT WAS ONLY THE LANTERN OF AN ITINERANT SOBA SELLER, BUT ANY LIGHT AND ANY HUMAN COMPANIONSHIP WAS GOOD AFTER THAT EXPERIENCE.
AH! AAH!! AAH!!!
HERE!
WHAT IS THE MATTER WITH YOU? ANYBODY HURT YOU?

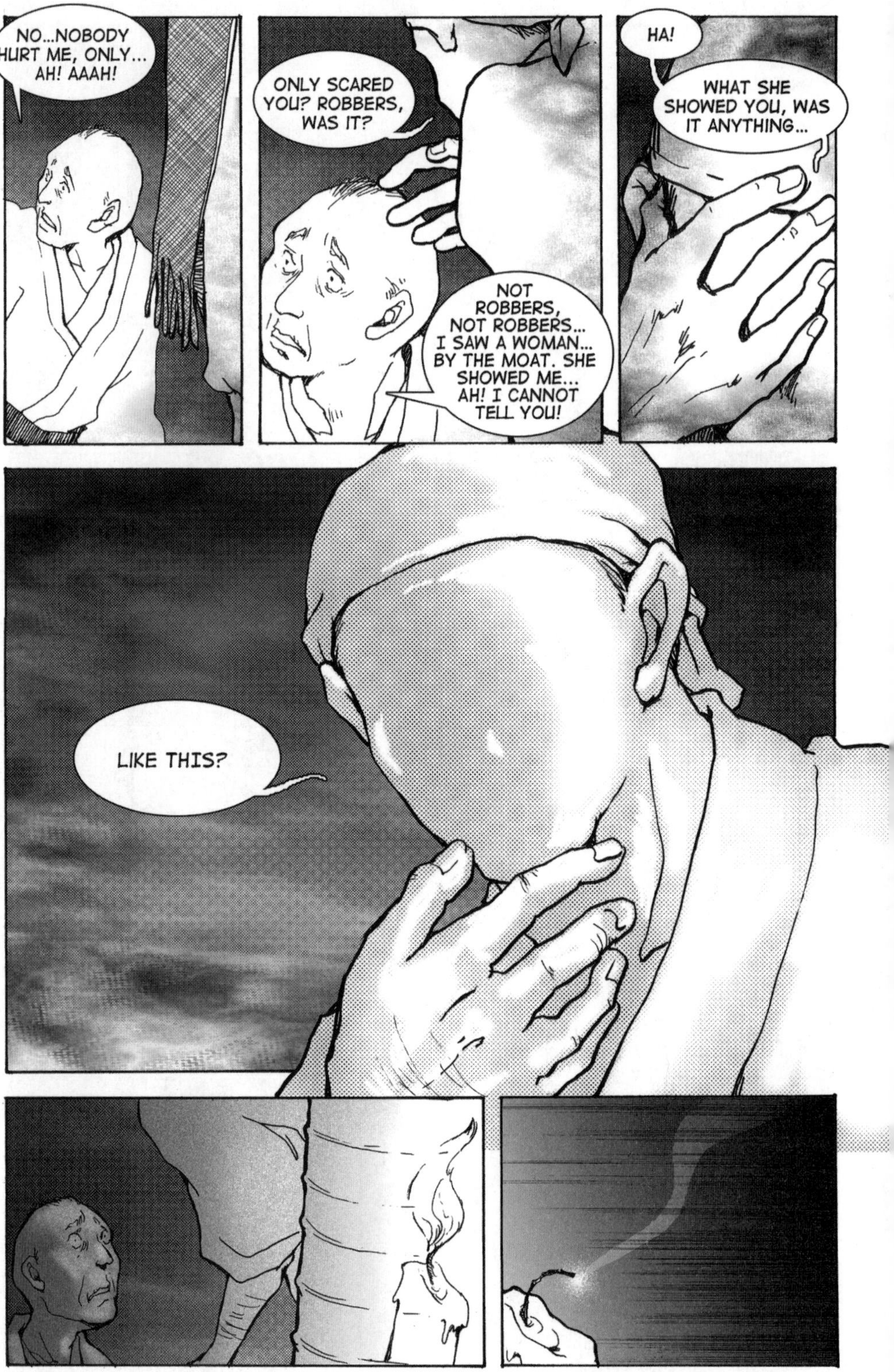
NO...NOBODY HURT ME, ONLY... AH! AAAH!
ONLY SCARED YOU? ROBBERS, WAS IT?
NOT ROBBERS, NOT ROBBERS... I SAW A WOMAN... BY THE MOAT. SHE SHOWED ME... AH! I CANNOT TELL YOU!
HA!
WHAT SHE SHOWED YOU, WAS IT ANYTHING...
LIKE THIS?

鮫人の恩返し

THE GRATITUDE
OF THE SAMEBITO

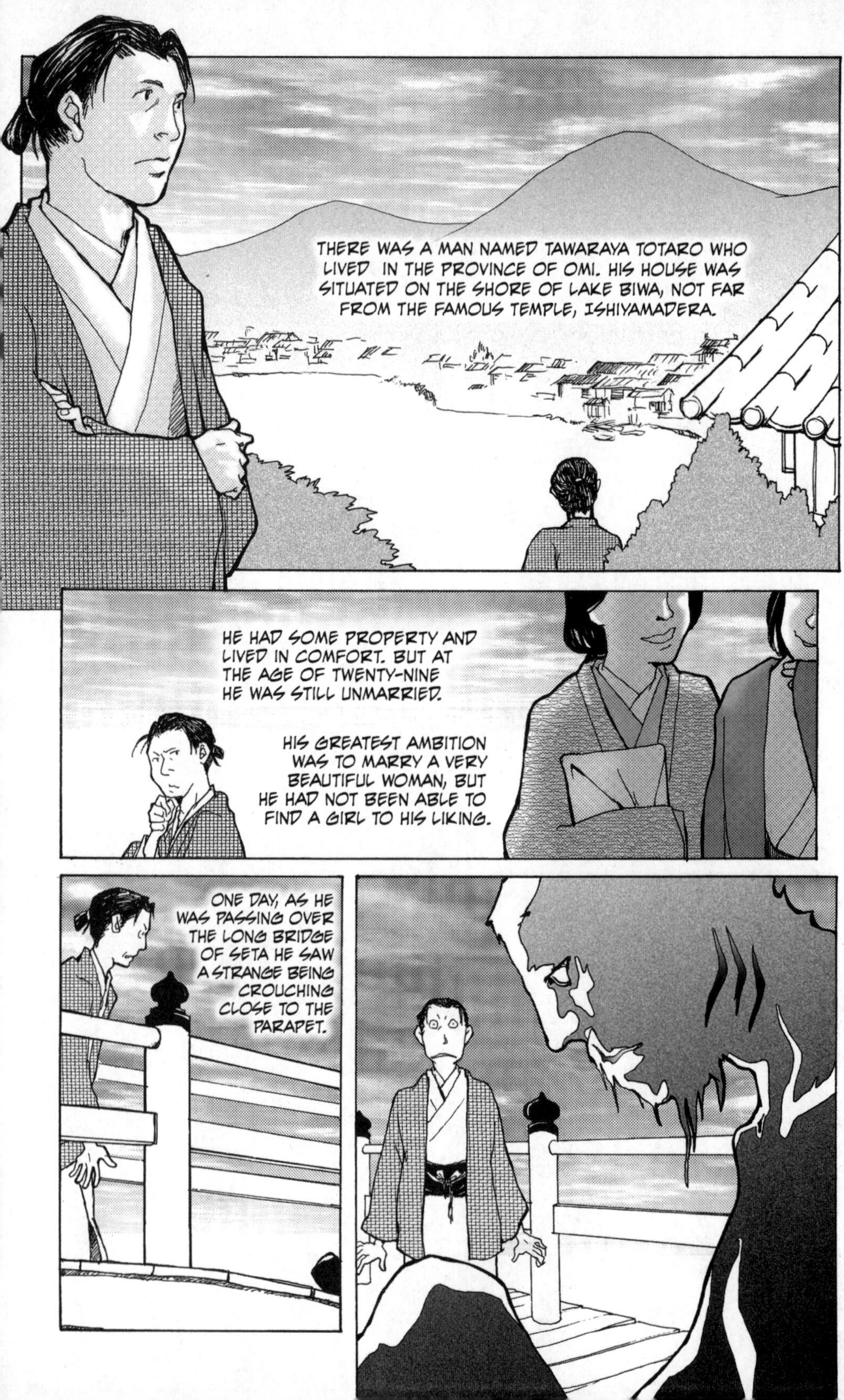
THERE WAS A MAN NAMED TAWARAYA TOTARO WHO LIVED IN THE PROVINCE OF OMI. HIS HOUSE WAS SITUATED ON THE SHORE OF LAKE BIWA, NOT FAR FROM THE FAMOUS TEMPLE, ISHIYAMADERA.
HE HAD SOME PROPERTY AND LIVED IN COMFORT. BUT AT THE AGE OF TWENTY-NINE HE WAS STILL UNMARRIED.
HIS GREATEST AMBITION WAS TO MARRY A VERY BEAUTIFUL WOMAN, BUT HE HAD NOT BEEN ABLE TO FIND A GIRL TO HIS LIKING.
ONE DAY, AS HE WAS PASSING OVER THE LONG BRIDGE OF SETA HE SAW A STRANGE BEING CROUCHING CLOSE TO THE PARAPET.

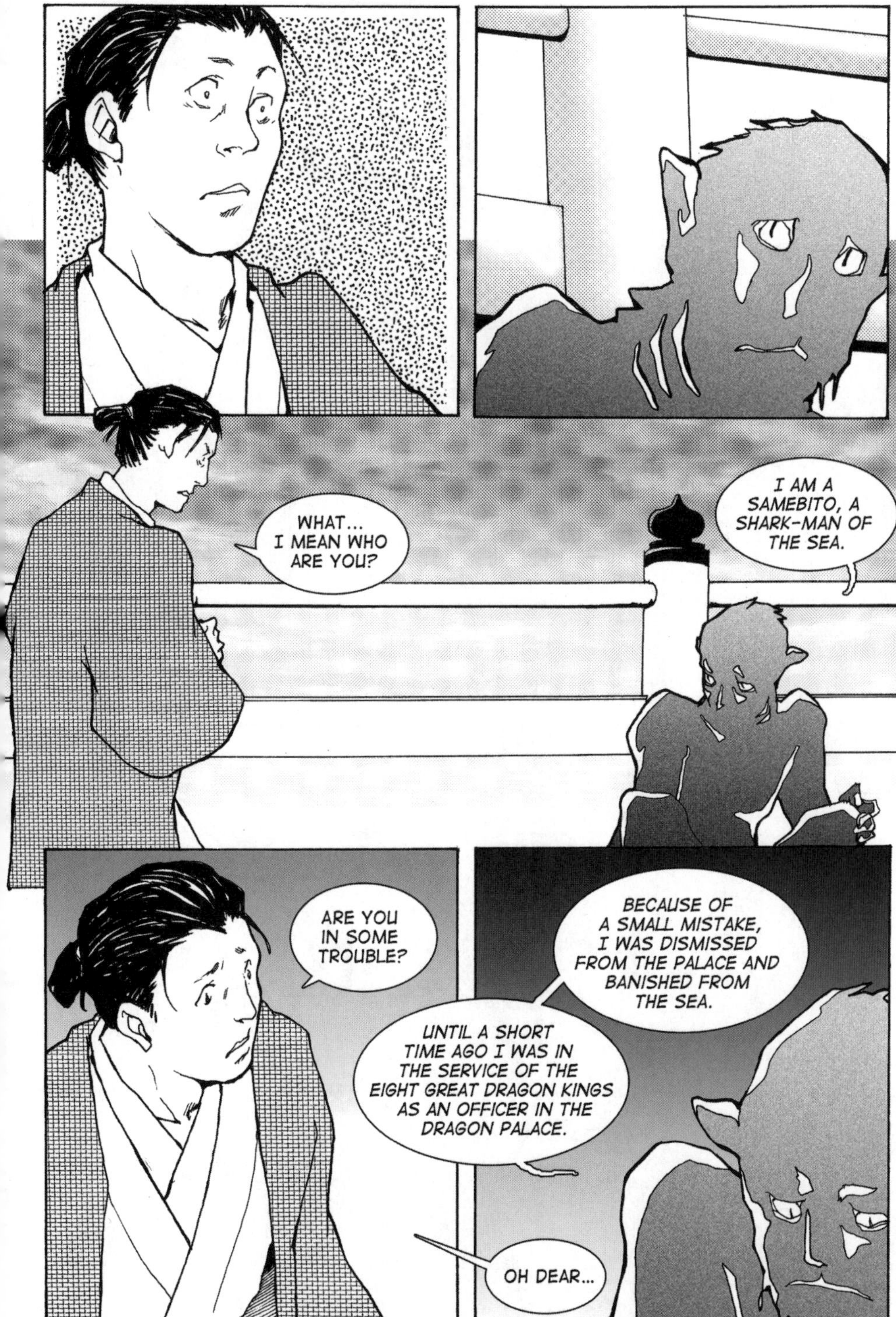
WHAT... I MEAN WHO ARE YOU?
I AM A SAMEBITO, A SHARK-MAN OF THE SEA.
ARE YOU IN SOME TROUBLE?
UNTIL A SHORT TIME AGO I WAS IN THE SERVICE OF THE EIGHT GREAT DRAGON KINGS AS AN OFFICER IN THE DRAGON PALACE.
BECAUSE OF A SMALL MISTAKE, I WAS DISMISSED FROM THE PALACE AND BANISHED FROM THE SEA.
OH DEAR...

SINCE THEN I HAVE BEEN WANDERING ABOUT HERE, UNABLE TO GET ANY FOOD, OR EVEN A PLACE TO LIE DOWN.

IF YOU CAN FEEL PITY FOR ME, PLEASE, PLEASE HELP ME TO FIND SHELTER, AND SOMETHING TO EAT!

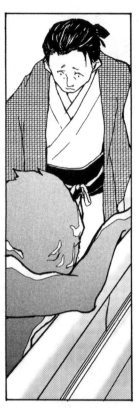

THIS PETITION WAS UTTERED IN SO PLAINTIVE A TONE, AND IN SO HUMBLE A MANNER, THAT TOTARO'S HEART WAS TOUCHED.

COME WITH ME.

THERE'S A LARGE POND IN MY GARDEN. YOU CAN LIVE THERE AND I WILL GIVE YOU SOMETHING TO EAT.

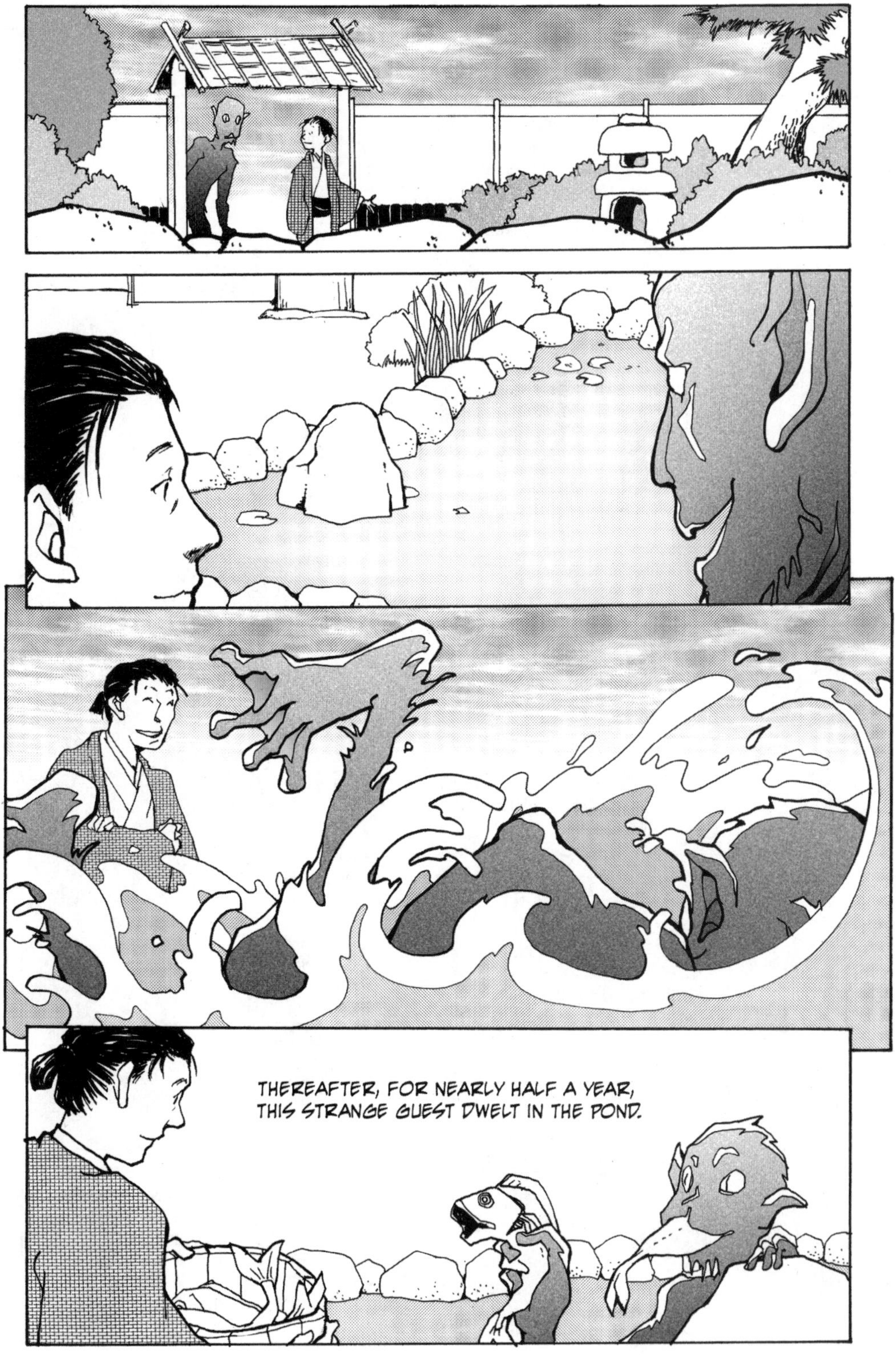
THEREAFTER, FOR NEARLY HALF A YEAR, THIS STRANGE GUEST DWELT IN THE POND.

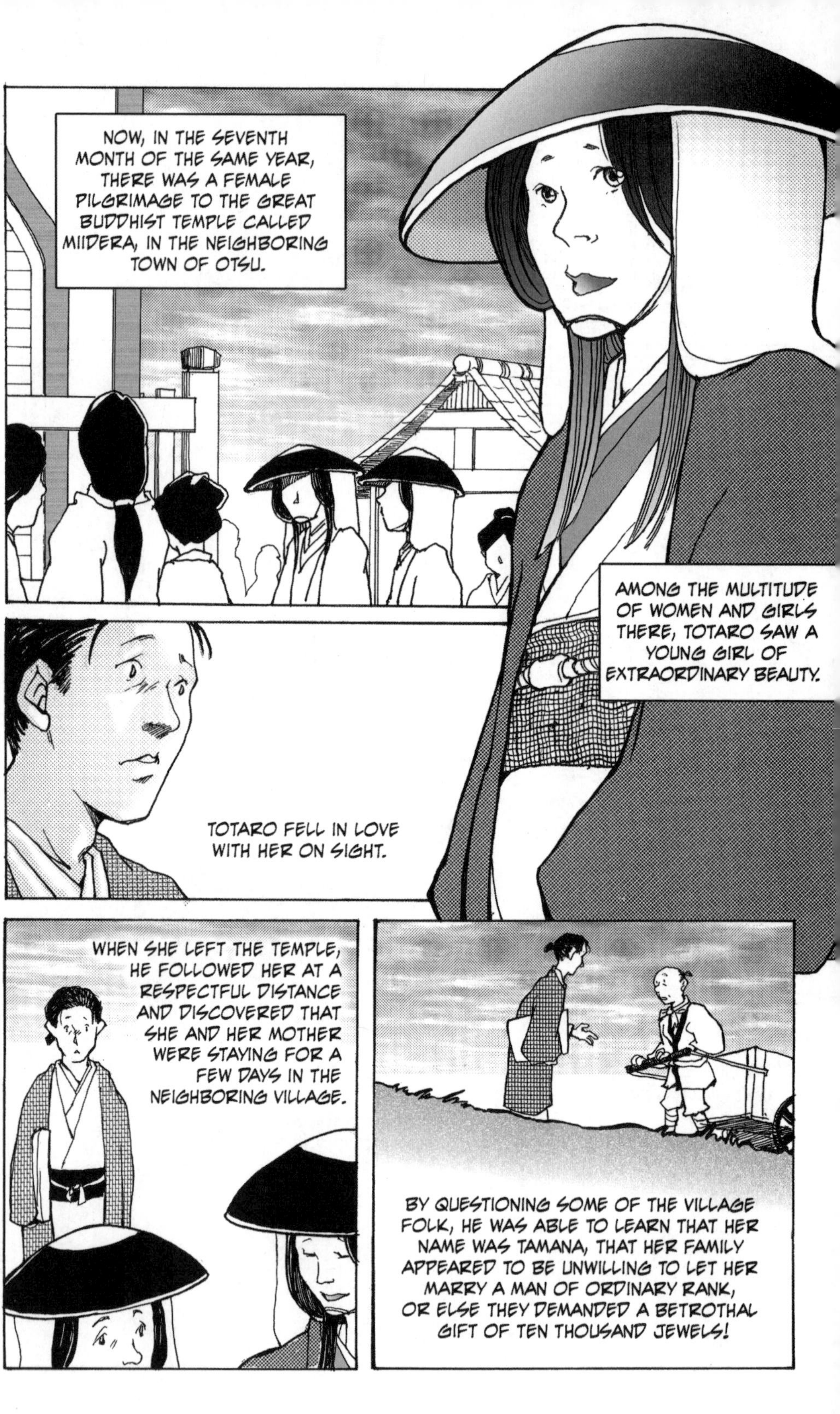
NOW, IN THE SEVENTH MONTH OF THE SAME YEAR, THERE WAS A FEMALE PILGRIMAGE TO THE GREAT BUDDHIST TEMPLE CALLED MIIDERA, IN THE NEIGHBORING TOWN OF OTSU.
AMONG THE MULTITUDE OF WOMEN AND GIRLS THERE, TOTARO SAW A YOUNG GIRL OF EXTRAORDINARY BEAUTY.
TOTARO FELL IN LOVE WITH HER ON SIGHT.
WHEN SHE LEFT THE TEMPLE, HE FOLLOWED HER AT A RESPECTFUL DISTANCE AND DISCOVERED THAT SHE AND HER MOTHER WERE STAYING FOR A FEW DAYS IN THE NEIGHBORING VILLAGE.
BY QUESTIONING SOME OF THE VILLAGE FOLK, HE WAS ABLE TO LEARN THAT HER NAME WAS TAMANA, THAT HER FAMILY APPEARED TO BE UNWILLING TO LET HER MARRY A MAN OF ORDINARY RANK, OR ELSE THEY DEMANDED A BETROTHAL GIFT OF TEN THOUSAND JEWELS!

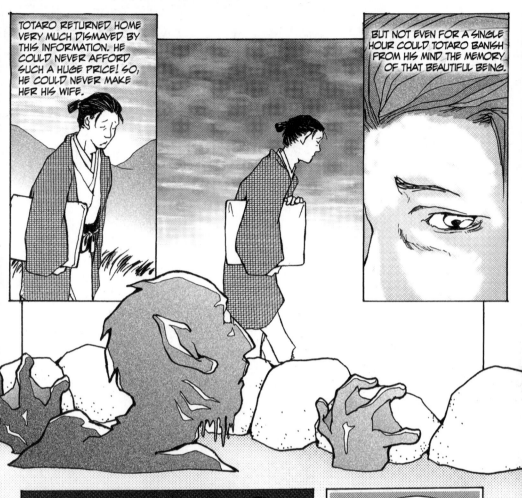

TOTARO RETURNED HOME VERY MUCH DISMAYED BY THIS INFORMATION. HE COULD NEVER AFFORD SUCH A HUGE PRICE! SO, HE COULD NEVER MAKE HER HIS WIFE.

BUT NOT EVEN FOR A SINGLE HOUR COULD TOTARO BANISH FROM HIS MIND THE MEMORY OF THAT BEAUTIFUL BEING.

IT HAUNTED HIM SO THAT HE COULD NEITHER EAT NOR SLEEP, AND IT SEEMED TO BECOME MORE AND MORE INTENSE AS THE DAYS WENT BY.

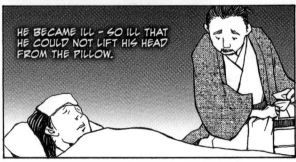

HE BECAME ILL - SO ILL THAT HE COULD NOT LIFT HIS HEAD FROM THE PILLOW.

ALMOST ANY KIND OF SICKNESS CAN BE CURED BY PROPER TREATMENT...

EXCEPT THE SICKNESS OF LOVE. THERE'S NO CURE FOR IT.

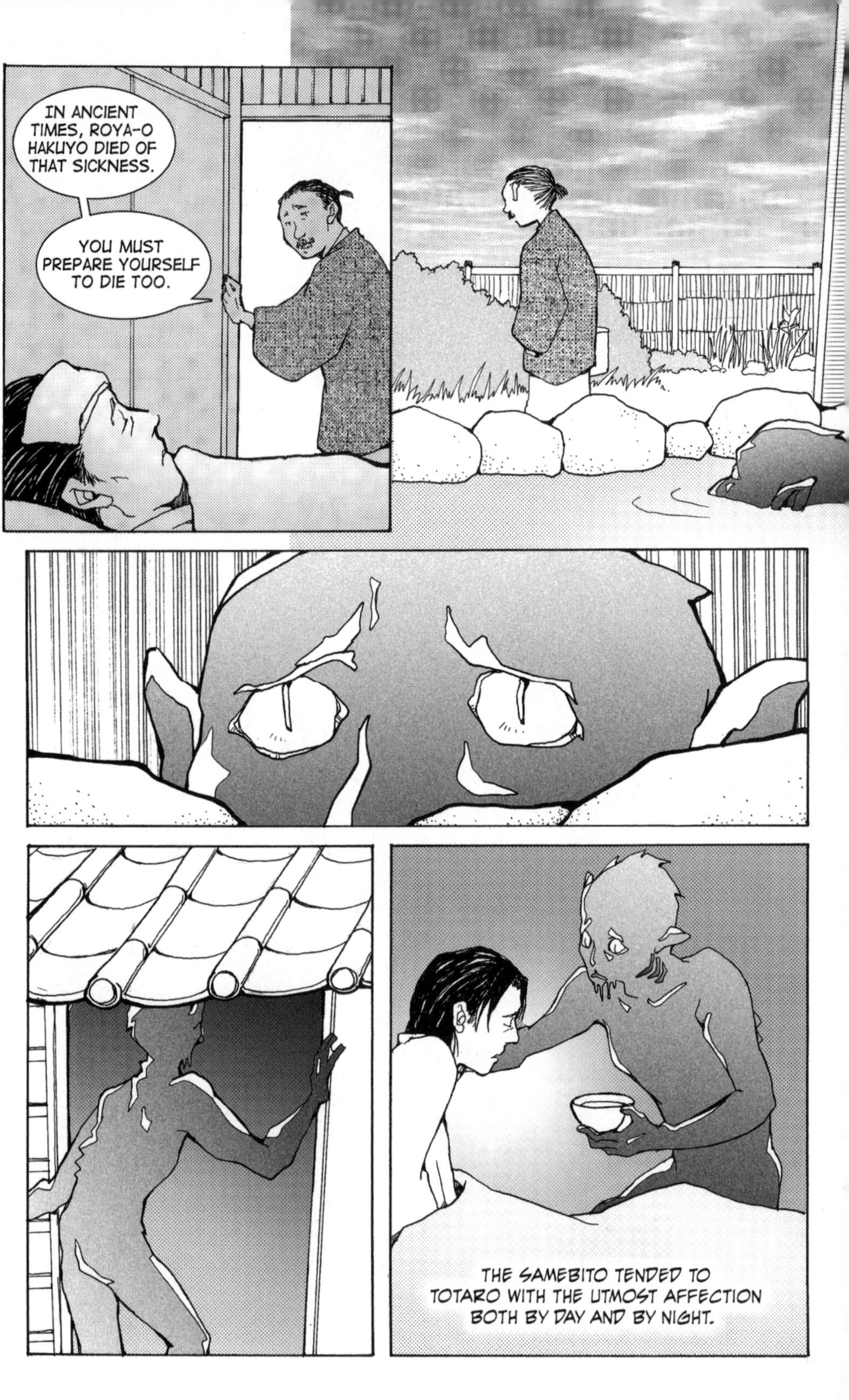
IN ANCIENT TIMES, ROYA-O HAKUYO DIED OF THAT SICKNESS.
YOU MUST PREPARE YOURSELF TO DIE TOO.
THE SAMEBITO TENDED TO TOTARO WITH THE UTMOST AFFECTION BOTH BY DAY AND BY NIGHT.

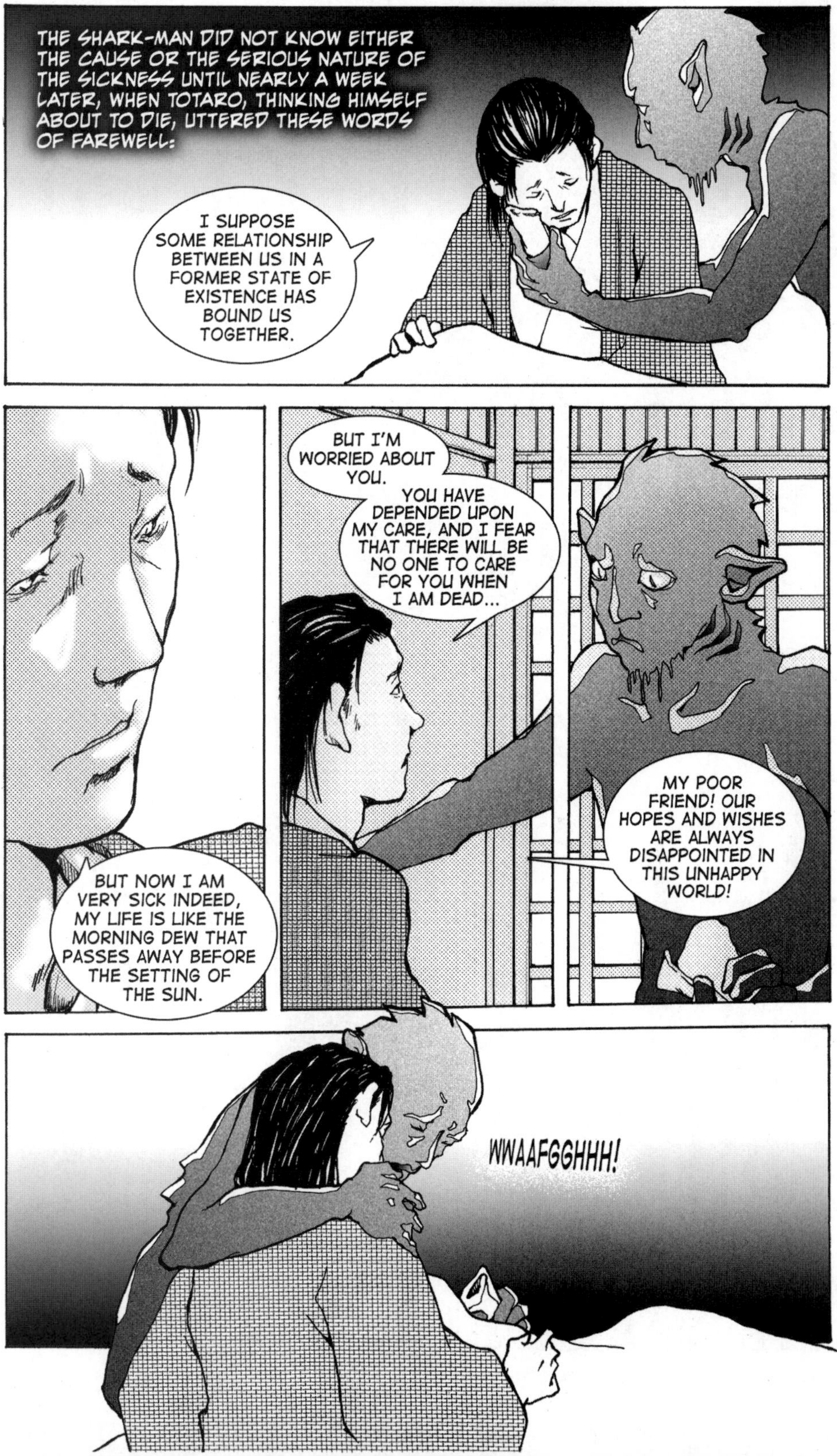
THE SHARK-MAN DID NOT KNOW EITHER THE CAUSE OR THE SERIOUS NATURE OF THE SICKNESS UNTIL NEARLY A WEEK LATER, WHEN TOTARO, THINKING HIMSELF ABOUT TO DIE, UTTERED THESE WORDS OF FAREWELL:
I SUPPOSE SOME RELATIONSHIP BETWEEN US IN A FORMER STATE OF EXISTENCE HAS BOUND US TOGETHER.
BUT NOW I AM VERY SICK INDEED, MY LIFE IS LIKE THE MORNING DEW THAT PASSES AWAY BEFORE THE SETTING OF THE SUN.
BUT I'M WORRIED ABOUT YOU.
YOU HAVE DEPENDED UPON MY CARE, AND I FEAR THAT THERE WILL BE NO ONE TO CARE FOR YOU WHEN I AM DEAD...
MY POOR FRIEND! OUR HOPES AND WISHES ARE ALWAYS DISAPPOINTED IN THIS UNHAPPY WORLD!
WWAAFGGHHH!

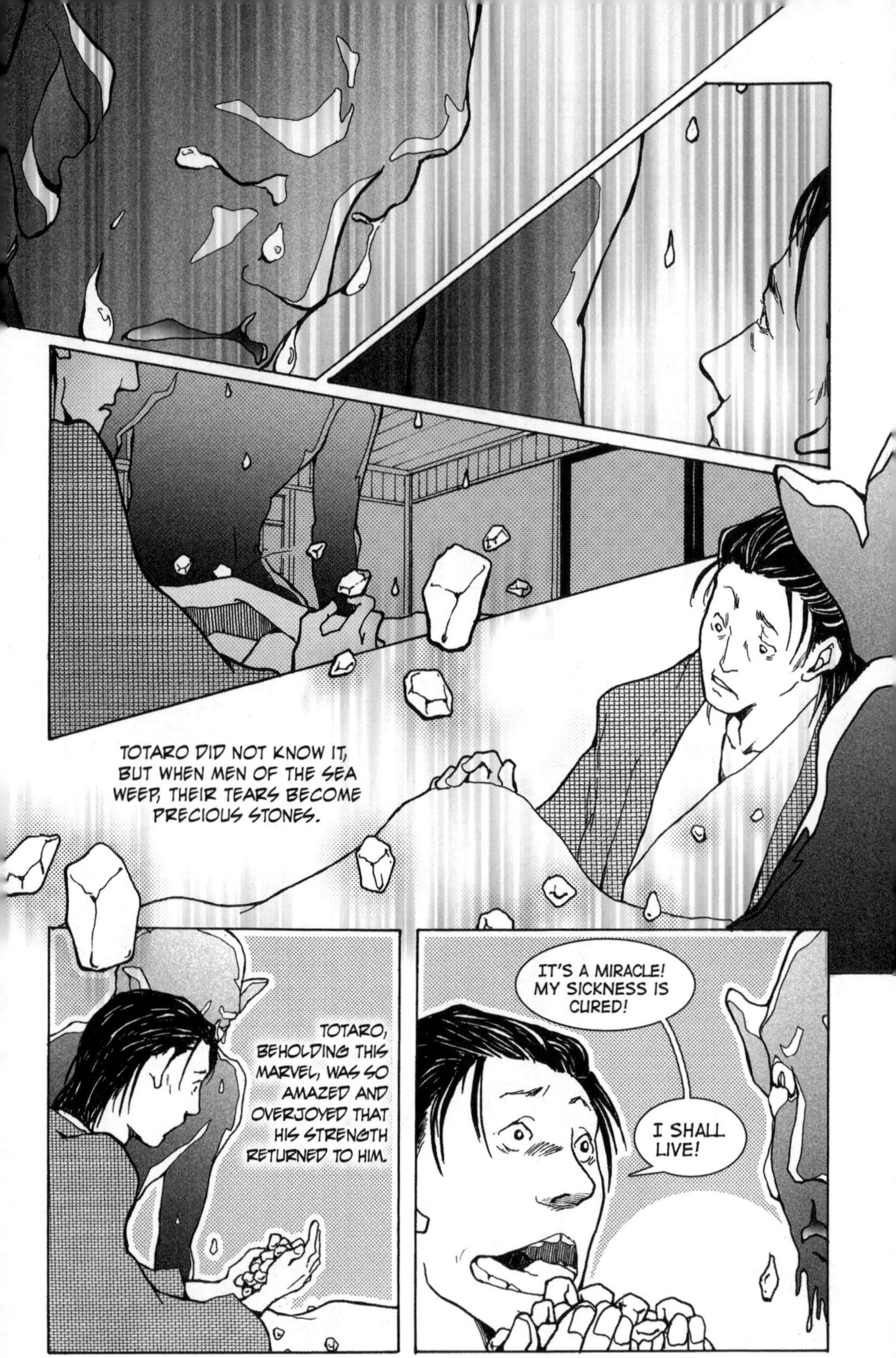
TOTARO DID NOT KNOW IT, BUT WHEN MEN OF THE SEA WEEP, THEIR TEARS BECOME PRECIOUS STONES.
TOTARO, BEHOLDING THIS MARVEL, WAS SO AMAZED AND OVERJOYED THAT HIS STRENGTH RETURNED TO HIM.
IT'S A MIRACLE! MY SICKNESS IS CURED!
I SHALL LIVE!

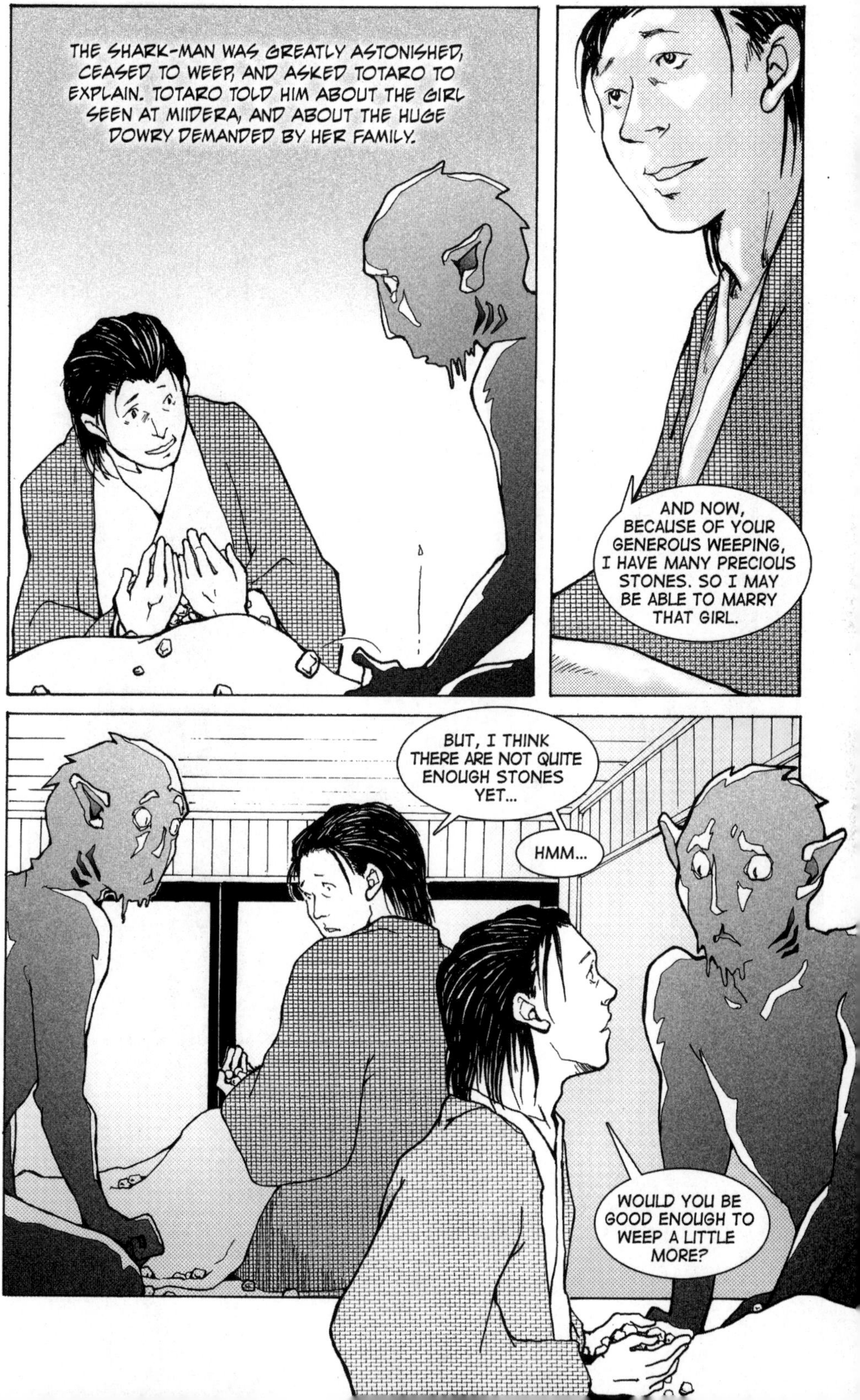
THE SHARK-MAN WAS GREATLY ASTONISHED, CEASED TO WEEP, AND ASKED TOTARO TO EXPLAIN. TOTARO TOLD HIM ABOUT THE GIRL SEEN AT MIIDERA, AND ABOUT THE HUGE DOWRY DEMANDED BY HER FAMILY.
AND NOW, BECAUSE OF YOUR GENEROUS WEEPING, I HAVE MANY PRECIOUS STONES. SO I MAY BE ABLE TO MARRY THAT GIRL.
BUT, I THINK THERE ARE NOT QUITE ENOUGH STONES YET...
HMM...
WOULD YOU BE GOOD ENOUGH TO WEEP A LITTLE MORE?

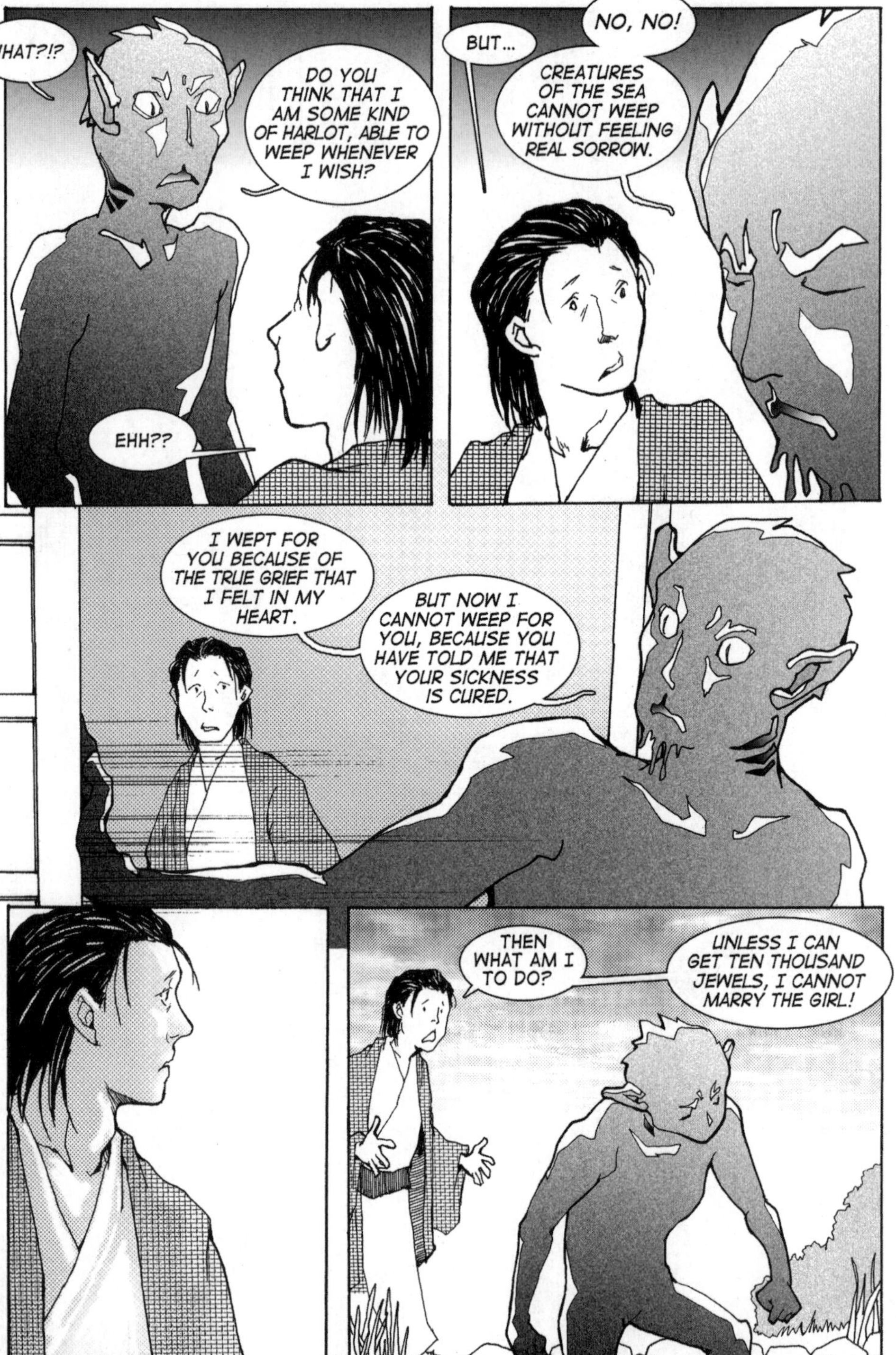
WHAT?!?
DO YOU THINK THAT I AM SOME KIND OF HARLOT, ABLE TO WEEP WHENEVER I WISH?
EHH??
BUT...
NO, NO!
CREATURES OF THE SEA CANNOT WEEP WITHOUT FEELING REAL SORROW.
I WEPT FOR YOU BECAUSE OF THE TRUE GRIEF THAT I FELT IN MY HEART.
BUT NOW I CANNOT WEEP FOR YOU, BECAUSE YOU HAVE TOLD ME THAT YOUR SICKNESS IS CURED.
THEN WHAT AM I TO DO?
UNLESS I CAN GET TEN THOUSAND JEWELS, I CANNOT MARRY THE GIRL!

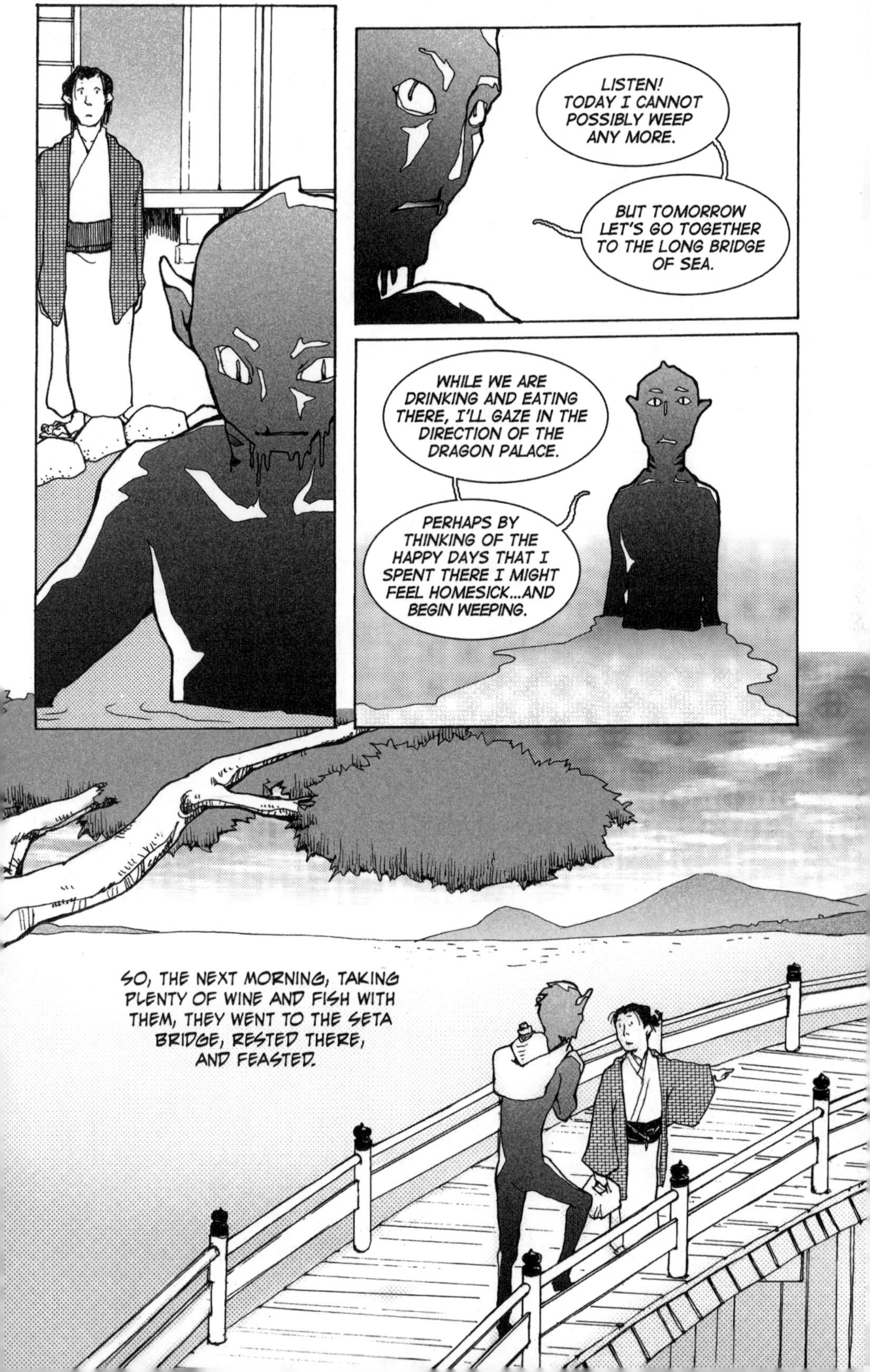
LISTEN! TODAY I CANNOT POSSIBLY WEEP ANY MORE.
BUT TOMORROW LET'S GO TOGETHER TO THE LONG BRIDGE OF SEA.
WHILE WE ARE DRINKING AND EATING THERE, I'LL GAZE IN THE DIRECTION OF THE DRAGON PALACE.
PERHAPS BY THINKING OF THE HAPPY DAYS THAT I SPENT THERE I MIGHT FEEL HOMESICK...AND BEGIN WEEPING.
SO, THE NEXT MORNING, TAKING PLENTY OF WINE AND FISH WITH THEM, THEY WENT TO THE SETA BRIDGE, RESTED THERE, AND FEASTED.

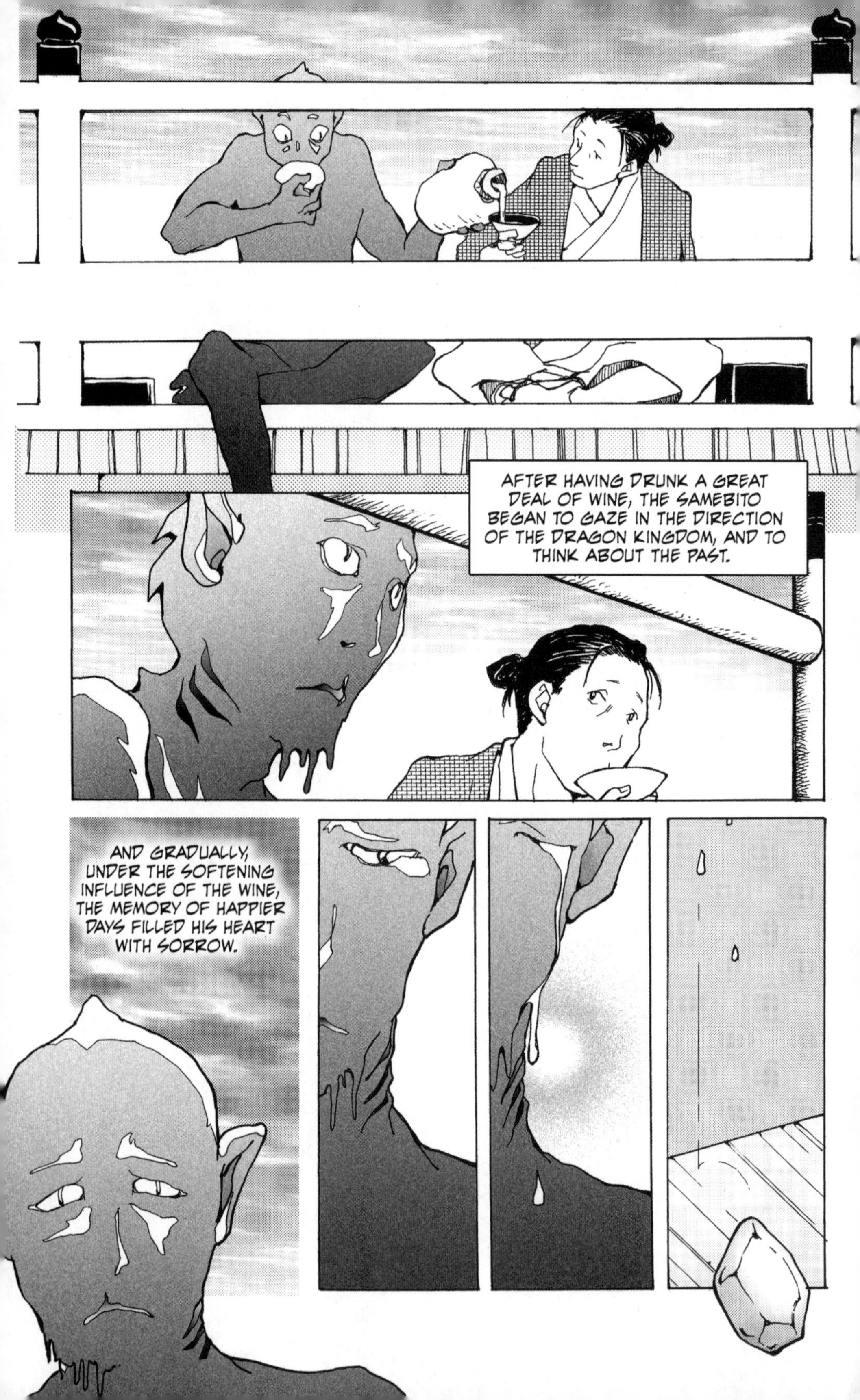
AFTER HAVING DRUNK A GREAT DEAL OF WINE, THE SAMEBITO BEGAN TO GAZE IN THE DIRECTION OF THE DRAGON KINGDOM, AND TO THINK ABOUT THE PAST.
AND GRADUALLY, UNDER THE SOFTENING INFLUENCE OF THE WINE, THE MEMORY OF HAPPIER DAYS FILLED HIS HEART WITH SORROW.

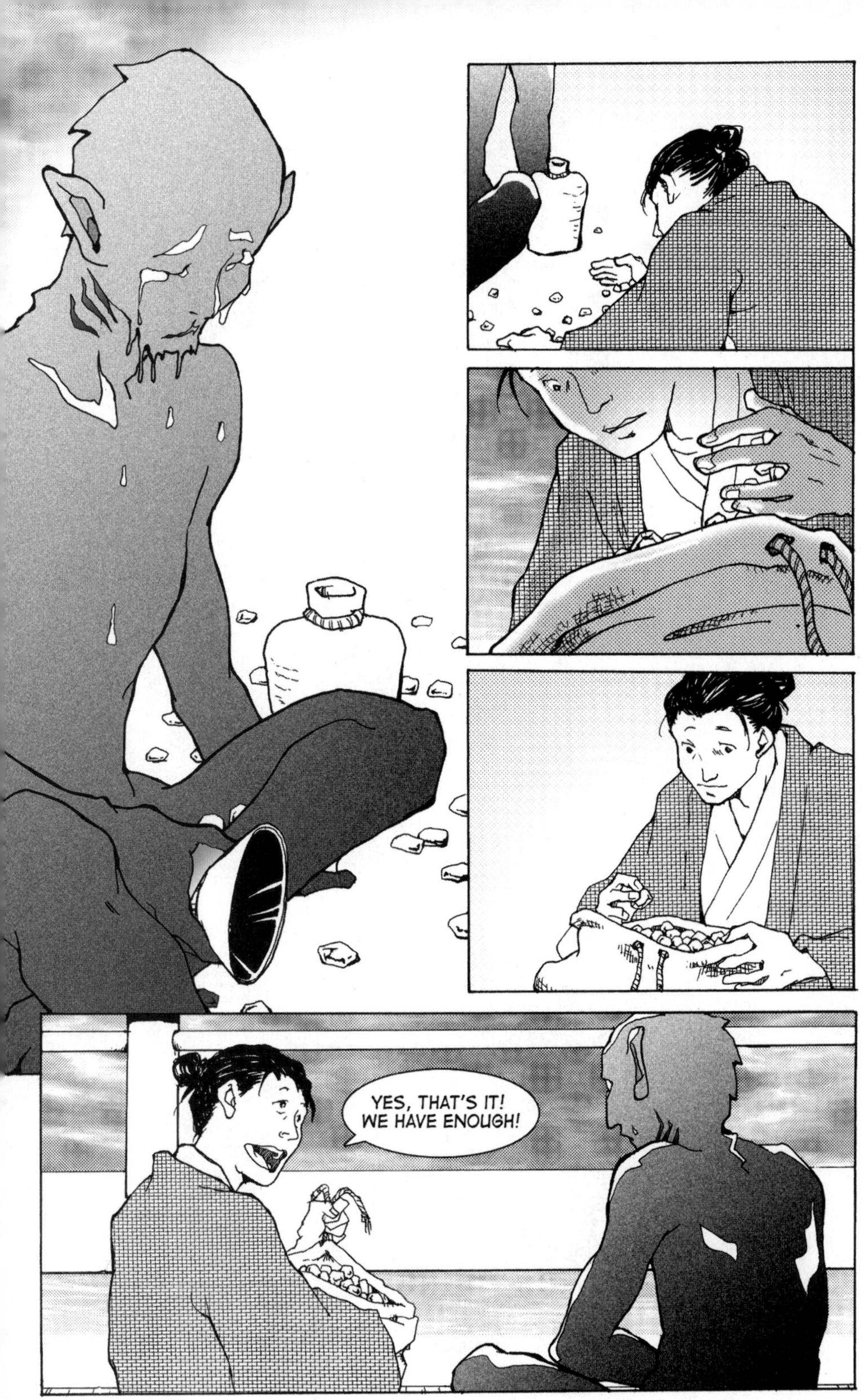
YES, THAT'S IT! WE HAVE ENOUGH!

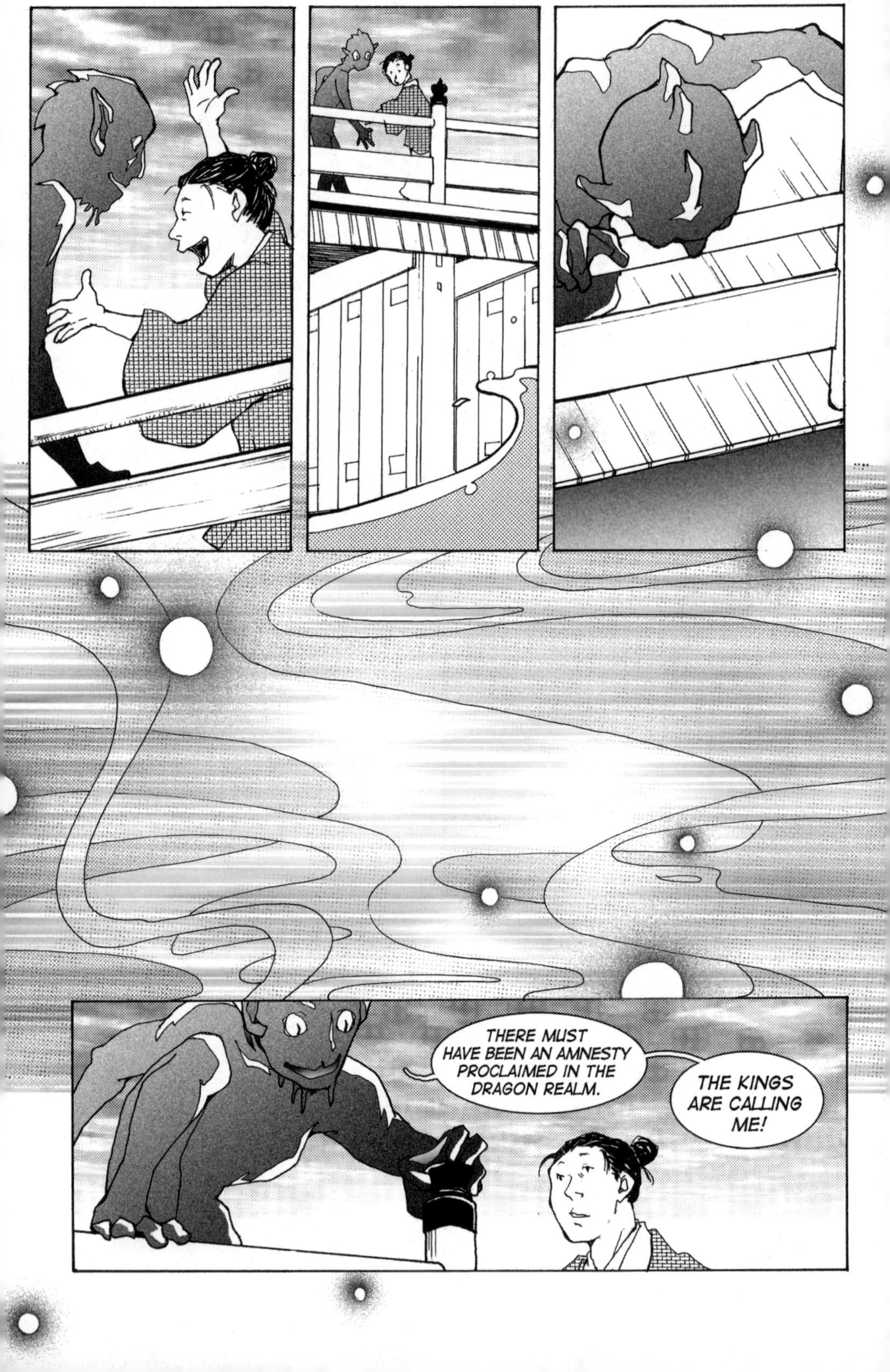
THERE MUST HAVE BEEN AN AMNESTY PROCLAIMED IN THE DRAGON REALM.
THE KINGS ARE CALLING ME!

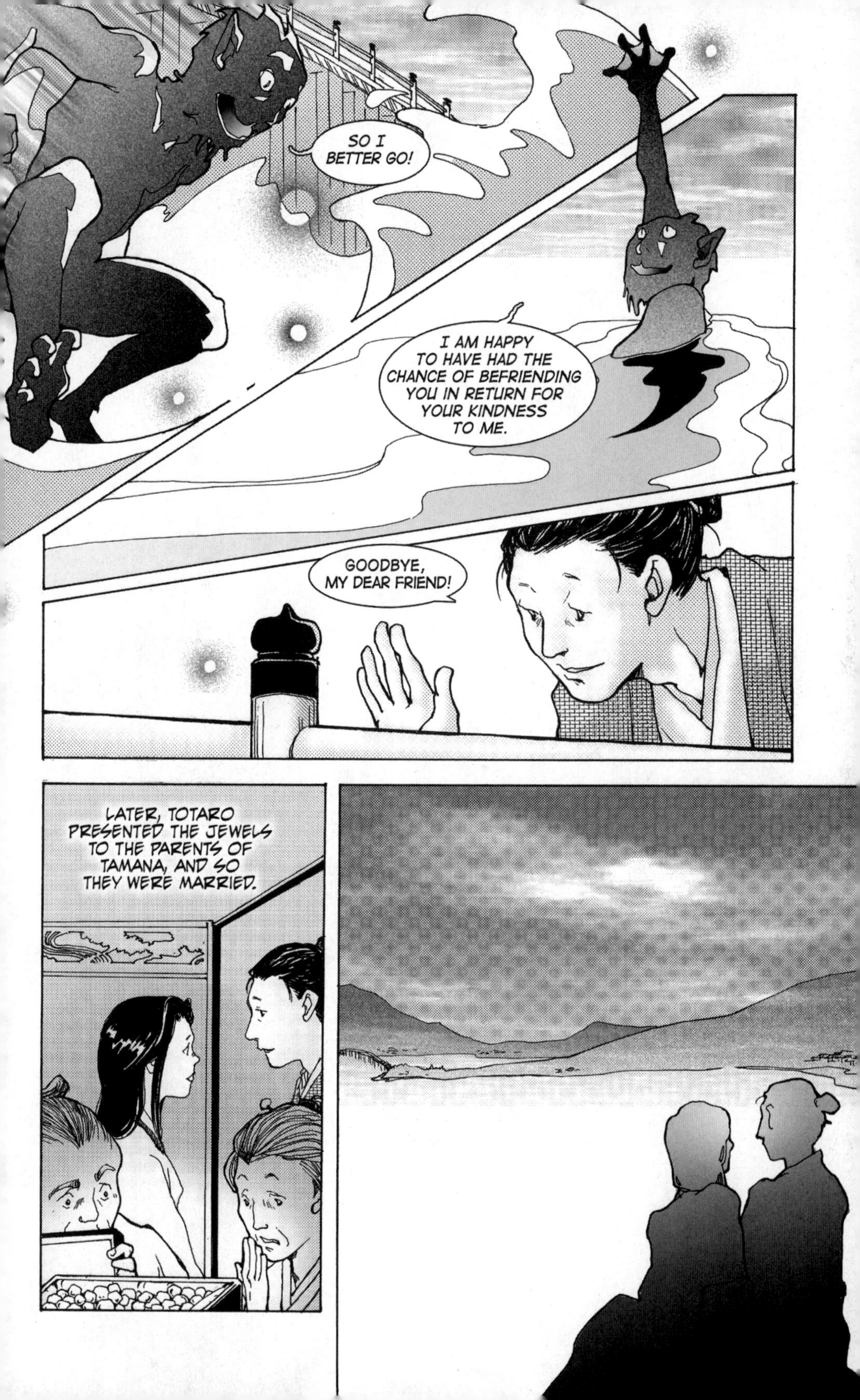
SO I BETTER GO!
I AM HAPPY TO HAVE HAD THE CHANCE OF BEFRIENDING YOU IN RETURN FOR YOUR KINDNESS TO ME.
GOODBYE, MY DEAR FRIEND!
LATER, TOTARO PRESENTED THE JEWELS TO THE PARENTS OF TAMANA, AND SO THEY WERE MARRIED.

THE END

Author's Note

The stories here are just a few from the many collected by Lafcadio Hearn (adopted Japanese name, Koizumi Yakumo), an Irish-Greek writer who lived in Japan from 1890 until his death in 1904. Some of these folktales were Japanese versions of older Chinese tales, such as those in *In Ghostly Japan* (1899), which draw from the tradition of Chinese divination. Hearn found many of the tales in old Japanese texts, such as the thirteenth century *Heike Monogatari* or the *Hyaku-Mo-nogatari* (from a Buddhist influenced mystery storytelling game popular during the Edo period). Others were told to him personally, such as "Yuki-Onna," which he heard from a farmer in Chofu. Some were related to him on quiet lamp-lit evenings by his wife, Setsu, recalling stories from her childhood. In the era of western colonialism of Asia in the late nineteenth century, rediscovering this folklore felt like a connection to "the soul of the Japanese people." In these stories, Hearn saw the influence of Shinto and Buddhism, as in "Diplomacy," which involves the Shinto notion of lingering ghosts whose anguish in death results in terrifying hauntings.

These tales were originally published in English in over a dozen books, including *Kwaidan: Stories and Studies of Strange Things* (1904). Our visual versions of the stories "Hoichi the Earless," "Diplomacy," "Of a Mirror and a Bell," "Mujina," and "The Snow Woman" are all based on the stories in *Kwaidan*. Our version of "The Gratitude of the Samebito" (which means "Sharkman") is drawn from Hearn's book *Shadowings* (1900). Much of the wording of the text we have used is the same as in Hearn's books, with adjustments to accommodate the visual format of a graphic novel. Michiru Morikawa has done a wonderful job of making these stories come alive on the page with her very beautiful illustrations.

These stories are not horror in the sense of blood and guts, or stuff that makes us jump out of our seats—although, the "Mujina" story is pretty unsettling, the murderous snow woman in "The Snow Woman" would terrify anyone, and I certainly would not want my ears ripped off by a stern ghost in the middle of the night like poor Hoichi. Instead, the stories are—as the subtitle indicates—macabre.

On a personal note, I myself have several small connections with Lafcadio Hearn. Like him, I am a half-Irish writer living in Japan. In fact, I live in Kumamoto, the same town where Hearn lived. My grandparents' family name is Mulhern, an Anglicized version of the Irish name *Ó Maoilchiaráin*, roughly meaning "descendant of the followers of Hern." Like Hearn, I also teach English classes, and within sight of where Hearn himself taught English in Kumamoto University 120 years ago. On his lunch break, Hearn would walk up the hill near the university, probably walking right past where I live and am writing these words. So, for me—and for many others—his influence lives on in these intriguing stories of myth, mystery, ghosts, and magic.

—SEAN MICHAEL WILSON
Kumamoto, Japan

About the Author

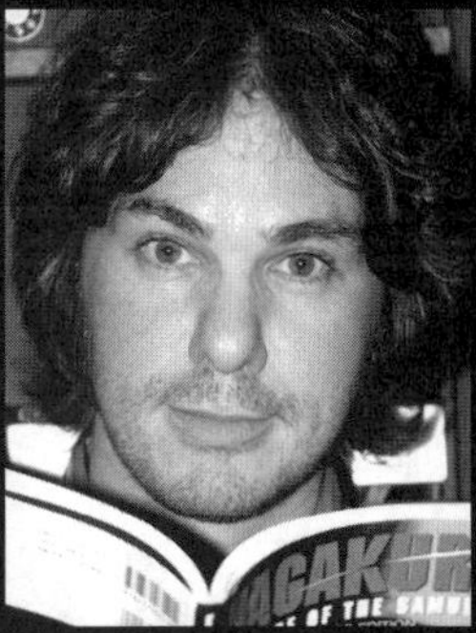
HAGAKURE

SEAN MICHAEL WILSON is a Scottish comic book writer who lives in Japan. He has published numerous comics and graphic novels with a variety of U.S., U.K., and Japanese publishers, including *Hagakure, The Book of Five Rings,* and *The 47 Ronin*. He is also the editor of the critically acclaimed *Ax: Alternative Manga*.

MICHIRU MORIKAWA is a Japanese illustrator and manga artist and winner of the 2005 International Manga and Anime Award. With Sean Michael Wilson, she has created the graphic novels *Buskers, Yakuza Moon, The Demon's Sermon on the Martial Arts,* and *Musashi.*

Also Available from Shambhala Publications

GRAPHIC NOVELS BY SEAN MICHAEL WILSON

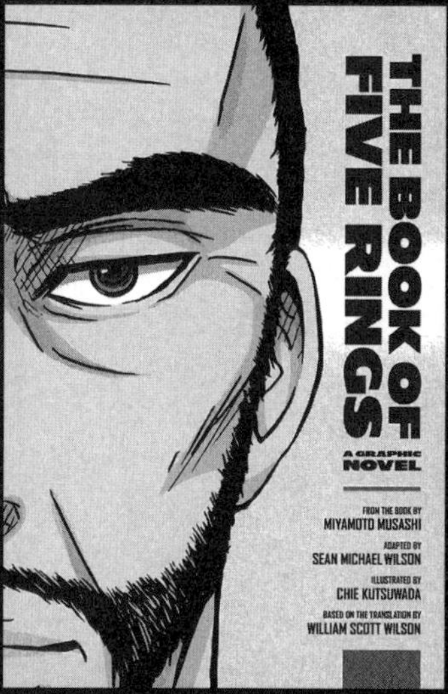
THE BOOK OF FIVE RINGS
A GRAPHIC NOVEL
FROM THE BOOK BY
MIYAMOTO MUSASHI
ADAPTED BY
SEAN MICHAEL WILSON
ILLUSTRATED BY
CHIE KUTSUWADA
BASED ON THE TRANSLATION BY
WILLIAM SCOTT WILSON

THE BOOK OF FIVE RINGS

"Truly a tribute to the original [classic]. There is a tremendous amount of depth and insight into this work, an exploration of the five elements of life (the 'five rings' of the title) that represent the cosmic Buddha. Readers get complex but eminently readable explorations of each ring and are led to see them all together as an overriding philosophy that enriches and broadens the life of any reader."

—Jason Sacks, *Comics Bulletin*

"This graphic adaptation of Musashi's seventeenth-century treatise on the martial arts makes careful, effective use of imagery to emphasize both the narrative and instructional aspects of the original text. . . . Musashi's lessons, in their focus on preparation and mindfulness, can easily be applied to most areas of life. Kutsuwada's art is delicate and clean, balancing the physiological dynamics of swordplay with a clear-eyed appreciation of Musashi's natural environment. An engaging, thoughtful update of what could be esoteric."

—Publishers Weekly

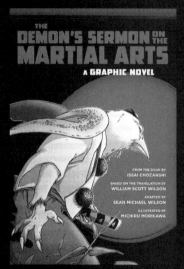

THE
DEMON'S SERMON ON THE
MARTIAL ARTS
A GRAPHIC NOVEL
FROM THE BOOK BY
ISSAI CHOZANSHI
BASED ON THE TRANSLATION BY
WILLIAM SCOTT WILSON
ADAPTED BY
SEAN MICHAEL WILSON
ILLUSTRATED BY
MICHIRU MORIKAWA

THE DEMON'S SERMON ON THE MARTIAL ARTS

"As a book of philosophy, it's fascinating; a dreamlike exploration of consciousness, life, and death. Michiru Morikawa's artwork is the perfect match for the text, her eerie, detailed illustrations—especially the lovely renderings of various animals—perfectly fitting the poetic feel. Recommended."

—Jason Thompson, *Otaku USA*

"Wilson and Morikawa capture all the wisdom and beauty of these original texts and enhance them with the visual vitality and playful charms of modern manga. Their faithful retellings of these allegorical fables and philosophical reflections prove how timeless and rewarding they truly are."

—Paul Gravett, editor of *1001 Comics You Must Read before You Die*

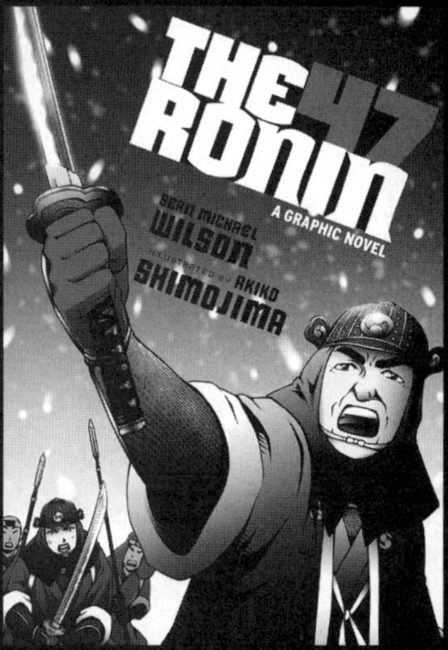
THE 47 RONIN
A GRAPHIC NOVEL
SEAN MICHAEL
WILSON
AKIKO
SHIMOJIMA

THE 47 RONIN

"A masterful retelling of one of the greatest stories in Japanese culture. An engrossing, engaging, emotional, and unforgettable epic."

—Jonathan Ross, BBC television presenter

"Wilson uses exactly the right scenes to tell this famous story, creating a quick, engaging read."

—*Library Journal*

"A dignified telling of a dignified story. It's violent when it needs to be, precise and calm when it's called for, and never once loses focus."

—BleedingCool.com

"Readers interested in accurate Japanese history rather than Hollywood embellishment will enjoy this well-done retelling of the legendary event."

—*The Japan Times*

MUSASHI

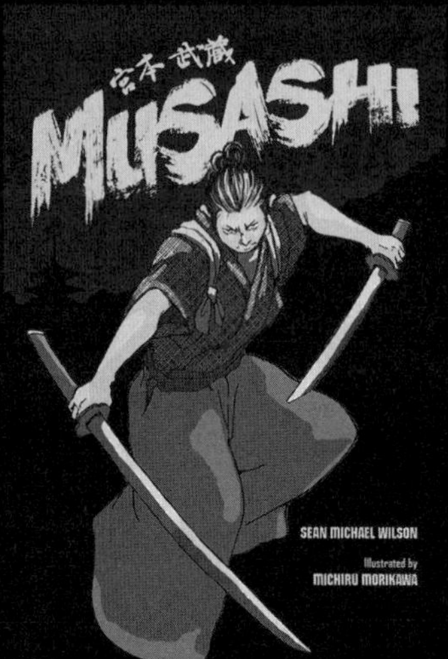
宮本武蔵
MUSASHI
SEAN MICHAEL WILSON
Illustrated by
MICHIRU MORIKAWA

"If you are into the martial arts, this is a book that should be in your personal library—along with *The Book of Five Rings: A Graphic Novel*. A beautifully fully illustrated book. 5 Stars."

—Joseph J. Truncale, author of *The Samurai Soul*

"Based on William Scott Wilson's biography *The Lone Samurai*, this work includes much historical material. The detailed black-and-white artwork provides a strong sense of the era. Well-drawn facial expressions and body language convey emotions in the often wordless art panels. . . . Pacing is deliberate, examining milestones in Musashi's life. The man himself remains enigmatic, shown speaking in only a few panels. Readers expecting only duels and bloodshed will be surprised by Musashi's disciplined, meditative qualities. This dichotomy of developing technical skills with sword as well as an enlightened and philosophical mind will appeal to fans of Star Wars's light-saber-wielding Jedi and their Jedi way."

—School Library Journal

"Morikawa's art, with its atmospheric compositions, gives the book a feeling of dignity and grace. Wilson and Morikawa also do a good job conveying Musashi's strategies even in short, two- to three-page fight scenes. . . . As a one-volume introduction to the real historical figure, this is a very fine synopsis."

—Jason Thompson, *Otaku USA*

COLD MOUNTAIN
SEAN MICHAEL WILSON
ILLUSTRATED BY AKIKO SHIMOJIMA
A GRAPHIC NOVEL
THE LEGEND OF HAN SHAN AND SHIH TE
THE ORIGINAL DHARMA BUMS

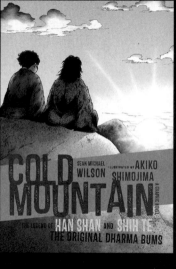

COLD MOUNTAIN

"If you're new to Han Shan and Shih Te, you'll find *Cold Mountain* to be a thoughtful, thought-provoking introduction. And if you're already old friends with them, perhaps you'll see something new in their fresh faces. Recommended."

—Amanda Vail, *Otaku USA*

"The poetry of the manga here expresses the poetry of this pair of 'mad men' of Cold Mountain. Read the wise verses of Han Shan and Shih Te and, like the sage, your face will also break into a great big smile."

—Paul Gravett, author of *Comics Art* and editor of *1001 Comics You Must Read Before You Die*